Tales of the Raven's Daughter

Collection One

BY

ERIN HUNT RADO

For my beloved Paul, the Wizard Pauldin, and for Kitty, my bestie of many years who gave me my main character's name.

A big thank you to Christopher Fain for all those late-night chats, a shout out to Wild Collective in Escondido, California - they are the Fookin' Wyld - and a huge hug to my good friend Caitlyn for some really nifty ideas.

I would also like to acknowledge my editor, Samantha Mueller of Finished Fiction, and my proofreader, Timothy Repasky.

CONTENTS

6 Fantasy Stories - 1 Epic Adventure!

Tales of the Ravensdaughter is a six-part novella series. Each story is a stand-alone tale, but all six build upon one another to complete a single narrative arc.

Each novella is meant to be read in one sitting with an average time of about an hour. The goal is to create a reading experience that mirrors a streaming experience, allowing folks to enjoy a satisfying moment of epic true fantasy.

Author's Note

Tales of the Ravensdaughter begins with Alerice Linden reacting to a recent personal assault. However, the series is about reclaiming one's power in the face of trauma.

Because of the assault, Alerice embarks upon a life she could never have imagined. By accepting her trauma - though never forgetting it - she discovers a power she is ready and willing to wield. Then, when Alerice comes upon some truly helpless victims, she uses that power to save them.

I hope my readers will find this acceptable. And now I invite you to enjoy *Tales of the Ravensdaughter*.

THE BEAST OF BASQUE

Tales of the Ravensdaughter

Adventure One

When the Serpent Father Fire
Loves the Mother Water Wind,
When L'Orku's breath of thunder
'Cross the mighty sky ascends;

When wings of ravens black
Stir shadows in the mist,
The Realme may kiss Mortalia
And a new child will be blessed.

from the Scrolls of Imari

Alerice watched the revelers stuffing their faces. They were of little concern. Her target was the evening's host, Gotthard, mayor of Navre. She could still smell his scent on her skin. She could still hear his taunt after he had assaulted her and murdered her cousin. "Fly away, little bird, or this lion will catch you."

Alerice could not bear the echo of his disdain. Needing to think of something else, she focused on Gotthard's wife. The bejeweled sow sat guzzling beside her husband. Had she been the reason for Gotthard's attack? Had she been encouraging him to assert wanton dominance over every person in the city?

No, Gotthard was Gotthard. Untouchable by law, he was assured of his own righteousness, and he deserved the cup that Alerice had just placed before him.

She hid at the side of the feast hall dressed as a serving page. Candle sconces on the walls and candelabras on the tables could only illuminate so much, and there were more than enough shadows to conceal her. Shadows had always been her allies, and secluded within them Alerice took the measure of her mark.

Gotthard entertained Lord Andoni, the Prime Cheval of Navre, and with good reason. The Cheval had appointed Gotthard as mayor, which had given him license to go wherever he pleased and take whatever he fancied.

Three nights ago, he had fancied Alerice after a chance encounter had gone terribly wrong. A furious Gotthard had been leading some of the constabulary to round up his drunken notary. Alerice had been trying to pry the notary away from his cup, but when Gotthard had seen her, he decided to show the notary how innocent people would pay for his staff's errant behavior.

Alerice's fists clenched as Gotthard and Andoni engaged in jovial chitchat. Time was of the essence if she was going to escape. Serving pages were already gathering in the hallway. If she could make it past them and out the kitchen's back door, the shadowed streets outside would conceal her.

If Gotthard would just drink his damned cup.

Gotthard rose to toast his guest, as did the assembly.

"Friends," he began, flashing a grin that far too many people found charismatic.

Alerice tensed, for the up-twist of Gotthard's lips caused the memory of that expression to flash across her eyes. She had seen it when he had forced her down over a bar table and cast her skirts up over her back. The fabric had felt like a shroud. She had locked her jaw, for she had refused to give Gotthard the satisfaction of hearing her cry out. However, she had managed to look back at the beast.

Just in time to see him kill Cousin Jerome! Jerome protected the tavern. He had tried to stop the assault, and what had Gotthard done? He had ordered the constabulary men to take hold of him and force him to watch. Then Gotthard had ordered one of them to stab Jerome as Gotthard finished with Alerice, grabbed her scalp, and cast her aside.

Thinking of Jerome brought tears, which Alerice desperately fought back. She turned and pressed her brow into the wall to prevent a rush of anguish. For these past three nights, she had been completely numb, unable to feel a single thing, pleasurable or painful. Now she suddenly felt everything – and now was not the time.

But poor Jerome. Poor Cousin Millie, Jerome's wife, who worked in Gotthard's kitchen and had helped her gain entry a moment ago. Poor Uncle Judd, Aunt Carol, Grammy Linden, and Jerome's three brothers who were no doubt spoiling for revenge. Gotthard had ruined an entire family in one heinous moment, and then he had proclaimed Alerice guilty of Jerome's murder to exonerate himself and prevent her from seeking refuge with those she loved.

"Sukaar, Father Fire," Alerice silently prayed. "Imari, Mother Water Wind. Give me strength in this moment."

Alerice felt her emotions drain away, and she turned back to her task. She wanted to shove a dagger into Gotthard's heart, but she could not get close enough to stab him and flee.

It was best to let the cup do its work, but she would make herself known. Partly to call Gotthard out, but mostly to show everyone that a small person was capable of standing up. Her father had always taught her to stand up when she could make a difference. Now she meant to.

"For the Cheval is indeed a noble man, and we praise him for his good graces," Gotthard said. "To the Cheval."

"To the Cheval," all assembled repeated.

Alerice drew out a small knife as the revelers drank. Gotthard took one swallow and another, but then stopped mid-draught. He rankled his nose and glanced at the cup, which he handed to his wife, who eagerly drained it dry.

Did he drink enough? Was this going to work?

The only sound Alerice could hear was her own heartbeat. The only sensation she could feel was her quickening breath.

Gotthard licked his lips while offering Andoni a smug little bow. Andoni responded by standing and extending his arm in brotherly friendship. Gotthard took it in a hand-to-forearm grasp. Then he began thinly smacking his lips.

A sudden *bleetch* erupted at the head table as Gotthard's wife vomited up the bloody contents of her stomach. All turned to her aghast and Alerice prayed that Gotthard would likewise splay his innards.

His wife moaned and vomited again. The Reef of Navre leaped up from his seat at a lower table and hurried to help her.

Then Gotthard doubled over, clutching his gut. He reached for the Reef and caught hold of his tunic, but he too vomited over the dinner and flatware, his blood and bits of food mixing with those of his wife.

Gotthard hoisted himself upright despite his obvious pain, and Alerice launched the blade at him. It sank into his shoulder, attracting all eyes.

She stood out from the shadows and tore away her page cap. Her blonde hair tumbled down past her shoulders as she summoned the full measure of the rage that was deservedly hers.

"There's a peck from this little bird! Mayor Gotthard murdered my cousin, Jerome Linden!"

"Take her!" the Reef shouted, gesturing for his men to advance from the hall's corners.

Alerice turned and bolted down the hall. She hurled herself at the pages, scattering their dessert trays. She heard the clatter of metal on stone as she sprinted into the kitchen.

She made for a table filled with pots awaiting washing, and knocked them all to the floor. The head cook stood bolt upright and the rest of the staff watched in shock, allowing Alerice to shoot for the back door.

One of the Reef's men entered and called for someone to shut the door. Alerice saw Cousin Millie respond, which was a ploy to keep the Reef from suspecting her. Alerice grabbed the copper pan that Millie had placed on a nearby stool and smacked her across the jaw with it to send her toppling backward. Then she hurried out into the night's blessed shadows.

***

Alerice knew every nook and cranny in Navre. She had come to the city at the age of five. Uncle Judd had taken her in at her mother's request after her father had died in Lord Andoni's ranks, serving honorably during the campaign against southern invaders.

Uncle Judd had praised Alerice for her quick wit and natural charm. He had doted on her as his own daughter, likely because he had been blessed with four boys and needed an angel to brighten his day.

Alerice had eagerly learned to manage a household, but while she was an adequate cook and seamstress, sophisticated chores had been her delight.

Uncle Judd owned the local brewery, and Alerice soon began taking stock of how much grain arrived each day, how much water the brewery drew from the nearby river, and how many barrels were properly ripened. She had been quick to learn ledgers and tallies, and how to make certain that inventory went unpilfered.

When Alerice had reached the age when most girls would have been sold in marriage, Uncle Judd could not bear to part with her. Instead, he had cooked up a scheme with Grammy Linden to marry her to Cousin Jerome, all the while placing them both at the new tavern that Judd had acquired in a card game.

Alerice had always wondered if Uncle Judd had cheated to win the establishment, which he renamed the Cup and Quill. While he had never spoken of the matter, she had been happy to learn the inn-keeping trade.

There had been so many things to manage – larder stocks, meats and cheeses, breads and treats. And the girls. They kept rooms upstairs and sold their company during the evening hours. Even though Mistress Dora kept track of each 'busy lassie', Alerice had seen to the tidiness of their lodgings and knew she would manage the girls herself one day.

And that day had come when Uncle Judd had placed her in charge of the Cup and Quill. She and Jerome had shared a quick cousins' kiss to end their engagement, which everyone knew had been little more than a sweet deception. Jerome had married Millie shortly thereafter while Alerice had 'taken the apron'.

Folk had likened it to taking holy vows. As the new mistress of the Cup and Quill, Alerice had plied each of Uncle Judd's management lessons with firm precision. Cousin Jerome helped as best he could, although he had doted upon Millie as any newlywed husband should. Even so, Alerice had been able to balance his married life with her independent one to make the Cup and Quill one of the most popular public houses in Navre.

Until the three nights before when Gotthard had shattered her world and sent her hiding in the city's backstreets, where she had been forced to slip silently to and fro, stealing food wherever she could find it and huddling for warmth whenever a hovel presented itself.

After the attack, Alerice had waited for the moment when she could steal back to the brewery without attracting attention. She would stop only to bid her family farewell, for lingering would implicate them in Gotthard's trumped-up charges regarding Jerome.

Yet as Alerice had waited, she had crawled behind the apothecary. The rear door's inner bolt had been secure, but not the side window's. Fortunately, Uncle Judd had insisted that she learn to read more than ledgers. She held a basic understanding of tinctures and medicines, and thus she had been able to identify the ingredients necessary to mix a swift-acting poison as the trauma of what Gotthard had done had begun to take hold of her exhausted wits.

In that instant, she had formed a new plan, one she could execute as Gotthard hosted Lord Andoni.

***

Alerice cast a weary gaze upward at her new traveling companions, three circling ravens that cawed into the night sky. She plodded down the open road on the bare back of a stolen plow horse. She wore stolen clothes, and a stolen pack containing stolen food rested across her shoulders. She was a thief. She was a murderess, and she was... alone.

She would never see her family again. She would never be able to curl into Uncle Judd's arms or have Grammy Linden sing her to sleep. She had never had the opportunity to say goodbye to any of them. After killing Gotthard, she did not dare go anywhere near the brewery.

Had standing up to that beast been worth it? Gotthard had taken everything from her – her dignity, her livelihood, and her self-respect. The last was the worst, for now that all was done, Alerice could not justify killing him. She certainly could not justify killing his wife. Indeed, who was she to have taken such action in the first place?

The ravens cawed again in low, throaty tones. More joined them until there were at least a dozen. They might as well have been vultures. Alerice was already dead in her own eyes. She could never use her own name again. She could never confide in another person again.

Had this all truly happened in a few scant days?

The horse clip-clopped on down the treeless road. More caws sounded and Alerice looked up a third time. Clouds shadowed the moon, creating a gray background for the ravens' flight. As they circled, her thoughts swirled.

Then she smiled, for she found herself back in her bedroom at the Cup and Quill. Somewhere in her oh-so-sleepy mind, she was aware that the plow horse had stopped moving and stood quietly in the open, but she paid it no heed as she bent forward and nestled against a broad horsehair pillow.

Something *thunked* into Alerice's pack with enough force to jolt her forward. The plow horse startled and whinnied, and then hurried off as Alerice toppled from its back onto the roadside. She landed on her hip as her pack flew off of her shoulder, a crossbow bolt sticking out of it.

Another bolt *whizzed* in, landing a hand's width from her head, and Alerice looked up to see three mounted men galloping straight for her. There was no

8

mistaking that the Reef of Navre rode in the lead position.

The clouds parted overhead and the moon seemed to spotlight her. Alerice's heart leaped and she ran, but there was no outpacing her pursuers. In moments, three horses surrounded her and three men jumped down to the grass, two with loaded crossbows trained on her, and the Reef fitting a fresh bolt into his.

Alerice froze and stared at him. The Reef leveled his bow and shot her in the shoulder. The impact knocked her to her haunches, and she cried out in pain.

"That's for pecking the mayor, little bird."

The other two men laughed as the Reef said to them, "What do you know, Tom? You did see someone ride away on old Pat's plow nag. Guess we'll have to wrangle it up and return it to him."

"Guess so," Tom said. "Funny how the ravens led us straight to her."

The Reef looked up at the dispersing flock. "Yes, funny." He paused to listen to the receding caws before he looked down at Alerice. "The gods below must really want this one."

Rage and fear welled up within Alerice as the Reef stepped close. She drew her dagger from her belt and crouched to spring up at him, but he rushed forward and dropped to a knee beside her, tossing his crossbow down so that he could place his gloved hand over hers and control her blade. Then he grabbed her by the hair and wrenched her head back.

The intimacy was terrifying. Alerice tried to summon the courage to fight, but she had no hope in besting him – and she was well aware, that he was well aware, of this fact.

She scratched at his face with her free hand, but Tom advanced to take hold of her arm. She struggled and kicked, but the third man came forward to step hard on one of her thighs. The Reef adjusted his position to kneel on the other.

"I should take you back to Navre," he said, looking her over with the confidence of a hunter watching an animal struggle in a steel trap. "I should hang you for what you did to Gotthard and his wife, but I think I will kill you here instead. I'll let the wolves take your flesh, and whoever wants you below take your soul. And that will be the sad end of tiny, little you."

He forced Alerice's hand toward her body and pricked the dagger into her ribs. She did not cry out, for the shoulder pain numbed her to the cut. Instead, she locked stares with him and breathed hard through her nose.

"You see," the Reef continued. "If I hang you, your family will have the right to claim your body. They will bury you at their brewery, and take solace knowing what happened to you. Instead, I will take this knife of yours, and leave it on their doorstep, and let them wonder. They'll know it's yours, won't they?"

Alerice could not deny that they would.

"Of course, I could arrest them all as your accomplices," the Reef added. "But why would I ruin Navre's beer supply?"

The men agreed, and Alerice's eyes narrowed as she struggled one final time to free herself. The one man pressed harder on her thigh, and she grunted in pain. Alerice glanced up at him, and then leveled her stare at the Reef and spat in his face.

He did not seem to mind. "Now, that's a kiss goodbye."

The Reef drew close. His beard stubble scratched Alerice's skin, and she thought he was going to force his lips onto hers, but he exhaled on her cheek as he wrenched the dagger from her grasp.

"And by the way, thank you," the Reef said softly. "With Gotthard gone, I am free to rise."

The Reef shoved the dagger into Alerice's ribcage. She screamed at the searing pain, and her body tensed as the steel pierced deeply. Somehow, she felt the dagger's tip touch her heart, but then she felt nothing further.

***

Something poked Alerice's shoulder. It poked a second time and then a third, each time deeper than the last. Alerice tried to wave it off, but she could not lift her arm. She was able to move her shoulder ever so slightly, but nothing more.

"What do you know?" someone said. "It lives, and it's awake."

What do you mean, it lives and it's awake?

Alerice tried to voice the thought, but all she could manage were a few thin moans. Was she waking from the nightmare that she longed to escape? Was it all finally over?

"Hello, mortal..." the same person said in a sing-song tone.

"Uhmph," Alerice groaned before she contracted her gut to force enough air through her chest to comment, "mortal?"

"Ah, would you listen to that. It also talks."

"Unh. Of course... I talk." Alerice thought she should punctuate her statement with something equal to the present sarcasm, but her thoughts swirled too greatly to summon a retort.

"Come, come, little flesh pot. Let's wake up all the way. They're waiting to see you."

Alerice sighed internally. None of this made any sense. However, the one thing she could comprehend was that the someone engaging her was going to keep doing so until she rose from her slumber, for that's what her present state must be. A slumber the likes of which she had never known.

The someone addressing her began tapping on her forehead, which was the most exacerbating sensation thus far, and Alerice finally found the strength to heft her arm and flail her hand about her brow to bat the someone away. Then, slowly, she opened her eyes.

A spry youth came into her line of sight. He hovered over her, his ice-blue eyes dancing. His whitish hair seemed alive with tiny sparks of different colors. His lips were deep peach, and he grinned with curiosity before he reached out to tap Alerice's brow once again.

"Please stop that," she said, moving her head away.

"Oh!" the youth exclaimed as he raised an eyebrow and inspected Alerice more closely. "It has manners."

"And please stop calling me 'it'." She drew in a deep breath as she began to feel more stable, and blinked widely a few times before she focused on the youth again. "My name is Alerice Linden. Of Navre."

"Well, that's interesting. Not that I either know where Navre is, or care for that matter, but Alerice... I do like that name. It's pretty, and I suppose it suits you because, for a mortal, you're somewhat pretty yourself."

"Why do you keep calling me 'mortal'?" she asked.

"Well, you're hardly anything else. Now, Alerice Linden of Navre, can you sit up?"

"I... think so, but I'm having trouble moving. I've never felt like this before."

"Oh, that's not surprising. You've never been dead before."

"What?"

"Ah, I didn't realize that you were hard of hearing. I can speak louder if it helps!" the youth shouted.

"No, I can hear everything you say, but did you just say I was dead?"

"Yes, and I must admit that's puzzling. Normally, mortals leave their bodies above while their souls come to us. But you came in as a complete package, didn't you. You even had a crossbow bolt stuck in your shoulder, but I took that out. You're welcome, by the way. Now, once more. Can you sit up? I'll help you if you like."

"Thank you," Alerice said softly.

"My pleasure," the youth said in a slightly higher, more feminine register. Alerice focused on rising as he reached down and lifted her torso away from her body so that she sat up within the shell of herself.

She looked down at her legs and then around and over her shoulder at her torso and head. Her body lay peacefully with her arms at her sides, still dressed in the clothes she had stolen.

Alerice blinked, dumbfounded, but then as she looked back at the youth, she startled in alarm. He had become a maiden with soft rose lips and waist-long whitish hair shimmering with colors along its length.

"What... are you?" Alerice gasped.

"You mean, who am I?" the maiden asked.

"No, I mean 'what' are you? Are you spirit? For I fear that you are not flesh."

"Yes, you do have that part right. My name is Oddwyn, Herald to the King of Shadows and the Raven Queen."

"Shadows? Ravens?" Alerice said to herself. "Then that means..."

A quick flash of her final moments with the Reef shot across her mind's eye, and Alerice found herself reliving the strike of her own dagger into her heart.

"Ohhh, there's that little memory angst you mortals do," Oddwyn cooed in a voice as sweet as any loving sister's. "It gets me every time. Since you're a bit overwhelmed right now, I'll try to explain things. You are in the Realme, both your spirit and your body, and again this is quite puzzling. That's why the king and queen want to see you."

"In the Realme?" Alerice asked.

"Yes," Oddwyn said, again presenting himself as a youth. "The Evherealme. This is the Convergence."

Alerice looked about, finding four towering filigree arches crafted of shimmering silver-veined stone. Each bore glyphs the likes of which she had never seen. They were set at quarter opposites to one another, and four smaller arches rested between each to form a wondrous octagon. A filigree stone copula rose high above, supported by the arches. Its apex seemed to extend toward infinity.

An ether of black, midnight blue, and deep teal pulsed within each arch, and Alerice could see the same ether wisping about the copula's filigree.

Then the ether in several arches began to swirl, and people floated through. They appeared thin and ethereal, some old, some young, and even a few abandoned babes. The moment they entered, pale spirits came to meet them, taking their hands and guiding them a few paces before they all vanished.

Alerice startled again, for the Convergence was both beautiful and demoralizing. She felt her heart sink as she turned her face aside to hide a sensation of utter loss.

"Now, what's all this?" Oddwyn asked, gently reaching out to take Alerice's chin and turn her face back. "Don't cry. As I said, you are very interesting."

"Please just leave me be," Alerice said as she saw more souls entering through the Convergence arch near her, only to be led away by more pale spirits.

"Now, now. The Realme's master and mistress are waiting to see you. You should feel honored to have the chance to speak to them."

"Should I?" Alerice said, finally finding enough strength to encase her loss in sarcasm. "You said your name was Oddwyn? Would that be short for 'odd one'? The name certainly suits you if this is so."

"Hmmm. And I thought you had manners. Well, if this is how you wish to converse, then let's be flat about it. First, being odd is a perfectly wonderful state of self. I would rather be odd than be anything else, and anyone who does not see the truth in that statement is... what's the phrase I'm looking for... oh yes – a dead mortal."

Oddwyn gestured his thumb at more souls entering the Convergence through other arches.

"Like them. Dead, dead, and dead. Second," he said with a hard flick on her brow. "Accept your situation and get up. Leave your body where it lies. It's not going anywhere. You're coming with me." Oddwyn held up his fingers to snap, even as the tri-colored ether in the arch behind Alerice began to swirl. "Now."

***

Alerice found herself standing in a space that seemed both vast and intimate. It bore no architectural definitions, but it was definitely a 'place'. She had no idea how she had traveled here. She suspected it had been through the Convergence arch, but as she glanced about to find it, she discovered the youthful Oddwyn standing beside her.

He wore an iridescent tunic of turquoise and lavender, accented by indigo and pearl. His shirt was crafted from some shimmering ethereal material, and his light-blue trousers tucked into white boots.

Oddwyn flashed a 'what are you looking at?' expression before he gestured that Alerice should look ahead.

Though she had not seen anything a moment ago, Alerice now beheld two otherworldly figures standing atop a dais.

Oddwyn stepped forward and bowed to them both. Then he turned toward Alerice and proclaimed, "Mortal, lower your gaze in awe. Bend your knee in respect, for I present to you the King of Shadows and the Raven Queen, master and mistress of the Evherealme."

Alerice stared wide-eyed at Oddwyn, half-paralyzed in fear and completely uncertain of what to do. Oddwyn gestured that she should look down, which Alerice did while offering a small curtsey. Then, she glanced back up at Oddwyn, who half-rolled his eyes at her meager gesture and returned to her side.

Alerice looked up at the two majesties, and her breath came up short, for she recognized what Grammy Linden had often described as the King of Shadows and his wife, the Raven Queen.

No stories of allegorical lore told to children by the fireside could have prepared Alerice for this moment.

The king was tall. The tone of his long, open robe shifted as though affected by the movement of light. His face was long and pale. His eyes were dark gray and he sported a thin beard trimmed close to his jawline. His crown was crafted of shimmering smokey crystals. Longer crystals adorned his pauldrons while an intricate crystalline trim ran along the border of his robe's vertical opening, its hem, and its cuffs. The king's physical form hidden, within his robe, seemed to shift, as anyone might expect of a shadow.

The Raven Queen stood in a gown of sleek feathers that fluxed from black to purple to emerald. Her arms were white as willows. Her crown was crafted of a silverish metal Alerice had never seen, even for an inn mistress well experienced in coin. Her black hair flowed nearly to her feet, billowing as if buoyed by unseen currents. Her eyes were the deepest amethyst, and her lips the deepest red.

Behind the king stood two Shadow Warriors.

Behind the queen stood two Raven Knights.

The Shadow Warriors' breastplates were etched with wispy curls about the articulations. The same curls adorned their arm and leg plates, but what unnerved Alerice was the lack of faces within their helms. She could only see gray-blackness therein.

The Raven Knights' helms were metal bird skulls. Golden orbs shone through the eye sockets. Sprays of metal feathers rose up from the top-back of the helms' crestlines. The edges of the layered plates along their arms and legs were fashioned to resemble metal feather tips, and Alerice could not be certain if their long, black, feather-trimmed cloaks weren't wings.

Oddwyn drew a breath and proclaimed, "Your Majesties, I present to you Alerice Linden of Navre."

Not having the slightest idea what more was expected, Alerice curtseyed again.

The King of Shadows and the Raven Queen nodded in response. "You are welcome to the Hall of Eternity," they said, their voices at an octave from one another.

Alerice shivered and reached out to take Oddwyn's hand. Oddwyn looked at the gesture, then at Alerice. Then Oddwyn became a maiden once again, her tunic transforming into a lady's belted demi-gown with sleeves that extended over the tops of her fingers and a length which displayed her light-blue leggings and white boots. She gave Alerice's hand a reassuring squeeze.

The king gestured to his right while the queen gestured to her left. In response, the hall took on the semblance of a columned rotunda with shimmering statues of male warriors along the king's hemisphere and women of the arts along the queen's.

Great glyphs appeared about the floor, giving it a mosaic quality. Thrones appeared upon the dais, the king's crafted with bunched spears along the sides, and the queen's crafted with raven heads looking out at side angles. Their dazzling golden eyes matched those of her Raven Knights.

The king and queen sat in a unified motion, the Shadow Warriors and Raven Knights advancing behind them. Then they bade Alerice to step forward.

Alerice gave Oddwyn's hand one final squeeze, prayed that the gods above would somehow protect her, and stepped toward the dais. She was shaking. She could not help it, but no matter how terrified she was, she made up her mind to endure the moment.

"Set your fear aside," the queen said in a dark honey voice.

"No," said the king. "Wear your fear openly. Show it for all to see. Only by exposing it shall you master it."

"Yes, Your Majesty," Alerice forced herself to say. "But if you wish to see my fear, then may I ask, do I have reason to fear you? If I am dead, do you have further harm in store for me?"

Both the king and queen seemed pleasantly surprised by her response, as did Oddwyn, whom Alerice could not see but somehow sensed that he had presented himself as a youth again. She thought she heard him chuckle, but she remained fixed on the Realme's rulers, for whatever lay in store did so at their deciding.

The Raven Queen gestured her willow-white palm toward Alerice. As if touched by a comforting whisper, Alerice felt her heart strengthen and her shaking abate. She looked into the queen's amethyst eyes, suddenly feeling release from all mortal notions. In those eyes, she found the freedom of an unencumbered spirit, and along with it the joy of having known a life well lived.

"You are a good person, Alerice of Navre," the queen said. The king scoffed, but the queen paid him little heed. "At least, you have always tried to be good. I see this as I measure you."

Alerice wanted to accept the compliment. Grammy Linden would be pleased, for she had always cautioned the children in her care to live good lives. Grammy had always said that folks would be judged on their merits or faults one day. Knowing this, Alerice lowered her head, for her most egregious fault hung heavily over her.

"Forgive me, Your Majesty, but I am not good. I am a murderess, plain and simple."

Alerice felt the king taking pleasure from her admission, but she could also feel the queen pressing her amethyst gaze.

"You are damaged, Alerice," the queen said. "But before that damage, how did you live your life?"

"I always tried to stand up," Alerice replied, still unable to lift her head. "I never watered down the ale. I never cheated customers. I looked after the 'busy lassies', and I tried to host everyone at the Cup and Quill with equal measure. But I've killed two people, and I cannot escape that."

"And so you believe that one wrong choice discounts a life of good ones?"

Exactly why Alerice felt the courage to look upon the Raven Queen, she did not know, but she had considered this moral debate before, only now she was the culprit, not the inquisitor.

"Your Majesty, if a man steals to feed his family, he is still a thief. He may not be in the eyes of his neighbors, but he is in the eyes of those who rule. I took two lives, which is far worse than taking bread. I metered out justice. Who was I to do so?"

"A victim with no advocate," the queen stated. "There was no one to stand up for you. There was no one to stand up for other victims. You knew this as you plotted your course. You apportioned justice to a man who required it but would never have faced it, and if he had never injured you, you would have remained serving good ale and welcoming guests because, at heart, you are a good person."

"But I killed Gotthard's wife," Alerice said.

"Which was not your intent," the queen replied. "Your focus was on the wicked, as it should have been. There are folk above who applaud you for your actions, if you wish to know. What I wish to know is, if you had the power to hold the wicked accountable, would you wield it?"

Alerice had no reply. She had never thought of herself as judge and executioner, and she was not certain she wanted that responsibility. What if she made a mistake and judged the wrong person? What if she made things worse by killing someone wicked, but who had a good family?

"Your Majesty..." Alerice heard herself saying. "I have always tried to be good. Keeping faith with good deeds is something someone does when no one else bears witness, and it's always made sense to me. But I'm a modest person. Yes, I try to stand up when I can, but my father also cautioned me not to throw coins into other people's games. I am not the type to claim righteousness."

"But you could be," the king said. "If you were properly inspired. Look at you, girl. You have strength. Do you think you would be standing here without it?"

Alerice had no idea what to say, and as Grammy Linden had always cautioned, moments like these were the perfect time to say nothing.

The queen smiled.

"This one is mine," she said.

"Ah, let's see," the king replied.

"No," the queen asserted. "This one is mine. You had yours, My King, and we both know how well a driven man has served you. I will take this woman and her good deeds under my wing. I will help redeem her of the crime she accuses herself of committing, for her nature proffers true service."

"Indeed it does," the king said. "That's why I desire her."

The King of Shadows rose from his throne, and before Alerice could blink, he stood before her. He placed his hand upon her upper arm so that she could not back away and looked down at her.

"Alerice of Navre, I offer you power to defeat any enemy, either here in the Realme or above in Mortalia. You have the courage, and the will, to do this. I see it within you. You say you are modest, but I see pride, pride that you can use to your advantage. Take up my sword and swear your soul to me. You will never be a victim again, I promise you that."

"But My King," the queen said. "Another mortal already bears your blade. Do you intend to retrieve it from him?

The king did not reply as he pressed his dark-gray eyes into Alerice's soul.

Alerice felt icy tingles within her breast, and though they were not born of fear, she knew that she was not aligned with this immortal. And yet he had said...

"Mortalia, Your Majesty?"

The Raven Queen also appeared before Alerice and took hold of her other upper arm, though in a gentler manner.

"Mortalia is our term for the living world, and you are one of its unique souls. Sometimes, the gods above and we below intertwine. Sometimes our worlds kiss one another, and when such moments of divine currents flow together, mortal children are blessed with the gift to 'walk between'.

"That is why your whole self came unto the Convergence, your flesh and your spirit. That is why, if you swear to one of us, we can restore you to walk again among the living. But you will also be able to walk among the Realme's many worlds.

"If this notion appeals to you, swear yourself to me and I will give you my dagger to replace your own. With it, you may right wrongs done to others. You may stand up for those who have no voice, those who truly need you, and in so doing you may discover your own path to self-forgiveness."

Alerice looked between the king and queen, finding their desire to claim her distressing. Never in her life had she entered into an impulsive bargain. She had seen far too many of them at the Cup and Quill, and they rarely ended well. Now these immortals were asking for her to swear her soul?

"How can I possibly answer you?" Alerice said.

She regarded their hands, shrugged them off, and then backed away toward Oddwyn.

"You are telling me that I have some sort of special blessing? I don't believe in stories like that, and it's not likely I will start now. I don't know what to make of any of this, and now you both ask me to swear to you without knowing what this truly entails?"

She shook her head before she continued. "You could be asking me to do something dreadful. How am I to judge? Yes, Grammy Linden told me many stories of people who walk on after death, in the woods, or about the mountain tops, or along the seacoasts, but I have never heard tale of a spirit who roamed contentedly."

Alerice regarded the king, for he was correct in that she did have strength, perhaps even pride. "Forgive me, Your Majesty, but I have no enemies to defeat. This is because I've made none, and I do not wish to start. Even Gotthard was not my enemy. He was just a vile excuse for a man."

Then Alerice looked at the queen. "And while I sense that your manner is more appreciative of goodness, you are still the ruler of souls that can never see their families again, so how compassionate can you be?"

Alerice looked back and forth between them once more, then looked at their stalwart Shadow Warriors and Raven Knights, and then about the hall, where her eyes darted from face to face of the statues that seemed to be scrutinizing her.

"I... I just want to go home," she finally said, burying her face in her palms.

Alerice felt the Realme's master and mistress disappear from before her, and then she felt a gentle grip on both of her shoulders. She lifted her face to see the maiden Oddwyn looking at her with a supportive smile.

"They can, you know," Oddwyn said softly.

"They can what?" Alerice asked.

"The souls here can see their families. Some can even whisper to them and guide them. And you're special in that regard because you can do the same thing and still remain fully fleshed." Oddwyn resumed his youthful appearance to add, "Not that flesh is always a good thing."

Alerice smiled at Oddwyn's manner and his/her clear attempt at humor. "I'm sorry," she said.

"For what?" Oddwyn asked.

"For calling you 'odd' earlier. I shouldn't have done that."

"I've already told you that I prefer being odd."

"Yes, but I said it in a bad way. That was wrong. I didn't mean to disparage you."

Oddwyn paused and then simply said, "Thank you." She resumed a maiden's form and brought Alerice into an embrace. Alerice wrapped her arms around Oddwyn's gentle spirit and was about to sob once more, but for some reason she felt her own soul voiding itself of angst.

Alerice glanced up at the King of Shadows and the Raven Queen, once again seated upon their thrones. They were not intervening to help her, and yet she felt she had the ability, indeed the empowerment, to withdraw from Oddwyn's embrace.

It was the Evherealme itself bolstering her. Alerice could sense it deeply within her. Somehow she felt in perfect tempo with this domain of endless time. Somehow it was a part of her, and she was a part of it.

Perhaps she had been blessed at birth. Perhaps Grammy Linden had known about it and never told her, but Alerice could not deny her love of shadows, where she had always felt the safest, and shadows were the very fabric of the Realme.

But more to the point, this everlasting master and mistress had not only offered her their weapons. They had offered her a new life, which was something Alerice now required. She could never return to her old life, for she could never return to Navre. If she were to walk again in the living world, she may as well do so in service to the Realme's king or queen, for at least then she would have the means to defend herself. Also, if these two wished her to willingly enter into service, she had the 'coin' to buy what she now wanted more than anything.

Alerice patted Oddwyn's shoulder and then stepped up toward the dais.

"Rulers of the Realme," she said. "I don't understand any of this, but I do believe wholeheartedly that the Reef killed me on the road. If that is so, then everything you are telling me must also be true, and though I have no idea what you will demand of me if I swear to you, I ask for only one thing in return."

The King of Shadows leaned forward, the upturned corner of his lips belying his affirmation that all mortals had their price. Alerice noted that the queen did not shift her posture, but was certainly focused.

"I ask that you protect my family," Alerice said. "And I hope that I may see them again one day, but only if it's safe."

"That's what you want?" the king asked. "Nothing more?"

"Nothing more, Your Majesty," she said. "For I wish nothing for myself." Alerice looked between them again as she considered her choice.

"Sir," she said to the king. "I appreciate that you wish to inspire me, for wicked people should face justice. However, I would prefer them to be measured as the Raven Queen has measured me. Let her apportion justice. I do not wish to."

The King of Shadows sat back while the Raven Queen leaned in. Her knowing smile and her head raised in pride provided Alerice with the clear answer of which weapon to accept. She took a solid step before the queen and knelt down on both knees.

"And so if you will protect my family, I will take up your dagger, in place of my own."

***

"Well, don't you cut a sleek figure," Oddwyn said, his ice-blue eyes dancing.

"Do I?" Alerice asked.

"Mmmm," Oddwyn replied.

The two stood in a grove of thick-trunked trees, the leafed branches of which stretched out overhead. The Raven Queen had restored Alerice to her mortal body, which Alerice had not been comfortable with at first.

After all, the vow of service had been an unnerving experience. The Raven Queen had risen from her throne and appeared before her. She had offered her dagger for Alerice to take, but as soon as Alerice had gripped its smooth, black handle, the Raven Queen had placed one hand over hers and her other palm atop Alerice's brow. Then she had guided the dagger's pommel over Alerice's breast in order to form a connection between mind and heart.

Alerice had felt the queen's power fill her. She had heard the queen ask, "Will you obey me, and act in my name? Will you remain steadfast to me as I remain steadfast to you? If these are your choices, swear upon your soul that they are."

Alerice was not certain of any formal response, so she repeated the queen's words. "These are my choices, and I do swear upon my soul."

After that, Alerice had felt her mind swirl. A strange sense of transition had overtaken her, as though she moved through multiple windows. Within each window she sensed a different world that she felt she could revisit and explore. She had heard voices whispering to her, voices she felt could guide and advise her, and when the swirling was over, she had felt the Raven Queen withdraw and saw Oddwyn approach to take hold of her and lift her up off her knees.

"Take her to the Convergence," the queen had said. "And lay her down."

"Yes, Great Lady Raven," Oddwyn had replied.

From there it had been a matter of helping Alerice settle back down within her body. The Raven Queen had accompanied them to the Convergence, and as soon as Alerice had stepped into her flesh as she might step into a long, thin sack, sat down, and lay back, the Raven Queen had instructed her to close her eyes.

20

When next Alerice opened them, while drawing in a deep breath, she had risen up whole and sound. Both the queen and Oddwyn had smiled, and then the Raven Queen had told Oddwyn to 'proceed'.

"I can't really see myself, you know," Alerice said as she ran her palms down the sides of her newly fitted tunic of black metal scales. Each scale lay flat along her body. The tunic buckled closed on either side, and Oddwyn had helped Alerice don the armor, which remarkably felt no heavier than a bodice.

The tunic spanned Alerice's torso from her neck to the width of her hips, and should she require more outfitting, Oddwyn had also offered her pauldrons and a gorget. She had refused the extra gear, for the tunic would easily suffice. After all, she could not imagine the Raven Queen sending her into battle.

Oddwyn buckled a black belt about Alerice's waist that was studded with the same white metal that composed the queen's crown. Apparently, it was a Realme amalgam that had only rarely seen the light of the living world. The queen's dagger, a Realme weapon, rested in a sheath affixed to the belt, and Alerice found her hand naturally drifting toward it. She gripped its handle, and then ran her fingers about its hilt.

"I'm glad you chose the dagger," Oddwyn said. "A sword would never suit you, although you should see the king's blade in action. If you throw it, it will always strike the target. Then all you have to do is hold your hand high overhead, and it will reappear in your palm."

Alerice smiled and drew her Realme dagger. It appeared to be a common blade, and yet as she gazed upon it, she could see shifting lines shimmer and flux. Indeed, the blade felt alive.

"Does this also reappear in your palm?" she asked.

"Yes, and it will always strike its mark as well, but it will also guide you to the target that most requires striking. That may surprise you when the time comes, but trust in the blade's integrity. That's my one piece of advice."

"Oddwyn, my friend," Alerice said with a smile. "I seriously doubt you ever limit yourself to one piece of advice."

Oddwyn regarded her and then offered, "It depends on what the advice is. Sometimes I only say things once. But there's something else the blade can do. Look at it more closely."

Alerice did, and soon saw that the blade's shifting lines blended into a surface that brightened before the weapon presented the scene of her family in Uncle Judd's home.

Alerice could see her own face reflected in the dagger's surface even as she gazed upon the sight of her loved ones stricken with worry. The Reef must have made good on his promise to return her dagger, and her family must have discovered it. She could see Cousin Chessy along with his younger brothers,

Clancy and Little Judd, pacing about, longing to take action. She saw Uncle Judd argue with them and Aunt Carol pleading with them. Grammy Linden sat with Millie, both keeping out of the fracas.

"Try saying something to them," Oddwyn suggested. "There's a good chance they can hear you whispering in their heads."

"Really?" she asked, hopeful that this might be true. Oddwyn simply gave her a slow, reassuring blink, and so Alerice focused on the blade.

"Millie?" she called, figuring that her cousin-in-law would be the most receptive. As she watched, she could see Millie's expression change as though listening. "Tell them I'm safe. Tell them that I escaped the Reef. Tell them I will send them a sign not to worry. I love you all, Millie. Don't let the boys do anything foolhardy. Make them listen. I know you can."

The blade brightened again, and then returned to its proper hue.

"You can't do that for too long, or do it too often, so save the moment for when you truly need it. In the meantime..." Oddwyn presented Alerice with a small crossbow.

"It looks like a toy."

"Well, it shoots like a spitting serpent," Oddwyn said. "And it will always have a bolt ready for you. Try it."

"Very well," Alerice said as she took hold of the bow. It was half the size of a proper crossbow, and as light as a child's plaything. Yet as Alerice hefted it to aim at a tree, the bow string pulled back of its own accord, and a glimmering black bolt appeared in the flight groove.

"Nice trick," Alerice exclaimed.

She squeezed the trigger into the tiller, and the bolt *whizzed* out with surprising speed. It struck the tree's trunk, and dissipated in a burst of dark light. Alerice stood silent in surprise, and then regarded the weapon.

"The bolts can kill most anyone in Mortalia or the Realme," Oddwyn said.

"Most anyone?" Alerice asked.

Oddwyn cocked his head. "You had best prepare yourself for an adventure, Alerice of Navre. You have no idea how long the Raven Queen has been awaiting a champion. I dare say that she has a long list of tasks in mind, and not all the personages on her list are going to be mortally wounded by a bolt from your bow."

Alerice lowered the weapon, wondering what to do with it. Oddwyn's countenance changed into that of a maiden, who gestured for Alerice to give it to her.

"It goes here," she said in her soft voice as she unbuttoned a strap on Alerice's belt and slipped the crossbow in so that the catch rested on the opposite hip from the Realme dagger.

Alerice regarded the Realme's Herald, and then could not help but ask, "Oddwyn, why do you keep doing that?"

"Doing what?" Oddwyn asked as she stood and looked Alerice over.

"...Changing hairstyles," Alerice said, deciding that a euphemism would be the most tactful way of addressing the fluctuations in gender.

"Do you wish to take issue with my expression?" Oddwyn asked matter-of-factly as she raised an eyebrow.

"Well, I'd be lying if I said I wasn't curious."

Oddwyn sighed through her nose. "Mortals... Very well. For me, there are times when the headiness of youthful moments best conveys my strongest self. Then there are times when I embrace the softness of my soul. I am a spirit of both reflections and quite happy to move between them."

"But, it's rather confusing."

"To you. But that's because you expect to see something specific when you look upon me. Perhaps when you do look at me, you should prepare yourself to see something different than what you expect. I see no reason to change myself in order to suit you or anyone else."

Alerice was about to mull this over, for no one had ever put the matter of personal identity so plainly before. However, a swirling ether of black, midnight blue, and deep teal appeared between two tree trunks, and the Raven Queen appeared in an opening portal.

She stepped forward into the grove. "Oddwyn," she said.

Oddwyn curtseyed, smiled at Alerice's outfitting, and then moved gracefully to the portal, where she stepped through. The queen banished the ether, and bade Alerice to accompany her.

The Raven Queen led Alerice to the edge of a rise overlooking a road. They stood in the hill country where the highs and lows of the landscape rolled out as far as the eye could see. Upon the hills, Alerice could see more stands of trees, terraced fields, and vineyards.

"I am sending you to the town of Basque," the queen stated. "Your first task it to slay a beast of two faces that has recently begun to feed upon innocent souls."

Alerice looked up at her matron. "I'm sorry, what?"

The Raven Queen stood tall as she gazed into the distance. A flock of ravens flew in and circled about her head. She raised a willow-white hand to greet them, and they alighted on to it one by one before they flew to the ground at her feet.

Alerice made a mental note that a group of such birds was commonly known as an 'unkindness', but then a group of crows was also known as a 'murder'. How wrong the common folk were to have named a flock of any black birds in such a manner.

"My Queen?" Alerice said. "You ask me to slay a beast with two faces? Doesn't that seem the stuff of fancy?"

"The beast is hidden," the queen said in her voice of dark honey. "You can expose it if you trust in yourself, but it must die and you must be the one to kill it."

"Does it breathe fire or fly or do any beast-like things I should know about?" Alerice asked. She was attempting to be sincere, but as she heard her own words, she could not help but think how ridiculous this all seemed.

"Use the weapons I have given you. Use your good judgment, and use this, for now that you are mine, I mark you as such."

Alerice was not certain what the queen meant, and she nearly startled as the Raven Queen turned to her. Then the queen appeared directly before her. Alerice stood straight as the Raven Queen took her cheeks in her palms and lifted her face up toward hers. Then the Raven Queen kissed Alerice on the brow.

Alerice experienced the same mental fluctuations that she had when swearing her allegiance to the queen, and she required a moment to gain control of her senses, even after the queen had concluded her kiss. The queen floated backward to allow Alerice some space as Alerice felt a pulsing sensation upon her brow

She drew her Realme dagger to see her reflection. An iridescent black mark now appeared to be inked onto her forehead. At the center rested a short, thin oval with a pointed bottom tip and capped with a dot. From either side, S-curls fanned out, much like the shape of bird's wings.

The Raven Queen held up her willow-white hand, and the mark began to glow. At once, Alerice could see the town of Basque as though her spirit was being thrust toward it. She saw herself standing within the town's central square, and then she saw herself looking at the backside of a building, which Alerice thought was an inn or public house.

Then Alerice startled awake to find that the Raven Queen had vanished. She stood alone on the rise, looking along the road below and knowing that she had a long walk ahead of her.

Just then, Alerice heard a horse neigh and snort, and she turned about to find a magnificent black mount. It was not as tall or bulky as a plow horse, nor was it as sleek as a strider. It stood at a height Alerice considered to be perfect for her. Its mane, tail, and feathered fetlocks were luxurious, and Alerice knew from their glossy sheen that this animal was another gift from the Realme.

The horse bore black tack studded with the queen's white metal. It shook its head, waiting for Alerice to approach. She sheathed her dagger and walked up to the creature, knowing that they were bonded on this, the first of many tasks.

The horse nickered and pressed its head to Alerice's shoulder. She scratched it behind the ears, and then saw a pair of black gauntlets draped over the saddle horn. She pulled them on, noting that they fit perfectly. She moved the reins over the horse's neck and prepared to mount, but then she felt the mark upon her brow activate and heard the Raven Queen's voice ring clearly in her mind.

"This is your Realme pony, for my champion does not walk. You may name him whatever you wish."

"Oh, that's easy," Alerice said as she mounted and took hold of the reins. "Come on, Jerome. Let's go to Basque."

***

Alerice had been riding throughout the day, and evening was drawing in. A while back she had thought it strange that the Raven Queen had not placed her closer to Basque, but as the day had progressed she had made good use of the time by testing Jerome's gaits. His trot had been surprisingly comfortable. His canter had covered much more distance than Alerice had expected, and his gallop had been by far the most exhilarating experience Alerice had ever known. She had felt as though she had flown as he ran, and she couldn't be certain if she hadn't. Who knew what a Realme pony was capable of, and she was only too happy to find out.

In the end, Alerice had settled into a walk, for she did not wish to spend Jerome needlessly. She had hoped Basque was only one more day's ride away, but she had no frame of reference regarding the distance for she had not encountered any other riders on her journey.

Trees lined the roadside, which comforted Alerice, for they provided ample shadows to protect her should the need arise. True, she now possessed weapons and armor, but she did not know the use of them nearly as well as she knew her beloved shadows.

She wondered where to make camp and what goods lay in store in Jerome's saddlebags, but she noticed a faint glow ahead and decided to take the chance that she might come across a helpful person who had also stopped for the evening.

Alerice approached a small campfire burning in a makeshift pit, and reined Jerome to a halt. Whoever had lit the fire had piled some rocks about it to form a ring, and had crafted a spit on which roasted a good-sized rodent. However, that person was nowhere to be found, and Alerice was not certain of the best course of action.

She removed one of her gauntlets and placed her palm on Jerome's shoulder. She trusted in his ability to sense things she could not, and as the horse did not appear to be nervous, she decided to take the initiative.

"Hello?" she called. Her voice faded into the trees, but no one responded. She decided to throw caution to the wind, and dismount. Then she paced to the fire pit, and looked about.

"Hello?" she called again.

Alerice heard the scrape of a sword being drawn, and turned about to find a man standing in the shadows not far from her. He leveled his blade but did not approach. Alerice took confidence in the fact that she bore ranged weapons, and if he decided to attack, she would have the advantage.

"Good evening to you. My name is..." Would it matter if she used her true name? Basque was nowhere near Navre, so the Reef could not possibly reach her here. Besides, she now had the Raven Queen's protection. "My name is Alerice Linden. May I join you tonight?"

The man hesitated before he stepped forward, broadsword still leveled. He was of a good height with strong shoulders. His weather-worn tunic bore a military cut, and Alerice noted a regimental badge of a broadsword set point-down between two bull's horns on the upper-left chest. He sported a wide-brimmed hat, which Alerice wondered was customary for the local folk. His salt-and-pepper hair did not quite reach his shoulders.

The man paced toward Alerice, who continued to judge the distance between them, and then paused to look her over. Alerice could see his hazel eyes dart from her black scale mail to her dagger and crossbow to Jerome. Then the man's shoulders dropped and he exhaled a single, dejected word. "Damn."

"Why damn?" Alerice asked.

The man sighed, somewhat crestfallen, and then sheathed his sword. He looked Alerice over once more, and then folded his arms across his chest as though resigned to fate.

"Do you speak?" she asked.

"Yes," he answered.

His voice belied the firmness of an experienced man of action, and Alerice had no doubt that this fellow had seen many battles. She smiled at him, for a man of honor would not harm her. Of course, she did not know if he was a man of honor, for he was clearly not assigned to any present service.

"May I ask your name?" she said.

His lips smacked open, but he still did not speak. Then he glanced about at the fire and the short grass and seemed to decide there was enough room for two.

"Kreston," he said. "Kreston Dühalde. Unsaddle your horse and sit down if you like."

Alerice eased her stance. She nodded before she crossed over to Jerome and led him off the road. Unbuckling his bridle and removing his bit were simple tasks. Jerome even lowered his head so that she could reach. Ungirthing his saddle, however, was another matter, for she had not fastened it in the first place, and it did not seem to loosen with any ease.

Kreston watched her efforts, and then crossed over to her. He nudged her aside, and with a few quick motions, he loosed the girth strap, hefted the saddle off Jerome's back, and plopped it down. He also handed Alerice the saddlebags as he looked at her with a slight scold in his expression.

"You look like you've done that before," she said.

"When you've saddled as many horses as I have, it's second nature. Let me know if you want help getting him ready in the morning."

"Where's your mount?" she asked.

Kreston head-gestured to the trees, where Alerice could make out a stallion's outline safely sequestered among the trunks. She nodded again and moved her arm under Jerome's jaw to place a palm on his cheek to guide him in the same direction.

"Always keep your mount hidden when you can," Kreston advised. "That way an enemy will think you can't flee."

"That's good advice," she said. "I suspect you've known as many enemies as you have horses."

He straightened and looked at her. "Yes."

"You have got to be joking," Kreston said with a chuckle. "A two-headed beast? In Basque?"

Alerice giggled despite herself. "I know, but I have this... this matron, and that's what she told me to look for. It's absurd, but I've recently come to appreciate absurdity."

"You must have," he said. "Now, what is this stuff?"

Alerice regarded the bottle she had pulled from one of her saddlebags. "I have no idea. Let's just call it Realme Brew."

"Realme Brew? Now that's a first."

"For me too, and I've seen just about every bottle there is."

Alerice and Kreston had both decided to take their ease, and the bottle certainly helped dissolve any wariness. Alerice wondered if Oddwyn had supplied it, for she suspected that both he, and she, was a spirit who enjoyed mortal brews.

They had shared the roasted rodent and filled their cups, and soon it would be time for sleep. However, with at least one drink remaining, they had decided to chat.

"So where do you hail from, Alerice Linden?"

"Oh, I'd rather not speak of it. You?"

"Torvale originally," Kreston said. "But I didn't stay there long. My father was a bastard, and my family blamed me for crippling my mother in childbirth, so I left for the army and never looked back."

"And you fought and won?"

"I fought. I didn't always win."

A moment passed as Kreston recalled a memory, but then Alerice watched him look her over. She looked down at her armor, noting how her scales glistened in the firelight.

"Who'd've thought that a maid as comely as you would don a tunic like that," he said. "Your hair, Alerice. Your smile."

Alerice hid an appreciative grin.

"How I wish you weren't wearing it, though," he said. "You must have such a lovely breast."

"Must I?" she asked coyly. "And what would be the good of it to you?"

"Alerice Linden, I've learned to live in the moment. You're a handsome lass, make no mistake. Enjoy the compliment, for I'll go no further." He drained his cup and then set it down so that he could fold his fingers behind his head and gaze up at the stars. "But if you had a bodice in that pack, I certainly wouldn't mind if you wore it instead of all those scales."

"Well, this has become comfortable, actually, and I'd rather keep it on."

"Suit yourself," he said.

The dying fire crackled, and the embers illuminated the circle of rocks. Alerice finished her cup and looked about for a place to curl up. She had found a cloak inside Jerome's saddlebag, and she folded herself within it, noting that it suited her as much as her bed's blanket back at the Cup and Quill.

"Never get comfortable," Kreston cautioned.

"What?" she asked.

"Never get comfortable. The day you think you are in command of your world is the day that your world comes shattering down. Have you ever taken a first watch? Maybe you should try it to get into the habit."

Alerice sat up, noting the road and the stand of trees nearby. "Do you think someone will happen upon us?"

Kreston likewise sat up. "Someone can always happen upon you. Some 'thing' can always happen. The question is, are you ready when it does?"

Alerice could not help but recall the night of Gotthard's rape and Cousin Jerome's death. Then she recalled the moment of the Reef's attack that had ended her life, and emotions welled up against her will.

Kreston sat up more alert and leaned in toward her. "Hey, sorry. I didn't mean to spark a bad thought."

"It's all right," she said. "There's nothing to be done about it now, except serve my matron, I suppose."

"She sounds like a kooky, old bat. A two-headed beast."

Alerice nodded to hide her grief, and watched Kreston get to his feet and take a stance.

"So how do you know if it's any good?" he asked.

"How do I know if what's any good?" she replied.

"Your armor. How do you know if it's worth anything when it truly counts?"

"Ummm, I suppose I don't."

"You mean you've never tested it?"

"No, and if I told you how little a time I've had it, you wouldn't believe me."

Kreston smirked and looked about the ground. He found a tree branch and hefted it as he might heft his broadsword.

"Let's test it."

Alerice regarded him and doffed her cloak to stand up. "Here and now?"

"No better time," he said. "I promise, no leg or head blows. You're not wearing a helm, and your leggings have no scales. Torso only. Yes, Alerice Linden?"

Alerice didn't mind the challenge. She had deliberately drunk half of what Kreston had drunk, and this was not the first time a man wanted to roughhouse with her. After all, she had grown up with four male cousins.

Alerice stood before Kreston. There was something about him that she trusted, though she was not certain why.

"Very well," she said. "Let's have a blow."

"First, a gut jab," he said to prepare her. "Someone will always want to stick you like a pig when you're in a melee."

He aimed the branch at her midsection and thrust. He did not fully pull his blow, and the impact knocked Alerice's breath out. However, the armor proved itself and she recovered her stance, waiting for more.

"Good scales," he said. "Now, how about a side shot? I'll wager that this two-headed beast has arms that will splay you out if given the chance."

Alerice watched Kreston pull the branch back and then swing for her liver. His blow was true and she fell aside to her knee, but the armor prevented any injury. She coughed and stood.

"You don't give up easily, do you?" he said as he swung for her opposing hip.

This time Alerice dodged the blow by shifting her stance just enough for the branch to pass her by. Kreston swung through, and as she saw his surprise that he had missed his mark, she rammed her shoulder into him and knocked him to the grass.

Kreston recovered and jumped to his feet to face her, but his hazel eyes seemed to go wild. He swung for her side again, but then redirected his blow to swing for her head.

"Kreston," Alerice said as she ducked. "You said no head blows."

"Shut up, Landrew!" Kreston shouted to some invisible person at his side as he swung for Alerice's legs. "I'll get the men out of this! Just take the damned hill!"

"Kreston," Alerice said, clearing some distance between them. "Who are you talking to?"

"I told you to shut up, Lieutenant!" he roared. "Take the hill, you little sack of shite!"

"Kreston," Alerice called, clearing more space. She watched him engage in a one-sided battle against foes who must have seemed real in his mind, and waited until he had spent the last of his energy flailing the branch about.

In a short while, he fell to the grass, panting, and as he finally dropped the branch, Alerice felt it was safe enough to approach him.

He clutched his side as if wounded. He reached for something in the distance, and stifled a cry of, "Landrew."

Alerice retrieved the branch and gently pressed it into Kreston's shoulder.

"Kreston?"

"Damn it," he muttered. "Damn it." He glanced at her, though he did not seem to know who she was, and stammered, "They're all dead, Field Marshal. They couldn't take the hill."

"Kreston," she said with a firmer shove. "It's Alerice. I'm here with you on the road to Basque. There's no one else about."

Kreston began to rub his head through his wide-brimmed hat, pressing harder and harder until he clutched the leather and pressed it into his skull. Then his eyes snapped open and he startled as he looked about. He looked up at Alerice and scrambled to his feet.

"Get away from me!" he shouted. She did not, and he locked stares with her to say, "Alerice Linden, get as far away from me as you can. Forget you ever met me. Ride away and never look back. Whatever you seek in Basque, find it on your own."

Alerice still did not move. Kreston snarled and then stepped forward to strike her on the jaw hard enough to fell her to the grass, dazed.

Alerice did her best to regain her senses, but as Kreston bolted for the trees, she was aware of one thing. He had jumped onto his horse's bare back and dug in his heels to ride away into the night.

***

Alerice had not seen Kreston the next morning. He had not returned, and Alerice knew that it was not best to wait for him.

Her dreams had been a constant vision of Basque as the Raven Queen had presented it when kissing her brow, moving quickly toward the waiting town, standing within the central square, and standing behind the building she now knew was a public house.

She had woken alone, wrapped in the safety of her cloak. She had glanced about to find Jerome, who was enjoying some sweet grass near the base of the trees. Kreston had left his horse's tack behind, along with his own saddlebags, and Alerice had decided to cover them with some fallen branches in hopes that no one might discover them until he returned to claim them.

Her jaw ached from his punch, but she bore him no ill will, for she knew that when a man was haunted by 'battlefield voices', he was not always the master of his own mind.

The journey to Basque had only required half the day. Alerice was aware of the figure she presented, a blonde woman dressed in black scales riding a prancing black mount. Farmers had gawked and folk had pointed, but she had kept her eyes forward as she made for the town.

Folk had continued to whisper about her and shuffle away when she gazed upon them, and so having no idea where to begin her search for a two-headed beast, she did what all inquiring travelers do – head for the busiest tavern.

In Basque, this was the Pink Rose.

Alerice felt strange entering, for the moment she had crossed the threshold, she recalled each time a notable personage had stepped foot inside the Cup and Quill. She had been able to take the measure of nearly every one of them – be he a rowdy local, a well-established merchant, or a man of war and fortune. She tried to put the last image out of her mind as she paced in, for it reminded her of Kreston.

Knowing that she would be the topic of town gossip for weeks to come, she decided to give the people a good show, and so she held her head high as she found an empty table near two men playing cards.

The first one looked up twice from his hand as she approached. He pointed to his gaming partner to do the same. They blinked with incredulity as she brushed aside her cloak and drew up a chair, and they began to snicker as she looked toward the bar for the master or mistress.

Alerice did not regard them as she rubbed her still-throbbing jaw, but as they openly displayed their scorn, she placed her crossbow and dagger on the table. She half-glanced in their direction, and then she jammed the dagger into the tabletop, causing it to flash brightly as it had when presenting the scene of Uncle Judd's home. She had not expected this to happen, but the surprise inspired the men to collect their cards and coins and move to another table.

"Well, aren't you a woman of mystery," the inn mistress said, coming forward with a full pint. "This one's on the house. We're going to have such traffic in here this evening if you return to join us that I don't mind advancing you a cup."

"Thank you," Alerice said, taking a sip. The beer was watered down, and Alerice wondered if the people in Basque had ever known a decent cup of brew.

"My name is Arrosa," the inn mistress said. "I'm known for the finest blooms in Basque. It's my specialty."

Alerice noted the carved roses painted bright pink that dotted the support beams and ceiling coffers. She spotted sprays of freshly cut roses decorating the bar.

Then her gaze fell onto a pretty young lass hurrying to bring a customer a goblet of wine. The girl could not have been more than twelve or thirteen, nearly the age Alerice had been when Uncle Judd had invited her to wait tables. It was natural for family establishments to employ their young ones, for how else should they learn their respective trades? Still, there was something about this girl that did not seem right.

Her complexion was a bit too pale. Her cheeks were a bit too pink, and her dark blonde curls were a bit too perfect. Alerice sensed resentment hiding behind the lassie's forced smile, which she evidenced by tensing as the customer stroked the back of his finger along her face. Indeed, Alerice bristled upon seeing the gesture, for Uncle Judd would never have allowed any patron to express such familiarity with a young thing who was barely old enough to fill out her bodice.

"Ah, I see you've spotted my Honey," Arrosa said. "Honey," she beckoned to the girl.

Honey responded by hurrying to Arrosa's call. She stood before the inn mistress, who placed hands on her shoulders to turn her about and face the tavern's new guest.

Alerice watched as Honey slowly lifted her blue eyes. The girl's resentment became palpable as their gazes met, for Honey seemed to be thinking a poignant question. However, then Arrosa pressed her thumb into Honey's back and the lassie's face lit up with a beaming smile.

"Good day, black mistress," she said in a tiny voice as she offered a tiny curtsey.

Alerice wanted to reach out to Honey, for her façade of welcome could not disguise her apprehension at Arrosa's touch, but Arrosa bade Honey to resume her duties as she sent her to wait on other eager men.

"She's my eldest," Arrosa said. "Though I look after my brother's and sister's children as well. Some help me here, some work the stables behind. Since last year's blight, folks have had trouble feeding their families, and since Basque is on the crossroads to several cities, there's plenty of work for them to do here."

"I see," Alerice said, doing her best to maintain her guise as mysterious and aloof.

"Is the brew to your liking?"

"Mmmm," she replied as she took another sip. Then she placed the tankard down, slid it to the side, and leaned in toward Arrosa. "Actually, I'm searching for something. I've heard a tale that there is a beast here in Basque. One with two faces, two heads. One that feeds off innocent souls."

Arrosa blinked and nearly laughed out loud, but Alerice rose up to stand tall before her. She projected the empowerment of her charge as a servant of the Evherealme, and though she was not certain how she managed it, she felt the Raven Queen's mark upon her brow pulse. As she watched the inn mistress' eyes widen, she was sure that the mark had flashed.

"This is my task," Alerice said in a voice of complete confidence. "And I shall not disappoint the matron who has sent me here."

"But..." Arrosa stammered, evidently uncertain what to say. "There is no beast. Beasts are cottage tales that grammies tell children to frighten them into doing their chores."

"Let me make myself clear," Alerice said, taking a half-step forward, which caused Arrosa to back away by the same measure. Inwardly, Alerice was chortling, for this farce was fast becoming hilarious, but outwardly she presented herself to be what the Raven Queen had outfitted her to be – her champion.

"Look at the mark on my brow. Look at my blade lodged in the table. I am a creature who knows other worlds, and if I say a beast dwells in Basque, I know of what I speak. You say you wish me to return here this evening..." Alerice looked about the tavern, noting that all eyes were fixed on her. "Then I shall, and I will find this two-headed creature, and I will save the innocents it threatens."

"Yes, mistress..." Arrosa said, though her voice trailed off for she did not know Alerice's name.

"Alerice, daughter of the Raven Queen."

"Raven's... daughter," Arrosa stammered as she curtseyed. "I will do my utmost to serve you." She looked twice toward the bar, her eyes landing on a man who had just appeared. "'Enri," she called. "Let's have another round for our guest."

"Let's have two," Kreston said.

Arrosa turned about to find him standing at her side, not at all certain of how he had approached without anyone having seen him.

Alerice brightened as she beheld him, but he maintained a character complementary of hers, and together they hid a knowing smile as the inn master hurried over with two tankards.

Kreston took a seat opposite Alerice and accepted the brew. Then he placed a coin on 'Enri's platter, and bade him to leave them in peace.

The tavern's collective gaze turned back to whatever had previously occupied them, and Alerice found herself blending comfortably into the shadows, Kreston following suit.

He looked her over, his intimidating demeanor melting into one of concern. He reached out to touch her jaw, noting the bruise he had inflicted and how she flinched the moment his fingertips brushed her skin.

"Oh damn it, Alerice," he said, his voice low. "I'm so sorry for last night."

"Kreston, what are you doing here?"

"I had to seek you out. I had to tell you that I never meant to hurt you, and I never would have laid a hand on you if I had been able to think clearly. But, I'm not always able to, you see, and striking you has been eating away at me since I did it. I knew where you'd be headed, and in a town like this, it's natural that this place would be your first stop. I just hope you can forgive--"

"I have already," she said, ending his plea. "Kreston, you're not the first military man I've met. My father died in Lord Andoni's southern campaigns. I remember a time when he brought home a wounded comrade and asked me to watch him one night. He told me not to get too close, because the man saw ghosts in his sleep, and I was only four.

"And he did see ghosts. And when he woke up, he cried out and ran for the back door, and my father had to catch him and help him see sense. So don't worry. You struck me because you feared you would harm me, and while you do pack a wallop, at least you didn't truly injure me."

Kreston looked her over, and then sat back. "You think about others a great deal, don't you?"

Alerice smiled, and sipped again from her mug. Then she spied something below the crown of his hat that she had not been able to see in the previous night's darkness.

"What's that mark on your forehead?"

"That's, uhh... Nothing. An old scar I earned doing something stupid."

It was not a large step for Alerice to link a scar on a man's brow and the blow that would have caused it, and from there to the madness of memory that such a blow might induce. She said nothing further as she sipped her brew once more.

Kreston took up his tankard and raised it to her before he drank – at which point he spat the brew onto the table and regarded the mug.

"That's the worst stuff I've had in years. How can you even drink it?"

"Practice," she mused.

Kreston moved the tankard aside and stood up. "Come on, let's go find your beast."

***

The sun had reached the western horizon as Alerice stood with Kreston in the town's central square. She felt as though she was completing a part of her envisioned task by doing so, but the simple act of surveying the town answered no questions. Rather, it clearly marked both Alerice and Kreston as strangers, and all folk in all towns bore a natural avoidance of anything as strange as a blonde woman in black scale armor and a tall man in a wide-brimmed hat bearing a broadsword.

Alerice had left Jerome in the stables behind the Pink Rose, along with her cloak and gear. Kreston had done likewise with his mount. The two sported their weapons as they walked toward the door to a local chapel. It was dedicated to the brother deities Gäete, God of Storms, and L'Orku, God of Thunder, and Alerice thought it might be a good place to search out lore regarding a two-headed beast.

The chapel's headmaster invited them in, knowing he was in the presence of a woman who must know the Evherealme, but while he paid respect to Alerice and the great Raven Mother whom she served, he could spin no tales of a beast of Basque.

Rather, he wished to engage on a variety of other topics, including the queen herself and the King of Shadows, until both Alerice and Kreston had become quite bored with his pedantic prattles. Kreston took the initiative to impose his military countenance upon the scholar while insisting that Alerice attend an upcoming rendezvous with the night's spirits, for if she failed to appear and appease the gods below, the entire town might face the Realme's displeasure.

"Where did you invent a story like that?" Alerice asked Kreston as they quickly paced away from the closing chapel doors.

"Oh, you'd be surprised at some of the stories I know."

Alerice next stopped by an apothecary's shop to see if mixtures and magic could reveal any clues to the beast's whereabouts. However, she knew an odd-water shop when she saw one, and she could see that the apothecary himself was a curator of all things curious and nothing substantial.

Alerice decided on her own to leave before Kreston invented another story to explain their sudden egress.

"This isn't working, Kreston," Alerice said as they walked past the central square once more. She paused to take stock of the town's buildings, noting that windows shuttered as she gazed upon them. She was fast losing confidence in her ability to live up to the Raven Queen's expectations, but she was not certain if she should say anything to Kreston.

"I'd like to know your business," a man said from the side.

Both Alerice and Kreston turned to find the Reef of Basque approaching with a crew of five men. Alerice tensed, which Kreston seemed to sense, but she decided to cast a full bet that the Reef firstly, was not acquainted with the Reef of Navre, and secondly was the last man who could possibly point her in the direction of some two-headed monster.

"My name is Alerice, and I have been tasked to uncover a creature somewhere within your town. Now, before you laugh or consider me a madwoman, allow me to assure you that I am quite sincere, and I would greatly appreciate knowing whatever you might know about such a creature."

Some of the Reef's men chuckled, but the Reef waved them to be silent as he stepped forward. He regarded the bruise on Alerice's jaw, but she held her head high as though it was a mark of service. Then he regarded Kreston's worn military tunic and its badge of a broadsword set point-down between two bull's horns.

"Crimson Brigade? King Kemen?"

Kreston nodded.

"Crimson Brigade?" Alerice asked, noting in the daylight that the emblem was, in fact, dark red. "I've heard of your ghost."

"Really," Kreston said.

"I heard things didn't go so well for your regiment," the Reef said.

"No, they didn't," Kreston said.

The Reef offered nothing further as he regarded Alerice.

"My fair woman, I appreciate your sincerity, so as a token of good will on behalf of my town, I will suggest that you make up your bed tonight and sleep well. Then I would have you take your leave in the morning. Whoever told you that a beast dwells here in Basque is either sending you on a fool's errand or is mad themself.

"There are no such things as beasts. They do not live in this humble place. I have been the Reef here for over a decade, and if a beast did exist, I would have already slaughtered it. Stories would have already circulated about my deeds, and the lore would have spread to wherever you are from."

Alerice thought the words over, seeing sense in them. Indeed, any story of any mythical creature being brought down by a courageous Reef would have reached Navre, no matter from how far away. Perhaps the Raven Queen was testing her faith with this task. Perhaps she wanted Alerice to follow her instructions blindly in order to present her with a true task sometime soon. The queen had promised Alerice a chance at self-forgiveness, and she had to admit that for the last day she had not been consumed by the guilt over poisoning Gotthard. Perhaps this was the reason to send her on a fool's errand.

Alerice placed a hand on the Reef's arm.

"Thank you for your advice, sir. Yes, my friend and I shall leave in the morning."

***

"I should have known better than to think I could do this, Kreston," Alerice said as she moved Jerome's saddle onto a patch of hay to make up a place to lie down. She could not bear to make another appearance in the Pink Rose that evening, and in her mind she was already riding away at dawn.

"You know, in my career," Kreston said as he reclined against his own saddle, watching her, "I've made good decisions and I've made terrible ones, but the one thing I can hold as my own is knowing that most of my ideas were well-founded. In the long run, the better ideas outnumber the bad ones."

"I'm sure that's true," she said. "But you've had a career of life choices. I'm just a tavern maid. I can keep a ledger. I can inspire men to settle grievances over a pint. But I can't pretend to be I'm something I'm not."

"And what are you pretending to be?" he said, sitting up.

She humphed to herself. "You wouldn't believe me if I told you."

"I might."

"No, you wouldn't. I don't believe it much myself. Let's just say that the headmaster at the chapel was right when he recognized that I was in service to the Raven Queen. I mean, at least I think I am, but maybe I've actually gone mad since..."

She wanted to trace her actions back to Gotthard's attack, for indeed an act that savage could have made her mad. For all she knew, she had never been to the Realme at all. The Reef might not have actually killed her. Rather, she might be lying in bed at Uncle Judd's this very moment, suffering from some lasting delusion.

In all honesty, wasn't this more believable? The King of Shadows and the Raven Queen? Oddwyn and the Evherealme? Or a broken mind trying to console itself from Gotthard assaulting her and killing her beloved Jerome before her eyes.

"Alerice, what are you recalling?" Kreston asked.

"I don't want to think about it," she said, averting her eyes. "I just... I just want to wake up."

Kreston grimaced, and then threw hay into Alerice's face.

"Hey!" she exclaimed, but he threw another handful, and another. Then he stood up and started kicking hay onto her lap and legs.

"Kreston, what are you doing?"

"Seeing if you're awake," he said flatly as he kicked more hay into her hair. She got to her feet and pushed him away, but he pushed back, forcing her against a beam supporting the stable's roof.

"So, are you awake?" he demanded.

"Stop it, Kreston. If you're hearing battlefield voices right now, I'm sorry but I can't help you because I'm not in my own right mind."

"Father Fire, you're not!" he cursed. "And if I were hearing battlefield voices, you'd know it. Right now the only voice I'm hearing is yours, and all I see is a frightened little girl. You don't trust your senses. You don't trust yourself. I can't believe this is always how you've been. You're made of better stuff, so I'm thinking that something bad happened to you recently, and now you're falling apart when you need to form a plan and get the job done."

"What job? This is all fantasy. There is no beast here, let alone one with two heads that feeds on innocent souls."

"Damn it, Alerice, that's not what *she* said to you!"

Alerice froze. Then she straightened. "What *who* said to me?"

"*Her*," Kreston said with a sneer. "Sorry, I mean *Her Majesty. She* did not say a two-headed beast. *She* said a beast with two faces."

Alerice stood stunned. "How do you know about the Raven Queen?"

Kreston sighed. "Oddwyn told me, and before you ask..."

He doffed his hat and ran his fingers through his salted brown bangs. What he had claimed was a scar was in fact a mark upon his brow that bore a striking similarity to Alerice's own, only his was a series of varying striations that looked as though they had been carved by fingernails.

"You?" Alerice asked. "You are the king's man that the Raven Queen mentioned."

"Yes," he said. "That's why I swore when I met you. Oddwyn told me that *she* had taken a new champion, so when I lit my fire by the roadside, I expected to meet someone like myself. I never expected *she* would choose a person who had clearly never seen a battle in her life."

"The queen said you did not serve the king well because you were a driven man, not one of good deeds."

"Oh, I serve the King of Shadows exactly the way he wants me to. Now if I were you, I'd think about what it is that you're supposed to find, because I can tell you that *she* is not to be denied."

Kreston hid a shudder that belied a past Alerice longed to discover. However, the Reef of Basque would force them both to leave in the morning, and now was not the time to pry him open.

"But what if I fail her?" she asked.

"*She'd* only send you back until you get it right. You pledged your soul, Alerice, and *she'll* never let you go. They never let you go, and they won't ever stop using you. You will belong to them for the rest of your life."

"You mean belong to her, to the queen, not to them both," she said. Kreston paused and then agreed. Again, Alerice knew there was more to him than he was allowing her to see. "I suppose I should reach out to her for guidance."

"If you do, I don't want to be anywhere nearby," Kreston said as he turned to leave. However, before he paced away, he turned back, a question clearly on his mind.

"Do you mind if I--"

"Please," Alerice offered.

"All right. What did you ask for? What did you get in exchange for taking the Realme's power?"

"How do you know I asked her for anything?"

"Alerice. Everyone who seeks them out asks for something."

"Did you?"

"Yes. I asked the King of Shadows for the power to defeat my enemies. He gave me that and more."

"And did that work well for you?" she asked.

"In some ways."

His reply only whetted her appetite to know more about him. However, she said, "Actually, I did not seek them out. Rather, they sought me. I had died and woken up in the Evherealme. Oddwyn brought me before them both. The queen told me that..."

"Everything had aligned at your birth, which is why you had always loved the shadows?"

Again, Alerice looked Kreston over. "You too?"

He nodded. She reached out to touch him, but he moved away.

"The queen offered me her dagger," Alerice continued, "and the king offered me his sword. They wanted me to choose."

"The king offered you his sword?" Kreston asked.

"Yes," she replied, but the consequences of that offering suddenly struck her. "And the queen reminded him that another mortal already bore it. If he had reclaimed his sword and given it to me, would that have affected you?"

"Probably," Kreston said.

Alerice thought it was best to refocus the conversation away from him. "Actually, I did ask for something."

"I knew it. What?"

"I asked for the queen to protect my family."

"That's all?"

"You know, the King of Shadows said the same thing. It's possible that I've been wrong in thinking better things of you, Kreston Dühalde. Perhaps you are his man, and well-suited to his tasks."

Kreston controlled a quick flash of anger, then turned away.

"Just summon *her* and figure things out," he said as he left the stables.

Alerice watched him go, but then sensed a presence off to the side.

"It's best to leave him be," Oddwyn said from the corner.

Alerice turned to find him. He stood near a rack of bridles, hands on his hips, one eyebrow raised.

"Kreston tries to help sometimes," Oddwyn continued. "But when he walks away, it's best to let him go. Trust me."

"Oddwyn, why didn't you tell me that the king's man was still alive and likely to find me?"

"Because that's not how the Raven Queen wished things, and I do what she wishes me to do, just as you need to do what she wishes you to do. And please, no more complaints. It's a waste of time."

Oddwyn advanced and reached out to brush Alerice's blonde bangs from her face. "You haven't really learned how to use this, now have you," he said, rubbing his thumb across the Raven Queen's mark. "It's time you learned."

Oddwyn flicked Alerice's brow quite roughly, activating the mark and forcing Alerice's spirit from her body. Oddwyn caught her limp figure and laid it down, even as he turned to her and said, "What are you waiting for? Go find what you seek."

Alerice wanted to ask what that was, but just as with the vision conveyed in the queen's kiss, she found her spirit pulled away from the stables and toward the backside of a building.

It was a public house, and the pink blooms in the nighttime garden informed Alerice of precisely which house. Her spirit hovered behind the Pink Rose, and as she floated closer she saw a familiar sight.

Arrosa was greeting men at the rear door. They slipped her coin, and she took their hats and cloaks. They had come for the company of 'busy lassies', a trade Alerice knew quite well from managing the Cup and Quill. However, as Alerice watched, she saw Arrosa produce Honey and offer her to one of the men.

The inn mistress was selling the company of a someone that young? Knowing she needed to see more, Alerice flew into the back rooms of the Pink Rose. She did not question how she traveled, but rather allowed her intuition to guide her – and what she found appalled her. Arrosa and 'Enri were putting all the young ones, lads and lassies, to work as company for men who were eager to have them. They could do nothing but accept their fate. Some even bore sprays of Arrosa's pink blossoms as they walked to their bed chambers.

It suddenly struck Alerice that the tavern's name was not chosen for the flowers, but for the young flesh sold, for the innocent souls so horribly abused, all under the direction of two schemers who certainly deserved to be held accountable.

"Oddwyn!" Alerice called, hoping Oddwyn might help her return to her body. "Oddwyn, can you hear me?"

Alerice sensed no reply, and though she was fairly certain that she could return to her body on her own, she realized that she needed help to see this matter through. She pressed her lips together, and commanded herself to seek out Kreston.

Kreston stood beside a building, his sword in hand. He threw the blade into the building's half-timber, where it lodged deeply. Then he held his hand high overhead. The sword appeared within his grasp, and Kreston prepared to throw it again.

"Stop that, will you," Alerice called to him.

Kreston froze. "Alerice?" he called, looking about.

She was not certain how to present her spirit in the living world, and so she drew near to him – and flicked the mark of the King of Shadows scratched upon his brow.

Kreston reacted to the strike by backing a few steps, then he stood straight and activated the mark himself to extend his own spirit toward her. He did not venture out from his own body, lest he collapse, but he did lock stares with her.

"Alerice, what is it?"

"The inn master and mistress. They are selling their young ones for pleasure. Hurry and get the Reef. I will go help Honey and the others."

Alerice flew away, not hearing Kreston's warning that the Pink Rose was certain to have men protecting it.

***

Alerice settled down into her body, and then forced herself to draw in a deep breath as she opened her eyes. She exhaled and sat up, taking stock of her composure.

She was whole and sound. The comfort of her black scales bolstered her as did the Evherealme itself. She dove through Kreston's thrown hay for her belt, and securing it, she buckled it about her waist so that her weapons hung at her sides.

***

Alerice crept out from the stables, staying in the safety of the shadows. Arrosa greeted what appeared to be the evening's last lonely man, and as she closed the rear door, Alerice crept further forward.

She did not have a plan, apart from forcing Arrosa and her husband to surrender the young ones. Would this work? Would they harm the lads or lassies if the moment became dire? Did the Reef already know of their business and condone it?

Alerice put the last thought from her mind. The Reef must be a better man than that, for only a horrendous person could condone the nightwork of the Pink Rose. Besides, the Raven Queen had said the 'beast' of Basque had *begun* to feed upon innocent souls, so the Pink Rose's trade must be new. Even Arrosa had said that the young ones had come in since last year's blight. She would give the Reef a chance to prove himself, and if he did not, she would take some other action to get the young ones to a safe place.

For now, the rear door. Alerice saw that she must step out from the shadows to reach it, for two lanterns burned brightly on either side of the jamb. She must be quick, or she would be seen--

"Who are you?" a man called out.

Alerice turned and found one of the two men who had been playing cards. She stepped forward to confront him, uncertain if she should draw her dagger or crossbow.

"You're that little puffed-up nothing from this afternoon," he said. "Hey boys," he called over his shoulder. "Here's that little black bird I was telling you about."

Alerice watched as three more men came forward, and though she could see they meant to attack her, she found her senses rankling at being referred to as a 'bird' by yet another man confident of his own domination.

She stood her ground, unbuttoning the leather strap holding her crossbow. She hefted and leveled it. The bow string drew back of its own accord, and a gleaming black bolt appeared in the flight groove.

"What's that supposed to be?" the lead man demanded as all four encroached. "The little bird has a toy bow."

Alerice hesitated, not because she wasn't prepared to fight, but because she

42

had never been faced with a moment of kill or be killed. This was not the same as poisoning Gotthard. This was taking a life in order to protect her own, and she searched for the cool clarity that Kreston must have possessed in his many battles.

She fired into the lead man's shoulder.

"Father Fire!" he swore as the bolt sank into him and burst into a dark flash that knocked him to the ground.

Alerice watched him growl in agony. She had aimed the shot to wound him in hopes that his accomplices would flee. However, two men locked stares on her and charged.

Alerice lifted her crossbow again, but before she could shoot, a broadsword's point erupted through one man's chest, splattering his blood across her black scales.

The other man skidded to a stop and turned, only to find Kreston holding his hand high and his broadsword reappearing in his grasp. Kreston leveled the point and then drew back to throw, but the fellow – apparently possessing some amount of wit – ran off into the night, the fourth man following him.

Kreston advanced, stepping on the leg of the wounded man as he strode toward Alerice. They regarded one another then glanced down at their foe. The lead man – likewise possessing a decent modicum of sense – scrambled away in the opposite direction.

***

The rear door to the Pink Rose opened into the back hall, admitting Alerice and Kreston.

"I told you to summon the Reef," she said in a low voice.

"I did," he said, ice in his veins as he focused on the task at hand.

She led the way to the bottom of a staircase and gestured for Kreston to remain while she crept upward. Kreston watched her ascend, but then caught sight of two young lads and beckoned them to come to him for protection.

Alerice made her way along the upper hall, noting the closed doors. She would need to find the inn master or mistress before she hurried any young ones down to Kreston, for she could not risk the couple injuring any of the remaining girls or boys.

"I don't know what you think you've come for," 'Enri said from behind.

Alerice turned and saw him emerge from a door she had just passed.

"And I don't know who you think you are," he continued, "but you're leaving now, or I promise you that more than one of our little beauties will pay for it."

'Enri held no hostage, but he had the same look Gotthard had sported when striding into the Cup and Quill. What gave a man such a delusional predisposition? How dare he claim anyone to be his?

"Beast," she growled.

"Is that the best you can say?" the inn master chuckled.

Alerice's hand moved toward her dagger, which seemed ready to jump into her grasp. She turned her hip slightly so that 'Enri could not see her draw it, but suddenly one of the men who had come to purchase a young one's company ventured into the hall on Alerice's opposing side.

He charged forward, and she threw the dagger into his heart. This time, she had no hesitation about doing what needed to be done. This time she was ready to take a wicked life that was threatening not only hers but the lives of innocents – a decision reinforced when she saw a girl Honey's age hurry to the door and cry out at seeing the dead man's rolled-up eyes.

Alerice rushed to the lassie and hid her from view even as she raised her hand. Her dagger appeared in her palm, and she threw it into 'Enri's throat, killing him.

One face of the monster slain. One more to find.

Alerice descended the stairs, the lassie and several others in tow. She took stock of Kreston, who had gathered a few more lads, and prepared to leave by the rear door. However, as she bade the young ones to be silent, Alerice heard voices in the now-closed tavern.

She made her way through to the front of the house, appearing in the shadows of the bar.

"You know?" the Reef said to Arrosa.

Alerice saw the Reef's five men as well, but watched the inn mistress play the moment with cool lubricity.

"There have been several of us who have turned blind eyes to the rumors we have heard," the Reef continued. "Largely because none of us could imagine a thing so rotten as selling your young ones for pleasure."

"And you would take the word of strangers over mine?" Arrosa said. "We know one another, Darmond. Don't believe tales that will damage your reputation when they prove false."

"Prove false?" Alerice said as she advanced. "I'll show you what's true." Alerice turned back to see Kreston leading his group forward. She crouched down and held out her hand. "Come here, Honey. No one's going to hurt you ever again. You have my promise on that."

Kreston urged Honey to take a few steps forward, but the lassie gained confidence the moment she gripped Alerice's hand.

In that moment, Alerice understood the palpable sensation of Honey's initial resentment. When they had first met, the girl had indeed been thinking a poignant question, and it was undoubtedly, "Why are you letting bad things happen to us? Why don't you protect us?"

Well, now Alerice was. She drew Honey in and held her close to steady her, even as she leveled a stare at Arrosa, who in her eyes was viler than Gotthard.

Honey took a step on her own, gazing up at Arrosa. Then her blue eyes narrowed and she spat on the floor before returning to Alerice's side, where she pressed in.

"There's at least a dozen of them, Reef," Alerice said. "Arrosa and her husband likely collected them from parents unable to care for them. They are the proof of her crime."

"And her husband's," the Reef said. "Where is 'Enri?"

"Dead," Alerice stated in a voice of complete confidence. "Along with another man upstairs."

"You killed them?" the Reef asked.

This time, the empowerment that Alerice displayed was no charade. This time, she projected the bearing of someone who knew she was in the right, in the charge of the Raven Queen herself, and in holding the Reef's gaze, Alerice became well aware, that he was well aware, of this fact.

The Reef ordered one of his men to take hold of Arrosa and remove her via the front door, through which he and his crew had entered and remained open. Then he regarded the young ones.

"Right now, this is the safest place for them. There's no room for them at the constabulary, and it's obvious that you intend to protect them. I'll send food and blankets, and we'll see what we can do for them in the morning."

The Reef sent one of his men to clean up upstairs, and ordered the remaining three to guard the Pink Rose throughout the rest of the evening.

The Reef began to exit the tavern, but turned back. "Thank you. Apparently there was a beast here in Basque. I should have believed the stories that people had begun to tell me."

***

Alerice rubbed her bruised jaw as she watched Kreston load the last of the lads and lassies onto a hay wagon. Docents from the chapel dedicated to Imari, Mother Goddess of Water and Wind, were busily sorting things out with the Reef prior to departing. They had come forward to see to the welfare of each child, and they were settling finalities as they prepared to depart.

Kreston looked over at Alerice and smiled. He held his hat in hand, and was about to cross over to her, but he suddenly froze and looked past Alerice's shoulder.

Alerice turned to see a tri-colored swirl of black, midnight blue, and deep teal appear behind her, and she watched as the Raven Queen stepped through the portal.

Alerice looked back for Kreston, but he had vanished. She then looked about at the town folk, but was shocked to see them going about their business with no hint of alarm.

"They cannot see me," the queen said in her voice of dark honey. "You can, though. And you can see them, the innocents who needed you. This is why I sent you here. In your old life, you kept to your purpose, and I imagine it would have been another typically unremarkable life when you had finished it.

"In your new life, you have found purpose. You once claimed to be modest, but you acted in the right, and I am proud of you for doing so."

Alerice looked at her matron, but then she noticed that half a dozen ravens had begun to circle overhead. As she watched them caw and glide, she was suddenly reminded of how a similar flock had mesmerized her when riding the stolen plow horse away from Navre.

She furrowed her brow and looked into the Raven Queen's amethyst eyes. "You sent the ravens to identify me to the Reef."

"I did," the queen stated.

"But you must have known that he meant to kill me. Why did you help me die?"

"Because only through death could you begin your new life."

The queen floated forward, placed a willow-white hand on Alerice's shoulder, and guided her to turn about. Alerice watched the wagon driver climb into his seat and take up the reins to the two-horse team. Kissing to the lead, he set the wagon in motion, driving the young ones away from Basque.

"And knowing what you can now do," the queen continued, "knowing the potential of what you might yet be able to do, would you still want the life you knew before your death?"

Alerice caught sight of Honey. She had climbed out of the wagon and onto the seat next to the driver. He pulled her close, and the lassie snuggled into the crook of his arm.

"No, My Queen. I would not."

"Do you still condemn yourself?" the Raven Queen asked. "Killing Gotthard was no different from killing 'Enri. You stood up to stop the wicked. Do you still feel shame?"

Alerice took a centering breath and turned to her matron. "No, My Queen. Though I will still try to remind myself of modesty."

The Raven Queen nodded. Alerice turned back to the town and searched for Kreston, but he was nowhere to be found.

"I no longer doubt the Realme," Alerice added. "I do not doubt that I am yours to serve as you wish me to, and I am ready to live the life you have granted me."

The queen placed her willow-white hands on Alerice's armored shoulders.

"Good," she said. "You have many discoveries awaiting you, Alerice. You shall pass between worlds, between the Evherealme and Mortalia. You shall become something that I have not had in my service for many generations – a Realme Walker. All this now lies before you, my Ravensdaughter."

THE THIEF OF SOULS

THE THIEF OF SOULS

Tales of the Ravensdaughter

Adventure Two

The children who walk shadows
Will know the Evherealme.
It floats within their dreams
A place they may call home.

Their souls will grow and prosper
As through the Realme they stride.
They will find nourishment,
A source of lasting pride.

from the Scrolls of Imari

A lerice sat astride Jerome overlooking the faraway town of Basque. She had no idea where she might venture next, but she knew that at some point the Raven Queen would call upon her.

She motioned Jerome down the road, putting Basque to her back. It was past midday and the weather was mild. A breeze played in her blonde hair, and she felt the need to doff her black scales and simply ride in the comfort of her black shirt.

Not that her armor was a discomfort. Quite the opposite, for it had felt like a second skin the moment Oddwyn had helped her into it. Still, the seduction of the soft wind was too irresistible, and so Alerice reined Jerome to a stop and started to unbuckle the top of the four leather straps under her left arm.

A broadsword *whooshed* past her shoulder, startling Jerome. Alerice reached for her saddle horn to steady herself, and the reins to steady him. Then she watched as the broadsword landed in the road a short distance before her, its point burying into the packed dirt.

She smiled to herself, and turned in the saddle to find Kreston mounted not far behind. He held his hand high overhead, and the broadsword reappeared in his grip. Then he brought its hilt before his hazel eyes in a salute. Alerice drew her Realme dagger and returned the gesture before she waved it.

"I thought you could use some company," Kreston called as he urged his horse forward.

"I can always use company," she replied, waiting for him to come abreast.

In moments his blood bay stallion stood next to Jerome, and Alerice looked Kreston over. He still wore his wide-brimmed hat, but he did not seem so eager to hide the mark of the King of Shadows upon his brow.

"Where did you go earlier?" Alerice asked. "After you had put all the children in the wagon, I looked for you but I couldn't find you."

"I thought one of the young ones had run off, and I went to find him," he said. "But it was one of the local lads, and the mother wanted to chat, so that delayed me. Where are you bound?"

"In all honesty, I have no idea." Alerice looked about at the rows of vineyards chasing up and down the hillsides. "But it's such a nice day, don't you think? I thought I would enjoy the ride."

She looked up at the few puffed clouds and at the upcoming rise in the road. Then she glanced at Kreston, who was trying to hide a smile as he gazed at her. "What?"

"Nothing," he said. "You're right. It is a nice day."

***

The cottage inn was a homey place. Alerice and Kreston had been pleased to discover it, and even more pleased to discover that the ale was not watered down. Dusk would be rolling in before long, but for the moment the two had found a table outside of the cottage, where they had set their tankards and gear. However, they both retained their weapons, for Kreston had suggested they spar.

"Why do I have a sword again?" Alerice asked, looking over the blade that Kreston had borrowed from the cottage's master.

"Because it's a superior weapon to a dagger," Kreston said, brandishing his own blade. "You can't beat a sword for range in combat, and if you're going to be a champion, it's only a matter of time before you go into an armed conflict."

"Do you think so?"

He *swooshed* his blade in a quick figure eight. "I know so. Now, go on your guard."

Alerice presented the broadsword in a two-handed grasp. Kreston looked her over with a little frown, and then approached to readjust her grip and stance. He pushed her slightly from side to side and front to back, noting how she needed to bend her knees and set her balance.

Alerice found herself enjoying the fact that Kreston instructed her as he might any man. He certainly was not going to ease back on any detail because she was a woman.

However, she still did not feel comfortable with a sword. She preferred the litheness of a dagger, with which she had some experience given the years of Cousin Jerome's tutelage.

"Ready?" Kreston asked. Alerice nodded and leveled the blade. "Good, aim right here," he said, pointing to his midsection. "Right for the gut, and when I parry, try to swing for my flank."

"Kreston," she said, lowering her guard a bit but still maintaining her readiness. "The last time we sparred, your 'voices' got the better of you. You shouted for someone named Landrew to take a hill. I think you called him your lieutenant."

Kreston paused. He stood up straight and lowered his blade a fraction, his eyes closing and his head bobbing a bit as he seemed to sort through past memories.

"Kreston?" she called.

"It's all right, Alerice," he said, eyes still closed. "I'm just trying to put things in the right pockets so that doesn't happen again." He continued concentrating, then added, "But just in case I can't, get away from me this time."

Alerice saw Kreston open his eyes and she nodded, then stood back on her guard. He patted his midsection again to indicate where she should aim her thrust, and she charged, point trained on him. Unfortunately, she overstepped her mark and by the time she managed to thrust, he had sidestepped and grasped her broadsword near the hilt.

This caused her to stop short, and she lost her balance. He grabbed her scale mail shoulder and hauled her back into her stance.

"Too much forward motion," he said. "You've got to step into a thrust, not run into it. Otherwise, you'll swing for my back and not my flank, or worse..." He yanked the blade from her grasp. "I can disarm you. Now, try it again."

Kreston handed the sword back and motioned for Alerice to return to her starting position. She did, hefting the weapon again as she turned to face him.

"How much longer are you two going to dance?" Oddwyn asked from the side.

"Oddwyn!" Alerice exclaimed, turning to him and beaming at his youthful guise.

Oddwyn smiled back and offered a flamboyant bow. Then he regarded Kreston with a straight-backed military salute.

"Oddwyn," Kreston said, semi-tolerant of the gesture.

Oddwyn strolled forward, taking in the moment.

"Kreston, why are you teaching her swordplay? She'll never be a natural with that weapon."

"See?" Alerice agreed. "That's what I've been saying."

"Well, someone needs to help her prepare."

"Oh, you're right about that," Oddwyn said.

Kreston cocked his head to the side. "And I suppose you think you can do a better job?"

"Kreston... why do you always say things you know you're going to regret?"

Kreston humphed and then gave Oddwyn a 'by all means' sweep of his broadsword.

Oddwyn briefly assumed the guise of a maiden in order to blow him a kiss, and then slipped back to his youthful countenance as he stepped before Alerice.

"Mind if I borrow your body for a moment?"

"What?" she asked, incredulous.

"Oh, sorry. I forgot you can be hard of hearing sometimes. Mind if I borrow your body?!" he shouted.

Alerice recoiled, then shook her ears clear and regarded him. "How can you do that? I'm using it?"

"Sweet Alerice. You truly do require elucidation when it comes to matter of flesh and spirit."

Oddwyn reached out to her cheek, to which she responded by relaxing ever so slightly. Then he quickly reached up to her forehead and gave the Raven Queen's mark a solid flick.

Alerice's soul startled from its natural inertia so that her astral eyes opened within her physical ones. Her astral head shook from side to side as she attempted to make sense of what was happening. However, Oddwyn stared deeply into her, commanding her attention.

"This is your spiritual being, Alerice," he said, his voice ringing within the metaphysical space about them. "The queen's mark upon your brow is more than just a beacon you can use to reach out to her. It's more than your connection to the Realme. It's a means to expand your consciousness in ways you never imagined you could. Take a look about you."

Alerice did. Immediately, the fullness of a new world filled her mind. She saw Kreston standing behind Oddwyn, but she also saw the mark of the King of Shadows blazing brightly on his brow. She saw creatures crawling about and up the nearby trees, their bodies alive with sensory alertness. She saw the aura of those trees glow with the full breadth of their long lives. She heard birds singing in multi-toned melodies.

She closed her eyes, mesmerized by the splendor about her, and began to drift away on ethereal currents, but Oddwyn tapped the Raven Queen's mark, waking her.

"Now, don't go flying," he said as he placed his hands on her shoulders. "You're not ready for that. But if you will allow me, I'd like to work through you, for this is something you can now do. You can allow a spirit to inhabit your flesh. We'll keep it short since this is your first time. Just call out to me when you've had enough."

"All... right?" she said, not at all certain of what she was allowing.

"All right," Oddwyn said in her female register, even though he still maintained his youthful appearance.

Oddwyn reached to Alerice's cheek once again, and then slipped into her body shoulder-first.

Alerice's eyes snapped open with a look she had never presented, and she leveled a gaze at Kreston.

"Oddwyn?" Kreston cautioned. He raised his broadsword and went on his guard. As he looked at Alerice, he noticed that her eyes had turned ice blue.

"Kreston," Alerice responded, placing her hands behind her back to reach for something. Bringing that something forward, she presented two thin cylinders, one in each hand.

Kreston regarded one, then the other, then Alerice.

"What are those supposed to be?" he asked.

Alerice struck a ready pose, and with two quick flashes of light, poles popped up from the cylinders, blades embedded along the inside and outside lines of both.

"They're pixie poles, you little teat!" Alerice shouted as she lunged forward.

She began flailing at Kreston with martial mastery, for Oddwyn was no stranger to combat. Kreston plied his long-practiced skills of battle, but the two blades out-numbered his single broadsword, and Alerice moved so quickly that Kreston had difficulty controlling the distance between them.

Poles struck at his shoulders, flanks, and legs, and Kreston was forced into a series of parries, unable to find the right moment to riposte. He backed about the table on which he and Alerice had placed their tankards. He jumped and dodged about their horses' saddles, bags, and tack. Even the cottage's woodpile offered little protection.

What made the challenge worse for Kreston was that he was not fighting Oddwyn. He was fighting Alerice, and the last thing he wanted to do was harm her.

"Always remember, Kreston," she shouted as she smiled and stalked him. "Don't 'fooke' with the Odd!"

"Two weapons to one isn't fair, Oddwyn," Kreston replied, trying to clear some ground.

"No, but it's fun," Alerice said as she lunged once more.

Kreston had reached his limits with this absurd moment, and he plowed forward, colliding with Alerice chest-to-chest. Then he reached down to draw out Alerice's Realme dagger.

Kreston pushed Alerice off-balance so that she landed on her rump, and leaped over her, sprinting a few paces so that he could turn, sword in one hand and dagger in the other.

"Right," he proclaimed. "Now, it's two to two."

"Nice move," Alerice said as she got to her feet. "All right then."

Alerice charged, as did Kreston, and the combat resumed sword to pole and pole to dagger as both martialists employed their skills.

Alerice was lighter and faster, but her flesh prevented Oddwyn from unleashing the full speed of his spiritual self. Kreston aimed strong blows meant to overpower an opponent and drain their muscles, given his greater strength and stamina.

"Oddwyn!" Alerice cried in her own mind. "Oddwyn, stop! This is too much!"

Oddwyn reacted by halting Alerice's body in full swing, and as Kreston's blade swung for her shoulder, Oddwyn parried and leaped her into a backward somersault. Then he scrambled her into a defensive stance.

"Kreston, hold!" he demanded through Alerice's voice. Suspecting a trick, Kreston grinned and prepared to advance, but Oddwyn caused Alerice to jump further away. "I said hold, damn it! I've got to release her."

Kreston stood down. Oddwyn's spirit leaped out of Alerice's body, allowing her full control. She cried out as she dropped the pixie poles and fell to her knees, clasping her hands to her head and wailed, reeling.

"Alerice!" Kreston called as he dropped his weapons and hurried to her. He gathered her into his arms and held her in a protective grip. She shook terribly, and he cursed himself for having engaged Oddwyn in the first place. "It's all right, Alerice," he said softly.

"It's cold," she muttered, burrowing into him.

"I know it is. I know exactly what you're feeling," Kreston said. He lifted her chin so that he could better see her face. Thankfully, her eyes had returned to normal.

Kreston looked about for Oddwyn and found him sitting cross-legged on the table, drinking from one of the tankards. Oddwyn regarded it with a 'not bad' look as Kreston stared daggers at him.

"You shouldn't have done so much with her. Not the first time."

"She's strong enough to cope," Oddwyn said, finishing the tankard and reaching for the other. "And she's got a lot to learn without the luxury of time."

Kreston understood the truth of the statement, but he refocused his attention on Alerice, brushing a lock of her blonde hair from her face and gently touching the Raven Queen's mark with his fingertips.

"Can you stand up?" he asked.

"I... I think so," Alerice said as her shaking began to abate.

Kreston nodded, but then Alerice saw him tense. A strange look came over him, and he stiffened. Then he grabbed Alerice in a desperate hold and called out, "Landrew!"

Alerice tried to back away, but he clutched her too tightly. "Kreston, it's me. Let me go."

"Landrew," Kreston said in a voice of strangled agony. He began rocking Alerice back and forth, the pain of a past memory surfacing. He looked skyward and called out, "Sukaar, Father Fire! Why did you take him? You should have taken me. I was the one who ordered him up that hill!"

Alerice managed to slip out from Kreston's arms and get to her feet. "Kreston. Come back to me if you can."

"Damn it, damn it..." Kreston muttered before he likewise got to his feet. He bolted to the side of the cottage.

An ether of black, midnight blue, and deep teal formed near some of the trees that ringed the cottage inn.

Oddwyn jumped off the table and hurried to Alerice's side, helping her stand at attention. The Raven Queen appeared, her ankle-length black hair flowing in the dusk's evening breeze. She stepped through the portal, accompanied by her two Raven Knights, and stood tall within the mortal world.

"Oddwyn," she ordered in her voice of dark honey.

"Yes, My Queen," Oddwyn said with a bow. He looked Alerice over to make certain she was sound, bowed to the Raven Queen a second time, and hurried past her and through the portal.

One of the Raven Knights watched him disappear, though the queen did not as she fixed her amethyst gaze on Alerice.

"My Queen," Alerice said with a curtsey, which she changed to a reverence, for a curtsey was a diminutive gesture suited to a simple maid. A reverence, however, was a bolder gesture in which a person places one foot back and lowers weight down upon the rear leg while keeping the torso straight, the shoulders back, and the head high. True, a reverence showed a touch of pride, but Alerice felt this display of deference was better suited to a woman such as herself, who wore black scale mail and bore a Realme dagger.

"Accompany me."

"As you wish, My Queen."

From the side of the cottage inn, Kreston watched Alerice retrieve her dagger, sheathe it, and move off. Yet, he deliberately kept *her* from his sight by blocking the image with the cottage's half-timbered corner.

When he sensed the area was empty, he swallowed hard as he closed his hazel eyes. However, he then felt a second presence arise behind him and he spun about. The King of Shadows stood, and Kreston fell to one knee, bowing his salt-and-pepper head.

"My King."

"Kreston," the king replied. "Have you recovered your wits?"

"I never lost them, Great Shade, but I could not remain where I was. You know that I cannot look upon *her*."

"I do," the King of Shadows said. He held his open hands before him, and his Realme broadsword appeared in his grip. He half-extended it to Kreston, who knew to reach out for it, head still bowed, but the king paused to look him over. He allowed the moment to linger before he bequeathed the blade back to Kreston and ordered, "Come with me."

Kreston swallowed hard once more, then summoned battle-hardened ice to fill his veins. "As you will, My King."

The Raven Queen, accompanied by her two knights, floated as she moved forward within the Realme. Alerice followed a half-pace behind her.

She glanced about, unable to keep her full focus on her matron. The Realme was a place of shifting composure. Sometimes it appeared to be a world of columned halls. Sometimes it displayed landscapes that stretched for miles.

Souls abounded in all shapes and sizes, but all were of the world she knew. Alerice saw no exotic creatures or mythical beasts. Rather, she saw clans and gatherings, some that were delighted to greet the family members who were being escorted to them by the guides Alerice had seen in the Convergence. She saw solitary souls reading or composing songs. She noticed some who wandered, haplessly confused, and she also sensed that some corridors led to places where she felt maleficent intentions.

Alerice wondered if she would be able to interact with any of these souls, for this was the afterlife of which Grammy Linden had so often spoken. If only her gram could see her now.

"You will be able to speak to the souls here at some point," the queen said, answering Alerice's thoughts.

Alerice looked up to the side of her pale face, sensing the link that the Raven Queen had crafted between them, as evidenced by the mark she now bore.

"Oddwyn's poles suited you well," the queen said. She lifted her willow-white hand, and the two cylinders appeared in her palm. "You should learn to use them."

The queen directed the cylinders to float to Alerice, who took hold of them, uncertain where to place them. Then she noticed that the cylinders bore metal rings at the base. She also noticed that two snapped leather straps had appeared on either side of her studded black belt. She used them to pass through the rings so that the cylinders rested near her Realme dagger and crossbow.

Alerice then thought of the experience of having Oddwyn possess her body, and she involuntarily shuddered, for the memory reminded her of how cold she had felt.

"It is called a meld," the queen stated. "As a Walker, you have the ability to invite souls into your flesh. You also have the power to expel them, which you must always bear in mind lest the experience overwhelm you and the spirits remain past the point of your acceptance."

"I will endeavor to learn this talent, My Queen," Alerice said. "That and the pixie poles."

"Good," the queen said, stopping before a vortex pulsing within the Realme's tri-colored ether. "Alerice, I have sensed something which concerns me," she said as she motioned for Alerice to stand abreast of her. "This is a breach of the Realme. They occur from time to time, largely when an outside influence, a mage or sorcerer, creates a state of flux.

"Commonly, a mortal instigates this flux for his own gain, and though he may temporarily tap the Realme, the mortal rarely possesses the stamina to maintain the breach. He either drains himself or dies, and the breach heals.

"But this breach has become pernicious. I have sensed souls slipping out through it, and the incidents have increased rather than decreased. I could seal this breach here, but I fear that the instigator, or I might more aptly say the thief, would only create a secondary and perhaps tertiary breach and continue to affect the Evherealme."

Alerice watched the vortex swirl and pulse in undulating currents. She wanted to touch it, but she restrained herself.

"Why 'thief', My Queen?"

"The souls that have slipped through did not do so of their own accord. They were taken, and the mortal responsible is the thief who stole them. I want you to venture through this portal, Alerice, and discover who is responsible. Then I wish you to report your discovery to me so that I may decide what action is best."

Alerice mulled the task over, and nodded as if to say, "Why not?."

"So, do I simply walk through, or is there something you need to do...?" she asked.

The Raven Queen smiled. She gazed down upon Alerice, pride flickering in her eyes as she beheld her champion. She blinked slowly in approval, and then set her amethyst sights upon the vortex. She held out her willow-white arms, and the dark, iridescent feathers of her gown glistened as she began to manipulate the portal.

Alerice watched with both fascination and anticipation, ready to take on the mantle of what lay before her. The memory of Oddwyn possessing her body somehow infused into her muscle memory, and she unconsciously fingered a pixie pole cylinder while gripping her Realme dagger. Then the Raven Queen opened the vortex, and the sight of a cavern appeared.

***

The roar of rushing water filled Alerice's ears while the kiss of cool vapor refreshed her face. She could see light ahead and saw dapples of brightness playing about stone walls.

She was in a grotto behind a waterfall. The stone was moist, and water pooled just below the rocks on which she stood. The light shimmered dimly on its surface, for the grotto created the most delicious shadows.

Alerice moved forward, trusting every part of herself that had ever moved within those shadows. Where other people would have required a candle or lantern, Alerice only required her sense of self, as she had since childhood.

She moved at an angle through the grotto and discovered the backside of the waterfall, a cascade roughly as wide as she was tall. Alerice felt her way along the stone walls, then noticed a strange indentation under her fingertips.

It was a glyph. Alerice traced it, noticing more glyphs of varying sizes. Was this some sort of sacred chamber? She centered herself and focused on the Ravens Queen's mark. She felt her brow pulse, and she recalled her astral gaze looking upon Oddwyn.

Alerice opened her spiritual eyes to examine the wall. The glyphs glowed with latent auras, marking patches of rock that appeared different from the surrounding stone. They reminded her of stories she had heard of great cities with burial niches crafted into underground catacombs.

Someone had created this array of glyph-warded niches, and being able to match these glyphs with others might help her discover the thief she sought.

Alerice emerged from behind the waterfall, stepping carefully from one slippery rock to another. Earlier, Kreston had instructed her to bend her knees in order to maintain balance, but she already knew this trick from carrying laden trays at the Cup and Quill. With a few steps and leaps, she alighted on the bank of a forest stream and looked about.

The trees were thin-trunked and covered with ivy. Lush ferns grew between them, as did a variety of scrub plants. The daylight was fading, for the sun had set and twilight colored the sky with blues and greens. She wondered how she would find her way if no moon rose. After all, shadows were one thing, darkness another.

Something rustled to her side, and Alerice looked to the right. She thought she caught sight of an animal, but then she also caught sight of what she thought must be a lantern's light. If someone was here, she made up her mind to discover who that someone was.

The thin glow of what Alerice was now certain was a lantern flitted here and there. Tracking it, Alerice caught several glimpses of antlers. However, she had no idea how a buck could be connected to a lantern, and she grew concerned that the glass might break and the poor animal would be burned. She did her best to stalk quietly, but there was no ending the incessant rustling she made as she moved through the ferns and undergrowth.

The light stopped and remained stationary, and Alerice sensed that her chance had come. She crept forward to the trees surrounding a small clearing. The lantern rested in the center, but as she looked about she saw no buck. Even more strange was a set of only two hoof prints, not four – a peculiarity that Alerice thought was best to investigate.

However, before she took a step, she felt the need to draw her Realme dagger. She also felt the Raven Queen's mark pulse upon her brow. Was she in danger? She did not sense any, but she trusted her intuition, especially since there were no shadows in the clearing's heart.

Alerice stepped forward cautiously, looking about for the buck. It must have been able to shake the lantern loose and bolt for the trees. Nevertheless, Alerice was relieved to have a light source with which to find her way out of the woods.

She bent down to claim the lantern, but just then the Realme dagger tugged her hand upward even as a crossbow bolt *whizzed* in. The dagger parried the strike, and Alerice startled before she rolled aside toward the trees and scrambled behind a trunk.

Something rustled not far away. Alerice peered out, knowing that the something was now stalking her. The Raven Queen's mark pulsed fiercely, and she ducked back just in time to avoid a second bolt, which sank into the tree at eye level.

Alerice reached for her own Realme crossbow, which she loosed from its keep-strap. She raised it, and the bow string pulled back of its own accord while a gleaming bolt appeared in the flight groove. Alerice readied the weapon, calling, "Come into the light. If I fire, you will die, and I have no desire to kill you."

Alerice scanned the trees and saw a rack of antlers.

"Are you a man wearing buck horns?" she asked. "If you are, be warned, for I am a..." She paused, uncertain how to present herself. Then throwing caution to the wind, she chose the bold approach. "I am a Realme Walker. I bear the Raven Queen's bow. Come into the light – now, please."

Alerice waited a moment more, and then saw the fern-thick brush part. A deer advanced into the clearing. Alerice sighed, for though someone was attempting to assault her, the deer might spoil the next shot if she got close enough to it.

Alerice emerged from behind her tree, both bow and dagger ready, and stepped closer to the deer – which stood up on its hind hooves. It had no forehooves. It had arms and a human torso. It had a half-human, half-deer face, and it even had bits of jewelry decorating two of the prongs in its three-prong rack.

It wore a corseted belt made of thickly woven fibers, the lower flair of which fanned out onto its spotted legs. A halter of the same woven fibers rose up from the top of the belt and joined at the back of the neck. More importantly than its garb was the fact that it held a crossbow, which it aimed squarely at Alerice.

"You're a Realme Walker?" the creature asked.

The voice was clearly female. Alerice tried to maintain her guard, but she had never encountered a being such as this, and though it bore antlers, it was clearly a doe.

"Forgive my astonishment," Alerice said with a slight reverence to indicate her salutation.

The doe looked Alerice over and made note of her armor. She approached on her two hooves, displaying no fear as she held her weapon ready.

"I would say that humans are always astonished to see a faun," the doe said. "But then humans can't see fauns. They always mistake us for animals, and the fact that you can see me makes me believe that you are indeed a Realme Walker. My name is Lolladoe. What's yours?"

"Alerice Linden of Navre. Servant of the Raven Queen," she added, deciding to be further bold in hopes of striking awe into this woodland wonder.

"Is that where you got the scales?" Lolladoe asked with a snort down her long nose. Her black nostrils glistened in the lantern light, and she licked them with her long tongue.

"Yes."

"They're brill."

"Brill?"

"Brilliant. Gods and trees, do I have to explain everything?"

"'Gods and trees'. Now there's an expression I've never heard before."

"I wouldn't expect you had," Lolladoe said.

Alerice was not certain what to make of this encounter, but there was one fact that she must address.

"Lolladoe," she said matter-of-factly. "Do I have any reason to fear you?"

"No. If I wanted to shoot you, I would have done it already."

"Then perhaps we should both lower our weapons."

Lolladoe pawed the grass with her right hoof, and then shrugged. "Sure."

Lolladoe tied the end of her crossbow to the side of her corseted belt and took another step forward. "Mind if I touch them?"

"Touch what?" Alerice asked as she affixed her bow to her belt and sheathed her dagger.

"Those scales," Lolladoe said with a lusting smile.

"...All right," Alerice agreed.

The faun reached out to pet Alerice's armor. She snorted again, and couldn't help but sniff the metal. Alerice felt uncomfortable at the intrusion into her personal space and was about to step back, but a sudden jolt of fear shot through her as the Raven Queen's mark pulsed brightly upon her brow.

"Get down!" she cried, pulling Lolladoe to the grass as a broadsword flew in. It missed Lolladoe by a hand's width, and then lodged into the same tree that bore the doe's crossbow bolt.

Both Alerice and Lolladoe looked up to regard it, but saw it vanish from sight. Alerice then looked in the direction the sword had come from, and scrambled to protect Lolladoe from the former captain who now came crashing into the clearing.

"Kreston!" she cried, standing and holding up her hands to halt his advance.

Kreston stood on his guard, broadsword in hand, ready to attack the downed faun. He looked between the creature and Alerice, finally focusing his attention on her.

"Are you all right?"

"Yes, Kreston. Stand down, please. And sheathe your blade. Lolladoe means me no harm."

"Lolladoe?" Kreston asked. "What's a Lolladoe?"

"Not what, who, stupid man," Lolladoe said, rising, her antlers bared for action.

Alerice placed herself in the middle of a potential 'man verses faun' conflict, holding palms up before them both.

"Kreston Dühalde, meet Lolladoe the faun."

Kreston looked Lolladoe over as she pawed the grass with her right hoof. "You have got to be joking."

Lolladoe regarded Kreston, then Alerice, then Kreston again. "He can see me too?"

"Of course I can see you," Kreston said.

Lolladoe raised her brows and licked her nose again. "Two Realme Walkers. The clan is not going to believe this."

***

Alerice and Kreston sat in the fauns' glen, the communal home of Lolladoe's clan. The clearing was spacious enough to accommodate several family groups, and while the child fauns played in the trees nearby, the glen's outer perimeter was protected by a thatched fence that kept predators at bay while disguising the glen from any human who might stray nearby.

Alerice wondered how this might be, for what man wandering through the woods would not find a thatched fence curious? Yet as she sat within the glen, Alerice sensed the wall had been imbued with protective magic, so it was quite believable that while she saw a wall, a common man might see only dense brush.

The central glen was capped by a series of thatched green draperies borne above by ropes and poles. Near the great center pole, which was a tall trunk honed into a three-dimensional carving of ancestral faun faces, a fire burned in a sizeable rock pit. The heat radiated out and about, contained by the draperies above to warm the air, and a cauldron hung on a wrought metal crossbar, for apparently the fauns were fond of soup.

Being herbivores, their culinary preference consisted of greens, herbs, and roots. The fauns had offered Alerice and Kreston a bowl, and while Alerice forced her portion down, noting that it was in serious want of salt and seasoning, Kreston had drunk his, set his bowl on the ground before him, and remained engaged in his staring contest.

Everyone sat on stools made from thin tree branches that had been soaked and woven. The fauns formed a circle with the bucks composing one hemisphere and the does the other.

Alerice noted with pleasant surprise that the fauns enjoyed adorning themselves. All wore some type of clothing, not because they felt the need to cover their half-human bodies, but because they enjoyed personal expression. They had a natural aversion to leather, but they saw no aversion to sporting re-worked scraps of fabric.

They also had a fondness for jewelry. Some wore golden loops in their long ears. Some had set cabochons into their antler points. Lolladoe was not the only faun to adorn her antlers with beaded metal hoops that did not fall off given that she placed them below a prong but above the branch-out from the prong below.

Not all bucks were warriors and not all does were domestic, but all were fixed on Alerice and Kreston with clear distrust.

"You claim to seek a thief of souls," Sheradoe, the black-spotted faun shaman, said.

"That is my task, yes," Alerice answered.

Sheradoe examined Alerice before she batted her liquid black eyes in approval. She licked her black nose, and then examined Kreston, seeming to peel him like an onion the longer she gazed upon him. "But seeking a thief is not his task," the faun eventually said.

Kreston did not respond, nor did he look at Sheradoe. Rather, he was engaged in a staring contest with the warrior bucks sitting opposite him. One was the clan's chief, Ketabuck, a dark-toned faun with white stripes down his back. He had fixed his steely black eyes on Kreston's hazel, and the two had not broken contact.

Alerice was concerned that Kreston might take some sort of initiative, given that he was a man of action and the moment was tense, but Kreston was obviously also a man of tact allowing her to lead the conversation.

In the back of her mind, Alerice wondered why Kreston had sought her out here in these woods. How had he found her, given that she had come to this place through the Raven Queen's auspices? She would ask him about it in time, but now was not the right moment.

"No, Sheradoe," Alerice said. "Kreston does not share my task of discovering the thief of souls, though he does guard my shoulder, and I guard his."

Alerice glanced at Kreston to see if he approved of the statement, but his gaze remained locked on Ketabuck.

"Well, if it is a thief you seek, you will not find him here," Sheradoe said. "We fauns have no care for the world of humans. We keep to ourselves, as you must certainly realize. That's why we are creatures of legend and myth. We may snatch a trinket or two from a human cart on the road or from a human home in the town of Vygar, but nothing more. Moreover, we are not magical beings. We do not conjure, so what use would we have for souls?"

"You don't conjure," Kreston finally commented as he looked away from Ketabuck and gazed at Sheradoe.

"No, sir," the shaman said.

"Then what's in that little brown pouch at your side?"

Alerice had not noticed the small canvas bag that Sheradoe bore on her right hip, but now that Kreston had brought it to her attention, she realized that it did radiate mystical energy.

"Sir," Sheradoe said. "I am the shaman of our clan, and I protect the talisman of our clan."

"And that's all you need to know," Ketabuck said.

"Well, I can feel the power of your talisman half-way across your glen," Kreston said. "So if you don't conjure, then you're holding something that is magically stronger than you are. Mind showing us what it is?"

The mark of the King of Shadows briefly pulse-glowed below Kreston's salt-and-pepper bangs. Alerice was unsure if he had caused this to happen, but it certainly punctuated his point.

"Sir," Sheradoe said. "You are marked by the Realme, and as such I understand that you may have an intuition most mortals will never comprehend, but I will repeat that we are not thieves of souls."

Alerice wanted to give Kreston an excuse to stand down, but he was right about the pouch.

"As you say, Sheradoe," she said. "But being a Realme Walker, I agree with Kreston that what you have there is very magical, and I wish to know if it is something that might give the Raven Queen cause for concern."

"There is no cause for concern," Ketabuck said, standing. His bucks and the warrior does, including Lolladoe, stood with him. Kreston rose to meet him, and Alerice rose to make certain that the moment did not devolve.

"And you are no Realme Walker," the big buck said, looking at Alerice. "At least not yet."

"Well, I've been at the game longer than she has," Kreston said. "And if you're not hiding anything of concern, then show us what she's got."

"Sir," Sheradoe said flatly, while remaining seated. "We have said our say. Your senses do not deceive you. I do have something precious at my side, but you must be content with my word that it is not a threat. Guile is a tool of men. Fauns have no use for it."

"I'm certain you don't," Alerice said to calm the moment. She looked between Kreston and Ketabuck, and then motioned for everyone to again take their seats. "If you say that what you harbor in your pouch is of no concern, I will accept your word, but if I have reason to suspect you, I will have no choice but to investigate further."

Sheradoe looked her over, then licked her nose before she said, "You two may stay the evening with us. We will offer you hospitality in hopes that you might see us in a different light, but you will leave at dawn. Go to Vygar's town, for it is there that you will find what you seek."

"I thought you said the town was called Vygar," Alerice said.

"I said the 'town of Vygar'," Sheradoe corrected. "Prince Vygar. His castle rests above the town. He is a mystical man, of that we are certain, and by the gods and trees, if anyone is a thief of souls, you will discover that it is him."

**

The town's name was Uffton, and Prince Vygar's castle was an edifice of four turrets and a central hall sitting atop the rise. The town itself spread about the rise in a horseshoe, and the main road passed by the town's front gates.

Alerice and Kreston had walked to Uffton from the fauns' glen. The distance had not been far, and neither of them had a mount, for Alerice had left Jerome at the cottage inn along with Kreston's stallion, a handsome blood bay named Captain.

Alerice had been able to gaze through her Realme dagger, as she had when viewing her family at Uncle Judd's home, to find Jerome happily grazing in the Realme. Oddwyn had even snuck him a few oats and carrots. She had no idea where Captain had gone, but she had the feeling that he was also being cared for.

Entering through Uffton's main gate had presented a challenge for unlike Basque, which was not a walled hamlet, Uffton was, and it was far less welcoming.

The Gate Master had questioned Alerice and Kreston at some length before accepting that her sole purpose was an audience with Prince Vygar. Once inside, all folk had avoided the blonde woman in black armor and the former military officer with a wide-brimmed hat and a broadsword. Indeed, there was an overall air about Uffton that made the hairs on the back of Alerice's neck stand up.

She had gleaned from the few townsfolk who dared engage her that Vygar's title was less royal and more self-honorary, but no one felt that the challenge to his rank was worth their life. This reservation, combined with a strange essence that clearly emanated from the castle on high, gave Alerice the sense that Vygar was a man of magical talents.

However, as she and Kreston walked past Uffton's central square, Alerice knew that she must ask the question buzzing about her brain, for she would never find another opportunity.

"Kreston?" she said as she slowed her gait and lowered her voice. "How did you find me in the clearing last night? I followed the Raven Queen into the Evherealme from that cottage, and from there I traveled through a vortex into a--"

"Waterfall grotto?" he said, completing her sentence. She nodded. "I know you did, and before you ask, I will tell you that I saw you walking into the Realme with *her*, and I called to the King of Shadows to allow me to follow you."

"Why?"

"As I said in the glen with those fauns, I have been at this game longer than you. I know the dangers that walking between worlds can bring. I followed you into the woods to look after you, and when I saw you and that thing--"

"Lolladoe."

"Whatever." He stopped walking and gazed upon her. "I couldn't let you do things alone. Not before you're ready. You're going to need my help, and I'd like you to let me guide you if I can."

"Kreston, I don't want you to take this the wrong way, but there are times when you worry me. Your memories of that Landrew person, for example. They strike you without warning, and they might compromise you at a critical moment. I may not be able to trust you."

"I know that, but let me try, just this time. If it doesn't go well, I'll leave."

She looked him over, and though she knew she was right to be mindful of her reservations, she nodded and continued toward the citadel.

***

Vygar's castle was surrounded by an unflooded trench. The drawbridge was down, and twelve men at arms stood guard along its length, six on either side. They wore studded armor accented with wolf pelts. Each bore a spear and a broadsword, and all eyed Alerice and Kreston as they passed.

Alerice summoned her charade of a confident, otherworldly warrior as she strode past, but inwardly she was thankful that she had allowed Kreston to accompany her.

Both Alerice and Kreston had been expected, and they soon found themselves in the high-vaulted central hall spanning the four cornering turrets. Colored daylight spilled in from long, painted windows, and Alerice noted that the multi-toned glazing dampened the sun's natural brightness.

The dais bearing Vygar's throne consisted of three white stone steps. His chair was crafted of the same material. Seated stone wolves flanked it, four on either side, and men similarly adorned to the drawbridge guards stood about the room to protect all points of entry.

Opposite the windows, a stone arch rose from the wooden floor, which Alerice found strange. Given the hall's breadth, the arch could not possibly lead to an adjoining corridor. It was simply crafted into the wall. A glassy black surface filled its interior, and Alerice could not stop herself from approaching it.

Then, the glassy blackness appeared to shimmer with life. It even crackled a bit, and she stopped short. Kreston came up to her side and nudged her to back away. She did as the shimmering congealed in the arch's black center.

The translucent form took shape, growing more opaque as someone drew near from the opposite side. Alerice watched the figure solidify... then saw a man step through the glassy arch into the hall.

He was young and quite striking, with silvery hair that flowed to his mid-back. He wore an ivory tunic studded with lines of lapis cabochons, and his cream trousers were tucked neatly into silvery boots.

He paused to regard Alerice and Kreston, then held his hands out to either side as if reaching for something near his hips. Two translucent figures appeared within more glassy black shimmer-crackles, and two white wolves paced out from the arch to run their heads under the man's hands. He stroked the beasts, and then nodded to Alerice before he led the wolves up the dais. The animals took up flanking positions on either side of the throne as the man sat down, petted their necks, and looked down upon his guests.

"I hear that you are Realme Walkers," he said in a voice that rang with magic. "I welcome you to Uffton. I am Vygar, known to many as the Wolf Prince."

"No kidding," Kreston muttered under his breath, but Alerice pressed her elbow into his ribs before she approached the dais and offered a reverence.

"My warmest greetings to you, Vygar, Prince of Wolves. I am Alerice of Navre, servant to the Raven Queen." She thought she should introduce Kreston, but for some reason she decided to hold that information in reserve.

"I have sensed your coming, Alerice of Navre. You search for something, do you not?"

"I do, sir," she said. The stone wolves on either side of Vygar's throne seemed to be staring at her, and she could not help but regard them.

Vygar looked along her line of sight, then sat back and smiled. "I see you have noticed my sentinels. They are my pack, if you will. They guard and protect, for no creature is like a wolf. They are killers, but they are also steadfast and never betray their kin. They hunt together in perfect precision, each one sensing the motions of the others, each knowing the others' thoughts. Never could you find better company, especially when in the heat of battle. Wouldn't you agree?" he asked Kreston.

"Wolves aren't men," he replied.

"No, they are much more pure of heart. Men can betray those they claim to love."

Kreston had no response, but Alerice could see that Vygar had touched a nerve.

"I seek a thief, sir," she said, taking a half-step forward to assert control over the conversation. "I seek a man of magical talents, and you are certainly one. What do you know of souls taken from the Evherealme?"

Vygar smiled and clutched the course hair on his wolves' necks. "You spent last evening with the fauns, if I am not mistaken."

"We did, sir," Alerice said, uncertain how he knew this but still waiting for him to lead up to his point.

"And being 'marked mortals' who know the Realme, you must have sensed the prize they keep in their glen."

Alerice folded her arms over her black scales.

"It would not have attracted your attention unless it was likewise of the Realme. The fauns keep this talisman hidden. So yes, as you see I am indeed a man of magical talents. I use my power to protect Uffton and its people. However, if you are looking for a key to the Realme's missing souls, I suggest you return to the fauns and demand that they reveal their treasure to you. It will lead you to the thief you seek."

"They said you'd do that," Kreston interjected.

"Of course they did. They ordered you away from their glen as well, didn't they? I have no doubt that they did because you cannot trust fauns. They hate the world of men. They steal from my people and they conjure within their forest. They are dangerous. I've sent hunting parties searching for them, and the men never return. If any beings are stealing souls from the Evherealme, it's the fauns. They are no doubt amassing an army to unleash on Uffton, and I would be the first to thank you if you rid me of them."

"You've got wolves," Kreston said. "Do it yourself."

"Wolf Price," Alerice interjected to stop Kreston from saying anything further. "If we return to the fauns, and we discover what they are hiding, and that something does not threaten the Realme, then what are we to think of you for sending us on a fool's errand?"

Vygar nodded. "A good question. Why don't you take the initiative to discover what they have that they cherish so much. Only after doing so will you know what to do next."

***

"He's an ass," Kreston said, lifting his tankard to his lips.

Alerice sat opposite him on a bench seat at a long table behind Uffton's only public house. She pushed her own tankard slightly from side to side, thinking.

"They're both hiding something," she said.

"You think?"

She looked out from under her brow at him. "One of them is the person I'm tasked with finding, Vygar or Sheradoe. The trick is to discover which one. I remember at the Cup and Quill--"

"Where?"

"My old tavern in Navre," she said. "There were times when I saw men accuse one another of cheating at cards. So you know what I'd do?"

"Deal yourself in?"

She looked at him again. "No, I would wait until they were about to come to blows and then I'd snatch their hands away. I'd turn the cards up on the table, and more often than not the cheat was usually the man who protested more."

"So how are you going to take hold of the cards this time?"

Alerice tapped her finger on the table before she took up her tankard and drank, but in doing so she noticed some boys playing 'knights' in the dark dirt.

"I have an idea," she said.

"I hate it when women get those," Kreston mused into his cup.

She leveled another look at him and then continued with, "If I can find a way to distract the fauns, can you find out what Sheradoe has in her pouch?"

"Probably."

"Then I will discover what Vygar is hiding in his castle. His magic is linked to that glassy arch, and I need a better look at it."

"His wolves could tear you apart, Alerice. I don't want you seeking out his secrets alone."

"Oh, I won't be alone."

***

"Oddwyn," Alerice said, as she approached the herald from behind.

"Alerice," he said, startling. He turned about from what appeared to be a spiritual dice table floating in midair. Opposite him stood three of the spirit guides whom Alerice had watched escorting new souls about the Realme.

She regarded them with curiosity and they regarded her with annoyance before they urged Oddwyn in some incomprehensible language to hurry up and throw.

Oddwyn looked between them and Alerice, and then said to her, "Just a moment."

"Oddwyn," she urged.

One of the guides muttered further gibberish to Oddwyn, but having been a tavern mistress for so many years, Alerice could clearly see that it had asked, "Are you going to play or not?"

Oddwyn took up an iridescent cup, rattled it about, and then cast out dice of different shapes that looked as if they had been carved from gemstones. The throw was a winner, and Oddwyn whooped before demanding that the others pay up.

As they begrudgingly did, Alerice's patience wore through, and she reached out to touch Oddwyn's shoulder. Then a wicked grin crawled into her lips, and she flicked Oddwyn hard on the back of his head.

"Ouch," he said, turning about.

"Oddwyn, I need you now. I need the queen's Raven Knights, and she told me that you would guide me to them."

One of the spirit guides had also reached the end of its patience, and began a heated conversation with Oddwyn, all the while pointing at Alerice. She knew the look of an irritated gambler wondering how long a fellow gamer was going to permit an intruder to remain at the table, and apparently not receiving a satisfactory answer, the spirit humphed and disappeared.

Its portion of the pot likewise disappeared, as did the portions from the other two guides who followed suit by disappearing one after the other.

72

Oddwyn regarded his missing winnings and called to the ether, "I know where to find you!" Then he took a deep breath, presented himself as a maiden, and turned to Alerice.

"Calmer," Alerice commented on Oddwyn's appearance. "Good. Now, I need the Raven Knights for a task in Mortalia."

"You spoke to her without first approaching me?" she asked coolly.

Alerice placed her hands on her hips. "Must I always solicit my queen through you?"

"Yes. I am the herald," Oddwyn asserted with measured authority.

"And I am her Ravensdaughter, and you were just playing dice when I am about the queen's business. She gave me these and sent me to find you."

Alerice presented a little black pouch from which she tumbled two gray cabochons into her palm. Their polished surfaces resembled eyes when Alerice moved them gently from side to side.

Oddwyn regarded the gems and looked up at Alerice. "She gave you two vision stones? This must be serious. Come with me."

The Raven Knights' golden eyes set into the sockets of their full-metal helms still pierced Alerice's soul, but she did not shiver as she had when she first saw them in the Hall of Eternity. This time she was their momentary mistress, for they understood the import of the gray cabochons she bore. She had requested them to help her complete the Raven Queen's task, and they had obeyed, for they were the queen's creatures.

The knights accompanied Alerice as she emerged from behind the forest waterfall. The moist evening air filled her lungs as she made her way forward into the dimming twilight. The plan was simple, and it must be conducted under the cover of darkness.

The knights would create a diversion allowing both her and Kreston to investigate Vygar and the fauns. Then they would both use the vision stones to report their findings to the Raven Queen, who would measure the situation and render a verdict.

Alerice knew Kreston was somewhere close, but she had not yet located him. She tracked her way along the stream's bank, but a rustle in the ferns to her side attracted her attention, and she turned. A small light drew close and she held her position, the Raven Knights standing tall behind her.

"Kreston..." she said, but her voice trailed off as Lolladoe passed through the brush, holding her lantern.

"You've forgotten my name so soon?" the doe asked.

"Lolladoe," Alerice said, looking about for Kreston. Not seeing him, she focused on the faun instead. "What are you doing here?"

"Tracking you. I saw you go into the grotto a short time ago, and I've been waiting for you to come back out, because I know you're not finished with my clan."

Alerice thought it best not to lie, though she did intend to obfuscate. "I'm not finished with any business here. As you can see," she said with a gesture of her head toward the knights, "I work in the Raven Queen's name, and I will not stop until I have completed my task."

"Did you question that Vygar?" Lolladoe asked.

"I did, and I did not find him credible. That is why I am returning to Uffton."

"Good," the faun said. "Then I'm going with you."

"No, I don't think so," Alerice said with a chiding smile.

"Yes, I do think so," the faun insisted. "I know the secret ways about that town, and unless you plan to attack all of Vygar's Wolf Warriors, you had best keep to the shadows."

Alerice wondered if Lolladoe knew what the phrase 'keep to the shadows' meant to Alerice, but concluded that the faun could not know her that personally. It was merely a choice of words, and moreover Lolladoe was right. She did need silent entry into Uffton, and if Lolladoe could provide it, all the better. If the faun clan was innocent, then Lolladoe had nothing to fear from the Raven Queen. However, if Sheradoe and Ketabuck were the thieves she sought... Alerice decided to put the last option out of her mind.

"Why do you want to help me?" she asked.

"'Cause I want to prove to you and that bonehead officer of yours that we fauns have true hearts. The entire clan knows that you suspect us, and we all know that the wolfy princeling is the one you want. I want to be there when you find out the truth."

"And so you'll ensure that I discover the truth you want me to see?"

"I'll guide you into the town. You can figure things out for yourself from there. But you'll see that what I'm saying is true. I promise you that," she said with a snort.

Alerice looked Lolladoe over, judging her motive to be well-meant, even if it was rather brash.

"You say humans cannot see fauns?"

"Yep."

"Then the towns people will see you as a deer if you stay near the tree line on the main road?"

"They always do."

"Then I will meet you there as soon as I can. I must... give something to Kreston. Oh, mind if I borrow that?"

Lolladoe looked at Alerice, and then looked down at her lantern.

Kreston paced in the clearing where he had first encountered Lolladoe. He bore no lantern, but the moon had begun to rise, and there was a tiny modicum of light bathing the forest in soft silver.

He heard rustling and turned. He saw a thin light approaching and went on his guard. However, he stood down as he saw Alerice emerging from the ferns, lantern in hand. He was about to step forward and greet her, but the two Raven Knights stepped in behind her, and Kreston's hazel eyes went wide. His hand flew to his broadsword's handle, and he backed to the opposite edge of the clearing, reflexes on a razor's edge as he looked back and forth between the two otherworldly warriors. He was ready in case they decided to attack.

"Kreston," Alerice said as she hurried to him. She bade the knights not to follow her as she approached. She hung the lantern on the protruding knot of a tree branch and said to him, "They are taking orders from me. They are part of the plan to discover the truth."

Kreston continued to eye the monsters, but they did not move. He did not fully surrender his guard, nor did he remove his hand from his broadsword, but he did give Alerice the majority of his attention.

"We will need to show the queen what we discover," Alerice said. "She gave me these vision stones so we can. Whatever the fauns have, hold the stone before it and the Raven Queen will be able to judge if it is what she seeks."

Alerice held out one of the polished gray eye-cabochons for Kreston to take. He regarded it, and then he stood straight and stared at it, fear creeping into him.

"Kreston?" she asked.

Kreston swallowed hard before looking down at her. "I... I can't touch that. I can't touch anything that comes from *her*."

Alerice noted the manner in which he punctuated the pronoun, but moved her open palm closer to Kreston for him to take the stone.

"This is the only way my plan will work, Kreston. Take it, please."

Kreston hid a gulp. He looked at Alerice as if to draw courage from her, and then held the vision stone in his sights as he slowly reached out. His hand began to tremble. He began to tremble. His fingers approached the stone's smooth surface, and he tried to force himself to take it, but the moment overwhelmed him, and he snapped his fingers into his palm as he yanked his hand away.

"Kreston..." Alerice stammered as she gazed at him with wide eyes.

"I can't do it, Alerice," he said sternly. "Give that thing to one of the birds."

Kreston looked at one of the monsters, then inadvertently locked stares with its piercing, golden eyes. He startled, feeling a shock shoot through him, and turned back to Alerice. Again, he tried to draw courage from her imploring expression before he summoned his own ice-veined self-control.

"Alerice, I will find what that shaman is hiding, but let one of those two things report it. I won't."

Alerice simply stared up at him, her brows furrowed, then curled the vision stone back into her palm and nodded.

***

Alerice followed Lolladoe up the rise toward Vygar's citadel. She bore a length of rope coiled about her black scale mail. Lolladoe had strapped her crossbow to her back, and being the stronger of the two, she carried a satchel stuffed with climbing spikes. Their plan was to slip down into the trench and then scramble up the walls surrounding the castle, for neither was about to enter via the drawbridge. That was the assigned path for one of the Raven Knights.

Lolladoe had much better night vision, given her large, black eyes. Her keen senses of hearing and smell also provided an advantage when it came to proceeding undetected. She had initially offered only to guide Alerice into Uffton via the section of town wall that had fallen into disrepair, but when she had learned that Alerice's target was Vygar's inner sanctum, desire to discover more about him had gotten the better of her.

She was remarkably silent, even when her hooves struck the town's stone streets, and she guided Alerice to the town's dirt roads as soon as she could to further muffle their progress. Before long, they were in place atop the rear of the castle rise, which Alerice noticed when looking down was the steepest part of the town's topography.

Lolladoe looked into the trench to gauge its depth, and then at Alerice.

"Your turn," she whispered.

Alerice nodded and closed her eyes. She summoned the strength of her spiritual self, which she was appreciating more with each passing moment. Then she called to her waiting Raven Knight.

She felt the Raven Queen's mark pulse upon her brow, and she ordered the knight to advance. Then she opened her eyes to see the last flash of the mark's glow highlight Lolladoe's astonished face.

Lolladoe licked her black nose. "Brill," she exhaled.

Kreston approached the thatched fence that marked the perimeter of the fauns' glen. Leveling an eye close to its weave, he could see the fire burning below the cauldron. He could see silhouettes moving about. Some of the beasts locked antlers with one another in playful combat while others handed comrades a drink.

None of them suspected his impending intrusion.

Kreston neither knew nor cared if these creatures were guilty. He neither knew nor cared if they deserved to be raided. His task was the shaman. The plan may involve the black monster Alerice had told to assist him, but he forbade any loathing thoughts to play in his mind, lest they spoil his initiative.

Kreston stared at the shaman. He would seize her pouch and then his part in this mission would be finished, the conflict of it all be damned.

Outside the gates of Uffton, one Raven Knight drew his sword, spread his long, black-feathered cloak into great wings, and leaped into the moonlit night.

Within the forest clearing, the other Raven Knight drew his sword, spread his black-feathered cloak, and leaped up through the treetops.

On the drawbridge of Prince Vygar's citadel, one Raven Knight alighted with enough of a spiritual shockwave that it jolted the twelve men at arms from their stances. The knight then held his blade aloft and cawed so loudly into the evening air that the men at arms to shuddered.

In the fauns' glen, the other Raven Knight plunged through the thatched green draperies, felling them and causing the parts that covered the cauldron to catch fire.

Vygar's men at arms recovered, brandished their spears, and charged.

Though not able to see the combat, Alerice knew that her plan was in the offing. She doffed her rope, the end of which was attached to a spike, and planted the metal into the dirt. Then she threw the rope into the trench, and rappelled down the wall.

Fauns bugled in alarm as they managed to escape the shroud of draperies. They quickly recovered their senses and trained their black eyes on the Raven Knight who stood before them in stalwart silence. They bugled again and charged, attacking it to rid their home of the grave creature.

Kreston hurried to the perimeter wall's gate and slipped inside the glen, keeping to the shadows as he looked for the right moment.

Alerice and Lolladoe hurried to the trench's upslope, where Alerice drew two climbing spikes and a leather mallet from Lolladoe's satchel. She hammered the spikes into the soil and began climbing. Lolladoe followed, passing her up more spikes. Both made quick work, but as Alerice reached down for one last set of spikes, her boot slipped.

Lolladoe caught the sole in her antlers and hefted Alerice back into place, grunting back the physical strain in order to remain silent.

Prince Vygar appeared at a window in one of the castle's forward turrets. He gazed down upon his men as they attacked a Raven Knight, and his blood ran cold.

He hurried back into his bedchamber, grabbed a long cream-colored robe, and threw it about his shoulders as he bolted for the door.

Crossbows at the ready, Alerice and Lolladoe made their way toward the scullery, which rested just behind the high-vaulted central hall. The door was unlocked, and Alerice gestured for Lolladoe to enter.

The faun did, sniffing to get her bearings as her black eyes adjusted to the dim interior. Dying embers glowed in the great cooking hearth, and above them Lolladoe could make out the shape of a carved-up joint of some large animal. She leveled an angry stare and snorted in disgust before leading the way further in.

Kreston watched the way in which the black monster did not engage any of the beasts. It defended against their feeble attacks, but it neither wounded nor killed them. He wondered if Alerice had given it orders not to harm anyone but rather to cause a diversion. What a stupid girl she was. Enemies must die, lest they seize the opportunity to kill. Any military man knew that.

Alerice and Lolladoe peered out from the archway connecting the citadel's rear turret to the central hall. They were about to enter when Vygar ran in from the opposing archway, hurrying for his great stone arch.

His two wolves ran in with him and sat at his sides to guard him as Vygar paused to center himself. Then he drew essence from the arch's glassy black surface, which began to shimmer. With a sweeping gesture of both arms, Vygar used the arch's power to set the hall's torch sconces alight.

Alerice recessed into the shadow her archway provided, beckoning Lolladoe back. Lolladoe looked about, her black eyes searching for her ally, and regarded Alerice with awe once she obtained her location.

"Shadows," Alerice whispered in explanation.

Lolladoe nodded. "I can see why you're a Realme Walker," she whispered back.

Alerice smiled, then affixed her crossbow to her belt strap so that she could draw out the vision stone from its nearby pouch and hold it up to capture Vygar's image.

In the Realme's Hall of Eternity, the Raven Queen sat upon her throne. The maiden Oddwyn stood on the dais' lowest step, watching her.

The queen held a gray orb in her willow-white hands. Its interior swirled as though made of mist churning in a globe. Oddwyn watched closely as she bade it rise up. Then her fingers gently pulled the air before her into two parts, separating the orb into hemispheres.

Oddwyn's ice-blue eyes danced as she watched the hemispheres float into place before the queen, domes upward. The Raven Queen gestured to one, activating it to project the image of Vygar standing before the stone arch in his central hall.

Kreston watched the beasts circle about the monster knight, not one of them striking a blow. They bugled, grunted, snorted and pawed the ground with their hooves, but nothing more.

Fed up with this ridiculous display, he stood forward from the shadows, attracting the beasts' attention. Then he drew his broadsword and caught Ketabuck in his sights. Sheradoe hurried to place herself before him, and though the faun chief tried to move her aside, she would not budge.

Kreston smiled, for the tactic of threatening the chief had drawn the shaman into the perfect position. He raised his blade, and then threw it at the shaman's side to sever her little brown pouch from her belt.

"No!" Sheradoe cried as her pouch flew open in midair. A stone popped out from it, and Kreston charged for it at full speed. Ketabuck likewise charged, but Kreston landed on the big buck's back and grabbed his antlers to twist them hard, jerking Ketabuck's neck and torso so that he fell to his side.

Kreston scrambled for the rock that had fallen from the pouch, which he snatched up as he continued running to clear some space.

He turned and stood, and as the warrior bucks recovered and trained their furious stares upon him, he held his hand high overhead, and the King of Shadows' broadsword appeared in his grip. This gave the bucks enough pause to stand off, and seeing that he controlled the moment, Kreston looked down and uncurled his fist to reveal a heart-shaped piece of polished red stone.

"Good sir!" Sheradoe cried.

Kreston glanced up at the faun, denying himself any empathy as he stared into her imploring black eyes.

Prince Vygar turned toward his throne and gazed upon the wolf statues. As he drew power from his stone arch, the wolves began to dissolve, head to tail. Their mineral composure floated as might too much salt in water, until Vygar commanded what remained of the statues to congeal into the shape of spirit wolves.

Vygar's own wolves stood and howled to them. The spirit wolves howled in return and flew forward to join them.

In the archway, Lolladoe shuddered in natural fear of a predator's cry, and held down one of her long ears to her angular cheek. She fumbled with her crossbow, and Alerice reached out to help steady it. Lolladoe drew closer to her, and Alerice made certain she was stable as she continued to hold the vision stone up at Vygar.

"This is your talisman?" Kreston demanded. "A stupid rock?"

"It's not stupid," Ketabuck stated, the rage in his voice barely contained.

"And it's not a rock," Sheradoe added, stepping forward even though Ketabuck tried to catch her arm. The faun chief was about to advance with her, as was each member of the clan, but Sheradoe motioned them back. "It is called the Heart of the Forest. It protects us and wards our glen. Prince Vygar hunts us, but as long as we have our talisman, he cannot find us, nor can any outsider."

Kreston humphed. "It didn't work too well this time, did it."

"The only outsiders that can find us are the ones we let in," Ketabuck half-shouted. "And we never should have let you in, or that girl."

Kreston's hazel eyes narrowed at the mention of Alerice, but he turned to the black monster behind him and held up the Heart.

"Here, bird," he growled. "Show *her* this."

The fauns tensed as the Raven Knight drew out the vision stone and held it up to catch sight of the Heart and the glen.

In the Hall of Eternity, the second hovering hemisphere activated to display the glen, the fauns, and the Heart of the Forest in Kreston's grasp.

Oddwyn looked questioningly at him, and then at the Raven Queen. "Why is Alerice letting him help?"

The Raven Queen did not respond as she began to measure the moment.

In his great hall, Prince Vygar sent his spirit wolves through his glassy black arch. Then he conjured the vision of his drawbridge to fill the arch's shimmering interior and watched as his wolves flew toward the Raven Knight.

On the drawbridge, the Raven Knight took hold of the last opposing spear. It had already cast eleven men at arms into the trench below, some wounded but most unscathed, for it had not been tasked with mortal destruction, only mortal diversion.

Yet as it disarmed the final mortal and used the man's spear to heft him down to join his comrades, the knight looked up into the moonlight to discover the approaching wolf pack.

It cawed long and loud, spread its cloak, and launched itself skyward for aerial combat.

Which Vygar witnessed through his arch. Sadly, the eight members of his pack, which snarled, circled, and then lunged with savage bites, were not sufficient to defeat a knightly spirit that bore armor thick enough to repel any spirit wolf's attack.

He required reinforcements, and so Vygar's eyes rolled back as he summoned the full breadth of his magical awareness. He reached out toward his arch, the keystone of which began to glow.

Hidden in their archway, Alerice and Lolladoe watched as the keystone presented a glyph. It matched the glyph Alerice had touched in the grotto.

Lolladoe looked at her. "You've seen that symbol before, haven't you?" she whispered.

"Yes," Alerice said.

Lolladoe snorted softly. "I told you."

Alerice did not respond as she made certain that her vision stone captured Vygar's every move.

Prince Vygar focused his arch on the grotto's niches, causing their glyphs to glow. They vibrated and then burst open. The anguished souls of wicked men flew out, howling with freedom.

Vygar called to them, "I command you to kill the Raven Knight! Fly to me!"

They howled again, summoned the weapons they had borne in life, and flew out from the grotto in a direct line for Uffton.

In the Hall of Eternity, Oddwyn looked at the Raven Queen. Neither she nor the Realme's mistress required words, for they had seen Vygar's interaction with the grotto's niches, and they now knew the identity of the thief of souls.

The Raven Queen held out one hand, and the hemisphere bearing the scene of the fauns' glen hovered into it.

"See to your brother in arms," she ordered before ending the vision. The scene faded in a cascade of misty gray dust as the hemisphere became inert.

In the glen, the Raven Knight cawed. The fauns all cringed while Kreston fell to one knee, lowered his head, and covered his ears. He dropped the Heart of the Forest to the dirt as the knight spread its cloak into black wings and leaped upward into the trees, its sword gleaming in the moonlight.

Sheradoe bolted forward toward the Heart of the Forest, but Kreston saw her and snatched it up before she could get close enough to reach it. He stood with it in hand, regarded both it and the faun shaman, and then tossed it to Sheradoe as he recovered his broadsword and turned toward the glen's gate.

Still hidden in their archway, Alerice and Lolladoe watched as Vygar's glassy black arch displayed a new round of combat, with the wicked souls flying in to aid the wolves and overwhelm the Raven Knight.

Lolladoe snarled and stamped a hoof, which pricked the ears of one of

Vygar's white wolves. It turned and barked as it stood on alert, prompting the same action from its mate. Both wolves arched their backs and snarled, alerting Vygar. Then they charged.

Lolladoe stepped from the archway and leveled her bow. She fired, killing the wolf as it leaped for her.

Alerice drew her Realme dagger and charged forward to kill the second wolf, which was about to sink its teeth into Lolladoe's leg. The beast whined as the dagger struck home, and landed with a thud on the hall's floor.

Vygar turned, furious, but Lolladoe had already fitted a second bolt into her bow and leveled it at him.

Alerice came forward holding the vision stone for Vygar to see.

"What shall I do, My Queen?" she asked.

In the Hall of Eternity, the Raven Queen responded in her voice of dark honey, "Await my knights."

In the sky above the citadel's forward turrets, the second Raven Knight joined the first. Together they dispatched the spirit wolves. The pack fought until its last member dissipated in a whisp of cloud. The wicked souls, having no loyalty and realizing that while they had been summoned, they had not been enslaved, fled away into the night.

The Raven Knights snapped back their winged cloaks, and swooped down to alight before the doors to Vygar's hall.

Alerice heard a mighty two-toned caw echo through the hall. The doors flew open so violently that they tore away from their hinges. Alerice leveled her dagger at Vygar, knowing what was about to happen.

Vygar regarded her, then the doors, but in the end offered Alerice one final stare. "Now you'll always be looking over your shoulder, for you've attracted attention."

"It wouldn't be the first time," she said.

Vygar smiled knowingly. "Arrogant girl."

The Raven Knights flew in and landed before Vygar. They took hold of his arms and forced him to turn about to face the glassy black surface of the stone arch. Securing him, they flew directly into it. The surface shimmered, but then crackled with such strain that parts of it shattered, shards cascading to the floor.

"Come on," Alerice said, sheathing her dagger and grabbing Lolladoe's arm to yank her forward.

"Where are we going?" the faun asked.

"Home, I hope."

Alerice ran to the arch and stood before its ruined surface, Lolladoe beside her. She centered herself before she touched a part of it that remained intact, and focused on the Raven Queen's mark. She watched it glow in her reflection, and extended her spiritual self into the glassy black void as she said, "My Queen. Please help us return to Lolladoe's clan."

In the Hall of Eternity, the Raven Queen's second hemisphere hovered above her open palm, presenting the reverse sight of Vygar's hall as though Alerice and the faun stood on the opposite side of a glass pane. With a slow blink, the queen conjured the image of the fauns' wrecked glen.

Alerice saw the image and understood the meaning. She clasped Lolladoe's hand in hers and asked, "Ready?"
"For what?" the faun asked, but the answer became obvious as Alerice prepared to lunge. "Ah, no!" Lolladoe exclaimed.
Alerice ignored the objection as she jumped forward, Lolladoe in tow.

In the Hall of Eternity, the Raven Queen watched the two disappear. Confident of their security, she focused the force of her eternal spirit at the stone arch.

In Vygar's hall, the remaining glassy black began to vibrate at increasing intervals until it could no longer bear the strain. It exploded into the hall, scattering shards that caught the light of the torch sconces.
The keystone began to vibrate even as it glowed once more with Vygar's glyph. Then it ruptured and the remaining arch fell to the floor in a cascade of stone and mortar.

The Raven Queen looked down upon Vygar, who stood between her knights. She commanded the hemisphere above her palm to become inert, and then commanded it to rise up before commanding its twin to rise opposite it. Folding her willow-white fingers into one another, she caused the hemispheres to fuse back into the original gray orb. Its misty swirls began to dance once again within its globe.
The Raven Queen bade her orb to settle into Oddwyn's hands before she said to Vygar, "The punishment for stealing from the Evherealme is imprisonment until death, which shall come mercifully swift to you as a mortal held within our world. I will not torment you, as you did to the souls you stole by sealing them within your niches. Your failure will be torment enough."

***

"What happened here?" Lolladoe exclaimed as she looked about the ruined draperies.

"She happened here," Ketabuck said, looking accusingly at Alerice.

"No, they happened here," another buck said. "Both her and her man."

"What do you mean?" Lolladoe asked. "Alerice was with me in Vygar's hall. He's gone now, and he'll never worry us again."

Alerice approached Sheradoe. "Was anyone hurt?"

Sheradoe snorted, but shook her head.

Lolladoe stepped up, looking her comrade over. "Alerice?"

Alerice turned to the faun and flatly stated, "I'm sorry, but I had to raid your glen. I had to discover what you were concealing. I was tasked with discovering a thief, and I found your clan suspect."

"You what?" Lolladoe demanded. Alerice said nothing further, drawing Lolladoe's ire. "I told you that the wolfy one was the man you wanted, and even though I helped you figure it out, you still attacked my glen?"

"The Raven Queen needed to take the measure of you both," Alerice stated. "I make no excuses for what I did, and I would do it again, for I am in her service. But I asked her that no one suffer harm, least of all your kin, and she agreed that she would only see what she needed to see and nothing more."

"And did she see?" Lolladoe asked.

"She did," Sheradoe replied, holding up the Heart of the Forest. "She saw our talisman. Your man held it up to the eye in the raven's hand."

"You know, he's not really my man," Alerice said, referencing Kreston.

"Shite, he isn't," Lolladoe said. "If this was all your idea and he helped, then he's your man." Lolladoe looked into Alerice's eyes and wanted to retain her fury, but the betrayal of a burgeoning friendship took hold. "Why didn't you just ask us about the Heart?"

"I did," Alerice said. "So did Kreston, but you didn't trust us."

"Realme Walker," Ketabuck said, coming before Alerice and standing tall. "We might have trusted you, but we did not trust him."

"Kreston? Why not?"

"There is something dark within his soul," Sheradoe said, some of the other fauns agreeing.

"He hears battlefield voices," Alerice said. "I think he failed in a fight when he ordered his lieutenant to advance on a hill."

"No, there's something more," Ketabuck said. "I knew it the moment I saw him. Some of us could smell it on him, secrets that eat away at him. If you keep trusting him, you will regret it."

Alerice gazed into the big buck's black eyes.

"Alerice?" Kreston called from some distance away.

Alerice turned to find him standing at the open perimeter gate. She brightened at the sight of him, but Ketabuck's words had spurred a wariness she could not conceal, and her expression faded into one more serious, which she was certain Kreston saw.

"It's time we left," Kreston said.

Alerice nodded, but then regarded the fauns before she looked at Lolladoe's liquid black eyes. "You were right, you know. You fauns do have true hearts."

***

Vygar knew only that his soul had already begun to languish. He could see nothing, for he lay in darkness so black that he could not find his hand when he held it before his face.

This was where he would die, and as the queen had said, his end would come mercifully quick, for no mortal held within the shroud of the Evherealme could find nourishment. Even if they did intend to maintain him, he would erode internally. He was finished, and as the queen had said, his failure would be his torment. It already was.

He had lost his rank, so let that be damned. He had lost his power and prestige, so let that be damned as well. He had lost his ability to serve the King of Shadows, so let that be damned the most.

"I would say that is a step too far," a voice rang out. The tenor might have been physical. It might have been spiritual. Vygar had no frame of reference. He only knew that he *knew* the voice. Indeed, he had conversed with it on many occasions.

Vygar's senses swirled in his mind, and he closed his eyes in the darkness – only to open them near a swirling vortex that pulsed with the Realme's tri-colored black, midnight blue, and dark teal ether.

"You let her see you open the niches in the grotto," the King of Shadows proclaimed from behind Vygar. The Wolf Prince spun about, and then fell to his knees, prostrating himself.

"I did, Great Shade. I blundered terribly, but I did not expect that the girl would be watching."

"And you called *her* arrogant," the King mused.

Vygar held his position, head down and eyes closed, trembling internally as he awaited the king's will. He hoped that somehow the Realme's master still had use for him, for he had just freed him. However, hope in the Realme was fleeting at best.

"I needed those souls, Vygar. The wicked men you freed. If you had left it to your wolves, yes they may have perished, but my wife would never have discovered your work, and the souls would still be encased. Now the queen will surely open the remaining niches, or rather she will have her child do it."

Vygar couldn't help but ask, "Her child, My King?"

"The girl, you fool. My wife's new pet. The girl has given my wife new confidence, and this presents a danger to me, for the queen may seek to expand her influence within the Realme. She may insist on measuring more souls before I have a chance to claim them, and I will not lose to my wife. So yes, I do yet have use for you."

Inwardly, Vygar breathed a sigh of relief, never once questioning the King of Shadows' ability to know his every thought.

"I want you to make that girl regret she ever took my wife's dagger," the king said. "I want you to haunt her steps and let her know that anything she touches will be vulnerable to destruction. I want you to make her question her every move and pay for every deed she believes is good. And you can start with those fauns. Now that I have seen their Heart, you will finally know where to find them."

***

Alerice tried to keep pace with Kreston as he strode through the woods. He was clearly tracking the way back to the waterfall, which was perhaps just as well. Ketabuck's seeds of doubt were already germinating, and they weren't helped by Kreston's silence.

What was the best approach? Should she confront him, or leave him be, or perhaps never see him again?

"Why don't you just say it?" he grumbled, slowing his pace. "You're obviously wanting to. After all, you're a woman."

"Kreston, if you're being condescending to anger or hurt me, it's not going to work. Any man would be asking the same question after hearing what I just heard."

Kreston stopped and turned sharply to face her. "Then ask."

She looked up at him. "Are you hiding secrets?"

"Of course I am."

Moonlight filtered through the trees, but with them both being creatures of the shadows, Kreston knew there was sufficient light to say what he needed to say.

"Look, Alerice. I've led troops into battle. I've seen men die on my sword. I've ordered spies executed. I've lied, I've stolen, and as you said to the clan, I'd do it again, most of it anyway, and the things I'd do differently, I wouldn't do that much differently. Do you honestly expect me to share my entire history with you, a woman I've only just met?"

"You could share some of it, if we're to be friends."

"And what if we can never be friends? What if all we can ever be is colleagues, and only then if our masters allow it."

"So there's a chance you might betray me."

"I wouldn't do it willingly."

"What kind of answer is that?"

"The only one I'm capable of giving you."

Kreston allowed the tension to permeate before he continued.

"What you haven't fully grasped, Alerice Linden, is that you are no longer free. I told you so in the barn in Basque. They own us, and they'll never let us go. We belong to them, and if they commanded us to fight one another, how do you think that would go?"

Alerice studied him, sensing desperation, which meant his tirade was as much a cry for help as it was his way of trying to put her off.

"Would you kill me if the King of Shadows ordered it?"

"Would you kill me if *she* ordered it?"

"Her name is the Raven Queen."

"You say it. I won't."

Alerice paused, for Kreston's plight was becoming more apparent with each passing breath. "Is that why you cannot touch anything of hers, because you fear her?"

Kreston stood tall and said, "It's not fear."

"Do you hate her then? Did she do something to you?"

He did not reply. Alerice knew that she had just guessed something significant, possibly something she could use to help him, but a faun's frantic bugle sounded into the night, and both she and Kreston looked in its direction.

"The clan," she said.

Alerice took a step in the direction they had come, beckoning for Kreston to follow her. He suddenly threw his palms to his skull and sank to his knees, strangling back a cry. The king's brand glowed brightly upon his brow.

Alerice half-turned back to him, but more bugles sounded and she knew that she must make a choice.

"The king," Kreston muttered. "The king. The king, the king, the king…"

Alerice could see the same look upon his face as the last time his battlefield voices had taken hold. She couldn't be certain if he was rambling about the King of Shadows or some mortal king he had once served, but there was no time to discover which, and likely no means by which she could help him overcome the moment.

She turned to the trees and hurried to aid the fauns.

***

A spirit mace cleaved into a faun's skull, cracking it open and spilling its brains. A spirit sword sliced into a faun's neck, spraying blood as the creature haplessly grabbed for it. The fauns scrambled for safety, but there was none to be had as Vygar attacked with red-hot fury, the souls of the wicked men at his disposal, courtesy of the King of Shadows.

The goal was nothing less than wholesale slaughter, made easy for Vygar as the fauns found themselves trapped within their own perimeter. They had no means to defend against otherworldly invaders bearing weapons that were frighteningly mortal.

A few fauns were able to escape through their open gate, but the souls pursued them and struck them down. Then they lifted their bleeding bodies and cast them back into the glen. Every member of the clan, from the strongest buck to the smallest child, fell victim even as Alerice appeared at the gate and beheld the massacre.

Vygar locked his sights on her. "I told you you'd be looking over your shoulder. You've earned His wrath, you wretched girl, and I am here to deliver it."

Alerice nearly tore her crossbow from its buttoned strap as she held Vygar in her sights. Its string pulled back, a gleaming black bolt appeared in the flight groove, and she loosed it. However, one of Vygar's conscripted spirits flew into the shot, and the bolt lodged in its ethereal chest, killing it with a dark flash of light.

Vygar held wide his arms. As wind seemed to circulate about him, his body transformed into that of a great silver wolf whose bright blue eyes pierced the night, and whose howl pierced Alerice's soul.

The wolf leaped high, clearing the distance to land before Alerice. She startled as it snarled, and reflexively reached for her Realme dagger, but quickly thought better of the tactic and instead flicked off the buttons holding Oddwyn's pixie pole cylinders.

She presented them, but she did not know how to activate them. Yet, she did not allow hesitation to hinder her, for if these weapons were of the Realme, then she could employ them by believing in her own empowerment.

She imagined the weapons extending as surely as she had ever imagined anything in her life, and to her surprise, the bladed poles extended and she stood on her guard.

"Alerice!" Lolladoe shouted as she vaulted over fallen kin and leveled her crossbow.

Lolladoe landed a bolt into the great wolf's flank, but it turned, caught her in its jaws, and shook her with enough force to snap her spine. The doe's bugle-scream echoed into the surrounding trees, even as the wolf shook its head in the opposite direction to cast Lolladoe's lifeless body over the perimeter wall.

"Lolladoe!" Alerice cried in horror before she watched the wolf turn to her once more.

She stood her ground, but the slaughter was complete. The clan was dead. Sheradoe, Ketabuck, and countless others had all bled out.

The wolf brought its snout close, its bloody breath falling onto Alerice's face. She glared, but its blue eyes narrowed as it said, "Run."

Oddwyn appeared through a portal behind Alerice.

"Give me those," he said as he jumped into her body.

Blades lacerated the wolf's face, and the creature whined before it leaped aside. It glared, knowing that it had lost the initiative. Still, it regarded the successful execution of the king's vengeance, and howled loudly. The conscripted souls flew to him, and the giant wolf charged forward and leaped, sprinting into the woods with the spirits in tow.

Oddwyn jumped out of Alerice's body, and examined her to make certain she was stable. She nodded that she was, but upon seeing faun bodies strewn about the glen, she dropped the poles and threw her hands to her mouth.

"Pick those up!" Oddwyn demanded.

Alerice was not able to obey. Oddwyn grimaced and slapped her cheek.

"I said pick them up."

Alerice went bolt upright, then did as he ordered. Oddwyn opened a quick portal to the Realme, grabbed Alerice's arm, and yanked her through.

***

"Oh, Oddwyn, what have I done?" Alerice asked, trembling.

"You didn't do this," he said. "The king did this."

Oddwyn was with her in the Convergence. Always the point of entry into the Evherealme, human souls appeared both alone and in groups through the four prime arches and the four secondary arches, where spirit guides escorted them away.

Oddwyn guided Alerice toward the arch being used the least, and took the pixie poles from her. He caused the blades to recess into their cylinders and tucked them into his tunic. Then he took her by the shoulders of her black scale mail and held her tightly.

"They're all dead, Oddwyn."

"I know. I saw."

"Is that because of me? Is Lolladoe dead because of me? Vygar said I earned his wrath. Whose wrath? The king's? You said he did this, but if I have offended the King of Shadows, why did he kill the fauns?"

"Alerice, listen to me," Oddwyn said with a strong shake. "I've seen this happen before, though not for a very long time. The king is not angry with you."

"He's not?" she asked, her voice belying her vulnerability.

"No," said a voice of dark honey as the Raven Queen appeared.

Oddwyn bowed but Alerice was too distraught to show deference. The Raven Queen permitted the lapse as she floated forward.

"No, my Ravensdaughter. The king is angry that I now have what he thought he had. A champion. Only you are strong and clear minded. His is--"

"Hiding secrets?" Alerice asked, knowing that she should not interrupt but unable to keep the words from leaping out.

"Wounded. Confused," the queen corrected. "Kreston Dühalde sought the King of Shadows because he was a broken man. He is still broken in many ways, but the same fate awaits you if you do not act this moment."

"What do you mean? I'll start hearing battlefield voices too?" Alerice envisioned Sheradoe's rolled-back eyes and Ketabuck's long tongue draped over his dead jaw. She could not bear the thought of being haunted by what she had witnessed, and she fell to her knees and buried her head in her hands.

"Alerice Linden of Navre, rise up to me," the Raven Queen commanded in a voice that voided the Convergence of all activity. Souls vanished, as did the spirit guides, and the ether in all eight arches fell dead.

The mark on Alerice's brow glowed brightly, and Oddwyn stood back as the queen extended her willow-white hand to the heart of Alerice's black scales to emit a brilliant gray light.

Alerice felt herself pulse with a might she had never known, nor ever expected she could know. She leaped to her feet and stood straight, looking at the Raven Queen and losing herself in the depth of her amethyst gaze.

"Alerice Linden, you have been struck with self-doubt," the queen said. "This blow has cut deeply into you, and you must bear it for the rest of your life. This memory will plague you if you do not find some way to master it. Yes, the fauns are dead. Yes, this is a direct result of your interaction with them, but let this be a lesson that you must now guard your actions with greater care lest more innocent lives suffer the same fate."

"But how can I act in your name if I know that someone I talk to, even casually, might get killed? This wasn't part of what you promised me."

"I gave you my word to protect your family. You asked for nothing more, and now you must come to terms that some of the things I will task you with performing have risks. But you are strong enough to cope with those risks. If you had not been, I would not have offered you my dagger, no matter what the conditions of your birth. Now will you remain standing, and remain my Ravensdaughter?"

Alerice felt her expression harden, even as she felt her hands clench into fists. Her vow to the Raven Queen had now crossed a line from the accomplishment of errands to engagement of war. Could she do this? Would she do this? And if she did this, what would she gain or lose personally?

Were these the same thoughts Kreston had once pondered? Was he the personification of the cautionary tale she now faced?

"If..." Alerice began slowly. "If I remain standing, may I know one thing?"

"What is it?" the Raven Queen asked.

"Does Vygar live or die?"

"He lives," she said. "He has returned to his citadel."

"No, I mean, does he get to remain alive? Vygar will kill again, and I cannot allow that to happen."

The Raven Queen looked down at Oddwyn. "Give her your poles, Herald."

Oddwyn reached into his tunic. He produced the cylinders and handed them to Alerice.

"And I will give her this," the queen said, gesturing to the large arch opposite them. The tri-colored ether began to swirl again, and images appeared. Though their forms were translucently nondescript, Alerice watched, and then smiled broadly as the spirits of the entire faun clan strode into the Convergence.

***

Alerice paced in even, deliberate steps along the rocks of the waterfall grotto. With each step, she swung a pixie pole at a glyph-sealed niche, exploding it. As the entrapped soul burst forth, either Lolladoe or Ketabuck slew it, for now in spirit form, the fauns were an even match for any incorporeal foe.

In his central hall, Prince Vygar had been inspecting the eight spirit wolf statues that the King of Shadows had restored to his dais. He had also been inspecting the conscripted spirits that the king had created as his new bodyguard.

However, he felt each strike to his distant glyph niches, and he spun about to his stone arch. It remained in ruin, for the king had refused to grant it back to him until he had proven himself to be a more worthy recipient of his power. Vygar again transformed into a great wolf and howled for his eight statues to come alive.

As before, they dissolved until their floating mineral composures took on astral lupine forms. Vygar howled again so loudly that the restored hall doors flew open, and he charged out, his wolves and his conscripts following.

Alerice stood downstream from the waterfall, the dawn's twilight beginning to lighten the sky. She bore the cloak of a Raven Knight, which the queen had lent her for this one task.

Alerice felt the security of its black, feathered drape protecting her back, and though she did not know how the cloak might convey her to where she needed to go, she nonetheless took hold of the cloak's sides and threw them open. The metaphysical fabric became wings, which beat down to bear her aloft. Soon soaring above the treetops, Alerice flew toward the waiting town of Uffton, the fauns' spirits with her.

Alerice alighted alone in Uffton's central square, where she stood tall, bladed pixie poles ready. It was not long before Vygar rounded a building and approached. She looked at the beast from under her brow, the smile of battle on her lips.

"You came back," Vygar said as he stalked forward.

"That's what all problems do until you take care of them," Alerice retorted.

Vygar snuffed derisively. "And you are indeed a problem."

He barked and his legions formed two ranks, his spirit wolves behind him and his conscripts further back.

"Right," Alerice said, clanging her pixie poles together.

The clear tone rang out, overwhelming the wolves' hearing. They shook their heads and whined, and when they were able to regain their senses, they startled, for they found themselves staring at a faun clan eager for revenge.

"Heart of the Forest!" Ketabuck shouted.

"Heart of the Forest!" the fauns repeated. Many bugled while others pawed the stone with eager hooves. Ketabuck charged, and they followed hot on his heels.

Vygar looked side to side as over a dozen fauns swarmed his spirit wolves, preventing them from forming into a coordinated pack. The wolves scattered, the fear of isolation spurring a frenzy that allowed the fauns to gain an immediate advantage.

Vygar looked further back to see his conscripts trying to advance, but they were cowards, only present due to enslavement, not desire.

A bladed pole slashed Vygar's right eye as Alerice leaped high with an uppercut. He howled and shook his head, but she descended with a downward cut to his left eye. Blinded, the great wolf howled in pain, unable to see – and yet fully able to feel his spirit wolves fall one by one to fauns hungry for revenge.

Then Vygar felt the searing pain of a blade sinking into his chest. In the next moment, he felt nothing but weakness as he collapsed.

Alerice withdrew her Realme dagger from the great wolf's side and watched as Vygar's body transformed into that of a man. She stepped next to him and bent down to wipe her dagger on his tunic, satisfied at the red blotches she left on the ivory fabric.

Then she looked up at the lightening sky, knowing the sun would soon rise. She watched the fauns approach the conscripted souls, all of whom fled given that their master was now dead.

Somehow, Alerice knew that the faun spirits might dissolve in the light of day, for they were new spirits that had not yet been properly tethered to the Realme. Alerice needed to make certain that the fauns were safely delivered back to the Raven Queen so she could place them. She must keep them safe. It was the least she could do for them.

Lolladoe approached and nodded. She was not able to speak, and Alerice noted that her spine seemed crooked, given the manner of her death. Alerice returned to the spot where she had placed the pixie poles, and lifted them from the stone. Then an interesting idea took hold, and she returned to Vygar's corpse.

"There's always the chance he could be risen," she said to Lolladoe. "I was, and he might be as well. But I can think of a form in which that's far less likely."

Lolladoe looked down at the hated mortal lying at her hooves, and then back up at Alerice. She smiled and licked her black nose.

"Would you like to do the honor?" Alerice asked.

Lolladoe regarded her questioningly, but then understood the meaning of her offer. Alerice closed her eyes and held wide her arms, and Lolladoe slipped into her body.

Alerice's eyes snapped opened, but now they were liquid black. She tightened the grip on her pixie poles, and then swung both in a low scissor cut.

Vygar's head popped from his body, and then rolled away into a ditch. Alerice snorted with pleasure, and then regarded her clan.

The air beside Alerice began to swirl in tones of black, midnight blue, and dark teal, but she did not notice. The faun spirits seemed to, but Alerice did not quite understand their pointing.

She turned about as Oddwyn appeared from the opening portal, making her startle and back away. Still in his youthful form, Oddwyn looked her over soon realizing the nature of her problem. He stepped forward and soundly flicked the Raven Queen's mark. Alerice nearly fainted, but Oddwyn caught her and ordered, "Shoo!"

Lolladoe leaped from Alerice's flesh, allowing her to collapse into Oddwyn's arms. He helped get her back to her feet and made certain that she was stable before he beckoned the fauns to gather. He also quickly checked to see if Alerice's eyes had returned to normal, which they had.

Oddwyn regarded the clan.

"The Raven Queen wanted me to give one of you this," he said, presenting the Heart of the Forest. The fauns all regarded their cherished talisman, with longing in their black eyes.

Alerice shook her head and tested her balance, and then also looked at the heart-shaped red stone. "How can you give it to any of them, Oddwyn?"

"Funny you should ask," he said. "The queen has imbued the Heart so that it may restore one of their bodies. The question is, which one should remain here?"

Alerice looked at Lolladoe. She stepped before the clan even as the first rays of sunlight pierced the sky and the clouds overhead came alive in shades of gold and pink.

"Could she please stay?" Alerice asked the fauns. "I promise I will do my best to look out for her."

Lolladoe smiled and held Alerice's gaze as Sheradoe and Ketabuck came up to place hands on her shoulders.

"Yep," Oddwyn said. "I had a feeling that would be your choice. And just because I tend to think ahead..."

Oddwyn reached into the portal and bent down to heft something heavy. With a few grunts and tugs, he dragged out Lolladoe's torso.

"You want to help?" he asked. "She's heavier than she looks."

Alerice helped Oddwyn lift the faun's corpse from the portal and arrange it on the street. Shadows began to recess as the sun rose, and the spirit fauns took shelter in what darkness remained.

"Hmmm," Oddwyn said, regarding their fear. "Better hurry. Lie down, will you?"

Lolladoe did as he bade and lay down into her lifeless shell. She did her best to hold still as the sunlight fell upon her, but Oddwyn placed the Heart of the Forest over her breast, and the faun's flesh drew down her spirit as water into a drain.

Alerice watched, but she sensed the remaining fauns calling to her in alarm.

"What are you waiting for?" Oddwyn asked. "Use the cloak."

"The cloak?" she asked.

"Gods above, Alerice. You're a Realme Walker. One of your tasks will always be shepherding souls into the Realme. Now hurry before you lose them to the daylight."

Alerice spread her wings wide and leaped toward Sheradoe and Ketabuck. She darted and flitted with surprising deftness, and before she knew it, she had taken hold of every last faun and tucked them safely within the metaphysical folds of her black feathers.

Alerice alighted next to Oddwyn, who said, "Just throw it into the portal. I'll sort them out in a moment."

She did as he bade, and Oddwyn closed the portal to ensure the cloak's safety.

"Alerice?" Lolladoe said as she opened her liquid black eyes.

"Lolladoe," Alerice replied, moving to take a knee at her side. She watched Lolladoe grip the Heart of the Forest, which seemed to give her strength, and placed her own hand over the doe's to offer support.

Atop the forward turret of Vygar's citadel, the King of Shadows looked down at the three figures in Uffton's central square. He looked at Vygar's decapitated body, and then he sighed.

"Kreston," he called.

Kreston stood at the turret's side, his hand on a crenelation. He glanced at his master, and then crossed to him.

"The girl stood up," the king said. "She fought back, and now she will sense the full measure of herself."

Kreston was not able to see much as he looked at the distant square, but then there was little he wished to see.

"I saw pridefulness in her the moment I set eyes upon her," the king said. "And in growing prideful, that girl shall fail, for if there is one thing my wife will not tolerate, it is an underling who thinks too much of herself."

The king turned fully to his captain.

"So when I place you in her path again, Dühalde, as I did this time, I want you to encourage Alerice to be bold. Do it by discouraging her. Tell her that she cannot accomplish something. This will only make her more determined. Keep telling her that she cannot help you, for she has already set her mind to try."

Kreston's gaze remained fixed on the town below.

"Do this, and my wife will renounce her," the King of Shadows said. "She will give Alerice back to Mortalia and have nothing to do with her. And if the queen does this, I will release you. And then you can take that girl and leave the Realme behind, and never look back."

The King of Shadows paused and then added, "And then you will have revenge on my wife for touching you with madness."

Kreston did not reply as he locked his jaw and closed his hazel eyes.

THE WIZARD AND THE WYLD

THE WIZARD AND THE WYLD
Tales of the Ravensdaughter
Adventure Three

Those kissed upon their birth
Will know Mortalia's ways.
Their hearts will always guide them
Through self-doubt and its haze.

For Walkers are true beings
Who rightly know their minds.
Inspired by the gods
Their worth is well-defined.

from the Scrolls of Imari

"I spy with my odd eye," the maiden Oddwyn said as she and Alerice rode along the ridge of a shallow river canyon. A blue waterway meandered below them, bending and flowing within the landscape's twists and turns. "Something black..."

"My armor?" Alerice guessed, more natural in the saddle now that she had become comfortable with flexing her legs in rhythm with Jerome's trot.

"No," Oddwyn cautioned in her gentle tone. "Something black, with a round crown, and an upturned brim..."

"And a black feather," Alerice added with a smile as she looked aside at her riding companion. Of course Oddwyn did not exactly ride. Rather, her mount was an ethereal pony that gently bobbed up and down as its hooves pranced in midair. Its multi-colored mane and tail accented its opalescent coat, and Alerice noted how the pony's overall look complemented Oddwyn's long white hair dotted with little bursts of color.

"And a black feather," Oddwyn said. "Do you like your new hat?"

"Yes, actually," Alerice said, running her fingers along the felt of her new wide-brimmed bowler, the left side of which was pinned up so that it could sport a plume. Oddwyn had brought it to her from the Realme, and Alerice was glad to have it, for she needed something to keep the sun from falling upon her blonde head. Not that the day wasn't pleasant. Indeed, the morning had been quite nice and the afternoon ride was comfortable, but the sun was the sun, and a bit of shade was most welcomed.

"You know," Alerice continued. "If you had something similar in white, we could be chessboard sisters."

"Hmmm," Oddwyn mused. "I hadn't thought of that." Smiling, she created a thin portal into the Realme. It appeared as a tri-colored slit of black, midnight blue, and deep teal, and Oddwyn reached into it as she might into a satchel. She rummaged about, reaching for something on the portal's far side, which to Alerice looked as though Oddwyn's arm had been eaten up to the shoulder by the airborne fissure. However, Oddwyn eventually exclaimed, "A ha!" and withdrew her hand.

She held the same round-crowned bowler crafted in iridescent white, only hers sported several plumes, each glimmering with a gradient of colors. She donned the hat, ran her fingers along the brim in a jaunty fashion, and then relaxed into the ease of her spirit pony's 'gait'.

Alerice smirked, but then her thoughts drifted to another companion, and she began tapping her gloved hand on the saddle horn.

"You're wondering what happened to Kreston, aren't you," Oddwyn commented.

"Um hmm," Alerice replied

"Listen to me, Alerice. If there's one thing I can assure you about Kreston Dühalde, it's that he always finds his way. I've never known him to lose track of where he's going, and I dare say that he'll find you before long."

"He can always find his way? You mean his 'voices' don't confuse him?"

Oddwyn did not comment. Rather, she deliberately looked ahead.

Alerice grimaced. "Oddwyn, what aren't you telling me?"

"Alerice, we're having such a nice time. Please don't spoil it."

Alerice considered whether or not she should press the matter, but a man's shout rose up from the river canyon, and she looked down to see Kreston in the distance, fighting the strangest beast.

The thing looked like some giant demon toad, only it had a humanish upper torso similar to the ones Alerice had seen on the muscle-bound men who used to heft full kegs out of Uncle Judd's brewery. It had a massive head with protruding teeth, and Kreston was fighting the thing on foot, doing his best to dodge its dripping, gray claws.

Alerice urged Jerome into a gallop and charged down the slope into the canyon as she drew her Realme crossbow. Her black bowler flew from her head, and though she briefly glanced back for it, she quickly reverted her focus to the task at hand.

Oddwyn watched Alerice go with some misgiving. Then she gestured to the bowler, which vanished as it drifted toward the canyon wall. It reappeared in her soft grasp, and Oddwyn petted its black crown and plume before she regarded Kreston with distrust.

"I spy trouble," she said.

Oddwyn looked ahead of her spirit pony and conjured a larger Realme portal. Then she kissed to her mount and rode into it.

Kreston tried to keep his footing on the river's marshy bank, but the beast towering above him made it all but impossible. As he backed for a swing, he slipped and landed hard in the mud. The beast brought down an arm's-length claw toward Kreston's shoulder, and he rolled aside to avoid being impaled. He leveled a strong slice at its cuticle, and while he caused some damage, the creature had thick skin. It howled and then struck again, and Kreston rolled in the opposite direction before he tried to scramble-crawl backward.

A crossbow bolt *whizzed* in and struck the beast in the eye. It bellowed loudly enough for Kreston to feel the sound reverberate in his chest, but while the shot dissipated in a black burst, it did not slay the thing.

Yet it did allow Kreston the opportunity to get clear and regain his stance, and he looked aside to see Alerice galloping in, Jerome neighing and rearing as she reined him up.

Kreston paused at the sight of her, hating himself for what the King of Shadows was forcing him to attempt, but the river beast launched itself forward in a great grunting hop, and Kreston found himself on the defensive once again.

On another portion of the rise above the canyon, a warrior band approached and stopped to observe the melee. Their faces and bodies were painted ash and black. Some decorated themselves in swathes and animal stripes, others in patterns and symbols. Most bore ashen torsos, while some blackened themselves entirely save for decorative ashen stripes and diagonals.

The men wore a hodgepodge of tattered cloth and armor. The women wore leather halters atop leather leggings, some trimmed with chain, others with fur.

Their queen, a battle-hardened woman with flowing berry-red hair trimmed in black cords tied with animal skulls, rode to the front of the horde. Her four pack leaders rode behind her. Her crown bore swept-back horns, and she had painted the skin about her eyes with black lines that swept up to her temples. The spaces between her teeth were also black, as were her lips, and her arms and legs were heavily inked.

The rest of the horde traveled on foot, a variety of weapons at the ready – and all were taken by the sight of two fighters battling a demon toad.

Some of the warriors fitted arrows into their bows and pulled back. A few grinned and joked in their tribal language while the pack leaders turned to their queen, who beamed at the discovery.

"Shall we ride in, Queeny?" Kara, a female pack leader, asked.

"Not until it gets interesting," Queen T'kyza replied.

In the canyon, Alerice brought Jerome a bit closer and leveled her crossbow for another shot. The bow string pulled back, and a gleaming black bolt appeared in the flight groove. She loosed, striking the gargantuan beast in the throat, for its eye had obviously not been a kill zone.

The toad howled as it reeled, but as it raised its head, its throat began to undulate. It then gave up a massive belch, and four fanged toadlings appeared in its jaws. They howled and leaped to the ground, flanking Kreston.

"Not good!" Kreston shouted as he found himself surrounded. Alerice leaped down from Jerome's back, grabbed the pixie pole cylinders from her studded belt, and hurried to Kreston's side as she caused the bladed poles to expand.

Atop the rise, the ashen-black warriors all whooped in excited surprise.

Some raised their weapons as might spectators watching sport.

"It just got interesting," Queen T'kyza said with a grin as she urged her company to charge into the canyon. They did with wild abandon. Yet as their whoops rang out, T'kyza noticed a blood bay stallion standing a short distance away. She ordered another of her pack leaders, a staunch woman named Shadow, to claim it. Then T'kyza urged her own mount forward.

Alerice and Kreston fought back-to-back, slicing into the toadlings' bites while dodging the giant toad's claws. While they certainly faced a dangerous moment, Alerice still found an odd pleasure in the heady thrill of team combat. The half-smirk on Kreston's face told her he felt the same.

Suddenly, arrows flew in to puncture the toadlings. Alerice and Kreston reacted to the multiple shots, and then to the whoops of the ashen-black mass of bodies bearing down on them.

There was no way to know if the incoming horde was friend or foe, and no time to discover their intentions. The greater toad kept slashing claws right and left, forcing both Alerice and Kreston to duck and dodge.

The frenetic band swarmed the river beast, one of their larger, black-painted men even leaping atop its back to ride it. In no time they brought it down and began stabbing into it.

Bewildered and even amused, Alerice was about to lower her guard, but Kreston urged her to keep her wits about her, lest these near-feral intruders become hostile. He was right to assume the worst, for no sooner had the horde dispatched the toad than it surrounded Alerice and Kreston, arrows and weapons trained.

"Nice poles," one of their men said from behind the vented bevor plate he wore over the lower half of his face.

"Nice armor," an ash-faced woman with black diamonds about her eyes said of Alerice's scales.

"So what do we do?" Alerice whispered to Kreston.

Kreston's eyes narrowed as he sized up the moment, his ice-veined military demeanor on full display.

A whinny sounded and the warriors parted so that Queen T'kyza could ride forward. The four pack leaders rode into surrounding positions, and the horde divided itself into quarters and took up stances about their mounts.

Alerice saw that one of the leaders had hold of Captain's reins, and while she could see Kreston thinking the moment through as though they were about to be taken captive, Alerice thought it best to try a different ploy.

She *clanged* her pixie poles overhead. The true tone rang out, startling the horde. Once the echo finished ringing within the river canyon, the ashen-black warriors whooped in response, banging their weaponry together.

Alerice *clanged* her poles a second time. The sound was met with a boisterous reaction, and Alerice smiled as she stepped forward and reverenced to the woman whom she knew must be the horde's leader.

"I am Alerice Linden of Navre," she stated. "Ravensdaughter of the Evherealme."

"I am Queen T'kyza of the Wyld," Queen T'kyza responded.

The warriors began a chant of "Queen-y! Queen-y! Queen-y!" which they repeated in an accelerating tempo until the words blended together. Then they whooped and banged their weapons together yet again.

Alerice extended her poles at the two Wyld nearest her, who struck them with their swords in salutation.

Queen T'kyza approved. "You fight well, Ravensdaughter," she said. "Do you drink just as soundly?"

"I'll drink anything you put in front of me," Alerice stated boldly.

"Then mount up," T'kyza said with a knowing smile.

Alerice saluted T'kyza and then retracted her bladed poles into their cylinders, which elicited a collective "Woah!" from the Wyld. As they stood amazed, Alerice crossed to Kreston and laid a hand on his shoulder. He regarded her, and then the situation, before he eventually stood down.

"You certainly have a way with people," Kreston said as he sheathed his broadsword.

Alerice smiled and then glanced about for Jerome, only to find one of the Wyld men holding his reins. She paced toward him, but a strange feeling touched her and she felt the Raven Queen's mark pulse upon her brow.

Alerice looked about, expecting to find her matron's impending portal, dread seeping into her at how Kreston might react. Then she looked up at the canyon's rim to discover an elderly woman leaning on a walking staff.

The woman gazed down upon the scene, and Alerice thought Kreston should be made aware of her presence. She turned to find and hail him, but as she looked back up at the rim to point the woman out, she saw no one.

Alerice had no idea what to make of the moment, or if she had truly seen the woman at all. Tucking the note of it into the back of her mind, she mounted Jerome and rode after T'kyza.

***

"He said his name is Mutt!" Shadow said of the Wyld who wore the vented bevor plate over the lower half of his face.

Given the raucous encampment and the bevor's muffle, Alerice could not quite make out what he had said. She stared at Mutt's dark eyes, the whites of which appeared quite striking against the black paint surrounding them. Somehow she knew that Mutt was smiling, and Alerice raised her cup to him.

Just then a quarter of the Wyld jumped to their feet and shouted, "Chaos!" into the night air. Their pack leader, Kara, stood before them as they raised cups, drinking horns, and weapons in salute.

"Decay!" another quarter of them countered, rising with their pack leader, a fierce mountain of a man who was ironically named Imp.

"Destruction!" cried the third quarter, as they stood behind their leader, Storm.

"Ruin!" Shadow said, rising with her pack to lead them in a great deal of weapon-banging.

Some of the Wyld grabbed drums and began pounding out a cadence. Others danced while still others pushed their clan members into one another until fights broke out.

Alerice looked aside at Kreston, who surveyed everyone.

"They're obviously not worried about giving up their position," he said. He glanced over his shoulder at the terrain and added, "Luckily, they've chosen the high ground, so any foes would have to sneak up from below."

Alerice looked about at the grassy hilltop, admiring Kreston for always being on the alert. Then again, it was second-nature for him to be concerned about possible points of attack, being a former captain.

"Have you known any mercenaries like these?"

"Mercenaries, yes. Like these? Never. But all mercenaries are loyal to comrades and coin. You think Vygar had loyalty with his wolves? That's nothing compared to these people. They will protect one another until the last of them falls, and if the coin runs out, they'll leave. And if you even think of trying to cheat them, think again."

"He speaks truly," Queen T'kyza said as she approached her Pack of Ruin. She offered her drinking horn for Alerice to touch with her tankard, which Alerice did before they both imbibed.

"Mmmm," Alerice said. "This is surprisingly good. Where did folk like you find a vintage like this?"

T'kyza smiled knowingly as she glanced at Shadow. "There's a traveler's rest not too far from here," she said. "They have a tavern called the Fire Inn."

"Which doesn't lock its back door," Shadow added.

"And we get the good stuff," Mutt said from behind his bevor.

"Yes you do," T'kyza said to Mutt in the type of talk one would use with an infant. She petted his head and Mutt responded as might a loyal hound enjoying his queen's affection. Then T'kyza regarded Alerice. "I send my four warrior packs on raiding parties when we're not employed. Keeps them fit."

"I see," Alerice said. "You are indeed wild, Wyld."

"We are that and more, Ravensdaughter," T'kyza said with pride. "We are an odd bunch, and proud of it. We come from all backgrounds, both simple and civilized. The one thing we have in common is that we were all rejected by the worlds into which we were born. Some of us are thieves. Some of us are rebels. We paint our faces to hide our faces, because no outsider need know our identities."

"And no one fookes with the Wyld!" Imp said in his deep baritone as he entered the conversation.

"The Wyld. The Wyld. We are the fookin' Wyld," some of them began chanting. Soon the entire company enjoined a distinct refrain as they circled their bonfire, the embers of which crackled high into the night.

Alerice could not make out a word they were saying, for they spoke in their tribal language, but Queen T'kyza decided to share the Wyld's fraternity with her guests.

"In common tongue!" she ordered.

The warriors did not miss a beat as they shouted,

"I was bane and I was banished,
I was cast away to languish,
Fights I seek, for I'm not finished,
I am a fookin' Wyld!

My face is ashen and is black,
Mortals fear my dread attack,
Fur and metal clothe my back,
I am a fookin' Wyld!

Queen and coin command my blade,
I've sworn an oath, my choice is made,
Destruction, Ruin, Chaos, Decay,
I am a fookin' Wyld!

With my clan do I now roam,
This is the true path I've known,
My blackened heart won't beat alone,
We are the fookin' Wyld!"

The resulting whoops echoed into the night. Alerice raised her tankard and took another sip, but noticed Kreston pulling back from the festivities. Quietly, she moved beside him.

"Does this spur bad memories?"

"No," he said. Then he drank.

"Are you concerned about something?" she continued, longing to have more than a simple response.

"I'm always concerned about something."

"Very well. So, are you going to tell me how you wound up on the wrong end of a demon toad?" she half-chided.

He sighed, and then looked at her.

"I wish I could. After you left me in the woods to help the fauns, I found my way back to the waterfall and then back into the Realme. I don't know how long I was there, but a portal opened up for me, and when I rode out, that river beast attacked. I think it wanted to eat my horse."

"It's a good thing Captain got away," she said.

"Alerice," Kreston added in a tone that refocused her attention. As she stared up at him, he said, "I wish I could tell you more. You understand that, right?"

Alerice paused, not certain what to make of his insistence. She wanted to say that she did understand, but in actuality she did not.

She also did not want to embarrass him by making him disclose a battlefield memory, and so she offered an awkward nod. Then she caught sight of his blood bay stallion, Captain, grazing next to her black Realme pony, Jerome, in the make-shift corral where T'kyza and the pack leaders kept their more common mounts.

"You know, Kreston. I've always wondered why you named your stallion Captain."

"Because he's a better beast than I am."

She smiled at him and again placed her hand on his shoulder. "Don't be so hard on yourself."

"Believe me, I'm not." Kreston regarded her hand, and then lifted it into his own. He gazed into her eyes, and then locked his jaw before giving her hand a squeeze that belied his inner conflict.

Kreston turned and paced away, only to be roughly pushed aside by Imp, who was clearly challenging him to a contest of strength. Kreston's cup flew from his grasp and he turned, but rather than becoming livid, he grinned wickedly as he tackled the man-mountain. The nearby Wyld whooped, and a few immediately placed bets as Kreston and Imp began to fight.

"You two should join us," Queen T'kyza said to Alerice.

"I appreciate the offer, but both Kreston and I have masters. I'm afraid neither of us are free to ride with you."

"Pity," T'kyza said. "We could use two folk of the Realme right now. Our next mark won't be as easy as stealing bottles from a tavern. There's a rogue wizard who resides somewhere near the traveler's rest, and this one's a problem. He's been harassing everyone in the region, and it's only a matter of time before the locals hire us to do something about him. And honestly, if they don't hire us, we might take care of it ourselves."

Alerice wasn't certain if T'Kyza made sense. Any wizard she had ever heard about spent his time in pursuit of knowledge, not launching vicious pranks. She was about to question T'kyza for more details, but the sight of Kreston and Imp divided her attention. Fortunately the two had started wrestling rather than throwing punches, which relieved her, for the last thing she wanted was to see Kreston with a broken jaw.

Even so, Alerice asked, "Can you please make sure that those two don't injure one another?"

T'kyza nodded and signed to a lithe warrior woman to have someone tell Imp to not run too recklessly. The Wyld woman signed back and scooted off.

T'kyza turned again to Alerice, noting her inquiring look regarding the exchange. "That's Wisp. She's part of Imp's pack. She's mute and uses hand expressions to speak."

"Interesting," Alerice commented. "But to your point about the wizard, don't most people like that devote themselves to study? I've never heard of a wizard going rogue."

"Then you haven't heard enough stories, Ravensdaughter."

"Oh, I used to be a tavern mistress. Believe me, I've heard quite a number of stories."

"Some, perhaps, but if there's one thing L'Orku's blade is meant for, it's skewering this mage."

Queen T'kyza patted the broadsword resting at her hip. The hilt was of a craftsmanship Alerice had never seen, cast with intertwined bolts of lightning on both sides and terminating in ram's horns at both ends. T'kyza noted Alerice's admiration and drew the weapon so that it caught the bonfire's light.

Sacred writing decorated the fuller. The edge seemed alive with energy. Alerice could almost feel its sharpness, and she knew that this weapon had been crafted by supernal hands as her own dagger had been crafted in the Realme.

"It was a gift from King Stradon. It was forged by L'Orku, God of Thunder, with help from his brother Gäete, God of Storms. Those two walk among men all the time, you know, hiding in army ranks while pretending to be soldiers. It's said that when they take a shine to a mortal, they present him with a gift. This was how Stradon got the sword. Sometime after that, Stradon hired my Wyld and me to fight his foes, and when he saw us in action, he knew that I was the only one to wield this blade."

Alerice could clearly see T'kyza's pride in the sword, but she also noted a hidden smile as the queen recalled this King Stradon. Despite the woman's fearful exterior, she was a soul who bore love's denial.

Just then, several Wyld horns blew into the night as the clan members assigned to sentry duty sounded an alarm. The Wyld's alacrity in striking up battle formations surprised Alerice, and as they ran to their posts, she hurried toward a rather disheveled Kreston. He responded to the alert with similar speed by drawing his broadsword and standing on his guard.

Alerice drew her crossbow, looking about as the Wyld formed a defensive ring around their encampment.

She heard the bellows of otherworldly creatures and expected that at any moment the Raven Queen's mark would pulse upon her brow. Strangely it did not. Rather, she saw the Wyld stepping forward, then back in anticipation of confronting enemy forces.

Whatever approached bellowed louder, and the battle joined as the Wyld attacked horned men and horned beasts encircling the hilltop.

"Weirdlings!" Kreston shouted as he pointed for Alerice to shoot.

She shot a gleaming black bolt at a horned man, and as it struck home, the impact's dark glow consumed him and he dissolved into charcoal dust. A similar fate awaited any other weirdlings, man or beast, that fell to the Wyld, and before long the night wind had carried the dust about the encampment, covering bodies and accoutrements in fine grit.

Alerice watched the last of the dust whirl about the bonfire's rising embers, noting that the attack did not seem as fatal as she had imagined. The Wyld whooped in victory, and even Kreston stood down and looked about for her. He was relieved to find her, but then his expression grew sullen and he turned away.

Queen T'kyza approached Alerice, sheathing her sword.

"Still think that wizard is no menace? These were his creatures, you know."

"Do I?" Alerice asked.

"What else would they be?" T'kyza insisted. "Horned weirdlings? You think those things just appear? There are no graves about this region, and no necromancer to raise the dead. Those beasts were the wizard's handiwork, make no mistake, and as soon as I judge the time right to take this matter into my own hands, I shall."

***

"Tell me again why we're seeking out a wizard?" Kreston asked as he and Alerice reined up not far from the traveler's rest, through which they had just passed.

"Because something about this doesn't make sense," she said, steadying

Jerome as she looked about the landscape of multi-colored wildflowers and stands of broad-branched trees.

Maneuvering Jerome forward so she could see farther, Alerice spotted a lovely estate with a manor house and gardens. She closed her eyes and reached out spiritually, using the Raven Queen's mark as her guide.

"Alerice, don't do that," Kreston warned.

She did not heed him as she ventured forth from her body, drawn to the estate, and more importantly its feeling of wonderment. She thought she saw a glistening, cascading fountain and she wanted to explore it, but someone took hold of her shoulder and gave her a rough shake. Her soul snapped back into her body, and when Alerice opened her eyes, she found Kreston next to her, looking at her with concern.

"I said don't do that," he said. "If that's a wizard's home, he could trap you."

Alerice tried to empathize with his worry, but not only did the estate beckon her forward, the entire landscape felt far too peaceful for her to be anxious.

"There is such ease here, Kreston. Can't you sense it?"

"Don't be fooled, Alerice. You've always got to be on your guard. You never know who or what might betray you."

Alerice looked deeply into him and noticed that he could not hold her gaze. Looking again at the estate, Alerice motioned Jerome forward.

"Kreston, I respect your caution, but nothing here feels untoward. I don't know how I know it. I just know it. Please come with me."

He paused and looked her over. "I hate that determined look of yours," he said.

She smiled and kissed Jerome forward.

***

Kreston did not offer more warnings as he and Alerice passed under the estate's decorative blue metal arch. Alerice knew he was on his guard, and he did have a point that malevolent forces could disguise themselves as benevolent ones, but she could not square the calm she felt or the beauty she beheld with hidden danger. There was simply too much sincerity at hand. She knew it as surely as she had known the peace of Grammy Linden's bedtime stories or the love Aunt Carol mixed into her bread dough.

Alerice took in the estate's brick and half-timber home. The windows were either painted glass or cut diamonds dotted with diagonally-set sapphire squares. Standing copper mobiles twirled gently in the breeze, and beautiful blooms grew in the window boxes.

The emblem of the estate was clearly a rampant gryphon. Alerice noted it in many places, wrought in gilded metal or painted on the exterior plaster. The gryphon was inlaid into the double-door entrance, which Alerice considered approaching. However, she felt a pull toward the garden, and so she dismounted on the lawn and passed under a smaller blue metal arch into a spread of manicured, blooming shrubs.

Kreston hopped off Captain's back and joined her, ever at the ready as he gripped his broadsword's handle.

There was no mistaking that the lean fellow standing in a long tunic and embroidered shoes was a man of magic. He wore his waist-long silver hair in braids woven with indigo cords. He stood before a rose bush bearing lavender flowers, and while Alerice saw Kreston tense as he brandished a sapphire-handled knife, she watched him use the knife to harvest a few roses, which he placed into a basket. Alerice had first thought the basket rested on a table, but upon closer inspection she observed that it floated gently near the man's side.

Alerice cleared her throat, but the fellow did not look up from his pruning.

"You must be aware, that I am aware, of your presence, Alerice Linden of Navre," he said in a sweet tenor that bore hints of whimsy and wisdom.

"Greetings, sir wizard," Alerice said with a deferential reverence in which she lowered her weight slightly onto her back leg while keeping her torso straight and her head high. "May I know your name?"

"Why, it's Pauldin, my dear."

Pauldin paused to snip and sniff one more bloom before he turned. The first things Alerice noticed were his eyes, rich blue with flecks of silver. They danced with hidden delight, and Alerice could not help but reverence a second time, nor could she hide her smile.

Pauldin returned her smile as he advanced. She stood up from her reverence and then stood tall before him as he reached to her head, moved her blonde hair back over an ear, and then waved his free hand to create a twist that secured the rose into place to rest beside her temple.

Pauldin reached to her chin and lifted her head to examine her. Apparently liking what he saw, he glanced at Kreston.

Alerice also looked at Kreston, only to see a hint of the trembling that he had displayed when attempting to take hold of the Raven Queen's vision stone. Unable to bear his discomfort, Alerice took Pauldin's hands in hers to redirect his attention. The wizard's fingers were long and graceful, and seemed to contain such power that Alerice felt only respectful admiration for them, and him.

"I knew you couldn't be a rogue," she said.

"Well, let's not be too hasty," Pauldin cautioned. "It depends on what manner of rogue. If you had known me a few hundred years ago, well perhaps not exactly that long, but still something approximating that general time, you might well have thought me quite roguish."

"Never..." Alerice chided. "Mischievous, perhaps, but certainly not roguish."

"Mind if I ask a question?" Kreston interjected, his matter-of-fact tone slicing through the pleasantries.

Pauldin regarded him, then nodded.

"Last night, the Wyld camp was attacked by weirdlings, both human and beast. Only a magical person can conjure such things."

"And you wish to know if I did?" Pauldin asked.

Kreston offered a "You said it" expression, which Alerice did not find tactful. Fortunately the wizard did not take offense.

"Of course I did not, dear sir," Pauldin said. "Though I must admit that I have dabbled in weirdlings once or twice," he said to Alerice with a twinkle in his eye. "Miniature creatures, you know," he added, holding his thumb and index finger a short distance apart. "So adorable with their tiny little horns and great big eyes, but quite a challenge if you don't keep them in the right box. They have a tendency to pick locks and escape."

Alerice chuckled, but a glance at Kreston reminded her of business. "Yes, well, good wizard, that is why we have come to see you. The Wyld have been blaming you for disrupting the region, and I want to ask--"

"My dear," Pauldin interjected. "We have the day to chat. For now, allow me to show you something dear to my heart."

"Of course," Alerice said.

Pauldin offered Alerice his arm, which she took. He gazed down upon her as he led her further into his garden, and she matched his steps on the right and then the left so that they moved in fluid motion.

"Are you coming, Kreston?" Alerice asked over her shoulder.

"Right behind you," he answered. However, Kreston paused to allow the two to glide away before he shook his head and rolled his eyes.

Centered in Pauldin's garden was a magical wonder that Alerice could only describe as a glimmering midair cascade. A deep-red rose hovered within it, the petals of which glistened with opalescent fire. Each petal seemed alive, and the sight of both it and the cascade stole Alerice's breath.

Pauldin paused to run his fingertips though the glimmers. They trailed along the path of his digits before falling back into place, and Pauldin sighed with the recollection of a fond memory.

"She bequeathed this to me, my dearest Allya. She was a sorceress of some renown when last I saw her. Now, however, I suspect that she has attained even further greatness in her quest for Sukaar's fire."

Alerice regarded the rose before Pauldin's words struck her. "You mean

Father Fire? Sukaar, the god himself?"

"Allya was determined to become his devotee. I suggested that she remain here with me, but she had a questing spirit, and the solitude of study would never have contented her."

"See?" Alerice said. "I knew you were the scholarly type." She looked about for Kreston, and found him standing a few paces away. "I knew that wizards spend most of their time with books."

Kreston did not comment, and more to the point he appeared bored, so Alerice decided it was best to say what she had come to say. "That's what I told Queen T'kyza. I said that it was not likely you would harass her Wyld."

"Unless you account for that little skirmish last night," Kreston said under his breath.

"Tsst," Alerice said, waving him down.

"The Wyld," Pauldin said derisively. "Those noisy, uncouth savages."

"Well, they're not all that bad," Alerice said, turning fully to Pauldin. "Kreston and I spent time with them last evening. They're good at heart."

"Hardly," Pauldin said. "My dear, you are sweet, but you are, unfortunately, blindly optimistic. The Wyld are a rotten clan. They have come to my estate more than once. They ride and run about, and cause me to fear for my safety. If I did not protect my garden, who knows what they would have already done to it."

"But..." Alerice countered. "Their queen told me that she has yet to seek you out."

"Which proves that those ashen-and-black individuals are liars as well as savages. The next time they approach, I may not strike a defensive posture. I have had my fill of them, and I may be required to demonstrate why it is not wise to attract a wizard's attention."

"Now I am confused," Alerice said.

"Go figure," Kreston grumbled.

Both Alerice and Pauldin regarded him before Pauldin assumed an avuncular demeanor.

"You have a great deal to learn about life, Alerice Linden. The people you trust may deceive you." Pauldin glanced fully at Kreston, who looked away, focusing his attention on the landscape outside the garden.

"But come in now and have some tea," the wizard continued. "You may both stay the evening and I would be glad of your company, for I have many stories that would please you both."

Kreston cleared his throat. Alerice and Pauldin regarded him one final time, but as he continued to gaze outside of the garden, his eyes narrowed.

"You said you would show the Wyld that it's not best to attract a wizard's attention if they came back here?"

"Of course I did, Captain Dühalde," Pauldin said.

Kreston reacted to the use of his former title, but then gestured his thumb to the landscape he had been surveying.

"Then this should be quite a show," he said.

Alerice looked in the line of Kreston's gesture, only to see Queen T'kyza leading the Wyld in a charge.

"Right," Pauldin stated, dusting off his hands and rolling up his sleeves. "This time shall be the last time."

"No, don't harm them," Alerice begged. "I can talk to--" She stopped short, for suddenly the Wyld appeared about the garden far more quickly than they should have. "...them," Alerice said to finish her thought.

The Wyld began whooping up a storm even as Pauldin pressed his palms together, his long fingers fanning out as he conjured a white-blue glow.

Alerice looked from the wizard to the Wyld, noticing that something was decidedly wrong. While the warrior clan seemed to threaten the estate with all the Wyld's boisterous enthusiasm, the bodies she beheld were not those of the true Wyld. They were painted ash and black, but they were smaller and did not bear individualistic designs.

"Kreston," Alerice said, moving to him. "Are you seeing what I'm seeing?"

"Yes," he said, confusion in his expression.

The glow between Pauldin's palms intensified before he cast his hands upward and out so that white-blue light radiated a magical shockwave.

"Pauldin, stop," Alerice said, but Pauldin was too deeply entranced to pay her heed. He formed a dome over the garden that sparkled with living dynamic, a meniscus of silver stars dancing about its surface.

Then, Pauldin made flicking gestures, and the stars shot out to strike the Wyld one by one until the entire clan had been laid to the ground.

They all jumped back to their feet, whooped, and yelled some more, and their queen vowed revenge. Alerice noted that no one was mounted, which was also quite wrong.

Pauldin centered his energy once more, and the dome began to vibrate. Alerice found herself stepping closer to Kreston, who wrapped a protective arm about her, but the false Wyld could sense the impending energy that was about to be loosed upon them, and they ran off in multiple directions.

As soon as the whooping faded off, Pauldin opened one blue eye and then the other. His garden was spared and his estate was secure. He drew in a centering breath and released the remainder of his power so that the dome vanished. Then he focused on his astonished guests.

"Are you certain you won't stay the night?"

"We need to get to the traveler's rest," Kreston said as he guided Alerice away.

***

The Fire Inn was aptly named. The courtyard was its centerpiece, and within it a great bonfire burned in a stacked-stone pit. Its tall flames licked the evening sky as folk took their ease and enjoyed the fabled libations for which the inn was rightly known.

Alerice and Kreston sat by themselves, Alerice drumming her fingers on their table's redwood top.

"Something is not right."

"Tenth time you've said that," Kreston said into his cup.

She looked up at him. "First Queen T'kyza says Pauldin has been attacking the Wyld, and then warriors who clearly are not the Wyld raid Pauldin's estate."

"I was there for both," he commented before he drank.

"What's causing this?"

"Why do you care?"

"Because I hate to see people ill-used. There's a third party at work here. There simply has to be."

"And I suppose you intend to discover who it is."

"Well..." she said, unconsciously rubbing the Raven Queen's mark upon her brow.

Kreston's gaze lingered on her brow, but he said nothing.

"More wine, travelers?" an old woman asked.

Alerice and Kreston looked up to find the inn mistress standing at their table, a bottle on her tray.

Kreston fished about in his belt pouch for a coin, but as Alerice watched him toss it onto the tray, she recognized the crone's face. It was the same old woman she had seen standing on the rise above the river canyon.

Alerice felt a pulse upon her brow, and knowing it was the Raven Queen's mark, she turned her head away. The crone looked her over, then bade Kreston thanks for the coin as she left the bottle and moved off. Alerice watched her walk over to another group, and then began drumming her fingers on the tabletop again, this time with more intensity.

Kreston placed his hand over hers. "Alerice, you cannot do this."

"Can't do what?" she said absently as ideas began to circle.

"You can't use *her* power for yourself, even if you think you're doing the right thing. We can only do what they allow us to do."

Alerice stared into him. "Is that what happened to you? Did you defy her?"

115

"Don't make this about me."

"But it is about you, partly. Are you ever going to tell me what the Raven Queen did to you?"

"Nope," he said before he released her hand and poured more wine into his cup.

"Why not?"

"Because it's none of your business."

"Kreston, how could it not be? I'm in service to her, and as you said in the woods the other night, if the king and queen commanded us to fight one another, how would it go?"

"All I can tell you is that I'm trying to avoid that. I truly am."

"Then let me help you. Tell me what happened."

Kreston slammed the bottle down and summoned the full force of the military officer he had once been.

"I said it's none of your business."

He commanded the tension between them, and only when he knew he had secured her silence did he add, "Listen to me, Alerice. *She* knows everything you do. And if you go off on your own, if you overstep the mark - you will fail," he concluded in three even words.

Kreston rose and held her in his sights. Then he took hold of the bottle and left with his cup to seek another table.

Alerice watched him go, not at all certain if she wished to pursue him. She looked down at the tabletop and began tracing the redwood grain.

Another tankard came to rest beside hers, and another body plopped down in Kreston's empty chair. Alerice looked up to find the youthful Oddwyn sitting opposite her. He was hooded and cloaked to hide his white hair and striking appearance, but he was a welcome sight.

"It's good to see you," she said.

"It's good to see you too, Alerice, but I wasn't sent here to enjoy myself. I heard what Kreston said, and for once he is right. You cannot follow this matter of the wizard and the Wyld. The Raven Queen already has misgivings that you've come this far. She doesn't have a task for you at the moment, but this is not the best use of your time."

"And what would be?" Alerice asked, folding her arms.

"Target practice? Pixie poles? Crocheting?"

"What?"

Oddwyn drew a breath to shout a repetition of his last suggestion, but Alerice quickly leaned in to silence him.

"I heard you, Oddwyn. I didn't ask 'what' because I'm deaf, but this is still wrong. These people need my help, and I can help if I'm given the chance."

"Alerice, our queen did not take you as a champion to help anyone she does not deem worthy of helping."

"She tasked me with helping those children in Basque."

"To build your confidence."

"That's all?"

"That's what she wanted of you, and you did well. You also did well exposing Vygar's theft of souls. So take my advice, and wait. She will task you with something soon."

Alerice regarded Oddwyn, not at all content. "I need to think," she said.

"I wouldn't, if I were you. I truly wouldn't."

Alerice took a breath, and then left her mug behind as she rose up. She said nothing further as she made her way out of the Fire Inn.

Oddwyn watched her pass the courtyard's dancing flames so that they briefly cast her blonde hair with burnt orange. Then he regarded her tankard, which he emptied into his own before he drank.

***

Alerice stretched out on the ground near a small stand of trees, reclining against Jerome's saddle. Jerome nickered from time to time as he grazed, hidden among the trunks.

She smiled as she contemplated her horse. Jerome never strayed. Rather, he always stayed where she needed him to stay, and she wondered if it was because he was a gift from the Raven Queen, and therefore bound to her somehow. At the Cup and Quill, she had heard tales of people bonding with animals 'familiar' to them. Perhaps that was what the queen had intended for Jerome, to become her familiar.

The sky above was popped with stars, and Alerice's thoughts swirled as she gazed up at them. Should she attempt to help the wizard and the Wyld, or should she take Oddwyn's and Kreston's advice to stay clear? The notion of not helping rankled her, for her father had been the one to instill in her a sense of right and wrong.

"You should always try to be good," he had told her as he rolled up his blanket and buckled it onto his infantry kit.

Alerice recalled the last day she had seen him alive. He was leaving to heed the call of Navre's Prime Cheval, Lord Andoni. Southern invaders were approaching, and Andoni needed all able-bodied men.

But her father was far more than that. While he was not an officer, he was still a leader, and while he never lamented that she had been born a girl instead of a boy, he had nonetheless trained her mind as he might a son's.

"And you are a good girl, Alerice," he had said. "But goodness takes more than doing what you're told. True goodness means that sometimes you stand up straight when folks tell you to mind your own business.

"Now, I do not suggest that you toss a coin into someone else's game every time, but as you get older, you will meet people who have been wronged. The world is full of them, and I'm telling you that there are times when if you measure the moment carefully, you will be able to judge for yourself if someone needs your help. Never be afraid to think, Alerice, and always try to stand up when you know down deep that it's the good thing to do."

Alerice recalled handing him a meat pie that her mother had baked and that she had wrapped up in the cloth she had chosen for his journey. She had only been five, and she recalled the tension that had taken hold of the farm as he prepared to depart.

When he had finished packing and given his kit one last look over, he had turned and caught her up in his arms. He had twirled about with her and tickled her, and they had both laughed. Then he had set her down upon a chair so that they shared an eye level.

"Be brave, my Alerice. Be strong. You are, you know. Both brave and strong."

She had nodded, and then gazed up at him, and then jumped into his arms.

"I love you, Dada," she had said.

"I love you too, my sweet Leecie," he had whispered back.

Alerice's thoughts drifted away in the cool night air, which played about the folds of her black shirt, for she had set her scale mail tunic down beside her. Listening to what she could recall of her father's voice, she drifted away in the soundness of his embrace.

Alerice woke to soft crackling and the smell of roasting meat. She opened her eyes, but the stiffness of having slept against her saddle struck her, and she winced before she stretched and sat up.

Kreston squatted nearby, tending a campfire and cooking an animal on a make-shift spit.

"Morning," he said as he rotated the little beast.

"Good morning, Kreston," she answered cautiously. She looked about to find Captain grazing next to Jerome, and noted that he was still saddled. "Did you just get here?"

"A short while ago," he said. "You still haven't learned to sleep with one eye open."

She nudged her rump further against her saddle to better sit up. "No, I suppose I haven't." She watched him stand and lift the bottle from last night. He stood and crossed to her to hand it down. "A drink this early in the morning?" she asked.

"It's water," he said.

She took the bottle and smelled it. He was telling the truth, and she drank a bit before handing the bottle back. He took it and drank a bit himself.

"Kreston, how did you find me?"

Kreston ran his fingers across the mark that the King of Shadows had scratched upon his brow. "You're not the only one who can use this thing to find another Realme Walker."

"Very well. Why did you bother?"

"I wanted to apologize for last night. I still don't think you should try to use *her* power for your own, but it's plain to me that you're going to try. You're one of those types who never stops when she sets her mind to something. For what it's worth, I admire that."

He looked her over, opened his mouth as if to say more, but closed it and paced to his saddlebag to stow the bottle.

"You care about me, don't you," Alerice commented.

Kreston paused and then exhaled as he turned to look at her.

"Alerice, I know you want to know about my past, and while I can't offer you much, I can say this. If I ever did anything to put your life in danger, I couldn't live with myself, and if I had one wish it would be for us both to be free."

"But you said yourself that we can never be free."

He crossed to her and knelt to take her hand in his. "But what if there was a way? What if the king and queen let us go?"

"Kreston, is that what you're not telling me? There's some secret way to be free, and you're leading me into it?"

"I don't know. It's not my idea, but if it worked, would you come with me? I don't know where we would go, but being able to go, to make our own choices, that would be the true gift."

She withdrew her hand and stood. Her black scale mail tunic caught her eye, and she looked down upon it. Then she looked up at him. "Kreston, what I think you're trying to tell me is that *you* are longing to be free."

He did not answer, but she knew that she had struck home.

"Then let me help you," she said. "That's what I asked you last night, and now I'm asking again."

"You can't help me as long as you're *hers*. The moment she orders you to do something you abhor, what are you going to do?"

"Is that what the King of Shadows has ordered you to do? Something you abhor?" She watched him clench his fists. "Kreston, what is it?"

"Alerice, stop."

"But--"

"Damn it, I said shut up, Lieutenant."

She looked at him askance. "What did you just call me?"

He calmed himself and added, "Look, Landrew. I know you don't think we have enough men to take the hill tomorrow, but the marshal has promised reinforcements, and we can trust him."

"Kreston?" Alerice pressed.

"Just see to your company while I see to the rest of the brigade. We'll toast our victory tomorrow night, right?"

Alerice swallowed hard, then summoned all her strength to demand, "Captain Dühalde!"

Kreston straightened, but grew annoyed. "What?" he snapped.

"Permission to approach, sir?"

He regarded her quizzically. "Permission? Landrew, you don't need permission. Just say what you have to say, man."

Alerice nodded and paced before Kreston, reaching to his face and taking hold of his head.

"Landrew?" he asked awkwardly.

She drew him close and pressed his brow to hers. She called to the Raven Queen's mark, not certain if it would clear his thoughts or send him into fits, but she had to do something to bring him back to reality.

She felt her mark pulse, and then felt him jolt. Still retaining her hold despite his reflex to back away, she quickly turned his head lower and kissed his brow. Then she took hold of his shoulders even as she saw his mark's latent glow shine under his salt-and-pepper bangs.

Alerice watched as Kreston startled and blinked. Then he looked down upon her, and she saw recognition in his hazel eyes.

"Alerice!" he cried as he gathered her to him. He held her tightly as he trembled and pressed his cheek against her blonde head. "Damn it, Alerice. Stop asking me questions. It's like... like there's a lock on my brain and everything you want to know is barred behind a door."

"I understand, Kreston," she said.

He released her and stared down at her. "No, you don't. I had my chance to do the right thing, but I gave in to anger and revenge. Do I want to be free? Gods above, yes, but I don't want to see you get hurt. You may not be able to believe anything I say to you. If I were in your place, I wouldn't trust me either, but that is the one truth I can offer."

She could see in his eyes that he wanted to come close, perhaps to kiss her, and despite her better judgment she wanted to kiss him. However, now was clearly not the time. She started to reach to his cheek, but decided to turn away and walk a few paces from him.

"Look," he said. "None of this is your fault. It's mine, and I'll clean up my own mess. You obviously came out here to think your plans through. Have you decided what you're going to do?"

"Yes," she said, gently but firmly.

"Then I'll help you."

***

Alerice waited with Pauldin at the same stand of trees where Kreston had woken her that morning. The wizard had refused to accompany her at first, but Alerice had insisted that he was being plagued by someone other than the Wyld, and the only way to discover what had been happening was to negotiate directly with Queen T'kyza. This could only be accomplished on neutral ground, and since this small grove was not far from the traveler's rest, and more importantly was secluded enough for a private meet and greet, it was the best possible location.

Besides, Alerice had impressed upon Pauldin that the Wyld queen wished to offer amends for suspecting that he was capable of malevolent craftwork. This last part was pure fiction, but Alerice had found herself adding it to create the dash of honey she had required to entice Pauldin to acquiesce.

Alerice scanned the horizon for Kreston. He had agreed to deliver a similar message to T'kyza, and he had expressed confidence that, as a former military man, he would be able to entice the Wyld. Now, it was only a matter of time to see if he had been successful.

Alerice did not know if her present course would work, or if it would anger the Raven Queen, but she was her father's daughter and she was going to stand up.

Pauldin had dressed formally in indigo robes embroidered with silver. He bore a sapphire-studded staff, which any common person knew was a wizard's way of imposing strength. Hopefully the Wyld would simply be themselves, but normalcy for them was fearsome enough to put anyone off their ease.

Alerice considered making small talk, but Pauldin's expression showed that he was politely tolerating her. Luckily, she heard a distant whooping and turned to see Kreston riding in on Captain, Queen T'kyza riding abreast of him.

The Wyld pack leaders rode behind them, and the Wyld followed in four ranks. Their ashen-and-black bodies struck a distinct contrast with the green-yellow grass, as did their leathers, furs, and armor when compared to Pauldin's elegant finery.

Before long, the Wyld had approached and the riders had dismounted. Queen T'kyza strode forward, gripping her sword of L'Orku. She paced before Alerice and offered her free arm in salutation. Alerice presented herself as proudly as she could and took the queen in a hand-to-forearm grasp. Then she beckoned Kreston to come beside her so that they stood as a two-person barrier between T'kyza and Pauldin.

Alerice regarded the Wyld, mercenaries hungry for action, and offered a silent prayer to Imari, Mother Goddess of Water and Wind, that this encounter might be blessed. She glanced at Kreston, who had folded his arms across his chest, seeming rather proud of himself.

"How did you get them to join you?" she whispered as she leaned in to him.

He leaned in to her and whispered back, "I made them a bet that they would have to meet you if I bested Imp in a wrestling contest."

Alerice scanned the Wyld for the great man-mountain, and when she found Imp he was standing a few paces back from the other pack leaders, a clear look of shame on his black-painted face. Even his own pack members snickered about his shameful loss.

Kreston smiled to himself.

"And what would have happened if Imp had won?" Alerice asked.

"I would have had to spit-polish all their armor, been their sparring dummy for at least a week, and bark like a dog whenever Mutt told me to."

Alerice saw Mutt prodding the ground near his pack leader, Shadow, and from the looks of things he was growling at Kreston from under his vented bevor plate.

"Good thing you didn't lose," Alerice said.

"You're telling me," Kreston agreed.

"And so, my dear?" Pauldin offered as he advanced. "Let us hear what these savages have to say in their defense."

"Our defense?" Queen T'kyza said. She ordered her Wyld to stay where they were, but they did not seem at all eager to heed her command. She glanced at Alerice, who stepped forward to present the wizard. "What does *he* have to say for himself?"

"No," Alerice stated flatly. "This is not how we are going to begin. I have asked you both to join me in order to give you important news, and we are going to begin with introductions. Wizard Pauldin, I present to you Queen T'kyza, fierce woman of the swept-horned crown. Queen T'kyza, I present to you Pauldin, the sapphire wizard."

Both Pauldin and T'kyza regarded Alerice, for neither had been introduced in such a fashion. Then they regarded one another, taking their time to gauge the other's measure.

"Good, now that's over with," Alerice continued. "As I said, I have asked you here because I want to inform you both that you are being deliberately set against one another."

"How so?" Pauldin asked.

"Yes, how and why?" T'kyza added.

"I must admit that I am not certain why, but Queen T'kyza, you are convinced that Wizard Pauldin has been harassing the region with his weirdlings."

"You were with us when they attacked," the queen said.

"I was," Alerice said. "But those weirdlings were not his."

"And how do you know that?" T'kyza demanded, placing her hands on her hips.

"Because I have been to his estate, and I have felt the goodness of his power. A man such as this, a scholar and deep thinker, does not waste time with frivolous schemes."

"That's all the proof you have?" T'kyza demanded.

"No, there's more," Alerice said. "When at his estate, Kreston and I watched as beings dressed as you and your Wyld rode in to harass him. But I could see that those creatures were imposters, and now you can as well," she said, turning to Pauldin. "Isn't that correct, sir wizard?"

Alerice watched Pauldin examine T'kyza before he said, "Your words are true, Ravensdaughter. This is not the queen nor are these the savages who have been plaguing me."

"Why would we want to?" T'kyza said. "We fight for coin. We don't spend ourselves stupidly."

"Indeed," Pauldin agreed. "So this is why they have come to ask my forgiveness?" he asked Alerice.

"Your forgiveness?" Queen T'kyza said. She looked accusingly at Kreston, and then at Alerice. "Your man said that the wizard wanted to apologize to us."

Alerice looked between the two, and then glanced at Kreston.

"Get ready for it," he muttered as he rested a hand on his broadsword's handle.

"Now, stop this, both of you," Alerice said, but she too knew that the damage had been done.

"Liar!" T'kyza said to Pauldin.

The wizard did not respond, but rather looked down at Alerice. "I will not dignify this savage with a reply. Let them be about their business and I will be about mine."

"Stop, please," Alerice insisted. "I need you both to listen to me. If we can't work together, we won't be able to discover who's toying with you, which means you will both face continued aggravation, and how do you expect that will turn out?"

Both Pauldin and Queen T'kyza paused, seeing the wisdom in her warning. They were about to listen to her once again, but a sudden volley of whoops and bellows sounded as a mass of horned weirdlings and imitation Wyld sprang up from the ground to encircle the grove.

"Wyld!" Queen T'kyza shouted as horns blew in alarm.

"Alerice!" Kreston said as he reached out to grab hold of her.

Alerice looked from side to side. "What's happening?"

"Magic is happening, my dear," the wizard said as he commanded himself to appear a few paces away from the nearest body so that he could press his palms together in a conjuring posture.

The Wyld fanned out to guard their half of the grove's perimeter, cursing in both their tribal language and in the common tongue that they had been deceived.

T'kyza looked accusingly at Alerice before she drew her sword and held it aloft. Its edges crackled with power, and as she led her Wyld to charge the weirdlings, she slew several with a single blow. As they had the previous evening, each dissolved into charcoal dust upon being struck down.

Pauldin threw his arms wide, and a distortion formed behind him that caused his robes to flow as though driven by the wind. Alerice could see that he was conjuring a portal, but it was not connected to the Realme, for it lacked the underworld's signature tri-toned colors.

She then heard a mighty screech, and everyone winced, including Alerice. When she recovered, a gryphon stood behind Pauldin, wings outstretched.

"Oh, right," Kreston exclaimed.

The beast turned upon the weirdlings and the false Wyld, reared up on its lion's legs, and beat its eagle's wings to flatten them to the grass. Then it screeched again so loudly that it nearly deafened Alerice. She threw her palms to her ears even as she saw the shockwave caused by its voice decimate all nearby foes, a wave of charcoal dust flying up from their wasted bodies.

Alerice drew and activated her pixie poles as she surveyed the ruin she had inadvertently wrought. To her one side, the Wyld fought like demons. To her other, Pauldin's gryphon snatched foes in its beak and snapped them in half. Whoever was playing with the wizard and the Wyld must have borne secret witness to her plans for a liaison.

In a final attempt to salvage the moment, Alerice *clanged* her poles together so that the tone rang out. However, no one reacted. Rather, the only response was a rip in the air before her that expanded into a portal of black, midnight blue, and deep teal.

A youthful Oddwyn stepped forward, a tunic of brilliant silver scale mail covering his torso. He bore bladed pixie poles of his own, and he fixed his ice-blue stare on Alerice.

"You. Queen. Now!"

Alerice startled, but Oddwyn shifted both poles to one hand, grabbed her hard by the arm, and shoved her through the portal. She turned back, only to see Oddwyn look at Kreston.

"You get to figure your own way out of this."

Alerice saw Kreston hold Oddwyn in his sights. "You serve them both, Herald. The king and the queen."

Oddwyn looked harshly at the failed captain. "A time is coming when we will all have to choose sides," he said.

With that, Oddwyn leaped through the portal, grabbing hold of Alerice and hurrying her with him as it closed behind them both.

***

"You were warned, not once but twice, and by two individuals whose advice you appreciate," the Raven Queen said, her voice of dark honey clearly conveying her displeasure.

Alerice stood in the queen's Twilight Grotto, a place where the dark-limbed branches of dark-trunked trees formed an interlaced grove. Thick bottom branches reached out between the trunks to create the lower portions of window panes that displayed scenes of the Evherealme.

Alerice counted six panes in all, and the Raven Queen stood statuesquely as she gazed into one that did not display a Realme scene. Rather it displayed the grove from which Alerice had just been plucked and the havoc her auspices had wreaked.

"Someone attacked us, My Queen," Alerice said. "I'll wager that it is the same someone who's been tormenting the wizard and the Wyld."

"Do not speak," the Raven Queen said with a wave of her willow-white hand.

Alerice's voice fell silent. She gulped to speak, but being unsuccessful, she stood and stared at her matron.

The Raven Queen turned, catching Alerice within her angered amethyst gaze.

"I told Oddwyn to make it clear to you that the power you wield is not yours. The power is mine, and you only have use of it by my will."

Unable to reply, and strangely not feeling the need to be obedient, Alerice set her shoulders and held her head high. This was not the first time she had been dressed down.

The Raven Queen allowed a moment to pass before she turned back to her window and bade it display a world of stars.

"What care I for the pettiness of Mortalia?" she asked, her voice slightly calmer but resolutely stern. "My care is for the Evherealme, its balance, its souls. Mortals are momentary. The Realme is eternal. I require you to help me manage it, to help guide souls to me so that I may measure them and place them. You do not bear my black scales to adorn yourself. You do not bear my dagger to empower yourself. You reserve yourself for me, and for no other purpose. This is now your sole reason to be."

Alerice swallowed, but then she felt the queen's power lift from her neck and she cleared her throat.

"My Queen," she said. "When you offered me your dagger, when you took my measure, you told me that I was a good person. I agreed, and I said that I had always tried to keep faith with good deeds. Now, you are asking me to act against my nature.

"People are being ill-used. It is not right. Do you wish me to be your slave or do you wish me to be my own person? Because I don't think you would have offered me your dagger if all you wanted was an errand wench."

The queen flashed Alerice a powerful glance before she floated to another of the panes. Then she cast her hand in a sweeping gesture so that the stars from the first pane appeared in all six.

Alerice could not deny the unnerving effect of feeling as though she floated untethered in the vastness. Indeed, she began having trouble maintaining her balance, and the only anchor which presented itself was the queen's willow-white face.

Alerice looked up at her, a creature both lovely and terrible, and she suddenly realized why Kreston trembled at the sight of her.

"You think of him when you should be heeding my words?" the queen asked.

"I..." She had no idea what to say. Of course the Raven Queen could sense her thoughts, but something inside Alerice spurred her to hold her own. "I would like to know what you did to him. It must have been something dreadful for a man like that to loathe you so much."

The Raven Queen paused, and then cast her hand about the grotto to restore five panes to scenes of the Realme while she directed the one nearest her to continue displaying an infinite array of stars.

"Alerice Linden, you cannot help Kreston Dühalde. What was done to him needed to be done, and I would discourage you from seeking any more from him. He is the king's man. He will be until his death, and, Alerice, it is unlikely that his death will come from old age. I would spare you that pain. I would have you focus on the tasks I assign, and nothing more."

"My Queen, I want to appreciate what you demand of me, and I would be lying if I said that serving you has not given my life new meaning. All I ask is that you allow me to use my own judgment from time to time. The mystery person who has been angering the wizard and the Wyld is magical. As with Prince Vygar, that person might affect the Realme. Allow me to discover who it is. You may find the identity useful."

"No," she said. "For completing your own task will merely embolden you. My husband noted your pridefulness when he offered you his sword. I now see what he saw in you: pride and desire, not the modesty you claimed."

"But these people are innocent."

"Innocent people die every day. Innocent souls cross into the Convergence and find their homes in the Evherealme. Your wizard and your Wyld are no different. Let them live their lives and let them die when their times come, but purge the thought of aiding them."

Alerice took a breath before she made one last attempt.

"My Queen, Great and Revered Lady of the Realme, you must know that I can't... No, I won't. I will not act upon their affairs if you command me, but what I ask is such a simple thing. It makes no sense to deny me. I will not grow as bold as you fear. That's not my nature. Perhaps it is for other mortals, perhaps even for Kreston, but I can content myself with knowing that I've helped someone. Please, My Queen. Denying me will place us at odds. It that honestly what you wish for us?"

The Raven Queen took a moment to review her champion.

"No," she said as she extended her willow hand. "It is not."

Clutching fingers into her palm, the Raven Queen commanded Alerice to appear before her. Before Alerice could draw another breath, the queen placed a palm on her brow and caused her mark to glow brilliantly within the grotto.

***

Alerice woke again in the stand of trees where she had attempted to broker peace. She wore no armor. She bore no weapons, and Jerome was nowhere to be found.

It was night. She stood in her black shirt, leggings, and boots. As she came to her senses, she immediately felt for the Raven Queen's mark. However, she touched only smooth skin, and in a heartbeat she realized that it had vanished.

Alerice fell to her knees in numb silence. She had no idea what to think or feel. She was not relieved. She was not bereft. She was simply... alone.

She looked at the grassy landscape, washed a dim silver by the quarter moon. She noted the dark trees overhead and how they matched those of the Raven Queen's Twilight Grotto. Visions danced before her mind's eye – drinking with the Wyld, invading Vygar's citadel with Lolladoe, discovering Kreston by his roadside campfire, and meeting Oddwyn in the Convergence.

The last memory spurred sadness, for of all her encounters she was going to miss Oddwyn the most. Whether a youth or a maiden, Oddwyn had become a friend. Should she have heeded his advice to not follow her own mind? Should she not have been so headstrong? Indeed, would regrets even matter at this point?

No, they would not. Of that Alerice was certain. She took a breath, and though she tasted the salt of tears, she gulped them back and got to her feet.

"I'll miss you, you sweet, odd thing," she said into the night air. She closed her eyes for a moment, and collected herself. As long as she had paid the price to see her intentions through, she would finish what she had started. It would be a long walk back to the traveler's rest, but she knew the way.

***

Alerice used the night's deep shadows to slip from place to place as she crept toward the Fire Inn. If she knew anything from all her years managing the Cup and Quill, it was that most problems could be solved over a drink, and there was no doubt that the Fire Inn had some of the best brew available. Besides, if the Wyld could raid the place because the inn mistress did not lock her back door, then Alerice could do the same.

She drew closer, already having formed a plan to outwit both Pauldin and T'kyza, for they had both revealed their true weaknesses. Now, if she could just find the right bottle, she might well be able to get them to work in tandem.

Alerice reached the Fire Inn's rear door, and as the Wyld had reported, it was not locked. Alerice slowly opened it, gave a silent prayer of thanks that it did not creak on its hinges, and slipped within.

The bonfire was still blazing in the courtyard. Alerice noticed it as she moved behind the bar and ducked low. It was most strange. The inn was closed and the entire traveler's rest was asleep, so why the need for the fire?

As she glanced over the top of the bar, Alerice saw its flames reaching tall as they burned brightly in the courtyard pit. However, as she was about to duck back down and examine the bottles resting on the bar shelf before her, a latent vision of what she had just seen registered, and she rose up again.

What she saw stole her breath. The elderly inn mistress approached the bonfire step by step. Alerice could not believe her eyes. The heat must have been roasting the crone alive, and though Alerice wondered if she should call attention to herself by shouting a warning, she remained still as she saw what she never could have imagined seeing.

The old woman reached to her own shoulders and drew off her skin as she might pull off a robe. Her flesh dropped to the firepit's stacked stone to reveal a creature of amazing beauty. The mistress had become a radiant woman with pearlescent skin and fiery red-orange hair. She stretched her arms upward, the bonfire leaping in response, and then stepped within the flames.

Alerice threw a palm to her mouth to strangle back her voice. She watched the woman bathe within the blaze, taking her ease in the luxury of its dancing licks. The woman reached out a hand, and a horned weirdling beast appeared before her. She stroked it as she might a pet, and Alerice had no further doubt that whoever or whatever this woman was, she was clearly the instigator she sought.

Alerice ducked back behind the bar. She examined and selected a few bottles, noted that a basket also rested on the shelf, and carefully loaded up her haul. Then she slowly lifted the basket into the crook of her arm, and turned to make her egress.

Alerice stole back out into the shadows. Now, she was going to need a horse. She regretted having to borrow one of the horses corralled nearby, but she needed to ride hard to both the Wyld encampment and Pauldin's estate if her plan was to work.

She slipped past the lone stable and from there to the collection of mounts. Her boots made a soft crunching sound as she crept, but it was not enough to wake anyone in the buildings nearby. She looked the horses over, some of which were sleeping with one of their back hooves cocked forward as they stood on three legs.

Then she saw a blood bay stallion, which meant...

"Don't even think about it," Kreston said as his broadsword scraped from its sheath.

Alerice felt him come up behind her and felt the flat of his blade land on her shoulder. She turned and made certain that the moonlight caught her face as she looked up at him.

"Alerice," he softly cried. He sheathed his blade and took her by the shoulders, then quickly looked her over and asked, "Where's your armor?"

"Kreston," she said, shifting the basket to her other arm.

He backed a step, realization registering on his face.

"You did it, didn't you," he stated. "You freed yourself."

"It didn't exactly happen that way."

"But you're free, Alerice. You're truly free."

There was no denying his look of joy. She nodded, and he stepped in again to take hold of her. However, she backed to maintain their distance. He stopped short, his eyes scanning hers, and he did not press forward even though she could see he was bursting to.

"Come with me," he said. "Please, Alerice. Do it now before they change their minds. Once the Realme has had you, it can always claim you again, but if you run, *she* won't want you. So, run now, I beg you."

Alerice set her stance, and she could see his hope fade as he read her expression.

"Oh gods above, Alerice," he swore, keeping his voice low. "What is the matter with you? You have your life back. You're insane if you don't seize this moment."

"All right, stop," she demanded. She waited until he brought himself under control, and then set the basket down. "I can clearly see what you want of me, Kreston, but have you considered what I want? You asked me to come with you, but now you're demanding it. But you, sir, are not free. You are still the king's man, so my freedom would be subject to his will if I went with you.

"And I'll have you note that I am not acting from the same desperation you are. You are thinking of yourself, and if that's the type of man you are, so be it. But I am going to see the wizard and the Wyld come to terms. Do you have any idea what that thing in the Fire Inn is?"

"What 'thing'?" he asked, glancing over his shoulder at the inn's rear door.

"Well, she's not an old woman, that much is certain. Now, I'll make you an offer. You've already said that I'm one of those types who never stops once I set my mind to something. You said you admired that. I will make Pauldin and T'kyza listen to me, and after that is over, I will consider going with you. You do care about me, and that counts for a great deal, but if you try to push me into doing what you want me to do, I will leave and never seek you out again. Help me, Kreston, and we'll go from there."

She was well aware, that he was well aware, that there was nothing more to be said.

"What do you want me to do?" he asked.

"Keep an eye on that sorceress, or whatever she is. I'll be back as soon as I can."

He paused, then stood straight and nodded his acceptance.

"Oh," she added. "And I need to borrow Captain."

***

Having tied Captain to a dead log some paces back, Alerice crept toward the Wyld's hilltop encampment. She could hear them snoring and grunting, and though she did not wish to remain downwind of them, she knew this was the best approach.

Topping the rise, she saw that they had all fallen asleep, no doubt secure in their fierce reputation and not suspecting that anyone would have the temerity to do what she was determined to do.

Alerice stepped lithely about their bodies, amused at the way some of them slumped over one another and others cuddled for warmth. Even Imp and Mutt seemed to enjoy lying back-to-back, which nearly caused Alerice to chuckle.

But T'kyza was her goal and the queen slept alone. Alerice found that stealing over to her side was a quick matter of skips and hops. She alighted beside the Wyld queen and located her sword. Yet as she reached down to take it, she saw T'kyza stir and open an eye.

Alerice clucked her cheek and winked as she snatched hold of the weapon's scabbard and shot away. She ran down the hillside as fast as she could, and bolted for Captain as she heard Queen T'kyza yell a furious alarm.

Alerice beat a heady trek toward Pauldin's estate, knowing that the Wyld were bound to be on her heels. Some groves had provided shadows in the setting moon that Alerice felt fairly confident had afforded her enough evasion to buy a few moments, but she had precious time to spare.

She bolted under the decorative blue metal arch and leaped down from Captain's back near the entrance to Pauldin's garden. She sensed movement within the home and noted that a light had begun to glow in one of the upstairs windows, but her prize lay just ahead.

She reached the glistening cascade, which danced in the darkness. She took a breath to screw up her courage, and then plunged in her hand to grasp hold of the fiery red rose.

She drew it out, relieved that the cascade's magic had not damaged her skin. However, no sooner had she turned to hurry back to Captain than Pauldin appeared before her in his embroidered nightgown.

"And just where do you think you are going, my dear?"

"Someplace where you will most likely follow," Alerice said as she drew T'kyza's sword and sliced into the cascade. Just as Alerice had hoped, the sword ruptured the magic in a flash of light, and Pauldin shielded his eyes.

Alerice pushed him off balance, and as the elderly man thudded hard against the ground, she ran for Captain, knowing this time that her very life might be in jeopardy.

***

Alerice rode for the stand of trees where she had left the basket and bottles. She had also stolen a few lanterns, a woven blanket, and some food on her way out of the traveler's rest. Now it all came down to preparing the place for her guests.

Counting the moments until they arrived, Alerice set T'kyza's sword down in the center of the blanket and crossed Pauldin's rose atop it. Then she used the burning candle from one lantern to light the others, even as the air about her grew dense.

Pauldin appeared in a soft flash of light. Alerice turned to him, a lump in her throat, but held her ground, for the unmistakable sound of the approaching Queen T'kyza and her pack leaders attracted Pauldin's attention.

The wizard struck a defensive stance and placed his palms together in preparation to conjure, but Alerice quickly stepped before him to take his hands in hers. She gazed up at him imploringly, and found him looking down at her with both adoration and admiration. She patted his hands and then gave him a quick kiss on the cheek before she turned to protect him as a furious T'kyza burst onto the scene.

"Stop!" Alerice ordered, her voice sounding into the night.

"Gods above, I will," T'kyza cursed. "This time you've gone too far, black bird."

"Excuse me," Pauldin interjected, "but if you will pause to look, you will see that Alerice no longer wears the Raven Queen's armor. She faces you here alone with no weapons but her wits, and if you will not listen to what she has to say, I will gladly *help* you listen."

Alerice glanced back at Pauldin, who winked. Then she struck a pose and stood tall before the Wyld queen.

"What is this stuff?" T'kyza asked, regarding her cup.

"Well, it's not quite Realme brew, but it's pretty close," Alerice replied, toasting her before taking a sip of her own.

"I must admit that it is quite tasty," Pauldin commented. "It reminds me of a particular distillation that I once savored nearly, oh how long has it been, let me think..."

"Just drink," T'kyza said, apparently having had her fill of the wizard's long-winded sentences.

"There's no need to be rude," Pauldin said.

"Very well, you two," Alerice said, standing up from the blanket on which she had been hosting her picnic. She looked at T'kyza and Pauldin, both of whom had agreed to hear her out. Then she glanced at the four pack leaders who had taken up sentry stations.

"I need to share with you what I have found. There's some type of sorceress at the Fire Inn, and I saw her with one of those weirdling beasts. She's the one who has been setting you two at odds, though I have no idea why."

"So, what is this matter to you?" T'kyza asked.

"Indeed, Alerice," Pauldin said. "I must admit that I have been wondering the same thing."

Alerice took a deep breath. "Look, I know that everyone thinks I should not concern myself, and everyone may be right. But, Your Majesty, it doesn't seem fair that you and your Wyld should be drawn into a conflict where you might face injury or death because someone is using you. Kreston said that if anyone ever tries to cheat a mercenary, watch out, and it seems to me that you have indeed been cheated.

"And, sir wizard, why should you feel any angst from a clan that would never seek you out if they did not feel provoked? You must certainly have better demands on your time."

Both T'kyza and Pauldin regarded one another, understanding in their eyes.

"And if you want to know the truth," Alerice continued, "you two are not all that different. Why do you think I stole what I stole from you? You're both romantics. You'd think you could respect each other's company rather than succumb to some sorceress' chaos."

"We like the chaos," Kara, leader the Pack of Chaos, said as she glanced back over her shoulder.

"That aside," Alerice continued, "I wanted to make you both aware of what is happening. I suppose that was my only goal. Now you know the truth, and now I've had my say."

T'kyza looked Alerice over as she sat back down upon the blanket. "And for that you gave up your armor?"

"It wasn't my first choice," Alerice said.

"You are quite a noble young woman, Alerice Linden," Pauldin commented. "The Raven Queen should think less of herself for not respecting you."

"Gotta admit the wizard's right," T'kyza said.

Alerice did not reply. Rather, she merely smiled to herself.

"So, I suppose we'll be riding then," T'kyza said.

"And miss the sport of challenging a sorceress?" Pauldin offered.

T'kyza glanced at him askance. "I'm listening."

Pauldin nodded, and then regarded Alerice. "Tell me more about this woman. What did she look like?"

"Well, I first thought she was an old crone, but then I watched her literally shed her skin and step into the bonfire at her inn."

"I'm sorry, she did what?" T'kyza said.

For a moment, Alerice considered responding the way Oddwyn might by accusing T'kyza of being hard of hearing and shouting her last statement. Instead, she said, "The woman had flaming red-orange hair."

"Flaming hair and stood within a bonfire?" Pauldin asked. Alerice nodded, and Pauldin set down his cup. "My dear, that is no sorceress. That is Belmaine,

Goddess of Passion and Chaos. If she is here in the living world, then some unseen force has allowed her entry, for Sukaar, Father God of Fire, keeps a close watch on her. Of all the four children, she is the most hazardous."

"Four children?" Queen T'kyza asked. "You mean the two brothers, L'Orku, God of Thunder and Gäete, God of Storms."

"With whom I'm certain you are well-acquainted," Pauldin commented in a knowingly avuncular tone. "They are sons of Sukaar and his wife, Imari, Mother Goddess of Water and Wind, but while those gods often assume mortal guise and walk among men, especially fighting men who welcome their presence, for it is said that when L'Orku and Gäete visit an army campfire the night prior to a battle, no harm will befall the regiment and no rain will fall upon the field--"

"Will you please make your point?" T'kyza demanded.

"Yes, please," Alerice added softly to hurry the information along.

"As I was saying," Pauldin continued. "While the brothers openly walk among men, even in mortal guise, their sisters move more subtly. Ilianya is the Goddess of Sleep and Dreams, also nightmares if you upset her. She rarely appears in the flesh. Belmaine, however, is the Goddess of Passion and Chaos. She wounds the heart and sets mortals against one another, and enjoys playing devious little tricks."

"Sounds like you know her personally," T'kyza said to Pauldin.

The wizard did not reply as he rose from the blanket. He offered Alerice his hand. As she took it and stood, he also offered his hand to T'kyza. She stared daggers at him and got to her feet.

"My friends," Pauldin said, "I strongly suggest that we dispel Belmaine before she causes any further damage."

"How do we do that?" T'kyza said before glancing down at her blade. She snatched it up and then then looked at the wizard.

"We must extinguish her fire," Pauldin said.

"And I suppose a bucket of water won't do the trick?" Alerice added.

"No, it certainly will not. However, there are ways of confronting a goddess, if one has the bravery to do so," he added, holding T'kyza in his sights.

The Wyld queen grinned as she tightened the grip on her sword's handle.

**

Kreston stole silently through the rear door of the Fire Inn. Whatever Alerice had seen, he knew he must also see it, for he fully intended to help her no matter what the King of Shadows had promised.

Kreston crept behind the bar, but the king's brand upon his brow began to pulse, and he knew he was in the presence of something magical. He cocked his head to the side so that when he peered out over the bar he would expose as little of his face as possible, and though this would only afford him a sideways glance, he required little more.

He rose slowly, cleared the bar's smooth wooden top, and looked toward the courtyard... but then he stood bolt upright, eyes wide and jaw gaping at the sight before him.

The most ravishing woman he had ever seen stood within the bonfire, her pearl skin glistening and her fiery hair tussled. Kreston blinked, unable to do anything other than gawk. The woman caressed a weirdling beast, which apparently adored her touch. Her other hand moved about her body as might a lover's.

Kreston swallowed hard and leaned in, but he accidentally toppled a few tankards onto the floor. He regarded them, knowing he had just given up his position, and looked up as the woman turned to him.

His breath came up short. Her naked breasts were beyond perfect, as were her belly and her hips, her thighs and the curves of her legs. Her face was that of a goddess, and her lips were the deepest crimson he had ever seen. Lust burst through him, and Kreston could not stop himself from crossing round the bar to stand in the open.

The woman held her arms wide, and Kreston's heart felt as though it was about to pound out of his chest. He took an unwilling step forward, for she was clearly beckoning him to lie with her.

"Come to me, Kreston Dühalde," she cooed in a multi-toned voice. "I am passion. I am your greatest desire."

"That, you are," he said, despite himself.

She drew fire into her hands and then shot up two small bursts from her palms. He became hard with sex at the very thought of entering her, and he nearly sprinted forward, for indeed she was his greatest desire...

But, was she? Kreston stopped short, for wasn't there another woman he held dear? What was her name? What was the color of her hair? Not red-orange like the creature before him, but simply... blonde.

Alerice Linden of Navre. That was her name. She was his greatest desire, and in a flash Kreston saw her face, her sweet smile, and recalled the softness of her gentle body.

He blinked, momentarily able to control himself, and he glanced back at the rear door, for he knew Alerice would be coming back, which meant she would be in danger from this fiery siren.

Kreston looked at the goddess in alarm, and she regarded him as might any spurned woman. She leveled a contemptuous stare and her eyes glowed red.

She again drew fire into her palms, and she shrieked as she hurled two flaming balls in his direction.

"Woah!" Kreston shouted as he dove back behind the bar.

One of the fireballs impacted the front of the bar, the other directly above him. Both set the wood ablaze, and as embers cascaded onto his leather tunic, he covered his head and shot for the door.

Kreston escaped the Fire Inn only to find himself in the center of the traveler's rest. He heard another shriek from within and knew full well that the business with the creature inside was far from over. He drew his broadsword and dove for the shadows, then took cover behind a cart.

Kreston turned and watched the rear door, expecting the woman to burst through. However, when nothing happened, he stood straight.

A great firepit erupted before him, centered within the traveler's rest. The woman rose up within it, far taller than she had been inside of the inn's courtyard. Flames clothed her body, and Kreston crouched back down as she gazed about the area to find him. His position was not nearly secure enough, and she locked her red gaze upon him, again summoning fire into her palms.

Kreston stood away from the cart and threw his broadsword into her heart. She reeled as it tore through her, and she shrieked again, but the Realme blade did not slay her. Kreston held his hand high and the sword appeared in his grasp, but there was no time for a second throw. She cast another fireball at him, forcing him to leap clear as it crashed against the cart, blasting it into flame-engulfed splinters.

Kreston ran while throwing his sword again, but he did not watch to see if the strike was successful as he searched for more cover. He heard her shriek and then held up his hand so that his blade again appeared in his grasp as he dove for some barrels.

He glanced out from the side to see the woman looking for him once more, and he noticed that she did not seem able to leave her firepit. Noting this weakness, Kreston looked about and found the town's water tower. It did not stand too tall from the ground, and if he could compromise the supports, he might be able to douse her flames.

A gryphon's cry pierced the night and Kreston looked up - then he looked up a second time to see Alerice riding before Pauldin on the great monster's back. He emerged from behind the barrels as Alerice jumped down and made for the water tower. He ran at top speed straight to her.

Still mounted on his gryphon, Pauldin held his palms out at Belmaine. He cast a magical cascade that flowed in midair. Only, this cascade was considerably larger than the one which held his rose, and it emulated the rush of a waterfall.

The goddess snarled at the wizard and then cast a sweeping gesture of her own to summon a great deal of horned weirdlings. They bellowed into the night, both human and beast, and charged the wizard. Pauldin urged his gryphon to rise up, and with a mighty wingbeat that flattened several weirdlings, it leaped aloft.

The wizard cast a rip in the air at ground level, which he widened into a sizeable fissure. Whoops echoed as the Wyld burst forth from it, all on foot though Imp held Captain's reins. Once through, Imp let the horse go with a slap on its rump that sent it over to the corral.

Queen T'kyza raised her sword of L'Orku, and the entire company shouted, "We are the fookin' Wyld!"

With a roar, they charged the weirdlings.

Alerice smiled as Kreston joined her at the water tower.

"That was one amazing entrance," he said.

"Glad you liked it," she quipped. She sized up the angle to their target and then took stock of the tower's supports. "I didn't expect that Belmaine would come out into the open, but it should make dispelling her easier."

Kreston looked over his shoulder at the melee and the fiery female centered within it. "Belmaine?"

"Goddess of Passion and Chaos."

"Passion," he commented. "That explains a lot."

"She the one who's been setting the wizard and the Wyld against one another."

Kreston noted Pauldin urging his gryphon to land once again, and as soon as it did, it snatched weirdlings in its talons, lifted them to its beak, and tore them to pieces. It also spared a few Wyld from the weirdlings' attacks, allowing them to slaughter more of the horned men and beasts, all of which dissolved into charcoal dust.

"Looks like they're working together now," Kreston said of Pauldin and the Wyld.

"We've got to put out her fire," Alerice said. "I don't know if mere water will do it, but even if it doesn't, it should be enough to compromise her so that Pauldin can contain her. What's the best way to topple this tower so that the flow goes into her pit?"

Kreston sized up a likely stress point and began hacking into it with his broadsword.

Pauldin dismounted and began to create more luminescent cascades that blinded the weirdlings, disabling them enough for the Wyld to attack and slay them. However, he did not see a particularly large weirdling rise up behind him, and he only managed to turn about when the thing bellowed and swung an axe for his silver head.

Mutt hurried toward him and quickly fell to all fours. T'kyza sprinted forward, leaped up onto Mutt's back, and flew high to swing her blade at the great weirdling's neck. With experienced grace of combat, T'kyza decapitated the creature and landed on balance as she searched for her next target.

Pauldin looked her over. "Not bad, my dear."

T'kyza nodded and gestured her blade in salute. Then she turned to Mutt. "Bite!" she ordered.

Mutt's eyes gleamed as he removed his vented bevor plate. He smile-snarled at the closest weirdling, his blackened, filed teeth ready to gnash. He howled and charged, tearing into the horned creature's leg and ripping open a wide gash.

Which Pauldin noted. "Evidently, his bite is worse."

"That it is," T'kyza said before she put fingers to the sides of her mouth and whistled sharply for more of her clan to join Mutt.

In her Twilight Grotto, the Raven Queen beheld the battle in one of the dark tree-branched panes. She watched as Belmaine summoned more weirdlings to attack the Wyld, and knew that the battle would eventually go to her, no matter how valiantly the mortals fought.

She slowly blinked her amethyst eyes as she beheld Alerice working with Kreston to topple the water tower. Then she gazed at Belmaine once again.

"You are aware of who this is," she said.

The maiden Oddwyn, still dressed in brilliant silver scale mail, surveyed the battle. "I do, My Queen."

The Raven Queen turned to her herald. "How is it that I did not see Belmaine enter Mortalia? I see everything in my grotto, Oddwyn, but I did not see this."

Oddwyn had no opinion, and did not attempt to offer one.

"Alerice, through her stubbornness, has exposed a flaw in the ether that I had not discovered," the Raven Queen stated as she turned back to the pane.

Oddwyn tried to hide a hopeful expression as she focused intently upon her mistress. She tried not to wring her hands in anticipation, but found herself doing just that and forced her arms to her sides.

The Raven Queen held out a willow-white palm, and a crystal vial appeared, the contents of which swirled in tones of light blue and glittering white.

"Give Alerice this," she said, gesturing so that the vial floated to Oddwyn, who eagerly took hold of it. "And kiss her for me."

Alerice put her shoulder to the water tower's compromised support beams as

Kreston finished his last hack. He joined her, and together they pushed with all their might.

The supports groaned and creaked, eventually giving way, and the tower crashed to the ground, spilling its contents in the direction of Belmaine's firepit.

The goddess saw the impending deluge and cast fire to turn the water into steam, but a great rush flooded her, diminishing her flames.

Pauldin stepped forward to conjure a luminescent cascade that flowed out and down to capture the goddess under a dome. Then, enduring the strain of his mortal magic verses her immortal power, he began to compress the dome to capture her.

Alerice hurried forward to help the mute Wyld, Wisp, slay a weirdling. Kreston reached in from behind to offer the fatal blow, given that Alerice bore no weapons. She saw Wisp offer thanks in sign language, and then nodded to Kreston, who quickly moved off to seek another mark.

Then Alerice felt a presence before her, and she watched as the air about her began to swirl in the tri-colored tones of black, midnight blue, and deep teal. She froze and waited for the Realme portal to open. When it did, she beamed to see the warrior-maiden Oddwyn step forward.

Oddwyn smiled, but quickly stepped before Alerice. She curled her middle finger into her thumb as if to flick her brow, but instead gently tapped her forehead. Then she brought Alerice's forehead to her lips, and kissed her.

Alerice reeled as she felt the mark of the Raven Queen pulse. She shook with a powerful surge, and then backed a step from Oddwyn to hold her arms slightly away from her body. Her black scale mail tunic appeared in layers upon her torso. Her studded black belt fastened about her waist with a strong cinch. Her Realme dagger appeared on one hip, her Realme crossbow on the other.

Alerice took an exhilarated breath and looked at Oddwyn, who extended an open palm, on which Alerice saw two pixie pole cylinders. She snatched them up, placing one in each hand even as Oddwyn did the same with her set. Together, they activated their blades.

Alerice was about to turn and charge, but a mighty neigh pierced the night, and she looked past Oddwyn's shoulder to see Jerome rearing. She hurried to him and leaped into the saddle, managing her seat as he reared again, his luxurious mane flowing and his long-stocking hooves pawing the night.

Alerice waited for the horse to land, and then looked down at Oddwyn, who produced a crystal vial and tossed it up.

"Cast it into Belmaine's fire."

Alerice nodded and sized up her line of attack, but then looked down once more. "It's good to see you again."

"Would you just hurry?" Oddwyn said before she launched herself into the fray.

Alerice dug her heels into Jerome's ribs, and he bolted forward. She tucked her pixie poles under one arm as Jerome leaped over several weirdlings, easily clearing them. Then she reined up at the side of Pauldin's cascade, stared into Belmaine's furious red eyes, and cast the vial into her pit.

The crystal shattered, splashing glittering blue-white foam into the flames. The fire died, and Pauldin directed his cascade over Belmaine's body. His magical luminescence adhered to her pearl skin as the foam crept up onto her legs. Both viscosities consumed her, and with a final shriek, she collapsed into the dying embers.

Alerice tucked the pixie poles before her saddle horn and drew her Realme crossbow. Its string pulled back, and a gleaming black bolt appeared in the flight groove. She shot it into the firepit's heart, where it exploded in a dark flash that made some of the nearby Wyld shield their painted eyes.

Jerome neighed in triumph and Queen T'kyza whooped, inspiring her clan to do likewise. Alerice looked about as the sounds of victory echoed.

Pauldin remounted his gryphon and gently urged it to approach Alerice. Jerome backed as the monster came near, but Alerice steadied him. Even so, she knew that a horse would never be comfortable staring into the eyes of a creature that was half-eagle, half-lion, and so parting with Pauldin would need to be brief.

The wizard offered a graceful bow. "I do hope you will call upon me sometime, dear Alerice. We have stories to share, you from your tavern and me from my adventures."

Jerome shuffled and then backed, and Alerice guided him to circle around back into place.

"Ah, yes," Pauldin said. "I understand the nature of common beasts."

"I wouldn't call Jerome common," Alerice said.

Pauldin smiled. "You may be right in that." He nodded to Alerice, and then found T'kyza standing before her four leaders and their Wyld packs. "You fought well, Your Majesty."

"We always fight well," Queen T'kyza said.

"'Cause we're the fookin' Wyld!" the Wyld said in near unison.

"And so you are," Pauldin said before he urged his gryphon to launch itself up toward the quarter moon.

Queen T'kyza watched him disappear, and then she sauntered forward to take a stance next to Jerome's shoulder. She gave him a few solid pats and then looked up at Alerice.

"I see your mistress has taken you back," T'kyza said, regarding the scale mail.

"So she has," Alerice said.

Oddwyn came up, and all nearby regarded her with curious interest. Queen T'kyza looked her up and down, but then Oddwyn changed into a youth, still bearing the silver scale tunic, and T'kyza went on her guard.

"Gods above, what is that?" she exclaimed.

"This, good comrades," Alerice said, "is the herald of the Evherealme, and while you are the fookin' Wyld, I caution you, don't fooke with the Odd."

Queen T'kyza had no idea what she meant or what to make of the youth, who briefly transformed back into a maiden to blow her a kiss before presenting himself as a youth once more.

T'kyza shook her head, and then regarded Alerice. "Come and find us sometime. You are always welcome for a drink, and Imp wants to challenge your man again."

Alerice nodded, but then looked about. "Where is Kreston?"

"Here somewhere, I'm sure," T'kyza said as she held her sword high and whooped in salute. Then she led the Wyld away, several helping themselves to spoils from the traveler's rest as they left.

Alerice rolled her eyes and shook her head before she dismounted. Then she looked full on at Oddwyn and drew him into an embrace, which he returned.

"Of all the things I would have missed about the Realme, I would have missed you the most," she said.

"Of all the mortals I have ever met, you are by far the most odd," he responded.

She released him and looked him over, not certain what to make of the statement.

"It's a compliment," Oddwyn said with a grin. Then his expression grew concerned, and he reached out to draw a lock of Alerice's blonde hair from her face.

"What?" she said, worried at his worry.

"Hmmm? Oh, nothing. Except this."

He flicked the Raven Queen's mark on her brow and then disappeared through a suddenly opened Realme portal.

"Oddwyn!" she grumbled as he vanished. Then she laughed to herself. She would soon ask the Raven Queen for an audience and explain that she was indeed grateful to be taken back into her service.

However, she vowed to remain modest and not grow bold from the success she had just achieved. The Raven Queen must have realized some advantage in her actions, and Alerice knew that the gift of serving her required adherence to her guidance. Even so, Alerice was proud that she had helped two parties escape manipulation.

She turned and looked about, but then she saw Kreston standing a few paces before her. She could see that he was dispirited, and she knew it was because she was once again in service to the Realme. She could see that he was masking his feelings in his ice-veined stoicism, and she knew that she had likely broken his heart.

She watched him clutch his blade's handle in an iron grip and raise it in salute, the hilt near his hazel eyes. She drew her Realme dagger to return the salute. He lowered his blade and sheathed it. Then he walked toward the corral to see to Captain.

RIPS IN THE ETHER
Tales of the Ravensdaughter
Adventure Four

The Realme will ne'er forsake them
These Walkers who defend
The king and queen below
For whom they make their stand.

Trusted by their masters
A Walker will not fail.
Honored by their masters
They welcome duty's call.

from the Scrolls of Imari

Alerice looked up at a dawn sky of pale blue green. The clouds were an opalescent mix of white, pink, and gold. A light breeze caressed her cheeks as it played in her blonde hair.

She and Kreston had taken their leisure on an oak-topped hill overlooking a sight Alerice had sometimes tried to picture, but never thought she would see – the Royal Range. It stood in the distance, its thin, snow-covered peaks scraping the sky like jagged teeth. As with the clouds, the impending sunrise had cast their caps in pinks and pale yellows, and Alerice awaited the moment when the sunlight would strike them.

Kreston had said that this was a sight few people ever beheld. The time of day and the time of year needed to be just right for the most grandiose effect. Fortunately, after leaving the traveler's rest and riding for a day and night, he had guided them to the perfect spot. Even though she knew she had broken his heart by retaking the Raven Queen's armor, she could not deny his company.

He had said very little as they rode, and she had done likewise. Captain had kept pace with Jerome, even though Jerome was a Realme pony and capable of covering greater distances.

There hadn't been any need to hunt for dinner, for the denizens of the traveler's rest had been so grateful to be rid of Belmaine, Goddess of Passion and Chaos, that they had stuffed both their saddlebags with meats and cheeses, and even a few treats. Alerice had asked for both water and ale so that she could dilute her cup after she and Kreston had stopped to camp. She was a tavern mistress, after all, and knew the advantage of drinking only half of what others drank.

Strangely, she had not felt the need to sleep. Nor had Kreston, which Alerice found odd considering all the physical exertion it had taken to dispel the goddess. Kreston had explained that increased stamina was a gift to Realme Walkers, and Alerice was obviously on track to living up to her birthright.

Still, they had sipped through the night and now enjoyed the morning as the campfire dwindled down to embers.

"So, I've been meaning to ask," Kreston said. "Your old tavern was called the Cup and Quill?"

"Um hmmm," Alerice said inside her cup.

"That's a strange name," he said. "Usually tavern names are stronger, like the White Hound or the Three Lions, or something."

Alerice shrugged. "It was Uncle Judd's name. The 'Cup' part was simple. It was a tavern, after all. I think he chose the 'Quill' because he loved writing poetry. He was actually good at it. I've seen some of the love letters he wrote to Aunt Carol when they were courting."

"Hmmm," Kreston commented, taking a bite of cheese before chasing it with a drink.

"The tavern's name was fun, though," Alerice continued. "Every so often we would have a contest. The person who wrote me the best love poem would win a free ale."

"Love poems, huh? You collected lovers in Navre?"

Alerice hid a blush. "No. And I wasn't looking for any, but when you have a, what did you call me once? Oh yes, a 'handsome woman' running a bar, and you have gents willing to abase themselves to win a free drink, well it was a unique way of promoting the establishment.

"And it worked fairly well. One of our poets wound up in the court of the Prime Cheval, Lord Andoni. Two others, I heard, went to Navre's sister city, A'Leon, and joined the court of its Cheval, Lord Bolivar."

"Sounds like the Cup and Quill was quite a place."

"It was, Kreston," she said with a recollecting smile. "I had many happy moments there."

Alerice could not help but drift off into nostalgia even as the sky grew brighter in the throes of the advancing sunrise. However, she could sense Kreston watching her, which he made known by clearing his throat to attract her attention. Then he drew a breath and recited.

"Upon the shore I think of thee.
Your eyes that dance with starlight,
Your hair caught in the moonlight,
Your lips I long to kiss.

Why did I e'er leave thee?
Your gentle, soft embrace,
The curve of your fair face,
Your heart that beats with mine.

No more again I'll see thee.
To battle I must go,
But please, love, this do know,
I'll cherish no one else."

"Kreston," Alerice exhaled. "A free drink to you, sir."

He smiled to himself. "I wrote it for a girl, Rachelle. She was..." He tapped his fingers on his stomach. "She was something special."

Alerice smiled and then teased, "I imagine that through your years you've known several women, Captain."

"Alerice, if it's all the same, please don't call me that. And yes, I've known women. She was the one I wanted, though."

"And you had to leave her. Do you know what happened to her?"

"Nope, and I didn't try to find out. Hopefully, she got married to a good man and had a good life. She deserved a good life," Kreston said with a little shrug.

"I know you're going to say that you don't."

"Let's just enjoy the morning, Alerice. It's going to be our last."

"Well, that's a sad thought."

"Reality is rarely a happy thought." He turned on his hip to face her. "But you serve *her*, and I serve *him*, and that makes us rivals. I can never trust you now, and you can never trust me. If they fight, we fight, and that's an end to it."

"I don't think she would ever order me to attack you."

"You don't know her."

"True, but the last time, she released me rather than forced me to act against my will. She knows I could never kill you."

He humphed a little laugh. "You couldn't kill me if you tried, but that's not the point. She still might try to use you against me, which is to say against her husband."

"Why do those two fight so much?"

"It's just who they are. It's who they'll always be. They're eternal. We're merely dots. Oh, turn around."

Alerice did as he instructed just as the sunlight crested the horizon opposite the Royal Range, and the tops of the jagged peaks turned fine gold. As though ladled with molten metal, the sunlight poured down the mountain sides to coat every surface, and Alerice's breath drew up as she watched the natural wonder play out before her eyes.

Kreston stood and came up behind her. She stood as well, and he advanced until he was at her back. She could feel his warmth, and she knew that he wanted to press against her. She held her place to see what he would do, but all he allowed himself was to touch a lock of her hair and move it off of her armored shoulder. Then he petted it flat with the palm of his hand, tensed, and stepped to her side.

"I..." he said, a quiver in his voice. He cleared his throat again and continued. "I told you it was a sight to see."

"It is, Kreston," she said, not turning to him. "Thank you."

"Don't mention it. Just give thanks to Sukaar, Father God of Fire, for the day. He lives in those mountains, and we must all bow to him when beholding his home as it's kissed by the dawn."

Alerice closed her eyes and offered Father Fire a short prayer. Then she sensed something and looked aside, away from Kreston.

The maiden Oddwyn stood near an oak trunk, petting Jerome. Alerice glanced back at Kreston, who was moving over to his spot at the campfire. Then she looked again at Oddwyn.

"I know Oddwyn's here," Kreston said, not looking up as he attended to his gear. "*She* obviously needs you."

Alerice said nothing further as she collected her things and headed in Oddwyn's direction.

Kreston did his best to avert his eyes as he saw Alerice and Oddwyn converse. He began rolling up his blanket and preparing his kit, but then he felt the brand of the King of Shadows pulse upon his brow. A shiver shot through him, and he gulped down his reaction so that he could summon that familiar ice into his veins.

"*Get below, Dühalde,*" the king said in his mind.

Kreston closed his hazel eyes and muttered aloud, "Yes, My King."

***

"You have alerted me to something dire, Alerice," the Raven Queen said in her voice of dark honey.

"My Queen?" Alerice replied as she stood in the queen's Twilight Grotto. The six tree branch-framed windowpanes displayed scenes of the Realme, one in particular being a field of flowers with blooms that glowed in rhythmic patterns.

However, the 'sky' above the blooms seemed troubled. It pushed and pulled against itself. Alerice tried to liken it to storm clouds gathering at a rapid speed, but the comparison did not seem right. The atmosphere seemed to bulge here and there as though it might rupture at any moment.

The Raven Queen had extended her willow-white hands toward the windowpane in order to align her essence with the fluctuations. Before her floated her gray orb, the interior of which swirled as though made of churning mist. The queen placed her palm over the orb to draw from its energy. As its swirling intensified, it emitted a grayish glow, and the queen directed its power toward the window.

The Raven Queen forced the orb's essence into the palpitating atmosphere. Alerice could see that the effort strained her, and she wanted to offer aid. However, she doubted that there was anything she could do.

Alerice watched the queen close her amethyst eyes as she exerted a significant amount of supernatural force. The atmosphere above the glowing flowers resisted her, and Alerice could feel the strain of their willful struggle. In the end the Raven Queen mastered the moment, and the 'sky' calmed into a steady hue of deep teal.

The queen exhaled and pressed her willow-white hands over her breast. The sleek feathers of her gown radiated their colors of black, purple, and emerald as the mistress of the Evherealme centered herself. Several moments passed, but eventually she recovered and stood tall. Then she turned and regarded Alerice.

"What you have just witnessed was an impending rip in the ether of the Realme," she stated.

"Yes, My Queen," Alerice replied.

The Raven Queen drew and released a thin breath, and then regarded her other windowpanes for any sign of danger.

"Upon occasion, outside pressures build upon the Realme's borders. When this occurs, a breach will try to form an abscess in our world. Anything may enter through this abscess, souls or creatures from other worlds. I have no idea what will transpire when it occurs.

"With my Eye," she said, gesturing to her gray orb, "I keep watch over the Realme. With my Eye, I can identify all breaches, as I did when sending you to Mortalia to deal with Prince Vygar. With my Eye, I can seal many rips before they abscess, as you have just seen, but the entrance of Belmaine into Mortalia was a breach I did not see, and this has given me cause for concern.

"If breaches open unbeknownst to me, then the Realme will become infected. I must bolster it against each breach, or else lance the breach and face the consequences of what will enter. I am more alert to the crisis now that you have shown me proof of Belmaine's infection above, and I have detected more potential abscesses than I am capable of managing.

"It is time to put you forward, my Ravensdaughter. It is time for you to go into battle to defend the Evherealme."

Go into battle, Alerice found herself repeating in her mind. She could not deny smiling at the thought.

***

The King of Shadows paced within his Hall of Misted Mirrors. A dozen elongated panes of varying sizes and shapes hung suspended in smokey tendrils. All were inert, save for the king's favorite, a large pane of black glass bordered in the same crystalline trim that adorned his long, open robe. A crown of dark crystals topped the pane to match his own crystal crown. Longer crystals jutted out from the top sides of the pane, matching the crystals which capped his pauldrons.

"Did you see what she did?" the King of Shadows asked as the pane relinquished the image of the field of glowing flowers and the nearly ruptured 'sky'.

"I did, My King," Kreston said as he stood at attention, his expression void as he stared 'eyes forward'.

"That damned Eye of hers," the king complained. "She used that damned Eye. Souls waited on the other side of that rupture, Dühalde. My souls. Do you think Prince Vygar has been the only one in Mortalia collecting them for me? Now I must derive another way to import them. I will consume them in any manner I choose, regardless of what the queen thinks. Do you hear me?"

"I do, My King," Kreston said. He was well-accustomed to the frustrated rants of superior officers, which was why he used the physical focus of 'eyes forward' to create a semi-meditative state that allowed him to absorb information while rendering no outward appearance of cogent thought.

The King of Shadows regarded him, and paused to look him over. He scoffed, and yet admitted, "You are still the best mortal to wield my blade, Dühalde. Of all the men I have taken into my service, you have been the most successful, and why shouldn't you be? You are a born Walker, a rare find. But you were also a man of battle. When I sent you to war, you killed with great acclaim.

"The Ghost of the Crimson Brigade, they called you, a specter who stalked the ranks and slaughtered anyone. You haunted the thoughts of all fighting men, or at least you did before my wife got her hands on you."

Kreston did not react.

"Be that as it may," the king continued. "It's my wife's gem that is the problem. The Queen's Eye, she calls it. She claims that it was made from the amalgam of willing souls, but those souls were never willing. She took them when she measured them, plucking them like prizes. Some of those souls were mine, and I want my tally before she assigns any more to their resting places. Do you know how difficult it is to harvest them once they settle?

"The only souls I may enjoy for my own pleasure are the ones you claim in battle or the ones she does not know about, which is why I want you to fetch her Eye for me. And I don't want any excuse about not being able to look at her. I know you cannot. If you so much as glance at her, you will fall into madness, and we both know how long it takes you to recover. So, use the girl, Dühalde. You have no difficulty tolerating her presence, correct?"

"None, My King," Kreston said, arching his shoulders a bit further back. "I will do as you command."

"Of course you will," the King of Shadows said. "Now, let's set the stage for a plausible encounter so the girl might still trust you."

Kreston locked his jaw, unable to hide a blink that was slightly longer than normal.

***

"Oddwyn, this place is beautiful," Alerice said, looking about at a landscape that could only be found in dreams. The sky was magenta and bore off-white star clusters that brightened the canopy above in gradient tones so that some areas appeared lighter than others. The clusters swirled as though stirred by ethereal currents, making the landscape seem alive as brightness congealed briefly in one place before moving about to another.

The topography resembled a flow of light gray stone that Alerice swore must have been molten at some point. How else could it have pooled in gentle cascades before it had hardened? The stone's composure bore the same shimmer as the arches in the Convergence, which made her wonder if it contained bits of the white metal composing the Raven Queen's crown.

The flows stretched as far as Alerice could see, and they glistened whenever the star clusters congregated overhead. The stone also reflected the sky's magenta, so it appeared pinkish in places. It was rough terrain, not soft or dusty, and Alerice's boot soles were able to grip it, allowing her to feel sure of her footing.

"It is nice, yes," the youthful Oddwyn said, looking about the landscape he had likely seen hundreds of times. "I've watched the queen change the color of the sky too. Sometimes this place becomes more purple, sometimes more blue."

"It's a good thing that the folk above fear death," Alerice commented. "If they knew how breathtaking the Realme was, they'd never want to live their lives."

"It's because they do live them that the Realme exists. It is due to the collected consciousness of mortals that the Realme has been able to craft itself in so many ways. This is one of the prettier ways, but don't be fooled, Alerice. There are many baleful places within the Realme."

"Hmmm," Alerice said as she continued to stare at the magenta landscape. "I'll try to remember that."

"Do," Oddwyn said as he adjusted the iridescent chain that he had wrapped about his silvery scale mail tunic.

Alerice regarded him, noting that he wore the same armor that he had as a maiden during battle at the traveler's rest.

"No woman of war this time?" she asked.

"Naw," Oddwyn said with a backward shoulder rotation and a slight side-to-side head toss. "I feel like scruffing it up this time. Got your poles?"

152

Alerice eagerly presented her pixie pole cylinders and caused the blades to pop out as she stood on her guard.

"Yep," she said.

"Good," Oddwyn replied, observing her look of determination. Then he regarded her stance, adjusted it a bit, and though she gave him a look of 'What are you doing?' he reached up and flicked his finger against the Raven Queen's mark upon her brow.

She shook off the flick and half-glared at him, but her mark began to glow, and she could feel the queen's essence flowing through her. Oddwyn then looked over his shoulder at the two Raven Knights, and next at Ketabuck, the faun chief who had brought forth a cadre of his best warriors.

"We're ready, Your Majesty!" Oddwyn called out to the stars above. He then let loose a great whoop, and as the fauns bugled in reply, Alerice found herself cheering as well.

In her Twilight Grotto, the Raven Queen had expanded the vision of the magenta landscape so that it flowed over each of her six branch-framed panes.

She stood stoically as she commanded her Eye to appear above her left palm, and then floated her right hand over it as though stroking it. The swirls within began to churn easily at first, but with another pass of her hand, they swirled more dynamically until the Eye gave off a gray glow. The Raven Queen held the Eye before the central pane, and said, "I open this rip in the ether of the Evherealme."

The queen's words rang out against the magenta sky, churning the star clusters. "Dispatch whatever enters so that I may mend and seal the breach."

Oddwyn leaned in to Alerice.

"You know 'dispatch' means to kill, right?"

"Oddwyn," she said, not taking her eyes off the stars. "Would this be a good time to tell you to shut up?"

"Probably," he said.

"Good, then shut up."

A flash tore across the magenta atmosphere, slicing through the star clusters and ripping open a long fissure.

The souls of mortals flew in as might clusters of leaves stirred up in a gale. Yet, while they filtered aimlessly above only to dissipate in batches, tension permeated the company as the atmosphere grew dense.

The landscape seemed to condense. Alerice looked about. She could see that the fissure created a rift through which the essence of the Realme and the essence of whatever world lay beyond exchanged some sort of balance, much the same way that air rises in a heated paper box. Only this pressure balance occurred in the reverse, with the Realme taking in the other world's essence rather than releasing its own to the other side.

Suddenly, oblong shapes appeared within the star clusters, buoyant for only a brief moment before they fell down to the pooled stone ground in a mass of heavy thuds.

Alerice watched the oblongs take shape, only to become brilliant green-yellow lizards, much longer than she was tall. One shook its head to clear its senses, and when the black slit pupils of its bright yellow eyes focused on her, it opened its jaws and hissed so loudly that Alerice thought she was back in Uncle Judd's brewery where a kettle was about to explode.

The beast roared at her and charged, its gait a waddle so quick that Alerice barely had time to jump toward it. She ran across its back and did her best to dodge its thrashing tail as she jumped off its flank.

Each of the oblongs took on the same lizard countenance, and the battle joined as Oddwyn loosed his iridescent chain. The Raven Knights took flight, and the fauns bugled again as they charged.

Alerice turned about and faced off against her lizard. The beast moved quickly, but she struck its jaw as it snapped at her. She sliced its forearms as it clawed for her. Dodging the tail was the most difficult feat, for it whipped in every direction.

Slaying Prince Vygar as a giant wolf had been easier, for then Alerice had been able to put out his eyes. She could not quite strike the eyes of this beast, for they were set too low and she would be within range of its claws. However, she did begin to feel the natural motion of her pixie poles guiding her as she swung one, primed the second, and then swung the second as she re-primed the first.

The lizard hissed again and prepared to charge, but Oddwyn's iridescent chain suddenly wrapped about its jaws to muzzle them shut.

"Kill it!" Oddwyn cried as he pulled on the chain with all his might.

Alerice lunged forward and sliced both poles deeply into the lizard's neck to splay it open. Its bluish blood poured out. She looked at it, then looked up to see Oddwyn leap over the lizard's back and then lunge forward to tackle and roll with her.

"Get clear!" he cried.

As they came to a stop and Oddwyn jumped away, he looked down at Alerice, who sat on the glimmering pooled stone.

"Its blood is acid. Don't let it touch you."

"Blood. Acid. Got it," Alerice said, as she jumped back to her feet and charged at another lizard.

The Raven Queen stood unmoving within her Twilight Grotto. Her Eye floated above her palm while her right hand extended to her central pane. Her amethyst eyes were open and fixed on the scene before her as she felt the abscess above drain dry.

Emptied of its infectious contents, she bent her mind to the task of sealing it.

The Raven Knights attacked the lizards with two-handed great swords. The fauns attacked with their razor-sharp prongs followed by both blunt force and edged weaponry. Oddwyn lashed out so precisely with his chain that he was able to blind several lizards so that Alerice could leap from one to another and slay them.

Alerice looked up to see the magenta sky further contract as the star clusters swarmed about the fissure to stitch it closed. She thought for a moment that the landscape might implode upon itself, for it had condensed a significant degree. She had no idea how she might escape if it did implode, so her only option was to keep fighting.

Suddenly a lizard hissed and reared up behind her. Alerice turned, ready for action, but a broadsword's point erupted from its chest, and Alerice had barely enough time to dodge the splatter of its acidic blue blood.

The beast's tongue lolled from its toothy jaws, and its head flopped aside as it fell forward, revealing Kreston and the king's two Shadow Warriors.

"Kreston!" she called.

He did not respond as he snapped for the Shadow Warriors to disperse and attack. Then he held his hand high overhead, and the King of Shadows' broadsword reappeared in his grip. He snarled as he hurled it at her head where it *whizzed* past her ear so closely that it stirred her hair.

Alerice looked over her shoulder to see the sword impale another lizard that had been about to charge. She looked back at Kreston, but his visage unnerved her. His eyes were fixed and his expression was as hard as the stone underfoot. He offered only a single nod, which she returned before she went her way, and he went his.

Each of the dozen panes in the Hall of Misted Mirrors tracked the souls that had filtered into the Realme. The only pane that did not was the prime pane, which displayed the conflict into which he had just dispatched Kreston and his Shadow Warriors.

The King of Shadows regarded it, and the battle's many participants, with derisive enjoyment, even as he collected the souls into pits below the other panes. Those souls, the remnants of mortals both cruel and kind, fell haplessly down, unable to escape as the king conjured more of the smokey tendrils that supported the panes. He transformed them into bars that sealed the pits. Then the king relished the plaintive moans that rose up as he continued to watch the magenta landscape.

In her Twilight Grotto, the Raven Queen began to tremble with the strain of sealing the breach. A tear formed in her unblinking amethyst eye and rolled down her willow-white cheek. It dripped off of the side of her deep-red lips as she continued to focus on her task.

In the magenta landscape, Alerice cut cleanly through a lizard's tail, causing the beast to roar and writhe. She dodged the spray of its blood, but noticed Oddwyn backing from a lizard of his own. He was drawing too close to the acid.

"Oddwyn, look out!" she cried.

Oddwyn turned in her direction, but a sudden burst of blood pressure from the lizard's body sent a viscous blue spray over him. Blood covered his hair and face, and splotched his silver scale mail. He grimaced and wiped his mouth clean, flicking the lubricious blue off of his hand as he shook it.

Alerice reined up, bewildered.

"I thought you said it was acid."

"To you, mortal!" Oddwyn shouted in disgust. "Yeck!" he complained before he launched his iridescent chain about the dying lizard's neck. Alerice looked Oddwyn over, and then regarded the beast. She leaped toward it and hacked its head off in a scissor slice of her pixie poles.

In her Twilight Grotto, the Raven Queen gave up a mighty exhale, and the panes about her went dark.

In the magenta landscape, the atmosphere above stabilized, and the star clusters began to swirl along their previous currents.

Kreston skewered the final lizard, and stepped back to avoid its blood.

Alerice paced toward him, but his expression was still void of emotion. Even though the fight was over and everyone should be enjoying victory, Kreston Dühalde, the confidant who had shared her drink and the comrade who had stood at her side, was simply not there. He was obdurate, unable to recognize her with any warmth.

Oddwyn approached, the Raven Knights behind him. He watched as the Shadow Warriors appeared to flank Kreston, who leveled a steely gaze at the knights.

Alerice watched as Oddwyn took in the scene. He dismissed the Raven Knights and offered for Kreston to reciprocate. Kreston gestured with his broadsword for the Shadow Warriors to disperse. They obeyed, leaving Oddwyn and Kreston locking stares with one another.

Alerice looked between them, and then she looked farther away to see

Ketabuck and the fauns leaving. She *clanged* her pixie poles to attract their attention, and as the clear tone rang out, she watched them pause and turn back. They bugled to her and raised their weapons in triumph. She raised a single pole to them in return.

Then Alerice turned back to Kreston, but she was unable to find any joy in his presence for what she beheld when she looked upon him truly frightened her. Kreston loomed tall, a deadly menace capable of wholesale slaughter. He was nothing short of a stone-faced reaper of souls that chilled her so greatly she stepped away from him.

"Why did you help us?" she managed to ask.

"The king ordered it," Kreston said in an icy tone that Alerice had never heard before.

"But why?" she pressed.

"Ask the king," he said. He was about to wipe the blue blood from his blade in order to sheathe it, when he suddenly let out a sharp grunt as his left eye crimped shut.

Alerice looked at the King of Shadows' mark on Kreston's brow, but it was not glowing. Still, he reacted by gulping back the words, "I will!", so he was definitely reacting to some unheard voice.

Kreston grunted once more and then gave his head a single strong shake. He pressed his lips together and drew a breath through his nose, but then relaxed his stance.

"The king knows about the rips in the ether," he said. "And if *she* can't do something about it, he will."

"The Raven Queen has this in hand, *Captain*," Oddwyn said, emphasizing Kreston's rank in the same tenor he used to refer to the queen.

Kreston's grip tightened on his broadsword, but Alerice stepped between the two.

"Fighting each other solves nothing," she stated. "Oddwyn, you and I will go to her majesty and learn what she intends to do. Kreston, I do not know if you are my ally or my rival right now. You said yourself that you serve the king, so it has obviously suited him to have you here. You are good in a fight, no one can deny that. And for what it's worth, I personally thank you for helping us."

Kreston drew another breath and his shoulders relaxed a bit more. He finally looked at her with a hint of humanity, for which she was most grateful.

***

"My husband sent his champion," the Raven Queen commented. "The King of Shadows will not assist me openly, but he offered his help peripherally. That is interesting."

Alerice stood at the foot of the dais in the Hall of Eternity. The Raven Queen sat upon her throne, her Raven Knights behind her. Alerice studied her matron, searching for clues that might give up her mood, but she may as well have tried prying secrets out of a porcelain doll.

The Raven Queen sat with posture so straight that she seemed to be supported by an internal frame. She gazed forward, her amethyst eyes looking into some vast unknown. Her voice of dark honey was calm and measured, and the only hint that she may have suffered strain came from Oddwyn.

He stood beside Alerice, still dyed half-blue from the lizard's blood. Yet he focused intensely on the queen, and Alerice could see that regardless of his appearance, which in a more jovial setting would be quite comical, the mood was very serious.

"There is another rip applying pressure to the Evherealme," the queen said. The Queen's Eye rested in her lap. She glanced down upon it, and then returned to her faraway gaze. "I do not have the strength to open and seal it."

Alerice glanced at Oddwyn, who glanced back. Then she looked up at the queen.

"If it opens, will you be able to contain it?" she asked.

The Raven Queen swallowed delicately. The flash of her willow-white throat was her only movement.

"I do not know," she said softly.

Oddwyn seemed ready to begin pacing, but he held his place. Alerice, however, began to reflect on all that she had learned thus far. Her gaze shifted to the eyes of the Raven Knights, glowing golden spheres in the eye sockets of their full-metal helms. She studied the edges of their arm and leg plates that were crafted as metal feather tips, and looked at the feathered edges of their long black cloaks.

She recalled wearing one of those cloaks as she had destroyed Prince Vygar's sealed niches in the waterfall grotto. She had smashed each of the glyphs with a pixie pole before she had marched out with the faun spirits in tow. The souls had burst forth and flown away, and she wondered...

"My Queen? Could a rift in the Realme be opened into Mortalia?"

Both the queen and Oddwyn regarded her.

"How do you mean?" the Raven Queen asked.

"Well, aren't there places in the Realme that meld into Mortalia, the way Mortalia melds into the Realme through the Convergence?"

"There are," the queen replied.

"So, if you could direct the energy of this new breach to open into Mortalia, then whatever comes through would be set loose in the living world. I can fight it there. So can Oddwyn and the knights. I could possibly call upon the Wyld, and perhaps even the wizard Pauldin. But if you can expel energy into a world where the Realme will not bear the strain, you can seal the breach while I dispatch whatever invades."

Alerice paused a moment and then leaned in to Oddwyn to whisper, "You know that 'dispatch' means to kill, right?"

Oddwyn glared at Alerice from under his blue-covered brow, but she winked at him and his gaze softened.

The corner of the queen's deep-red lips turned up, and life seemed to rekindle in her amethyst eyes.

"You will need a colleague," she stated. "You have lived a secluded life in your tavern, Alerice, and though you may have heard of some wonders, you have yet to meet someone truly wondrous. Pauldin is not the man for this task. The person you require is the lady he lost, the sorceress Allya."

"Yes, My Queen," Alerice said. "How do I find her?"

"I will open a portal to her," the queen said. "I will tell her the reason for your arrival. She respects the Realme and its balance with Mortalia. She will lend herself to this fight, and perhaps become a source of inspiration for you. Like you, she has suffered personally for a life of greater meaning."

"It would be my pleasure to meet her," Alerice said with a reverence.

"It would be my pleasure to meet her," Oddwyn mimicked under his breath as he folded his arms and rolled his ice-blue eyes.

"Oddwyn?" the queen asked.

"Nothing, My Queen. I was just wondering how long it will take before Alerice needs my help."

"You don't think I can meet a sorceress?" Alerice asked.

"I think you still need help in a fight," Oddwyn replied. "You're getting better, but you're not ready to go into full battle yet, not on your own."

"She is not going to go on her own, Oddwyn," the queen stated. "She is going to go with Kreston."

Alerice opened her mouth to ask "What?", but all that came out was a throaty, "Erhh..."

"Ahmmm..." Oddwyn similarly declared.

Then they regarded one another before Alerice spoke.

"But, can I trust him?"

"A valid question," the queen said. "I have told you that he is the king's man. That said, I must consider the reason why the king sent him to aid you in sealing this latest breach. It was because my husband wished to gain some advantage.

"The King of Shadows will never act against me directly, nor I against him.

159

He must have tasked Kreston with seeking what he desires. However, Kreston must work through you, Alerice, and if he fights at your side, you may be able to discover what the king wishes him to do."

Alerice glanced at Oddwyn, who grimaced awkwardly as if to say, "Are you sure about this?" Alerice set her shoulders.

"I will do as you say, My Queen."

"Alerice," the queen cautioned. "Remember that Kreston Dühalde is a man in great turmoil. What was done to him needed to be done."

Alerice considered the look she had just seen on Kreston's face – that of a man void of empathy whose only objective was to slay what lay before him. She shuddered at how cold his hazel eyes had become, and knew that perhaps the queen was right.

***

"Kreston, have you ever seen a fire opal?" Alerice asked.

"No," he replied. "Heard of them. Never seen one."

"I have. A wealthy man came to the Cup and Quill once, and he wore one centered in his amulet. They shimmer in colors of red and orange and blue-green."

"And?"

"And so I think this tower was crafted from giant slabs of them," she said as she beheld a magnificent stone structure that caught the daylight with a grace she could never have imagined.

Allya's tower looked to be hewn from polished opalescent blocks. It rose up two stories high and then spanned out into a pointed cap. The roofing tiles looked like wide, flat rubies, and the spike above appeared to be made of gold.

The tower stood on a rise in a rock basin, and a little lake had formed in the bowl. The surrounding stone presented colors of ruby, brown, and fuchsia. Festooning them were luscious draping vines bearing burgundy blooms. Fire spouts dotted the area, some flaming up in spurts, some burning constantly.

The energy of the place was that of a domesticated conflagration, alive and burning yet comfortable and hospitable. Alerice had no idea what source fueled the fire spouts or what water nourished the vines. She only knew that she could never have conjured such a place in her wildest dreams, and she was fairly certain that Kreston could not have either.

Alerice adjusted her studded belt and made certain that her weapons rested in their proper places. She felt for the Realme dagger at her hip, gripped it, and then gave it a pat. She took a confident breath, set her shoulders back, and prepared to step forward. After all, how often did one have the chance to make the acquaintance of a sorceress?

"Alerice," Kreston said.

She turned to him, but she had seen that guilt-ridden look before. He no doubt wanted to apologize for the way he had behaved when fighting the lizards, or more to the point, the way the King of Shadows had forced him to behave.

However, now was not the time. If he was being forced to plot against the Raven Queen, so be it. She needed his steel, and hopefully he could relax into simply being himself if she made that clear.

"Kreston, do you remember the evening we met?"

"Yes?"

"Do you remember that after you had heard your battlefield voices, you recovered yourself and then struck me across the jaw to prevent me from getting close to you?"

"Yes," he said, more regretfully.

"Well, I understand now that there are more than battlefield voices in your head. The king is there. Perhaps the queen as well. But we have work to do. Are you with me?"

Kreston stood straight and nodded.

Alerice softened her tone to add, "That's not to say I don't care about things that plague you. I do, and perhaps there is some way for us to sort it all out, but for the moment, we need to keep to our task."

Kreston offered her an "after you" gesture. Alerice smiled and turned toward the tower.

Alerice found herself looking about at a magnificent interior. Flaming golden sconces burned about the encircling walls. A curved staircase rose along the wall, ascending to the story above. Vaulting timbers joined at a central ring beam to support the roof, while vertical and horizontal beams jutted out from the curved ones to join the roof to the tower's walls. Fairy lights twinkled about the timbers in colors of pale red, white, and soft yellow.

Rich tapestries bearing images of Sukaar, Father God of Fire, hung on the wall before her, accenting the hall's most striking adornment – an altar standing in the tower's center, its rounded shape matching the hall. Its red stone bore wide black veins, and its golden top was dotted with cabochons of garnet and jet. The altar bore a hammered gilt basin in which burned an iridescent flame. Alerice stepped a bit closer to it and glanced inside. No fuel fed the blaze. It simply existed.

"So, where is she?" Kreston muttered from the side of his mouth.

Alerice did not know, for a portion of the tower's exterior had simply faded open a moment ago to admit them.

"Here, Captain Dühalde," a woman said from behind.

Both Alerice and Kreston turned to see someone truly wondrous, as the Raven Queen had proffered.

Allya was a woman of Alerice's own height. She had rich auburn hair with pearl-and-golden highlights. Her eyes were emerald, but the most striking thing about her was that the left side of her torso bore a tremendous scar.

Indeed, her entire left breast had been burned away, leaving only blistered blotches and crinkled lines that were both hideous and beautiful. They glistened with the same fiery opalescence found in the tower's stone.

Alerice saw hints of ivory and gold in the grotesque skin, but what made Allya's disfigurement all the more intriguing was that the sorceress wore it openly. Her shimmering green gown was cut one-breasted so that it fell from the right side of her neck to her left hip. Indeed, while her right breast seemed perfectly intact, Allya's great scar was obviously a source of pride.

Alerice met Allya's emerald gaze and reverenced. "Sorceress."

"Ravensdaughter," Allya replied. She then regarded Kreston. "Captain."

"Madame," Kreston said with a formal bow.

The three passed an awkward moment, before Alerice simply could not contain her childlike giddiness.

"This place is amazing," she exhaled.

Allya smiled. "I'm glad you enjoy it."

"Enjoy it?" Alerice said turning about as she held her hands out from her sides. "The whole tower is beyond belief. The stone basin outside is too. I mean, I've heard people spin tales of magical places. My Grammy Linden used to send me to sleep with them, but..."

Kreston stepped close to Alerice, grabbed the back of her studded belt, and gave it a yank.

Alerice collected herself as Allya came forward.

"Might I inquire about the burn?" Kreston asked.

"You may, Captain," Allya said.

"Actually," Alerice interjected. "He doesn't like being called Cap--"

Kreston yanked her belt once more, and stood his ground as Allya came before him.

She began running her fingertips about her scar, her hand moving over the many dimples and creases. The gesture was not meant to seduce, nor did Kreston appear to see it as such. Eventually, she passed her hand down to her hip and rested it at her side.

"This is unlike any wound you have ever seen, I would imagine," she said.

"It is, madame," he replied.

"That's because it was a gift. A loving gift from Sukaar himself. This..." She gestured to the area where her left breast had once been. "...is where he kissed me."

"Kissed you," Alerice said softly.

"Yes, Ravensdaughter. Just as the mark upon your brow is where the queen has kissed you." Allya glanced from Alerice's brow to Kreston's, but offered no comment on the mark left by the King of Shadows. "The gods above and below all claim us with signs we can never hide. Myself, I never wish to. I wear this scar openly so that all may see it and take heed."

"Of?" Kreston asked.

"Of this," Allya said gently as she raised her hands palms-up.

Fire shot up from her grasp. Alerice reflexively tried to step backward, but Kreston tightened his grip on her belt and forced her to stand her ground.

Allya, however, did step back to set her full body alight. Alerice could feel the heat. The sorceress smiled as flames licked about her face. Her green gown shimmered all the more brightly, reflecting the orange-gold of the dancing inferno, and just as with Belmaine, Alerice wondered if the sorceress was about to weaponize her scintillation.

"You needn't worry," Allya said in a voice that half-echoed about the tower. She drew the fire back into her palms, and with a graceful wave of both hands, she caused the flames to reduce down to red wisps that floated about her fingertips. "The Raven Queen has explained the reason for your visit."

Kreston released Alerice's belt and bowed once again. Alerice, however, was transfixed on the sorceress' scar, which now danced with light like embers glowing in a pit.

***

"By design, our world and the Evherealme are not meant to meld into one another, save for at a few specific points," Allya said as she led Alerice and Kreston from her tower's entrance, down the short rise, and toward the stone basin's little lake.

Alerice fought the distraction of the flame spouts above and around, doing her best to listen.

"The Raven Queen sent you to me as the best hope to induce a meld, though what we truly require is a devotee of Imari, Mother Goddess of Water and Wind. Such a devotee would be able to calm things better than I. However, I have not known the Great Mother to bless anyone in my lifetime, and so we must work with Father Fire's power to tear open a rift."

"But isn't a rift the sort of thing the Raven Queen has been trying to prevent?" Alerice asked.

"It is," Allya answered. "Yet, it is the only way for the queen to direct the energy of an abscess into our world. I will manage the breach here with your assistance, and she will lance it, forcing the energy to us."

"What assistance?" Kreston asked.

Allya paused to regard them both. "You two are Realme Walkers, but you cannot create your own portals. However, I need a gateway to the Realme in order to control whatever the queen sends us. She will not be able to create a portal because she will be overseeing the abscess, but you can create a joint one by using the king's Shadow Warriors and the queen's Raven Knights."

Alerice was not certain this was a good idea, for she had brought Kreston to fight, not solicit the King of Shadows.

"What about Oddwyn?" she asked.

Allya smiled. "Oddwyn is a dear soul, but I need more than he, or she, can offer. I need the two of you. While I concentrate the power of the Great Father, you will call for the warriors and the knights. You can use their essences, which in truth is their majesties' essences, to affect a gateway."

Alerice noted Kreston's tension.

"Is there any way I can open a gateway myself?" she asked.

"Just set it in motion," Kreston said flatly.

Alerice wanted to say something that might spare him the indignity of calling upon the king only to be denied, but she could see that he was ready to act, do or die.

"We need to take up positions about the lake," Allya said. "A triangle will give us the best advantage. I will move to the stone overhang just there. Alerice, stay where you are, and, Captain--"

"I see it," Kreston said, noting a flat boulder that completed the required formation.

"Very well, let's begin," Allya said.

Alerice watched Allya and Kreston move toward their places. Having no idea which weapons would suit the moment, she drew the pixie pole cylinders from her belt and focused her spirit on the mark of the Raven Queen.

She allowed her soul to 'open' through it as though she were opening her own personal portal to the Realme. She felt it pulse upon her brow even as she concentrated on the air before her. She willed the world about her to swirl with the signature tri-colors of black, midnight blue, and deep teal.

As she did, she wondered if she would be able to create her own portals someday. If she was destined to be a Realme Walker, she couldn't rely on portals crafted by others. Independence was key to agility, and if the Raven Queen needed her to perform at her best, she required autonomy.

"My Queen," Alerice called mentally into the ether.

Standing within the magenta landscape, Oddwyn at her side and her Raven Knights behind, the Raven Queen raised her willow-white face to the swirling star clusters. Her Eye floated above her left palm, and she smiled, for Alerice's voice did not simply ring in her mind. It echoed across the atmosphere with a clarity previously unknown.

Oddwyn looked up. Then he regarded his mistress. "That was strong."

"It was," the queen said as she held both palms before her so that the Queen's Eye rested above them. Focusing her amethyst gaze upon the gem, she caused its glow to intensify and its inner essence to churn.

"*I am prepared, Alerice,*" she mentally conveyed.

In the stone basin, Alerice felt the queen's words sounding through her. She saw the magenta landscape in her mind's eye, and she nearly reeled at the synergy of spirit she shared with the world below. She felt as though she herself was the gateway between Mortalia and the Evherealme. It was as though she stood at once between the two places, and wondered what might happen if she called upon the qualities of either world to meld through her.

"Alerice!" she heard Kreston call.

Alerice startled back to the present and regarded him. He stood upon his boulder, broadsword in hand.

"Get your poles ready!" he ordered.

It was an order, not that Alerice objected. In point of fact, she was glad to have a bit of direction to steel herself from the throes of the inter-worldly connection she somehow knew she had just created.

She activated her pixie poles so that the blades popped out, and stood on her guard. She then looked between Kreston and Allya, noticing that they regarded her in a strange manner, almost as though they were both awestruck. Precisely why, she had no idea, but it was best not to wonder, for it was time to get to work.

She raised one pole in salute to Kreston, who raised his broadsword in reply before he looked at Allya and gestured his blade in her direction.

Allya nodded to Kreston and to Alerice. Then she held out a palm toward them both.

All the fire spouts about the basin suddenly flared up as Allya called to Sukaar, Father God of Fire. She sent out flaming beams toward Alerice and Kreston, refining them until they became luminescent red-orange rays. She aimed her power at the marks upon their brows, and as they struck, stunning both Realme Walkers, she instructed, "Reach out to one another."

Alerice leveled a pixie pole at Kreston, who leveled his broadsword at her. Red-orange rays shot out from the tips of both weapons to complete the triangle.

"Tell the queen we are ready, Alerice," Allya commanded.

"Yes," Alerice said before she mentally called, *"Send the Raven Knights, My Queen."*

Alerice's words echoed across the magenta sky, affecting the starry swirls. The Raven Queen focused upon her Eye even as she drew down a bulge from the 'sky' above. It grew bulbous with multiple blotchy pockets that threatened to spew forth whatever contents they contained.

Oddwyn drew and activated his own set of pixie poles as he stood protectively at the queen's side. The Raven Knights each held up their two-handed blades.

Atop his boulder, Kreston tried to center himself enough to reach out to the King of Shadows. However, the energy swell filling him struck his senses. All he could see when he looked at Allya was a woman of such living dynamic that he felt alive in her fire. She was as intoxicating as Belmaine, Goddess of Passion and Chaos, only he did not desire her. He did, however, feel the power of a dozen horses in his heart as her strength filled him.

Then he gazed upon Alerice. How could she have known that she had just caused the air about her to dance as though she were a living portal? How could she have known that the mark upon her brow had glowed so brightly that he had nearly cowered before it as he might before *her*? And yet he had felt no fear or touch of madness. Clearly, Alerice possessed talents that she had yet to discover.

Kreston forced the myriad of sensations to the back of his brain. He concentrated on the accursed mark scratched upon his brow, and conjured the image of the king's prime pane hanging in his Hall of Misted Mirrors.

"Give me your Shadows, My King!"

The King of Shadows reacted to Kreston's voice emanating from his crystal-crowned mirror. He paused from the enjoyment of sending shock bursts into one of his captured souls and turned to the pane. He conjured the sight of Kreston standing atop a boulder in the stone basin, and upon adjusting the view to see through Kreston's eyes, he beheld the girl and the sorceress.

"To help them? I think not."

Kreston drew up his courage amid the rush of vitality to risk the tone that he reserved only when correcting a superior officer at a dire moment.

"You want the Eye? Give me your damned Shadows!"

The king reacted with incredulity. It would be a simple matter to draw Kreston back to the Realme for a reprimand, but as he paused to consider the moment, he activated another pane.

The Raven Queen stood in the open magenta landscape. She bore her Eye, which the king found deliciously enticing.

"*They're yours,*" he said to Kreston.

In the landscape, the Raven Queen bade her Raven Knights to take flight toward the globular distortion overhead. They spread their feathered, black cloaks into wings and launched themselves upward, flying at the abscess from opposite directions. Then they extended their two-handed blades and carved slices as they flew toward one another.

The queen caused her Eye to glow exponentially. An atmospheric pustule burst above her, and she directed her Raven Knights to circle about the incoming deluge. They began spiraling so quickly that they created a meniscus that held the abscess' discharge in place.

The Raven Queen directed them to come abreast of one another and fly up into the breach's center. They did, drawing the abscess into the vacuum of their wake. The Raven Queen then used her force of will to thrust the Evherealme's power after them, shoving the ulcerous energy into Mortalia.

In his Hall of Misted Mirrors, the King of Shadows watched his wife. He gestured for his Shadow Warriors to come forth, which they did, blending in with the surrounding smoke tendrils that bore the mirrors. With a quick wave, he banished them to Kreston's side.

"Here it is!" Allya shouted.

The little lake bubbled, then roiled, then erupted in a great upward splash that inundated Alerice and Kreston. Yet, focused on their course, they did not react as the Raven Knights emerged from the lake, followed by the Shadow Warriors.

Alerice and Kreston held wide their arms so that their respective guardians could flank them. The knights and warriors alighted abreast of them, and Alerice and Kreston tapped their strength while raising their hands to the lake.

As though their mental visions had joined, they both saw that a tremendous gash had opened along the lake's bottom. Together they used the Realme's power to seal it.

Allya collected the power of the roaring fire spouts to break the triangular beams she had created, and redirect the energy into the lake. She caused a bed of multi-colored coral to weave about the gash and stitch it closed so that Alerice and Kreston could step away.

Both Alerice and Kreston felt the break in Allya's contact and nearly fell to their knees. Kreston quickly regained his balance atop his boulder while Alerice stumbled a few paces before she found her footing. They both shook their senses clear, and then regarded each other as though they had successfully crossed the finish line of a race.

In the magenta landscape, the queen sealed the breach above. Oddwyn breathed a sigh of relief as the queen allowed her Eye to float freely.

"Knights, return to me," she said.

In his Hall of Misted Mirrors, the King of Shadows smiled as he called to his crystal-crowned pane, "Shadows."

The king then glanced at the exhausted soul beside him. With a final volley of shocks, he caused it to gyrate, scream, and rupture.

In the stone basin, Alerice watched the Raven Knights spread their cloaks and take flight. In the blink of an eye, they were out of sight. She looked at Kreston, only to watch the Shadow Warriors dissolve in dark gray wisps.

Then she regarded the lake, which had begun forming multiple bubbling domes.

"Kreston...?" she asked.

Kreston looked at the water.

"This isn't over," he called as he leaped down from the boulder and hurried for Alerice.

"Move to higher ground," Allya called out in a voice that, while physical, also resonated mentally. Alerice and Kreston could see the marks glowing on one another's brows, and as they met on the sandy lakeshore, they turned together and hurried toward the rise that led up to the sorceress' tower.

The lake's domes were on the verge of bursting. Allya summoned more power from the flare spouts and cast a ring of flame that evaporated several domes into fumaroles.

The domes centered within the lake exploded. Otherworldly neighs sounded as silvery, green-blue horses leaped forth from each. Their eyes burned red. Their front teeth were long and sharp. Their manes and tails were made of twined river grass, and their powerful bodies heaved as they blew foaming water from their nostrils.

"Kelpies!" Kreston shouted as he helped Alerice up the rise.

"What?" she asked, taking a stand with her pixie poles ready.

Kreston glanced over his shoulder as he protectively placed himself before her. "Kelpies. Water demons. Don't let them get near you. If you touch them, you'll stick to them and they'll drag you into the lake and drown you."

"Gods above!" Alerice exclaimed.

Four kelpies neighed, their terrible voices echoing about the stone basin.

They fixed their stares on Kreston and Alerice and charged, galloping atop the lake's surface and churning up foam in their wake.

"What do we do?" Alerice half-shouted.

Kreston glanced at her weapons. "Get your bow. You need range when dealing with these things!"

Kreston threw his broadsword at the nearest kelpie. It impaled the monster, which gave up a bloodcurdling neigh as the sword passed through its body. The kelpie reared, but then it congealed into a viscous blue-gray ooze that gushed onto the water's surface and dissolved.

Kreston held his hand high, and his broadsword reappeared in his grip. He threw it at the next kelpie, likewise congealing it into blue-gray ooze.

Alerice retracted her pixie poles and drew her Realme crossbow. She glanced up at Allya, who was directing her fire to move in from the lake's perimeter in order to close on more bubble domes.

Alerice aimed at one of the two incoming kelpies. Her crossbow's string pulled back of its own accord, and a gleaming black bolt appeared in the flight groove. She pulled the trigger into the tiller and the bolt struck home.

The kelpie reeled with a wild whinny. As the dark glow of the bolt's impact spread over its torso, the beast dissolved into its own clot of blue-gray ooze and sank below the water's surface.

Kreston advanced to throw his blade at another kelpie, which was nearly upon him, and Alerice watched in horror as he closed the distance.

"Kreston!" she called as she leveled her bow for another shot.

Kreston came before the monster, which reared and kicked its forehooves. He dodged and thrust his broadsword into the creature's chest. It reeled, but still bit at him, tearing the shoulder of his worn uniform. A crossbow bolt struck its red eye, and it reeled again before rupturing into a blue-gray oozy mass that soaked Kreston's head and shoulders.

He withdrew his blade and wiped his face clear as he turned toward the lake to size up any other targets.

In his Hall of Misted Mirrors, the King of Shadows moved before his crystal-crowned pane. He saw the Raven Queen standing with Oddwyn. Her Eye floated above her willow-white palms. The king smiled and traced the nail of his index finger vertically down the pane.

Standing atop the magenta landscape's light gray stone, Oddwyn and the Raven Queen surveyed the sealed breach. The work would hold.

Oddwyn looked aside to find the two Raven Knights flying in. However, he noticed a little crevasse open in midair near the edge of the starry clusters.

"My Queen?" he said, regarding her to make certain he had her attention, then pointing at the crevasse.

The crevasse tore downward and split in half. Bright green light shone out as it began to pull apart.

The queen's amethyst eyes widened, and she turned fully to the rift, directing her Eye to float before her so that she might draw upon its power.

"Knights!" Oddwyn ordered.

Alerice paced a step down the rise as she leveled her crossbow at another forming kelpie, shooting it before it could fully emerge from its bubble dome. She paced another step and then another as she continued to fire, grateful that her bow reloaded in rapid succession.

She saw Allya begin to blast kelpies with fireballs even as her still-flaming ring scintillated kelpies at the water's edge. Each disappeared in steam plumes that mirrored the basin's flame spouts.

Alerice watched Kreston throw his blade to slay another kelpie, and as its neigh rang out, she looked for another target. Just then a bubble dome appeared before her and a kelpie burst forth, showering her with lake foam.

Alerice tucked her head, and then wiped the water from her eyes and looked up. The kelpie sprang forth and vaulted over her, easily clearing her as Jerome had cleared the Wyld warriors when battling Belmaine. It landed behind her, turned about, and reared.

"Alerice!" Kreston shouted.

Alerice tried to aim her bow, but the kelpie lashed out with its forehooves and kicked her hard in the chest. She flew to the sandy lakeshore, her wind knocked out, and was unable to protect herself from the vicious teeth bearing down.

She caught sight of the kelpie's blazing red eyes as it snatched hold of her and tossed her up onto its back. Then it reared high and neighed wildly before it landed on all fours and bolted for the water.

"Alerice!" she heard both Kreston and Allya cry as she tried to leap down. However, her legs stuck to the kelpie's ribs and her hands stuck to its shoulders. She tugged and struggled, but in moments it had splashed into the lake and dove down.

Alerice barely had time to draw a deep breath as her head went under. She continued to struggle, all the while hearing the kelpie's neigh bubbling about her ears as might a ghost's haunting howls.

She tugged and tugged, but soon she felt dizzy. It became difficult to move, and she began to feel as though she were floating. She looked up at the water's surface, seeing twinkles of sunlight, and possibly hints of Allya's encircling flames, and while she knew she was in the utmost danger, she could not help but become transfixed by the softly enchanting spectacle.

Until a crossbow bolt *whizzed* in and a dark flash burst before her. She felt the kelpie rear under her, and then she felt nothing below her legs. She tried to kick in hopes that she might have the strength to move, but her body began to go limp.

Alerice felt someone grab her arm and yank her upward, dragging her toward the surface as though she were a lump of wet laundry. Before she knew it, her head splashed out from the lake, and she tried to breathe. Then she quickly fell into a violent coughing fit as her lungs did their best to expel the water she had inhaled.

Someone wrapped a strong arm about her and pulled her close. He swam with her to the water's edge, even as the encircling line of flames parted to permit them access to the shore.

Still coughing and unable to gain her bearings, Alerice felt someone sit behind her, his chest pressed against her back to prop her up. Then she saw a man's hands forcing her crossbow into hers.

"Fire it, Alerice," Kreston said over her shoulder. "You're the only one who can load it. Thank the gods you had one bolt ready when the kelpie took you, but you've got to keep shooting."

Still coughing, Alerice managed to comprehend what needed to be done. She leveled her crossbow at the few remaining kelpies. Allya's fire blasts landed on others while she shot, noting how Kreston helped her aim and pull the trigger into the tiller.

As the next few moments flashed past her eyes, Alerice finally saw her black bolt strike the last kelpie, which dissolved into blue-gray ooze that floated like dark scum on the water's foam.

Then the foam sank and the lake became calm. The encircling fire died, and Alerice looked up to see Allya standing tall on her stone outcrop, the scar across the left side of her body glowing brightly.

Alerice felt Kreston pull her close and hold her. She coughed one last time, and relaxed into him. He brought his cheek against her head, and she responded by nuzzling against it. Then she felt him tremble slightly, which caused her to move away.

"Kreston?" she asked softly over her shoulder.

Kreston released her and stood. She looked up at him, seeing his expression of anger and desperation, but also relief. He extended his hand, which she took so that he could help her up to her feet. She wobbled a bit, and he reached out to steady her.

Her crossbow rested on the shore. She bent down to take hold of it and looked it over. Then she noticed Kreston looking her over. Apparently satisfied that she was restored, he held his hand high and his broadsword appeared in his palm. He sheathed it, and Alerice turned to locate Allya.

Then she heard Oddwyn calling, "Alerice! Get down here!"

"Did you hear that?" she asked Kreston.

"Yes," he said, looking about. He pointed to the signature tri-color black, midnight blue, and deep teal of a nascent Realme portal. "There."

"Go!" Allya called in a voice that was again both physical and mental.

Alerice leveled her bow and charged for the portal, Kreston running behind her.

***

In the Evherealme's magenta landscape, seven wyverns circled above the Raven Queen and Oddwyn, churning the starry clusters into wild patterns in the wake of their flight.

Each Raven Knight had engaged a wyvern, slashing with their two-handed blades as the creatures fought back with claws and teeth. The remaining five targeted the Raven Queen.

Using her Eye, she attempted to seal the breach feeding strength to the beasts. Oddwyn glanced over his shoulder at the open Realme portal, but quickly shifted his attention back to a wyvern that had begun a strafing run.

He summoned his iridescent chain and began twirling it. The wyvern drew close and opened its jaws. Oddwyn leaped high and cast the chain, which coiled about the wyvern's mouth and lashed its jaws shut.

It immediately banked hard and beat its wings to gain altitude, drawing up Oddwyn and snapping the chain from his hold, which cast him across the landscape. Able to glide within the Realme, Oddwyn banked hard and shot back for the Raven Queen, sweeping her aside as the wyvern scraped the chain off its jaws with its hind claws.

Oddwyn looked up at the beast's yellow-green eyes, only to see one struck by a black crossbow bolt. The impact's dark glow radiated about the wyvern's head, and it breathed out a misaimed green fire burst as it reeled and careened, dead on the stone.

Oddwyn looked in the direction of the open portal, much relieved to see Alerice standing before it, crossbow aimed for another shot.

"Alerice!" he called, summoning a bladed pixie pole into his hand and raising it in salute.

Alerice raised her hand back at Oddwyn, but as he took up another protective stance before the queen, she glanced over her shoulder and said to an approaching Kreston, "The queen is here. Stay back."

She saw Kreston stop in his tracks and look past her. Then he averted his

172

gaze.

"I'll take care of this," Alerice said as she charged into the fray.

Kreston watched her go, never feeling more impotent in his life. How could Alerice jump into this fight when he stood by and did nothing?

His blood began to boil as he glanced askance at the Raven Queen. He stepped out from the portal, daring to behold what he could of her. As long as he did not look at her damned purple eyes, he could manage this.

Here, now, in the chaos, when the heat of battle caused the most confusion, he had a chance to do his master's bidding, though he hated to. He hated the king for enslaving him. He hated himself for having become enslaved, but he could not stand against the King of Shadows.

But get *her* Eye, and perhaps the king might finally release him. That's why the king had called to him in the previous battle, causing his eye to crimp. "Gain her trust," the king had said, and this he had done, though for reasons that were solely his own.

But now he could use that trust. Implicate Alerice, and the queen might release her. It was his only option, and so he began to stalk Alerice as she shot down another wyvern.

Above, the Raven Knights each slew their beasts and flew to attack others. The final two wyverns circled, looking down at their marks.

Oddwyn saw one targeting him, and he moved away from the Raven Queen to lure it off of her position.

Alerice saw the other gazing down upon her with its steady yellow-green gaze. She raised her crossbow, smiling as she aimed. The bow's string pulled back, a gleaming black bolt appeared in the flight groove, and she fired. The bolt sailed with ease, striking it down.

Alerice leveled her bow upon the final beast. The crossbow self-loaded again and she took aim, but Kreston appeared beside her and snatched the bow from her grasp.

"Kreston," she said, turning about to behold him. "What are you doing?"

Kreston looked down upon Alerice, ice in his veins, and grabbed her tightly. He pulled her close and pressed his brow to hers so that the marks glowing upon their foreheads touched.

"*Do as I say!*" he ordered in her mind, stunning her. "*Admit this was your choice!*"

Alerice trembled helplessly as Kreston placed the bow back in her hands, helped her level it at Oddwyn, and fired. The bolt struck Oddwyn in the shoulder, and he cried out as he fell. Kreston averted the queen's deadly amethyst gaze as she turned toward him, and then threw his broadsword at her with all his might.

He heard her scream. He heard Oddwyn call to her, and then he heard the glassy tinkle of the Queen's Eye falling to the pooled light gray stone.

Kreston bolted for the gem, diving for it and clutching it as he rolled forward into a stance. He turned about and hurled it into the still-open portal. Then he felt, more than heard, a hand catch it.

The King of Shadows appeared within the portal's opening, the Eye in his grasp. He held his free hand forward, and the broadsword he had bequeathed to Kreston appeared in his grip. He gestured it toward his side, and Kreston disappeared from his stance and reappeared to flank him.

The king held up the Eye to examine its inner gray swirl, and then shifted his gaze up at the remaining wyvern. With a surge of his own psychic force, he directed the Eye's energy at the beast. He called down the atmosphere's starry clusters to envelope it. Each luminous glow responded, leaching into the monster's scales and dissolving it midair so that its outline took on the stars' semblance before it joined their swirling cluster.

Oddwyn pulled the bolt from his shoulder, looked at it, and regarded Alerice. Then he looked at the felled queen, and cast the bolt aside as he dove for her, lifting her unconscious body into his arms.

"My Queen," he called as he moved her black hair from her willow-white face. He stroked her cheek, and she nestled against his hand. Oddwyn then presented her maiden self, and as the Raven Queen slowly regained consciousness, Oddwyn looked at Alerice, betrayal in her ice-blue eyes.

"Why?"

Alerice stared numbly at her crossbow. Unable to fathom all that had just transpired, she only knew one response, which she offered in a voice that did not seem to be hers.

"It was my choice."

Alerice watched Oddwyn regard her with a mixture of hurt and disbelief. She looked at the Raven Queen's body slumped in Oddwyn's embrace. Then she looked down at her bow – and suddenly she recalled everything.

Her head snapped up, and she glared at Kreston.

"What did you do?" she demanded.

The King of Shadows stepped forward to loom large. Even though he did not stand close, Alerice still backed a step.

"Go back to the witch," the king said, opening a portal and using the Queen's Eye to shove Alerice through it.

***

Alerice woke in a soft bed, wrapped in the comfort of a plush blanket. She wore only her black shirt and leggings. Glancing aside, she saw her scale mail tunic draped next to her, along with her studded belt.

She gazed overhead to find the interior of a roof's pointed cap. Support beams crossed above, dotted with fairy lights that twinkled in pale red, white, and soft yellow. A magnificent chandelier hung from the central crossbeams, but it bore no candles. Rather, iridescent flares sprang up from each dish to bathe the room in a warm glow.

Alerice smiled and turned to her other side to find Allya seated next to her in a carved armchair decorated with embroidered red upholstery.

"How long have I been here?" she asked.

"A few hours," Allya replied. "It's after nightfall. And you're welcome to stay the night. In truth, I wouldn't mind if you stayed a few days. You're quite a woman, Alerice Linden."

"Mmmm," Alerice commented. "Did the Raven Queen tell you my full name?"

"She did."

"Ah... oh!" Alerice said, sitting up. "The queen. Oddwyn. Allya, there was a fight in the Realme. And... And Kreston! Allya, he used me to attack them."

"Did he," Allya commented. "I didn't think he was that desperate."

Alerice looked at the sorceress. Then she pulled the blanket off and moved over to sit at the bedside.

"What do you mean desperate?" Alerice asked. "Kreston just betrayed me. How could he do that?"

"My dear, the King of Shadows tasked Kreston with capturing the Queen's Eye. I heard him say this when calling for the Shadow Warriors. He cannot disobey the king any more than you can disobey the queen."

Alerice considered her words and realized this was true. Both Kreston and the queen had warned her. Now it had happened, even though she did not wish to believe it.

"He was right to tell me that I could never trust him. I'll never make that mistake again."

"Alerice," Allya said gently. "I don't know if this will help, but for what it's worth, I can tell you that Kreston did not act according to his own desire."

"How do you know?"

"Because Kreston Dühalde is in love with you."

"With me?"

"Oh, yes. Quite deeply, I would say."

"Allya, anyone who loves someone would never betray them."

"Unless he believed he was doing the right thing."

Alerice looked Allya over. "What do you mean?"

"You should have seen Kreston's near-panic when the kelpie took hold of you," she said. "He threw his sword at it, but it dove underwater and he missed. He saw that you had dropped your bow on the shoreline, and he snatched it up as he dove in after you.

"Then when he brought you to the surface and swam with you to the shore, it was all he could do to keep himself from pressing you close. He focused his feelings into action, because that's what military men do. He helped you fight off the last kelpie, and then he shoved his feelings down as far as he could so as not to cling to you.

"You see, Alerice, I know the type of man whom the King of Shadows takes into his service. Kreston is one of those men, and now he may see you as his only hope to live, which is likely why he did what he did."

"Yes, he does see me that way," Alerice said before she drew and released a breath. "What... What sort of man does the king take?"

"All men of fighting stature have heard of the King of Shadows," Allya offered. "He is thought to have the power to defeat a man's enemies, and he bestows this power upon those who prove themselves worthy.

"So what type of man desires the king's power?" Allya continued. "There are two types. The first is a man of ego and ambition. This man craves power for power's sake and will do anything to achieve it. He will endure the physical rigors required in order to gain the king's attention, and will revel in the righteousness of wielding the king's blade."

"And the other?" Alerice asked.

"The other is the broken man who still has the strength to seek revenge. He is a lost soul, likely due to his own bad judgment or sometimes the victim of one bad decision. This is a man who, at heart, wants to right the wrongs he has created. He isn't seeking power for his own sake, but to correct some egregious error. I would place Kreston in this category."

Alerice nodded. "So does the Raven Queen. She told me once that Kreston is a broken man, wounded and confused. I've heard him call to a man named Landrew. I think that was his lieutenant. I think Kreston ordered him to attack a hill.

"Oh, and now that I think about it, when Kreston and I were in Basque, the Reef there noted his uniform and asked if he had been part of the Crimson Brigade. I said that I had heard about the brigade's ghost..."

Alerice's voice trailed as she recalled the sight of Kreston after fighting the Realme's lizard invasion, that of a stone-faced reaper of souls, a man capable of wholesale slaughter.

"Allya," Alerice half-gasped. "You don't think that ghost is Kreston, do you?"

Allya's silence spoke volumes. Alerice pressed her hand to her mouth and said softly into her fingers, "Gods above."

"As I said, the latter," Allya commented. "I believe he seeks to be free, but he's trapped."

"He is. And he wants to escape more than anything."

"Then Kreston may have betrayed you in order to accomplish that goal. But you are still in service to the Raven Queen. You still bear her armor and her weapons, so Kreston's attempt has likely failed."

Alerice began drumming her fingers on her thigh.

"I've got to do something."

Allya smiled. "I admire your courage, Alerice. And your fortitude. I can see why the Raven Queen wished to take you into her service. Do you know why she has not had a champion for so long a time?"

"Why?" Alerice asked, cocking her head slightly to the side.

"Firstly, because Realme Walkers are not born all that often, but mostly because no one seeks the queen looking for power or prestige. She prefers to take someone's measure. That is perhaps the difference between them. The king is impetuous, whereas she is methodical."

"I wish I could knock their heads together and make them both see reason," Alerice said. "I used to do it all the time at the Cup and Quill. I negotiated more arguments than I can recall."

"Yes, I can see that in you."

"But the king and queen are acting like a rival brother and sister, and the only thing children respond to is a strong parent, especially a father."

"I can't imagine what type of father could dominate the King of Shadows and the Raven Queen, Alerice."

"Nor can I..." Alerice said, but her voice trailed off as she began to study the blotches and crinkles of Allya's scarred body.

Allya regarded her line of sight, and then her own body, and she looked up sharply.

"You're not thinking of Sukaar?"

"He's the Father God of Fire."

"Alerice, listen to me," Allya said, leaning in. "You must be an accomplished person of magic for Sukaar to grant you his power, and while you are a natural Walker, you are nowhere near the level he seeks in a devotee."

"But, could it be enough for him to lend me the power to make the king and queen listen?"

"Sukaar does not lend anything. He gives his power to those who are willing to sacrifice to attain it."

Alerice settled herself and said, "Allya, I understand, but I need to be honest with you. This is not about Kreston. This is not about my service to an immortal who is at war with her husband. This is about the Realme.

"The king and queen behave the way they do because they face no consequences. Perhaps if they did, they might reconsider their motives. Does Sukaar have the power to make them listen? Is he wise enough to set them on a better course? The Realme will become more unbalanced as the king and queen argue. In the end, I don't believe that's what either of them want."

Allya sat back and considered everything for a moment. She looked about her bedchamber and gestured for the flames burning in the chandelier to rise up slightly. Eventually, she regarded Alerice, who had not broken eye contact.

"He does have the power," she said. "And he is wise enough, but Alerice, what are you willing to give up in order to have Sukaar do what you ask?"

"Whatever he takes," Alerice said.

***

Alerice stood with Allya in her tower's lower hall. Now that night had fallen, the fire burning atop the altar appeared far more brilliant. Alerice could not deny that she feared what she was about to attempt. However, she had set her mind to this task, come what may, and she trusted that Allya would do her best to intervene if the Father God of Fire became angry enough to wish her dead.

For some reason, she heard the King of Shadows' voice in her head reciting the admonition he had given when they had met.

"Wear your fear openly," he had said. "Show it for all to see. Only by exposing it shall you master it."

Very well. If she trembled a bit, let Sukaar see. Perhaps it was a good sign to show her apprehension and still stand tall. If she could do so in the Evherealme, she could do so now.

"Are you prepared?" Allya asked. "Because once I summon him, there will be a price to pay, no matter what happens, and he will know that you are the one who has requested his presence."

Alerice took a shallow breath, held it for a moment as she closed her eyes, and then exhaled as she set her shoulders and regarded the sorceress.

"I'm prepared."

"Very well."

Allya turned and paced to her altar. The iridescent flame lapped as it burned in the hammered gilt basin. Allya placed her hands into it and held them there as she aligned her spirit with Sukaar's essence. Then she began to chant.

"Sukaar, Father Fire, listen to my voice.

178

Sukaar, Father Fire, you are my love and choice.
Sukaar, Father Fire, come to my domain.
Sukaar, Father Fire, your power I maintain."

Allya repeated the chant, and as she did the flames grew taller. The iridescence gave off an otherworldly light, and Alerice could feel power building inside it. The flames burning in the sconces began to dim as though the altar was drawing in the air which gave them life, and as Alerice focused on Allya, she watched her skin glow in tones of living pearl, much as had Belmaine's. The sorceress' scar came alive with hints of light, again like embers glowing in a pit.

Suddenly, the flames died in the bowl, and as Allya continued to chant, Alerice saw something undulate in their place. She could not be certain at first, for the small mass that coiled and heaved appeared to be liquid gold. Yet as it grew more solid, Alerice saw the unmistakable shape of golden serpent scales.

The coils writhed, growing in girth until they filled the bowl to its rim. Ever expanding, the coils crested the bowl and began cascading over its sides. Alerice saw no head or tail, no fangs or rattles. Only the coils, which, as they grew still larger, took on a fiery quality as though an artist had brushed the golden serpent with tones of pink, pale orange, and ruby.

Then the coils expanded from the bowl, spilled out across the altar, and slumped onto the floor. They grew to the size of tree trunks, and Alerice found herself taking a step back as Allya finished her chanting and stood still.

"Stay where you are," Allya warned. "Let him examine you."

Alerice muscled her way through a nervous gulp and did as Allya instructed.

The coils expanded to her feet and began rubbing against her legs. Their sheer strength threatened to knock Alerice from her stance, but she employed a balance trick that she had learned when carrying heavy trays ladened with tankards – move one foot slightly behind the other and bend the knees. It had worked quite well at the Cup and Quill, and it worked quite well now.

"Allya, my love," a man's voice called from somewhere behind the altar. The coils continued to expand until they were so large that they filled the hall's inner circumference.

"My passionate father," Allya said.

She fell into a deep curtsey so that her front knee touched the floor, and she held the position. She gently reached back toward Alerice and offered a little hand flick to indicate that she should also assume a deferential posture. Alerice offered her customary reverence, but judging the move insufficient, she lowered herself to one knee while arching her back and setting her shoulders.

The serpent's head finally rose from the coils at the altar's opposite side, and

Alerice found herself looking at a spectacle so dazzling that she nearly felt the need to shelter her gaze.

The supernatural viper bore a diamond head and piercing eyes alive with flame. Its coils gave off light, and as with the stone composing Allya's tower, each scale seemed to be created from a fire opal.

Alerice's fear melted into sheer awe. She felt excited, even giddy. She found it nearly impossible to contain the same childlike fascination that she had felt for Allya's home, and she was glad that Kreston was not here to yank the back of her belt to silence her.

"Great God!" she exclaimed. "Father Fire!"

"Alerice," Allya cautioned. "I have not yet presented you."

"Allya, my beloved," Sukaar said as his head rose toward the ceiling timbers. The fairy lights intensified near him. "I am not offended. Introduce us."

Allya stood and offered a head bow. Then she gestured for Alerice to rise and stand abreast of her. Alerice did, unable to feel her own feet as she moved. Indeed, this was all too marvelous.

"Sukaar, Great Father Fire," Allya said. "May I present Alerice Linden of Navre, the Raven Queen's Realme Walker."

Alerice reverenced, for she now felt it appropriate, and waited for Allya to encourage the next move.

Sukaar tilted his head so that he could better examine Alerice. The flame within his eyes burned brightly, and in the next moment Sukaar transformed into a man.

His clothes were ruby velvet and gold, trimmed with black opal and garnet. His long hair was flaming red, though he had drawn his bangs into a woven knot at the back of his head. His eyes danced with the same fire as in his serpentine form, but then changed to a rich black dashed with gold.

He stepped forward toward Allya and reached a palm to her cheek. Heat radiated from his touch. Sukaar brushed his fingertips along her scar's pooled and cracked skin, red wisps floating from his nails as he lightly scratched her.

Alerice could see that Allya found the contact erotic, and watched as the sorceress reacted as any lover would when caught in the spell of her master's will.

Sukaar centered his fingers over the area where Allya's left breast had been, pressed them into her skin, and waited until she gave up a throaty moan of carnal delight. Then he withdrew and regarded Alerice.

"Look at me, pretty thing," he said in a voice so clear that Alerice knew she was his to command. "How do you find me?"

"You..." How Alerice found her voice, she had no idea. "You leave me speechless, sir."

"Clearly not," he said with a grin, at which point small shoots of flame danced about the corners of his lips. Sukaar paused to examine Alerice, and a moment passed before a hint of fire flashed across his black eyes. "A Realme Walker. I can see why my wife, Imari, Mother of Water and Wind, has decreed that you should be honored. You are indeed rare."

Sukaar held Alerice in his sights a moment longer before he turned to Allya. "So, my beloved. Why have you summoned me? Or rather, why did this sweet thing ask you to?"

Allya regarded her god and lover, and then her guest. "Alerice?"

Alerice knew it was her moment to stand up and make her case, but the initial inertia presented quite a barrier.

"Great God--" she began.

"You may address me directly," Sukaar said.

Alerice forced herself to nod sharply. "Sukaar, Father Fire. I ask for your help. As... you see and know," she said, gesturing to her black scale mail, "I serve the Raven Queen, but she and the king have begun to contest one another."

"When don't they?" Sukaar replied.

Alerice was not certain how to respond, and looked at Allya for guidance. However, Allya simply smiled and gestured that she should continue.

Alerice screwed up what courage she could and said, "Father Fire, I wish to settle things between them before they fall victim to their own shortsightedness and cause the Evherealme lasting damage."

"Why?"

"...Sir?"

"Why do you concern yourself with those two? You are mortal. They are everlasting. Do you believe they will heed anything you say?"

Alerice decided it was best to press her case as she had to the Raven Queen about the wizard and the Wyld.

"Sir, I have no idea if I will be successful. In truth, I may likely fail, and I may fail to persuade you to aid me. However, I have made up my mind to try, and I believe that with..."

She wasn't certain if she should continue her present thought, but she could see Sukaar waiting for her words, and so she said, "With the presence of an immortal father behind me, I might make those two see sense."

Sukaar looked Alerice over, then regarded Allya. Allya shrugged her shoulders with an 'It's true' expression, and Sukaar returned his attention to Alerice.

"Have you always been this straightforward?"

"Great God, when it comes to solving problems, I--"

"It was a comment, girl. I can see your entire life as I look at you."

"Of course you can, Father Fire," Alerice said with enough personal fortitude that Sukaar seemed to respect it.

Sukaar drew a step closer to Alerice, his presence taking hold of her as might a lord taking the leash of his hound. "My beloved Allya told you that there would be a price in summoning me, yes?"

"Yes, sir," Alerice said, trembling with a sensation not born of fear.

"Whether I aid you or no?" he asked, drawing closer.

"Um hmm," she managed to say, forbidding herself to move.

Sukaar stepped before Alerice and reached to her blonde hair. Wispy redness floated out from his fingertips, singeing it. She could smell the pungent odor even as he smiled as would a lover about to take a woman to his bed.

"I will aid you, Alerice Linden, Walker of the Evherealme. And the price shall be a kiss."

Sukaar took Alerice by the left side of her neck. His touch torched her hair and burned her skin. Alerice fought back her voice as he drew her close and kissed her cheek.

His power filled her even as his heat assaulted her. His kiss was as passionate as it was painful. Alerice could feel her skin crinkle and blister below his lips, and yet she felt the rush of his power fill her toe to top, enlivening her as she never thought any man could.

***

Souls flew into the Hall of Eternity. The King of Shadows stood within the center of the glyph-inscribed floor, holding the Queen's Eye. He raised his head, closing his dark gray eyes as he commanded the souls fly to him. He ordered them to enter his body, savoring each as he might a delicacy.

He soon reached his fill and stood silently, his grip tightening on the Eye. The souls flitted and circled above. With a sweep of his free hand, he chased them all from the hall so that they flew past the columns and the statues of fighting men and women of arts.

The Raven Queen sat upon her throne, her Raven Knights standing behind her. She stared forward, her amethyst eyes displaying no sign that she was cogent.

The maiden Oddwyn stood nearer to the queen than she might normally. She knew that the queen had deliberately detached herself from the moment, for she always took the measure of souls before placing them. The king's disregard for this process was something the queen could not abide.

Oddwyn glanced past the king's throne to behold Kreston standing at the base of the dais. Her ice-blue eyes narrowed upon him, for he bore sole responsibility for this travesty. He could stand 'eyes forward' all he wished. Oddwyn knew that Kreston was well aware of what he had wrought. Hopefully, it was eating him alive.

The King of Shadows held wide his arms and let out a satisfied exhale. Then he paced up the dais' steps, twirled about so that his long open robe parted and its crystalline trim caught the light, and sat as might a satiated glutton.

He held up the Queen's Eye and gazed into its swirling interior, musing at its mesmerizing nature, then grinned as he glanced aside at the queen. She remained fixated on some distant place. Dissatisfied at her lack of response, the king set his sights on Oddwyn. He offered the herald a kiss, though he made only a slight motion with his lips. The gesture resonated, and Oddwyn nodded her reluctant acceptance.

The king sat back in his throne, his Shadow Warriors behind him. He glanced at Kreston, who, like the queen, was immobile. Annoyed that no one present would grant him the attention he craved, the king began turning the Queen's Eye about in his fingertips. However, then a distortion within the Hall of Eternity caught his attention.

It caught Oddwyn's and Kreston's attention as well, for it was forming into a portal. Yet unlike all Realme portals, which bore the signature tri-colors of black, midnight blue, and deep teal, this one was ringed in crackles of fire.

The Raven Queen regained consciousness as she sat more alert, and all watched the portal widen.

Alerice stepped through. Her unburned blonde hair bore pearl, red, and gold highlights. Her black scale mail was now tinged with gold on each plate, and the left side of her face bore a hideous yet luminescent scar, as if she had been burned.

"Alerice!" Kreston cried as he took a step forward. He began to reach out to her, but he held himself in check.

Alerice stepped forward to the dais. Her eyes were amazingly bright. She reverenced to the Raven Queen, and then turned fully to the King of Shadows.

"Give me the Eye, Your Majesty."

"What did you just say?" the king demanded, rising.

"I'm sorry, Your Majesty," Alerice said with a grin. "I did not realize that you had trouble hearing me." She turned to Oddwyn and asked, "Oddwyn, do you want to shout the response, or should I?"

Though shocked at her manner and appalled at her injury, Oddwyn could not contain a smirk. However, she snapped to attention as the King of Shadows glared at her.

The Raven Queen rose and looked down upon her champion. "You bear his kiss."

"Indeed, she does," Sukaar said as he sauntered forward from the portal, which ignited into a full conflagration as he passed. "For I am here to help her with her task," he said to the king.

Alerice held out her hand. "Your Majesty?"

"I do not take orders from you," the king snapped.

"Of course you don't, you petty ghost," Sukaar said. "But you should, and while you might not listen to her, you both *will* listen to me!"

In a flash of flame, Sukaar transformed into a great golden serpent. His scales shone in opalescent hues that gave off red wisps. His body coiled about the Hall of Eternity, and he drew the dais, its thrones, and their occupants, to him in his coils as his giant diamond head hovered over theirs.

"Get away, Herald," Sukaar ordered Oddwyn.

Oddwyn did not need to be told a second time as she hurried to the side of the hall.

"This is not your domain, Sukaar," the King of Shadows protested.

"Shade, it never ceases to amaze me that you are so willing to state the obvious."

"Then why are you here?" the Raven Queen asked.

"Because of this child," he replied, his gaze bearing down on the Realme's rulers. "Alerice can see what you cannot, that you two have again set yourselves on a course that will only end in your reduction.

"You," he said to the queen. "You created a trinket that gave you too much control over the Evherealme. Your husband was bound to covet it. And you," he said to the king. "You took it like some petty thief. Now give the Eye to Alerice, for if anyone knows what to do with it, she does. She bears my fire, so challenge her at your own risk. She may not be able to stand the test of immortality against you, but she can diminish you."

The King of Shadows held up the Queen's Eye, then glared from under his brow at Sukaar.

Sukaar drew a breath and bellowed fire upon the dark couple. Kreston bolted away for his own safety. Alerice, however, held her ground, for the fire did not injure her.

The king and queen both recoiled at the blast, and then recovered. The king reluctantly held out the Eye, which the queen caused to float into Alerice's grasp.

Alerice smiled as she took the gem. She held it up before the two rulers, and then conjured fire to engulf it, burning it red hot. Its outer crystalline casing cracked, and the gray swirl within began to leach out. Alerice concentrated on the Eye a moment more, and then hurled it against the hall's floor where it shattered into a thousand shards.

Sukaar returned to his mortal guise, his red velvets trimmed in gold alive with power. He beckoned for Alerice to turn to him so that he might touch her scarred cheek.

"Alerice Linden, I give you a choice. Come with me and serve as Allya's devotee, or remain here with these two unworthy specters and serve the Realme. You shall remain a Walker either way, only in my service you shall be more than these two deserve. My wife, Imari, has decreed that Walkers should be prized, but I can see that you..." Sukaar also tilted his head in Kreston's direction. "That you have not been. Not as greatly as you should have been, in any case."

Alerice nuzzled against the god's hand and smiled. Then she withdrew and stood back.

"Father Fire, Great God and Lover, I will stay and serve the Realme. I was born to be its Walker, and I belong in the shadows."

Sukaar nodded, accepting her choice. He then gazed at the king and queen, imposing the full force of his being over them.

"I give you permission to remove my kiss and take her fire, though she is perhaps foolish after all to give it away. However, I will look in upon her from time to time. I will also seal the Evherealme from further breaches. Should anyone attempt to bring more forth..." he said, looking at the King of Shadows, "I will know of it."

The Realme's rulers said nothing as Sukaar turned and created another fiery portal. He strode toward it, not glancing back, and sealed it behind himself as he left.

Alerice watched it dissolve, and then turned to the dais. She took a knee before the king and queen, and looked up into their joined gaze.

The King of Shadows and the Raven Queen descended to her. They reached out together and touched her face. Extending their combined essence, they pressed fingertips against her curdled cheek and drew out all traces of Sukaar's vitality.

Her scar vanished, except for a trail along her jaw, and her blonde hair lost most of its highlights. Her damaged hair grew back to full length, and Alerice closed her eyes as the Realme's cool power filled her.

The king and queen withdrew, ascended the dais, and sat together upon their thrones.

Alerice rose and reverenced to them, sincerity in her deference. Then she glanced at Kreston before addressing the king.

"Your Majesty, I wish to speak with Captain Dühalde. May I have your leave to bring him back into Mortalia?"

The king offered a dismissive wave of his hand. The queen followed by creating a portal in the Hall's center.

Alerice turned to the man she sought. "Kreston?"

He advanced. Alerice joined him, and they walked abreast into the portal.

***

Kreston watched as Alerice skipped a pebble across the little lake below Allya's tower. The stone basin showed no signs of the kelpie battle. The flame spouts fired and spurted. The lush vines dotted with burgundy blooms swayed gently in the breeze.

She bent down to fetch another pebble, but Kreston was quicker to pick one up. He handed it over, and she smiled before she took it and skipped it across the lake.

"One question," he said.

"Only one?" she asked.

"Alerice, I've learned not to ask too many questions when people do things that are clearly insane."

"Is that what I did?"

"Yes. Not only were you free of them, you had power over them. And you gave it up? That is clearly insane."

"But I didn't want the power, Kreston. Sukaar is a demanding master. His life wasn't right for me." Kreston tsked his disapproval, and so Alerice continued with, "So what was your question?"

Kreston paused and then asked, "Why did you show them any respect? The king and queen?"

"Because they deserved it."

"No, they didn't."

"Yes, they did, Kreston. You said it yourself. They are eternal. You and I are merely dots. I'd say that's worth a little respect."

Kreston had no reply. He picked up his own stone and was about to skip it across the water, but he dropped it on the sandy shore.

"Alerice, why did you do it? Why did you maim yourself?"

"It wasn't my first choice," she said.

"No, but it was the choice you pursued. Why sacrifice yourself for them?"

"I didn't do it for them. I did it for the Realme. Perhaps I even did it for myself, just as you used me against the queen for yourself."

Kreston closed his hazel eyes and sighed. "I am so sorry for that, Alerice. I can't tell you how much."

"Kreston, look at me." He did, and she continued. "I forgive you. I understand that you did what you did because you were trying once more to escape. I see

186

now that you are a prisoner, and you are desperate for freedom. I would be too."

He gazed upon her, took her by the shoulders, and brushed back a lock of her blonde hair.

"But, your face, Alerice. Your lovely face."

"I still have it, just with a little scar to remind me. You must have scars to remind you of what you've done."

"Plenty, but I deserved each of them. You didn't. You did not come to the Realme of your own accord. I did. I sought the king's power, and he gave it to me. You? You were innocent."

"Perhaps I was once, but no longer. I'm keeping the armor, Kreston. I'm keeping my place at the Raven Queen's side, but I am not going to rest until I find some way to free you. I don't know why you wanted the king's power, and it honestly doesn't matter. I don't think that you intended to become his slave, and perhaps if you had known this would be your fate, you might not have sought him out.

"The Raven Queen would allow me to leave if I ever grew that discontented with her, but the king is obviously a much harder master, and that's not right. And you know how I set my mind to fixing things that aren't right."

Kreston smirked. His common retort would be self-admonishment. He had sought the King of Shadows because of what had happened to his brigade and his brothers in arms. He had sought to take revenge upon the commander who had betrayed him.

However, as he looked at her, he could not help but think that perhaps, and how, he had no idea, but perhaps she might be able to do what she intended. She might be able to help him find a way out of bondage and to atone for the crimes he had committed.

He pulled her to him, and she did not resist. There was nothing else to do but believe in her. Which made their kiss all the more sweet.

MISTRESS OF HER OWN GAME

MISTRESS OF HER OWN GAME

Tales of the Ravensdaughter

Adventure Five

A rare thing is a Walker,
So, gods below: Take care!
Groom them and protect them.
Do not let them despair.

For when a Walker rises,
Realme glory in their eyes,
Mortalia will breathe softly
As Walkers touch the skies.

from the Scrolls of Imari

A lerice had heard of mead halls, high-vaulted chambers with roughly-hewn beams supporting the wide roofs, and roughly-hewn columns supporting the beams. Two great tables stretched along the hall's sides while roaring pits blazed in the central troughs.

Alerice knew that remote clans constructed such halls as village centerpieces. She had heard of rowdy feasts, and roasting beasts, and flowing tankards. However, she never expected that she would find a mead hall in the Evherealme.

This hall belonged to the Hammer Clan, so called firstly because they bore war hammers, each unique to the warrior who wielded it. So called secondly because they were folk as hard as hammers, both in manner and appearance. Their men broad-shouldered and bearded, their women buxom and braided, Alerice thought their tales were myths conjured by boastful travelers to solicit free drinks. Now, as she supped with the clan's most noteworthy spirits, she could see the substance behind the fables.

Of course, Alerice did not actually sup. She was mortal, and the Realme held no nourishment for her. The roasting joints and foaming brew bolstered the many souls in attendance – and indeed there were many, for the Hammer Clan took pride in offering hospitality.

Alerice sat with the clan elder, Aric. Apparently, he had been quite eager to meet her, not merely because her fame was spreading as the Realme's new Walker, but rather because men of his clan were commonly named Alerick and he wanted to know how her parents had decided upon her name.

Alerice had not been able to answer him, for her parents had never discussed the matter. Nor had Uncle Judd or Grammy Linden, and so any possible connection to the Hammer Clan, no matter how remote, was an historic mystery.

Even so, this small detail did not stop Aric from proclaiming that Alerice was a descendant. The moment he had seen her in armor, with her blonde hair and black scale mail, he had declared that she must somehow be related. Never mind that he was twice her girth and could heft her slim frame single-handedly. He vowed that she was a clanswoman through and through, though Alerice suspected that Aric simply wanted bragging rights.

In truth, she did not mind the manner in which the clan folk pulled her to one side, pushed her to the other, and then slapped her back so hard that she doubled forward. They all meant well. They were a solid people, as roughly-hewn in life as the columns and beams supporting the roof.

Three spits turned of their own accord in the hall's central trough. Coals cooked the meat while movable flat stones regulated the heat. Alerice watched several warriors of varying clans walk to the spits and hack off juicy slices. She noted members of the Wyld, the ashen-and-black painted mercenaries she had met while ridding the traveler's rest of Belmaine, Goddess of Passion and Chaos. They were as noisy and jovial in death as they had been in life, and Alerice smiled to herself, for their queen, T'kyza, would be happy to know of their contentedness.

Alerice also noticed a new clan that called themselves the Painted Women. These were all fearsome females, most of whom had painted themselves indigo and purple. Some had skin the color of rich, brown soil. Some had skin somewhat copperish. All either wore their hair cropped in rows or had no hair at all. Indeed, those who sported bald heads made quite a show of decorating their scalps with white-and-yellow dots that accented their indigo and purple.

Alerice could see from their bodies that each Painted Woman was likely skilled in multiple weapons. She had no idea from which land they hailed, for she had never heard tales of these folk in Navre. Yet how wonderful it was to meet them in this congenial setting.

Alerice glanced at Kreston, who sat two bodies down from her. He pretended to drink as she did, sipping semi-visible brew from semi-tangible tankards. Two Hammer clansmen heartily slapped his shoulders, forcing him to nearly strike his chin against his cup. Then they moved off in the direction of what Alerice considered to be the hall's most striking accoutrement.

This was the great ever-flowing cauldron that floated at the hall's head. To Alerice, it seemed made of solid gold. It had twelve sides, each displaying a clansman's or woman's face amid woven geometric knots. Each knot was dotted with gemstones that winked as they caught the light.

No matter how many guests dipped their mugs, the cauldron never ran dry. Alerice suspected that, as Oddwyn had once stated, these wonders of the Evherealme existed due to the collective consciousness of the mortals whose spirits now inhabited it. The Realme was born of the imagination of the living, men and women, seekers and believers, dreamers and lovers. Indeed, the richness of legends long told had created the splendor inherent within the Realme's very soul.

***

"She called upon Sukaar, Oddwyn," the Raven Queen said as she watched Alerice from her Twilight Grotto. The great tree trunks rooted to the grotto's base gave way to lower and upper branches that stretched toward one another to form six living windows. Less consequential scenes of the Evherealme appeared in five, but the queen's prime pane displayed Alerice in the Hammer Clan's hall.

"She did, indeed, My Queen," the maiden Oddwyn agreed as she beheld the mortal friend whom she had not imagined would have grown so suddenly complicated. Alerice wore the queen's black scale mail. She bore the queen's dagger and crossbow, and yet she had called Sukaar, Father God of Fire, into the Realme so that he could subjugate both the Raven Queen and the King of Shadows. In so doing, Alerice had transitioned from eager servant to problematic ally.

"Sukaar robbed me of my gem, my Eye," the queen stated, her voice of dark honey belying her misgivings. "All because of my husband's covetous desire."

"Yes, My Queen."

The Raven Queen turned from her pane and fixed her amethyst gaze upon her herald.

"So, what am I to do with her?"

Oddwyn moved a lock of her own white hair sparkling with multi-colored light over her ear. "My Queen?"

"I believe you heard me, Oddwyn."

"Indeed I did, but…" Oddwyn shuffled in the awkward moment of wishing to speak her mind, but not daring to.

"You may tell me your thoughts."

"Great Lady Raven, I am honored. I honestly cannot recall the last time you asked for my opinion."

"Yes, this is true. However, I ask it now. Should I allow Alerice to place herself on display like this? Should I allow her to ingratiate herself with spirits of the Realme, especially to those who were bellicose in life?"

"Hmmm," Oddwyn said, softly rubbing her chin. "A good question, but if I may, I don't think Alerice is ingratiating herself. She is growing accomplished. Word of Sukaar's presence has spread far and wide. You simply can't keep something like that hidden. And everyone knows that not only did Alerice cause it to happen, she also willingly relinquished the power Sukaar offered her. I have to say that even I was amazed."

The queen pressed her lips into a deep-red line and gracefully turned back to her pane. "Will this not embolden her to look beyond the Realme? When she next returns to Mortalia, she may call upon other gods above. What will she ask of them? How will it affect the Evherealme?"

"I don't believe there's any way to know this, My Queen. I think we can only judge Alerice by what she has done thus far. She chose to remain in your service. She chose to meld with the Realme. That brings her closer to us." The maiden Oddwyn paused, then added, "Do you wish to know what the sorceress Allya told me?"

"Yes, Herald."

"Allya said that as she and Alerice and Kreston prepared to battle the breach of energy you sent them, Alerice was nearly able to create her own portal. Walkers cannot do that."

The Raven Queen neither moved nor responded as she beheld Alerice happily drinking and playing push-pull games with the warrior spirits who dwarfed her.

"Remember how loudly her voice rang out when she called her readiness to us?" Oddwyn continued. "She's unlocking talents that, personally, I did not know she had. It seems to me that the choice is simple. Allow her to leave your service now, and possibly offer Kreston's freedom in the bargain, or nurture her and inspire her and keep her close to you."

"Hmmm," the queen voiced before she lifted her willow-white face. "My husband noted Alerice's pridefulness when he first examined her. What if she grows prideful enough to challenge the Realme?"

"I don't think she will, My Queen. Not unless she feels she's forced to. It's not in her nature. When we all first met Alerice, she stated that she was modest, and I think she has demonstrated this quality several times. She may be prideful, and she's certainly willful, but she is not ambitious. I think she prefers to serve. She just prefers to serve causes that she feels are honest."

The queen said nothing further as she continued to observe her celebrated Walker.

***

"She called upon Sukaar," the King of Shadows complained as he stood within his Hall of Misted Mirrors. Twelve panes of varying sizes and shapes hovered about him, borne upright by smokey tendrils. All were inert, save for his favorite, a pane encrusted with the same crystalline trim that ran along the edges of his long open robe, and topped by the same crystals that formed his crown. "I wonder what our 'honey herald' is saying to the queen about it right now," the king added.

Behind the king floated a specter he had released from the barred pit nearby. This ghost had been a coarse man in life, raw and haggard and suited for ill deeds. Now, he was a mute thing, unable to comment, for he was barely able to comprehend.

The king raised his hand and shocked the spirit, forcing it to contort. The king shocked it a second time, and the spirit shrank in agony. Then the king bade it to regain its composure and stand ready. He would require it, and others like it, in the coming moments. Fortunately, given the manner in which he had briefly wielded his wife's gem, the Queen's Eye, his barred pit of souls was stocked to bursting.

The king focused his pane on the mead hall. The girl was jesting, and walloping, and clanking tankards. And what was his own champion doing? Sitting hemmed in by clansman looking cowed and foolish. Kreston Dühalde spoke little. He made little eye contact. He was allowing himself to be passed over when he should be standing up and outshining that doe-ish blonde child.

"This is humiliating," the king said. "He's languishing when he was once feared. He was such an excellent slayer. Once I brought him to heel, he strode the Realme even as he strode the battlefield. Spirits fled from him here just as mortals did above. But place a girl in his path, and he's ruined. No soul will fear him after this gathering. No soul has feared him since my wife locked his mind away."

The king turned to the spirit and was about to shock it until it ruptured, but instead he chose to banish the bars from the pit and bring forth the strongest spirits. They flew out, and he commanded them to retreat behind his mirrors, which they did, obscured by the many smokey tendrils.

The king turned his head back to his prime pane before turning his shoulders to face it.

"I need my captain back the way he was, burning with red-hot war. I need his wits restored. Otherwise, he's useless." The king shifted his mirror back to Alerice, even as his dark gray eyes came alive with a gambit.

"She wants to be the Raven Queen's Walker? Then perhaps she should learn what that truly entails."

The king turned back to his hall's interior, and with a summoning wave, he commanded all souls to appear before him. Extending both hands, he jarred and shocked them until they began to contort. The souls wailed their misery, but then they roared with vitality as the king transformed them into clawed shadow beasts. Some bore fangs, wings, and human torsos. Some bore elongated arms and animal hindquarters. The winged ones stretched their leathery flaps and screeched as they raised their clawed hands in hungry grasps. The animalistic ones sat upon their haunches while resting their great hands flat before them.

The king gestured to the mirror adjacent to his prime pane and conjured the sight of an abbey situated within a verdant vale surrounded by boulder-studded hills. He conjured a portal of black, midnight blue, and deep teal to open along the mirror's surface. Then, with a few quick waves, he commanded his shadow beasts evaporate in smokey wisps, which he thrust into the portal.

***

One of the Painted Women, Pa'oula, who sported purple spirals upon her brown skin, and one of the Hammer clanswomen, Frayla, who wore her hair in long red braids, grabbed Alerice's arms and yanked her from her seat. Aric and his nearby clansmen shouted happily, and pounded the table as the two dragged Alerice toward the great ever-flowing cauldron.

Kreston looked up from his mug, concern for Alerice's well-being clearly on his face, but the clansman beside him knowingly threw an elbow into his ribs, causing him to lose hold of his drink. Kreston glanced at the clansman, annoyed, but then focused on Alerice.

Half the gathering began to chant:
"Drink it down, we all do!
We all know it's Realme Brew!"

One clansman stood to say:
"I'll tell you of a drink that's true!
What's it called?"

The gathering responded with a resounding:
"Realme Brew!"

A Painted Woman stood to say:
"With hearty head and golden hue!
What's it called?"

"Realme Brew!" the gathering responded.

A Wyld who looked very much like the mute, Wisp, but who, in the Evherealme, was anything but mute rose to say:
"A drink that makes you rise anew!
What's it called?"

"Realme Brew!" all shouted.

Pa'oula moved Alerice before the cauldron, shoved a mug into her grasp, and gestured for her to dip and fill.

"Go on, give us a line," she said, her copper-brown eyes dancing in the mead hall's firelight.

Alerice wasn't certain what to say, but this was hardly the first time she had been invited to join an improvisational drinking game. She dipped her mug and then held it high. The foam slid down the side of her mug's metal belly. She smiled at it, almost thinking she could smell it. Then she looked at the sea of expectant faces.

"A drink that fills you, through and through,
A drink that's worth a ballyhoo,
A drink I never shall eschew!
What's it called?"

"Realme brew!" all shouted, elongating the last vowel in triumphant conclusion.

"Not bad, Walker!" Aric shouted. "A tad wordy, but not bad!"

His clansmen laughed before they drank.

Alerice glanced at Pa'oula and Frayla, who were gulping down their mugs. Though she knew it was a wholly symbolic gesture, Alerice brought her tankard to her lips, and took a deep draught.

Then she startled. She froze in place, and held the mug before her astonished eyes. She licked her lips, unbelieving because... she could actually taste the drink.

"Oh, come," Frayla said. "You must like it, right?"

"...I do," Alerice said. To check her senses, she drank again. The brew was sweet with a soft alcoholic tang. Its bubbles tickled up through her nose and into her brain. She felt the liquid slide down her throat and instantly warm her stomach.

She had no idea what was happening, for she had been pretending to sip from the several mugs the clan's folk had been placing before her, but this time the brew nourished her.

"Then why do you pause?" Pa'oula asked.

"Because, I can actually taste it."

Pa'oula slapped Alerice on the back, making her double slightly. She tried not to spill her mug as she regained her balance, but Pa'oula paid her no heed as she raised her cup to the gathering.

"You hear that?" she proclaimed. "The Walker can taste the brew!"

Every person in the mead hall roared with pleasure, many rising to toast Alerice while others pounded the long tables and chanted, "Wal-ker, Wal-ker, Wal-ker!"

Alerice made her excuse to Pa'oula and Frayla, and sidled back over to Aric. She resumed her seat next to him, and leaned in for a private aside, which he was happy to indulge.

"What just happened?" she asked.

"You tasted the brew," he said in a fatherly tone. "That means you are becoming one with the Realme, more so than you have ever been. Your spirit and your flesh are taking root here, and you will never be the same."

Alerice stared into his big blue eyes, not certain if this was a natural step for her to make. Could becoming rooted to the Realme portend danger to her mortal self? She had arrived at an unexpected crossroads and taken an inevitable step.

Alerice noticed Kreston staring at her. His expression was one of solemn comprehension, for he could obviously read her concern. His hazel eyes fixed on her, and he leaned in slightly as though he wished to reach out to her. She wanted to pull him aside and ask his counsel, but the sudden sound of disembodied, bloodcurdling screeches rang out in the mead hall, silencing everyone.

"Alerice!" the Raven Queen called, her voice echoing across the hall's towering ceiling.

Alerice saw Kreston recoil, and she quickly stood and raised her mug so that everyone looked at her.

"The Raven Queen!" she shouted in salute.

"The Raven Queen!" the gathering responded.

The air behind the great ever-flowing cauldron began to churn in a spiral of black, midnight blue, and deep teal. Alerice threw a leg over the long table's bench seat and hurried toward the hall's head.

"I'm here, My Queen," she called as she approached the forming portal.

"Alerice," the queen's voice rang out once more. "Hurry to my abbey. Protect my devotees."

Alerice stood before the portal, which did not seem to be opening quickly enough. Through its widening aperture, she could hear more screeches accented by grunts and growls. She heard cries and screams, and she knew that whatever awaited her was a scene of attack, perhaps even a massacre.

Alerice closed her eyes and centered within herself. As when anticipating the fight at the sorceress Allya's lakeside, she focused wholly on the Raven Queen's mark imprinted upon her brow. She felt it pulse, and judged by the comments from the clan's folk that it glowed quite brightly.

She also felt a warm pulse on her jaw along the remnants of Sukaar's fiery scar. She imagined it glowed like embers, as did Allya's great burn, but inured to the mutters about her, Alerice focused all the stronger on opening the portal.

She knew that she affected its expansion, for she felt a shift in its pressure. She raised a hand to the portal, and felt it swirl at her direction. Her other hand floated out to her side and inadvertently touched the rim of the great, golden cauldron.

Alerice felt a shock as she forged an unintended connection between the Realme and Mortalia. However, she had no time to discover what she had created as she opened her eyes to see the interior of a stone abbey on the other end of the wide portal. People ran about in wild panic as strange beasts, some winged and some on all fours, clawed and bit at them.

Alerice drew the Realme crossbow from her belt strap and aimed. The string pulled back of its own accord, and a gleaming black bolt appeared in the flight groove. She fired into the portal, striking one beast about to alight on a woman wearing black velvet robes. Then the bow reloaded as she charged forward.

"Now that's a Walker!" Aric exclaimed as Alerice hurried into battle. His kindred spirits agreed, but then they all regarded the still-seated Kreston.

Kreston saw all eyes on him. He suppressed a shudder at the latent sound of *her* voice echoing in his mind, and then pulled on a military visage as he stood.

Aric looked back at the still-open portal, and then once more at Kreston.

Kreston followed the Hammer clansman's line of sight, and then arched his shoulders as he stared into the man's eyes.

"It's the queen's business," Kreston stated. "I'm the king's man."

One of the Hammer men smirked, and then offered, "You were the king's man."

Kreston noted the chuckles that the comment solicited. He bit hard on his back teeth, summoning ice into his veins, and for the briefest flash he became what he once had been, that which he now loathed, the Ghost of the Crimson Brigade.

He stared at one accusatory face after another, a snarl crawling onto his lips. Then, he summoned the scratched brand of the King of Shadows to glow upon his brow as he drew his broadsword.

"Damn you all," he said as he turned and charged for the portal.

***

Alerice reached down to grab the woman in the black velvet robes. She yanked her to her feet, and struck a defensive pose before her as she leveled her crossbow and fired at one of the animalistic shadow beasts. The bolt sailed into the creature's heart and impacted with a dark glow that enveloped its body, returned its countenance to a simple spirit, and dissolved it in midair.

"So, that's what these things are," she said as she sized up the situation.

Alerice stood in a stone abbey where light spilled in from tall windows. She had never seen such a place as this, and though she faced attacking beasts, she could not help but notice the great vaulted ceiling supported by fluted wall columns that split apart into arches. Flat medallions secured each of the arches' juncture points, and the glyphs set into those medallions bore the same mark as the one upon Alerice's brow – a thin oval with a pointed bottom tip capped with a dot, and set on each side with S-curves that fanned out as might a bird's wings.

Resting in the abbey's nave was a two-man-tall statue of the Raven Queen. Its stone bore the same silver veins as the filigree arches in the Evherealme's Convergence. Her likeness was quite true, though Alerice doubted that the sculptors who had crafted it had ever been to the Realme.

But Alerice had no time to admire the craftsmanship, for the abbey was under attack by otherworldly beasts that could turn themselves into smokey wisps and then suddenly reappear in a different location. Recalling how the King of Shadows had sent Vygar and his band of ghoulish thugs to slaughter Lolladoe and the faun clan, Alerice did not hesitate to shoot the beasts as quickly as her crossbow could load.

"You're her, aren't you," the woman commented from Alerice's left.

"Who?" Alerice said as she shot a winged beast in the chest, dissolving its spirit with the dark glow of the bolt's impact.

"The Great Lady's Walker, her Ravensdaughter."

Alerice gave the woman a moment of her attention. Not only did she wear black velvet robes, she clutched a medallion made of the same silver as the Raven Queen's crown. The glyph cast into it was the same as on Alerice's brow.

This woman must be the abbey's priestess, and Alerice nodded to her as she continued to fire, sparing any devotees from the shadow beasts' fangs.

In the mead hall, souls had gathered near the ever-flowing cauldron, for in touching its golden rim, Alerice had inadvertently joined the cauldron with the portal, allowing the great vessel to retain access to Mortalia and display the abbey battle.

The gathering cheered at each shot Alerice landed, some taking bets as to which shadow beast she would slay next.

Kreston hurried in from the portal. He assessed the plight of mortals fleeing claw and bite, but then he accidentally gazed upon the statue of the Raven Queen. He froze, for the stone bore such a perfect likeness to *her* that he heard the sounds of the hilltop charge where he had lost his lieutenant, Landrew Mülton.

Kreston heard the screams of his brothers in arms whom he had ordered to take a hill that in retrospect could never have been taken. He saw Landrew splayed out upon the field, and was prepared to dive for him and cradle his corpse. If only he had not obeyed the marshal's order to commit the Crimson Brigade to charge that day.

He was about to lose his wits. He was about to go mad. He was going to lose his hold on the moment if he stared at her one heartbeat longer, and so he punched himself across the jaw to break eye contact, and did his utmost not to cower as he lunged for the nearest being, mortal or beast, and began cleaving into it.

Fortunately, he heard only roars and grunts, and he gave thanks to the gods above that his victim has been a beast, not a hapless devotee.

In her Twilight Grotto, the Raven Queen stood stoically as she watched Alerice confront the invasion of one of her most sacred spaces.

Graystone Abbey was a place the Raven Queen held dear. The verdant vale that cradled it rested atop a secret conduit to the Evherealme. She had only to extend her spirit toward Mortalia, and she could touch the thoughts of her devotees. Men and women came to die in the abbey, attended by the Black Mother, as the lady in velvet was known.

The Mother would see to their passing in peace, and assure them that the Raven Queen herself would take their measure and guide them to their places of eternity. To die within Graystone's walls was considered such an honor that towns would pay to transport their most wise and revered. The Black Mother did not acquiesce to admitting the rich and powerful simply for their status, for neither attribute counted among a person's merits or defaults.

Only the wealth of a person's heart mattered, and knowing this the Raven Queen would – upon occasion – appear behind the Black Mother as she tended to a person about to give up their last breath. The queen herself would measure a soul prior to entering the Realme, and in so doing, she had gleaned the spirits required to form her gem, the Queen's Eye.

Now the abbey was in chaos, and the Raven Queen knew well the reason. The King of Shadows had chosen to assault her cherished place. He had chosen to assault her Realme Walker, and everything that Alerice – her champion – represented.

The maiden Oddwyn still stood beside the queen, watching Alerice shoot down more beasts. Then she beheld a struggling Kreston Dühalde, and knew the reason for his anguish.

"He should not be there," Oddwyn said. "As long as he's compromised, he's a distraction."

The Raven Queen did not respond as she watched her Black Mother hurry devotees to the safety of the abbey's private prayer rooms.

In his Hall of Misted Mirrors, the King of Shadows watched the fight from his crystal-topped pane. He discounted the girl, for she would dispatch his shadow beasts in due course.

Rather, his mark was his own man, and Kreston was already in such turmoil that cracking his mind apart would be a simple matter. The king stroked the thin beard that ran along his jaw, and then transformed his face into the Raven Queen's. His crown of dark crystals became hers of bright silver metal, and his dark gray eyes became hers of amethyst.

He turned to one of his inert mirrors and gazed upon himself, causing his torso to haze over with some of the same smokey tendrils that bore up his twelve panes. As they wrapped about him, he saw only his wife's visage, and once he was satisfied with the guise, he turned back to his prime pane and placed his hand upon the surface.

Alerice moved closer to Kreston. As with the demon toad in the river valley before meeting the Wyld, she stood so that they could fight back-to-back. As she had then, she could feel him enjoying the joined combat.

She could sense him becoming himself again, a man who savored a good fight. He seemed happy to guard a comrade's shoulder, while knowing that a comrade likewise guarded his.

Until the Raven Queen's voice rang out from the lifeless statue. "Captain Kreston Dühalde!"

Kreston froze in his tracks, his head snapping toward the statue. Alerice saw the statue's face come alive with the queen's countenance, her amethyst eyes bearing down upon them both.

Kreston screamed and fell to the abbey's cut stone floor just as two shadow beasts attacked from either side, a winged one swooping in to land before Alerice and an animalistic one vaulting forward to attack Kreston.

Alerice only had one shot, and she leveled her crossbow to protect her comrade. Her gleaming black bolt impacted upon the shadow beast mid-vault, and its dark glow dissolved the creature in midair. Then, the winged beast struck Alerice with enough force to send her flying across the abbey and land hard against one of the fluted columns.

In the mead hall, the gathered souls exclaimed a collective, "Whoa!"

Some were about to demand payment of bets, but Aric advanced and *clanged* his hammer against the cauldron. A deep tone rang out, perpetuating as the cauldron reverberated. Knowing this was no longer a gaming matter, but one of life and death, he *clanged* his hammer against the cauldron again to silence it, destroying the latent portal.

He then turned to his kinfolk and guests.

"We will witness this no longer. The gods above will decide their fate."

In her Twilight Grotto, the Raven Queen cast her hand toward Oddwyn, causing the silver scale mail tunic to appear on her torso.

Oddwyn wasted no time in conjuring and activating her two pixie poles, the blades of which popped out as the queen cast a portal in one of her tree branch-outlined windows. The abbey appeared in a flash of black, midnight blue, and deep teal, and Oddwyn leaped through toward Alerice.

In his Hall of Misted Mirrors, the King of Shadows reclaimed his proper visage and watched for one final moment as the war maiden Oddwyn hurried to his wife's girl of a champion. Then he banished all sights from his mirrors, for he needed to see nothing further.

In the abbey, Oddwyn laid into a few shadow beasts, slaying them with lightning precision. Then she shot for Alerice's side, lifting her into an embrace.

Oddwyn watched Alerice regain consciousness, then wince and reach to the back of her head. Then she saw Alerice's eyes go wide as she looked past Oddwyn's shoulder, and Oddwyn turned to find the same winged beast that had struck Alerice looming large.

From the corner of her eyes, she saw Alerice reach for her Realme dagger and cast it into the beast's heart. Then Alerice stood up from her hold, and though she teetered a bit, she held up her hand so that the dagger reappeared in her palm.

Oddwyn also stood and looked about for any further danger, but the abbey fell silent and secure. Oddwyn nodded to Alerice, but then watched her eyes roll slightly. Oddwyn quickly slung Alerice's arm about her shoulder even as the Black Mother and the Raven Queen's devotees began to advance.

Oddwyn knew this moment would end in a mass of groveling, awestruck mortals if they did not leave immediately. She held Alerice close and moved to one of the abbey's many windows. A portal was already forming, and Oddwyn guided Alerice toward it.

However, as she prepared to leave, she noticed Kreston recovering his wits and standing up.

Oddwyn's ice-blue eyes narrowed, and she mentally ordered, *"Stay away from her, you useless wretch."*

She watched Kreston's shoulders fall and felt his heart sink, but neither mattered as she stepped through the portal with Alerice, heading for the safety of the Realme.

***

"How's your head?" the maiden Oddwyn asked.

"It still hurts, but I'm feeling better," Alerice said as she relaxed against what she would normally describe as a soft mossy rise were she in Mortalia. The 'sky' above swirled in tones of the same deep teal that composed a portal, only currents of lighter blues gave it a daylight hue.

Columns of the Realme's silver-veined stone rose about, each set independently about the mossy rise to form a circle. Black glyphs, the same color as the bolts that loaded into her crossbow, ran down the columns, but what Alerice found the most intriguing were the cascades of silvery glimmers flowing out from the top of each, creating sparkling miniature waterfalls.

The overall area was not vast, and Alerice could see that the 'nothingness' of the Realme surrounded more mossy rises so that the green faded away into the surrounding teal and lighter blues. Fortunately, she did not feel like going anywhere at the moment, though her mind buzzed with questions.

"We don't have healers or doctors down here," Oddwyn said in her gentle voice. "We have their spirits, though, and many have crafted this place of peace over the eons. It's a place for you to recover."

"Thank you," Alerice said, drumming her fingers on her black shirt, for Oddwyn had helped her out of her scale mail tunic so that she could rest more comfortably.

Alerice lolled her head to the side to regard Oddwyn more clearly, then she rolled onto her hip as she prepared to rise. Dizziness struck her, though, and she planted a hand on the moss to steady herself as Oddwyn came closer to help.

"Perhaps you should lie back for a while longer."

"No, I need to sit up," Alerice said, accepting Oddwyn's hand to scoot backward on her buttocks and gain her balance on the rise. She then looked Oddwyn over.

"May I please ask a favor?"

"Of course," Oddwyn replied.

"Please don't take this as any type of a personal comment, but may I please chat with your youthful self? It's not that I don't enjoy you as a Realme sister, but I miss my cousin Jerome right now, and I would find a gentleman's presence a bit more comforting. Plus, you do offer different advice between your male and female sides, and--"

Alerice stopped short, for Oddwyn had already presented his youthful appearance.

"Better?" he asked.

Alerice placed her hand on his and softly said, "Thank you." She drew and released a breath, and then went straight to her point. "Oddwyn, why did the queen call out to Kreston in the abbey?"

"She didn't, Alerice. I was standing next to her the entire time."

"But someone did. Her statue came alive and called, 'Captain Kreston Dühalde'. If the queen didn't do it, who did?"

"I don't know. Perhaps the king?" Oddwyn suggested with a shrug.

Alerice's brow furrowed. "He can assume his wife's guise and invade one of her sacred places?"

"Well, he can present himself anywhere in Mortalia, just as the queen can, and as far as him using her guise, I don't see any reason why he couldn't."

Alerice began to drum her fingers on the moss. "So the king did that to Kreston deliberately. He attacked the abbey, knowing that the queen would send me there, and knowing Kreston was with me in the mead hall. I mean, if the queen knew I was there, the king must have known Kreston was there, right?"

"Probably."

"Then why torture Kreston like that? Is the king angry with him? Or is this how it's always been, which is why Kreston wants so desperately to be free of the king's service?"

"I wish I could help you, Alerice. I truly do, but I have no idea why the King of Shadows does anything."

Alerice continued drumming her fingers as she focused on a column and its sparkling flow. Then she looked into Oddwyn's ice-blue eyes.

"Actually, there is something you can do to help me. I need to know what the queen did to Kreston. I don't wish to confront her about it the way I did about the wizard and the Wyld. I am comfortable serving her, and my soul is becoming more tethered to the Realme. I can feel it, and I don't want any discord with her.

"But I cannot sit by while Kreston suffers, and I'm not going to ask him what happened. I doubt he wants to speak to me right now, and he's probably feeling so lost that if he could end his own life, he would."

"The king won't allow him to do that, and even if he asked someone to kill him, the king would only restore him."

"Well, I heard you call him a useless wretch, and that wounded him deeply. I saw it." She shook her head and looked toward the brilliant sky. "Oh, Oddwyn. That poor man is utterly devastated, and as much as I care for the Realme, I care for him as well. Please, tell me what happened."

Oddwyn sighed. "Alerice, this is not a nice story."

"Life rarely is," she said. "Life has nice moments, and if a person is lucky, life has more merits than defaults. But I know Kreston's life has been difficult. I just need to know how bad it had to be for the queen to lock up his mind."

Oddwyn blew out through pursed lips before he said, "Kreston Dühalde was captain of the Crimson Brigade of King Kemen of Andelous. He had joined the army when he was ten, and rose through the ranks from runner boy to officer. He was a good leader. He took good care of his men. The Crimson Brigade gained a reputation as a fearsome regiment, and Kemen used that to his advantage. Sometimes, all he had to do was threaten to unleash the Crimsons, and his foes would negotiate rather than go to war."

"But something must have happened," Alerice said. "When Kreston and I were in Basque, the Reef there mentioned that things had gone badly. In Navre, I heard of the Crimson Brigade's ghost, and Allya all but said that the ghost was Kreston."

"Yes, he was," Oddwyn said, "and he'd still be that ghost if he could think straight. That's the reason the Raven Queen scattered his thoughts. Kreston had become a butcher, and one time it went too far.

"You see, the Crimson Brigade was betrayed. Their own marshal ordered Kreston to take a hill on a particularly rough campaign, and then denied him support. The brigade fell, and only a few men survived. Kreston discovered the marshal's plot to undermine the king by sacrificing the men, and he sought the King of Shadows for revenge."

"When you first presented me to the king and queen," Alerice said, "the king offered me the power to defeat any enemy. He must have offered Kreston the same."

"Oh, he did, and Kreston took it," Oddwyn said. "Like you, he didn't know he was a natural-born Walker. You people don't come along all that often, and when the king first saw Kreston, he offered him everything he wanted. Kreston killed the marshal and the rival lords who had put the marshal up to betraying the brigade.

"But then, what was there to do? Kreston had no more enemies, and the King of Shadows hardly wanted a 'champion avenger', which is how the queen sees you. The king wanted souls, and so he started sending Kreston into any type of battle, be it a small skirmish or a full-out charge.

"Kreston needn't have feared dying, for – as I said – the king always had me bring him back to the Realme for restoration. I did it several times. Just as soon as his soul entered the Convergence, the king would protect it while I fetched his body. The king would meld the two, and I would be there when Kreston regained consciousness. He sat where you're sitting now, we talked about what he was doing. He had a conscience back then."

"But over time, that conscience faded?"

"No, it was shattered. In one battle, Kreston found a wounded captain cradling a dead lieutenant, and it triggered the memory of his own lieutenant. He wanted to spare the captain, but the King of Shadows ordered his death. Kreston was forced to obey, and then he went wild. He slaughtered anyone nearby, and then a runner boy attracted his attention. He stalked the child and killed him. Then he murdered the rest of the boys, and after that he attacked the nurses.

"But some of the nurses were devotees of the Raven Queen. Some hailed from Graystone Abbey. They prayed to her, and she came aloft from the Realme to stop Kreston's butchery. Kreston fell to her feet and begged forgiveness. She granted it by affecting his mind so that he could no longer commit wholesale murder."

"That poor man," Alerice breathed as she closed her eyes and lifted her head in thought. She placed one hand on the moss for balance, and allowed the visuals of Oddwyn's story to filter through her mind. Everything about Kreston Dühalde now made perfect sense, and of all the wrongs she had encountered since the night Gotthard had raped her and killed Cousin Jerome, this was the worst she could imagine.

"No wonder he's so desperate for freedom," Alerice said.

"No wonder," Oddwyn said, returning to her maiden form.

Alerice opened her eyes and glanced at her, then nodded and folded her legs as she sat up.

"You must know that I want to help him, Oddwyn."

Oddwyn smirked. "Of course I do. This is *you* we're talking about."

"But this isn't going to be simple. Helping Kreston means I need to outmaneuver the king, and while I've solved many a problem at the Cup and Quill, I've never attempted anything like this before."

"Alerice," Oddwyn said, presenting his youthful self once again. "You really might want to reconsider what you think you can accomplish."

"See?" Alerice said smiling. "I told you that you had different types of advice to offer between your male and female sides. The little colors in your hair even glow differently."

Oddwyn glanced side to side at the bursts of color that naturally appeared in his white hair.

"Be that as it may," he said. "The queen will not allow you to confront the king. I can tell you that for certain."

"Confront how? Am I not allowed to speak with him?"

"No, you are allowed to do that, though she won't like it, and she'll know that's what you mean to do before you have a chance to ask her permission, which means she'll forbid it before you can bring the topic up."

"Well in that case," Alerice said, climbing to her feet. She felt steady and her wits were sound. Her judgment might be a different matter, but physically she was capable of doing what she fully intended to do. "In that case, you had best take me to the king now."

Oddwyn drew a breath to object as he looked up at her, but she silenced him with a clear, and yet controlled, "Now, please, Oddwyn."

***

Alerice found herself in a field she had seen when standing beside the Raven Queen in her Twilight Grotto. It was covered with small blooms that glowed in rhythmic patterns. Alerice had thought it lovely when gazing upon it through one of the queen's tree branch windows. Now that she was here, the sight of flowers dancing before her, as might birds shifting to and fro in midflight, nearly took her breath away.

Indeed, Alerice would have loved to take her leisure in this wondrous place, were not the King of Shadows standing a few paces off, his back to her.

Oddwyn stood next to Alerice, his posture rigidly formal. He gestured his ice-blue eyes toward the king as if to say, "There he is," and Alerice gleaned that he would have offered a palm in the king's direction if he felt it was appropriate.

Though still quite new to the Evherealme, Alerice found it interesting that Oddwyn was herald to both the king and queen, yet he, and she, clearly preferred the latter over the former. Alerice had declared her preference more boldly, and was proud of it. The king had noted her pride when he had first looked upon her. However, it was a pride that she would never give to him.

Alerice stepped across the blooms, their glows fleeing from her boots as she stepped. She approached the king and reverenced by placing one leg back and lowering her weight slightly upon it while keeping her torso straight. She did not wait to be addressed as she regained her stance, head up and one hand resting on her dagger.

"You should have accepted my sword," the king said, unmoving.

"Your Majesty," Alerice replied.

The king humphed a small laugh. "You wish to speak about Dühalde."

"I do, Your Majesty," Alerice said. "The man who currently bears your sword."

The king seemed to draw and release a breath as he turned to regard Alerice. She studied his calculating dark gray eyes and noted the tension along his jawline. His crown of dark crystals reflected hints of the glowing blooms, as did the crystals adorning his pauldrons and the crystalline trim about his long robe.

"You want me to free him," the king said.

"I want to know what you want of him, Your Majesty," Alerice countered.

"To serve me, girl. What else do you think?"

"But what manner of service, sir?" she asked. "Kreston wishes to be free of you. I don't know if he tried to escape before the Raven Queen took me as her own, but he has certainly tried since. Why do you want to retain someone who hates being tethered to you?"

"Because he's the best at what he does."

"Because he's a born Walker, as I am? Funny that you offered me your blade when you already had someone who knew the shadows."

The king looked Alerice up and down. "You're better. Dühalde is a man of action and experience, but your birth is truer to the Realme. That's why you're becoming part of it. Soon, you'll not be able to leave us, even if you wished to. Soon, you'll be as tethered to it as Dühalde is to me."

Alerice knew this was true, and while it might normally have concerned her, now was not the time to ponder such things.

"I told you to wear your fear openly," the king said, reading her thoughts. "Only then will you master it. It seems you have begun to learn how. My wife's black scales suit you."

"Thank you, Your Majesty," Alerice said, moving her torso slightly aside so that the glowing blooms reflected off her scale mail tunic. Then she leveled a stare and said, "Why do you keep Kreston as a prisoner? He may be the best at what he does, but he no longer wishes to do it. It seems to me that you'd be better served by a mortal who enjoys killing, someone who's a natural butcher rather than someone who's forced to be one."

"A Realme Walker is an asset I do not wish to give up," the king said. "I may be required to force his participation, but he knows better than to resist. He's done so before, and he'll not likely do so again."

Alerice could not help but shake her head. "So he has tried to escape. And still you enslave him. What a cruel thing you are."

"You think my wife is any better?"

"From what I've seen of her, yes."

"Then you have trials ahead of you."

Alerice lifted her chin a bit higher. "Perhaps, but as I told Kreston, the queen released me once rather than argue with me. Then she took me back, and I accepted. And as I said when Sukaar offered me his choice, I wish to remain with the Realme. I have always been a part of it, though I never understood why until I came here.

"But above all, I hate to see people ill-used. Kreston can no longer slaughter in your name. The Raven Queen will not allow it, and I would never do it, so two Walkers are before you and neither are of any use to you."

A moment hung between the Realme's master and its newest servant while the blooms danced as though wind drove their shifting glows.

"And what would happen if I did free him?" the King of Shadows asked.

"How would a man like Kreston Dühalde react if he could roam Mortalia again knowing the woman he loved remained in the Realme? Would he pine for you or write poems to you? Would he try to remain at your side? He'd have no blade, and I'd never restore him if he fell in battle. He'd die failed and broken. At least with me he has a sense of purpose."

"You know something, Your Majesty?" Alerice said. "You have a point. He does have purpose while he's with you, but he takes his ease when he's with me. I've seen it in his eyes. For a few moments, he relaxes and becomes the man he longs to be. If it is your desire to enslave him and the queen's desire to cripple him, then it is my desire to comfort him. My father always told me to stand up when I could make a difference, and when I first met the Raven Queen she rightly noted that I was a victim with no advocate. Well, perhaps I will become Kreston's advocate."

"Against me?" the king said.

"Only if necessary, Your Majesty."

The king smiled knowingly. "Girl, you are going to be far too busy to advocate for him. You wish to be my wife's Walker? Then it's time for you to get to work."

Alerice forced a confident look onto her face as the king turned to the field. With a sweeping gesture, he summoned the glow from every flower petal, draining them until they all withered and died.

"Alerice," Oddwyn urged, beckoning her to step away.

Alerice did, even as the king collected and compacted the glows to form the head of a translucent horned sea dragon. The beast was more ghost than corporeal, and Alerice inadvertently stepped backward as the king drew out a great eel's body from its neck. It bore a fish's fanning fins and tail. Long whiskers dangled from its jaws.

The king commanded it to turn in midair and regard Alerice, at which point Oddwyn hurried over to take her by the arm and move her behind him.

The King of Shadows noted the gesture, but paid it no heed as he conjured a spacious portal from the edge of the withered blooms. Within it, Alerice could see a seaside village of hearty, broad-shouldered folk, and she knew that this must be the home of the Hammer Clan.

The king commanded the sea dragon into the portal. It obeyed with a roar. A flicking sweep of its tail caused a whip of air so powerful it nearly hurled Alerice and Oddwyn to their knees. The beast then swam into the portal and dove into the waves with a massive splash. It swam along the surface, its tail churning water to foam, heading for the village's docks and their moored longboats.

The King of Shadows turned to Alerice and offered an "After you" toss of his hand.

Alerice saw the sea dragon rear up at the dockside, shocking the clan folk and spurring a wave of panic. Anger mounting in her, she placed a hand on Oddwyn's shoulder.

"Herald," she said. "Take us to the mead hall."

***

The Hammer Clan's village was normally a quiet hamlet. Located on an island inlet, its long dock hosted a small fleet. Fishing and trade were the clan's primary activities, for they enjoyed the bounties of the sea at their supper tables, and the metal they forged into magnificent war hammers was found only on their island, and thus was prized.

The clan had heard tales of many monsters that dwelled in the deep, but none had ever expected to see one rising up before them as some semi-transparent demon.

Chaos took hold as folk cleared children from the area while others armed themselves. Men and women ran to the water's edge, while one quick-thinking soul ran to the clan's alarm shield and began clanging out a steady warning.

The horned dragon fell sideways from its rise to cause a massive wave that flooded the dock, washing folk off their feet and sending others leaping into their longboats. A few fell into the sea and scrambled for help amid the wake churned up by the dragon's thrashing tail.

In the mead hall, Alerice appeared to find the warrior spirits asleep, some lying atop their long tables and others curled up on the floor. Some snored, some belched, and Alerice gave silent thanks that they were not alive, for the smell would have been quite pungent.

She hurried to the hall's head and drew out her pixie pole cylinders as she approached the golden ever-flowing cauldron.

"Oddwyn," she said, looking at the youthful herald who was fixed on her every move. "I'm going to need a portal. A big one."

"Oh-ho-ho, Alerice," Oddwyn gut-chuckled, for a key talent known to every Realme Walker was the ability to guide spirits into combat, and he could see what she meant to do.

Oddwyn hurried to the hall's far side and began transforming the spiritual wall into a churning swirl of black, midnight blue, and deep teal, and he glanced back at Alerice as she raised a single pole.

Alerice struck the cauldron with a tone that resonated clearly. The spirits startled awake, and Alerice struck the cauldron a second time. Brew gushed up over the cauldron's lip and cascaded onto the hall's floor as every spirit shook themselves alert and regarded her.

"Your mortal folk are in danger!" Alerice cried.

She gestured to Oddwyn, who threw open the portal to display the dockside havoc. Aric was the first to stand at the ready and draw the magnificent war hammer from his thick studded belt.

"Kinsmen!" he cried.

"Kinsmen!" his fellow spirits echoed.

"Come on!" Alerice shouted as she sprang over the flowing brew and sprinted for the widening portal.

The horned sea dragon dropped its massive jaw and sank its fangs into the dock, ripping it up from its moorings and consuming a few unfortunate men who could not clear the area in time. Hammer men and women lunged for the beast, doing their best to land a damaging blow. With a few strong head shakes, the dragon cast all aside, impaling some people with massive dock splinters and scattering the rest by forcing them to run for their lives.

The dragon spat out what remained of the dock and roared again, but as it raised its head, a black crossbow bolt lodged in its throat, the dark glow from its impact severely damaging the many floral glows that the king had used to create the dragon's translucent countenance.

It roared again, this time more piteously, but a second bolt lodged in its chest, and the subsequent black glow dissipated its luminous flesh, causing it to half-sink into the sea.

Hammer folk turned to find a blonde warrior in a black scale mail tunic standing on a rocky formation. Behind her the air churned in colors of black, midnight blue, and deep teal, and before the astonished clan's folk could catch a collective breath, the woman gestured to the aperture behind her and shouted, "Onward!"

A roaring rush of ancient voices hollered in response as spirits swarmed out from behind the woman's slim form. She raised her crossbow once more and fired into the horned dragon's eye even as the souls of the clan's mightiest warriors swarmed the beast, laying into it with a volley of unified hammer strikes that *clanged* against its head, back, and ribs.

From her vantage point, Alerice lowered her crossbow, for there would be little action left for her. Unlike protecting the souls of the forest fauns in Uffton, who had been recently slain, daylight had no effect on the souls Alerice had just brought into the living world. The spectral ancestors of the Hammer Clan were long-tethered to the Realme, and feared nothing of Mortalia. True, they would be far more effective at night, but Alerice took pride in their alacrity, and had no doubt that they would soon destroy the king's monster.

Then, the cries of children attracted her attention, and Alerice fixed her crossbow into her belt holder so that she could rush to their aid.

In the field of dead flowers, the King of Shadows watched the scene from his still-active portal. He had compacted its size, but it suffered no loss of clarity. The king nodded despite himself, for the girl was indeed learning what it meant to be a Realme Walker. Her fame would spread all the more quickly once she returned with the Hammer Clan's souls. There was no stopping her in the Realme where he was king, his wife was queen, and she, apparently, was becoming a legend.

"Do you see what she's doing, Dühalde?" the king asked.

He waved his hand, and the veil that had concealed Kreston vanished, allowing him to finally move and speak. He stood, shuddering from the experience of having been locked away while the king had spoken to Alerice. He had witnessed everything while enduring the torture of being unable to intercede. The king smirked at Kreston's anguish, the same way he smirked when shocking a soul to the point of rupture.

"I... I do, My King," Kreston panted, doing his utmost to gain control over himself. His hands were balled into fists. His breathing was quick and shallow. He could not summon ice into his veins, for his body shook with immortal cold, and yet somehow he was able to lock every muscle until he forced himself into near paralysis.

From there, he focused on his breath, inhaling and exhaling with the same cadence that drummers pounded during a funeral procession. Inhale, exhale, until he eventually lifted his hazel eyes to watch Alerice hurry a group of Hammer Clan children away from the water's edge where the horned dragon's thrashing fins threatened to sweep them out to sea.

With one final exhale, Kreston straightened and leveled his shoulders. Then he paced toward the King of Shadows, his deliberate steps crushing the withered flowers.

"She's doing quite well," the king commented.

Kreston offered no reply.

"I thought for certain that a girl so prideful would assume she needed to battle my creature by herself. Any man would assume that, don't you agree?"

"Yes, My King," Kreston said.

The king regarded Kreston with distaste, no doubt perturbed by his simple replies of "yes" and "no".

"Perhaps that's the difference between mortal women and men," the king said. "Perhaps they don't feel they have as much to prove. Who knows?"

Kreston cleared his throat to chase away the lingering effects of silent confinement. The King of Shadows turned to him and looked him over.

"She's right about you, though. You aren't of any use to me, not while my wife holds the key to unlocking your mind. Perhaps I should seek out a man who enjoys slaughter in my name. You certainly don't, and you can't, and with that girl determined to *comfort* you," he said with a mocking lilt, "you'll only grow more worthless."

Kreston's natural reaction would have been to stand 'eyes forward' so staunchly that he entered his semi-meditative state where he could absorb information without presenting any sign that he was cogent. However, he found a deviant pleasure in watching Alerice manage her battle, mostly because he knew it irked the king.

Kreston smiled despite himself, and then offered his master an unconsciously disobedient smile. As he became more aware of his expression, he allowed himself to wear it openly, for he was striking a blow against his enslaver.

The king's dark-grey eyes narrowed, and daring the dangerous without saying a word, Kreston simply held his head high. He tensed, ready for anything, and stood his ground.

The King of Shadows snarled, and then shouted as he backhanded the air before Kreston so forcefully that Kreston felt the strike land upon his jaw. His head snapped to the side so violently that he thought his spine might snap, and as he tried to regain his balance, he felt a power surge pound his shoulders strongly enough to splay him out onto the dead flowers.

Kreston tried to recover, but the king's power grabbed him by the throat and choked off his air as his master lifted him up and set him on his knees. The king then released his hold, stepped forward, and planted his palm over Kreston's brow.

Searing pain shot through Kreston's skull as he felt the King of Shadows scrape fingernails across his skin. They sunk in as though tearing off a layer of flesh. Kreston clawed at the king's hand, struggling to get free. The pain mounted, but then the King of Shadows shoved Kreston hard, and he fell to his side, panting.

Yet even through the assault, Kreston felt one distinct sensation. The mark that the king had once scratched upon his forehead pulsed one final time, and then ceased. Kreston's eyes snapped open, and he knew that the mark he had once sought – the mark that had proclaimed him as the Walker of the King of Shadows, the mark that had been the symbol of his shame – was gone.

Kreston's eyes went wide. A rush of emotions threatened to undo him, and he fought with every ounce of self-control to keep himself in check. He was free. *He was finally free.*

Kreston planted a boot and forced himself to rise. Then he felt for the

215

implement he had used to take far too many lives, the king's broadsword. It no longer rested at his hip.

Kreston nearly yelped in elation. Instead, he locked his arms to his sides. He longed to insult the king, to lampoon him, to curse him, but he did not dare say a single word. He would celebrate his liberty soon enough. The only initiative that now concerned him was escape.

"Escape?" the King of Shadows commented as he gestured to the still-open portal and the dying dragon. "Why do you think I left the portal open, you fool? You chose the girl over me. Go and take her."

Kreston swallowed hard, knowing he could never trust the King of Shadows. But, he had no other option than to take him at his word. He offered a thin nod and paced toward the portal, noting that he would need to jump into the water and swim for what remained of the dock.

Yet as he approached the portal's rim and the water's edge, the King of Shadows called out.

"Remember, Dühalde. There will be no more restoration after this. You die in Mortalia, you die."

Kreston could not help but smile. "Good," he said, and dove into the waves.

***

"See to your descendants!" Aric ordered his fellow spirits as he pounced upon the sea dragon's sinking head. As what remained of the beast began to lower into the waves, he struck it once, twice, then thrice on the skull, his war hammer sinking further into the creature's luminous outline with each blow. The creature flickered as would a candle spending the last of its wax, and then faded from sight, leaving Aric's soul to hover freely above the water's surface.

Alerice had collected the children and also some teens to her. The teens had not seen the need to seek her protection, but they had gladly approached the blonde warrior wearing black scale mail. Alerice had allowed them to touch and pet it, watching them admire it. She was happy to employ any handy device to keep them nearby until the adults came to claim them.

She did not need to wait long, for now that the danger had passed, the clan's folk began to collect themselves. Mothers and fathers hurried to her and began to sort through her brood. Smiling, Alerice was happy to greet each of them. She also glanced past them to watch other members of the clan stand in wonder as the spirits she had brought forth gathered on what remained of the dock.

The living folk gathered behind their current chief, who gripped his war hammer and threw his shoulders back as he strode toward Aric. Aric grinned and threw wide his arms, and the two leaders approached, exchanging familial greetings. There was no point in attempting physical contact, which both parties seemed to realize, and as much as Alerice was tempted to offer the two a means to touch, which would entail allowing Aric to possess her body in a Realme meld, the thought of his massive essence in her slim frame made her decidedly uncomfortable.

The last parent claimed the last child, and Alerice smiled before looking out to sea. Then she noticed a man swimming toward her. She watched with curiosity, for he was certainly not a member of the Hammer Clan. Then she noticed the man's familiar build, and her heart leaped.

"Kreston!" Alerice called, a wide smile filling her face.

Kreston waved in mid-stroke, and then dove under the water to make his approach. Alerice watched his submerged form glide beneath the waves, and she moved toward the low footing along the rocky outcrop where he was bound to surface.

He did with a smile, and he offered a happy splash as he treaded water.

"Hey!" she called as he soaked her boots.

"Hey!" he shouted back.

She was about to offer a hand to help him out, but she had seen that mischievous look on her cousins' faces at the brewery. It had always appeared as they planned a prank, and she stood back to regard him.

"You're not going to pull me in with you, are you?"

"Tempting, my dear. So tempting, but no."

"All right, I'll trust you," she said with her hands on her hips. "But don't make me regret it."

There was sincerity in Kreston's eyes as he said, "Alerice, causing you regret is the last thing on my mind."

Alerice smirked with mock suspicion, but knelt on one knee and offered a hand to help him climb onto the rocks. He scrambled out of the water and got to his feet. Then he shook his head and wiped his brow and eyes.

At which point Alerice noticed that the mark of the King of Shadows, the series of slashes he loathed so greatly, no longer appeared on his brow.

"Kreston," she breathed.

He met her gaze.

"I know. He let me go, Alerice. He set me free."

"Oh, Kreston," she half-cried out.

She was about to rush to him, but his clothes were sopping. She hesitated a moment, and then decided to throw caution to the wind. They both moved toward one another, and he folded her into an embrace, pressing her to him.

She felt him chuckle. She felt his joy. She could not have been more elated for him, and she did not resist when he simply could not contain himself a moment more.

"Alerice!" he cried aloud as he hefted her into his arms and spun about with her. She laughed with delight until she felt him beginning to lose his balance, at which point she wiggled a bit so that he might set her down.

He did, but he beamed so greatly that he stepped to the edge of the rocks, held wide his arms, and let loose with a mighty, "Ho-ya!"

From the corner of her eye, Alerice saw that he attracted a few glances from nearby folk. Fortunately they were so fixed on uniting with their most revered spirits that they paid little heed.

"Ha!" Kreston exclaimed as he turned back to Alerice.

She smiled and nodded. "Good for you, sir."

He let his arms dangle at his sides as he exhaled. "Good for me," he softly agreed. Then his expression became more reserved as he stepped toward her. "I wish I could say good for us."

Alerice drew and released a breath, then took a step back. "I know you do. But take this triumph and enjoy it. You deserve it."

"I don't know that I do. I have a great deal to atone for, but gods above, Alerice. At least I'm not *his* any longer."

"You're not worried that he might reclaim you? Remember what you said to me when the Raven Queen released me? That once the Realme has had you, it can always take you back."

"I did say that, and the queen did take you back. I guess I'll always live with the risk that the king might try to claim me again."

"Try?"

Kreston smirked. "I won't go back without a fight."

"No, I suppose you won't," she said.

Alerice watched Kreston come close. He moved a lock of her blonde hair behind her ear, and then ran his fingertips along the burn scar that Sukaar, Father God of Fire, had left upon her jaw. She knew that he wanted to kiss her, but he held back.

"You don't want to come with me, do you?" he asked.

"Kreston," she said. "It's not you. I don't want to go with anyone. I've never wanted to go with anyone, and I can't tell you how many times I've been asked. You think those men who competed with love poems to win free drinks at the Cup and Quill didn't mean the words they wrote? You think my uncle and aunt and grammy didn't want me to find someone? Even my cousins tried putting their friends forward."

"I understand," he said. "Who wouldn't want to marry you? You're so easy to love."

He cupped his hand to her cheek, and she cupped hers over his.

"You're a good man, Kreston Dühalde," she said. "And I want you to spend the rest of your life doing good things. Promise me you won't waste this chance."

"What?" he said, his expression suddenly concerned.

She pulled away from his touch.

"I said I don't want you to waste this chance," she repeated.

Kreston patted his palm over his ear, and shook his head. "I can't hear you," he said. He opened and shut his jaw a few times, then shook his head again.

"Kreston," Alerice said, taking hold of his shoulder and forcing him to lock stares with her. "Kreston, look at me. Can you hear what I'm saying?"

His expression conveyed that he could not, and she noted his anxiety as she looked about for help.

"He cannot hear you because I do not wish him to hear me," the Raven Queen said in her voice of dark honey.

Alerice looked up to see her matron standing stoically on the rocky outcrop. Kreston began to look as well, but Alerice pulled him close and forced his head away.

"Cause him to face the sea," the queen ordered.

Alerice maneuvered Kreston about, and guided him to face the waves breaking below their feet. He tensed, for he likely knew what was transpiring, and he lowered himself to his knees and struck a rigid pose.

Alerice placed a hand on his shoulder and gripped his wet tunic before she paced about his side and reverenced.

The Raven Queen floated down to her. She surveyed the clan meeting upon the ruined dock, and her amethyst eyes filled with disapproval.

"Look at what my husband has done," she said. "He assaulted my abbey because he wished to strike at me. He assaulted these people because he wished to strike at you. Alerice Linden, my Ravensdaughter, you will no doubt have qualms with what I am about to say, but I must task you with striking at him."

"But you said you would never openly act against him, My Queen."

"Nor am I," she replied. "But this is a specific task that must be completed now, while he has no champion. This task will prevent him from enslaving anyone else. I now send you to his shrine on the seaside cliffs where you will destroy his gateway and those who guard it."

"Those who guard it?" Alerice repeated. "So, you're sending me to murder people?"

"Alerice, if you could destroy the gateway by some other means, I would accept, but you cannot. You must strike while my husband is compromised. Without his shrine, he will not have a fabled place where men seek him out.

Without his gateway, he will not be able to send forth his Shadow Warriors to test the mettle of men who would serve him.

"Let Kreston be his last servant. He does not deserve another, and he certainly does not deserve a Walker. It is the Mother Goddess of Water and Wind, Imari, who has written that all Walkers should be cherished. Look how my husband has mistreated Kreston. Look at how he assails you. You must destroy his shrine, and this time I must command it. Come to your peace with this task, Alerice, but do not challenge me, for I will have you obey."

Alerice pressed her lips together. Then, she found herself asking, "How... do I find it, My Queen?"

"Call to me, and I will deliver you."

The Raven Queen held Alerice in her infinite amethyst gaze. Then she turned and raised a willow-white hand toward Aric and his Hammer Clan souls. Alerice watched the spirit warriors raise their hammers to her, bid farewell to their descendants, and then raise their heads. The queen gestured for them all to come to her, and Alerice saw them dissolve into glittering metallic wisps that flew to the queen as she faded into an opening portal of black, midnight blue, and deep teal.

Alerice exhaled heavily. Kreston responded to the sound of her breath, and quickly rose to face her.

"What did she tell you?"

"Kreston," Alerice noted. "You didn't say *she* the way you normally do."

Kreston paused, realizing this was true. "No, I didn't. Funny. But what did she say?"

Alerice sighed, turning about as she patted her hand against her thigh. Kreston stepped into her line of sight and pressed his gaze. She met his hazel eyes, and then shook her head.

"She wants me to destroy the king's shrine."

"The cliffside shrine?"

"You know it?"

Kreston looked at her incredulously. "Know it? Of course I know it. Where do you think I sought him out? Where do you think anyone seeks him out?"

"I wouldn't know," Alerice said flatly. "I'm just a tavern maid, remember?"

Kreston grimaced. "Well, you're hardly that any longer. You're a Realme Walker, and from what I can see you're becoming accomplished. The cliffside shrine has existed for ages. It's a fable told to every man in uniform. We've all heard the stories, especially on the nights before a battle when we don't dare keep a fire going for fear of giving up our position. Any man brave enough to seek the black fire and climb the cliffs can light the basin and call upon the King of Shadows. And he will answer, as he did for me."

"That's all? Get some black fire and light a basin?"

"You think it's easy? Monks guard the flame, and they can shadow-step so quickly that you won't be able to see them move. The cliffs are damned tricky to climb, and you can fall onto the rocks below. And then when you get to the top, if you get to the top, and light the basin, the king will send his Shadow Warriors to test you. You can't beat them. No one can beat them, but the king watches the fight, and if he thinks you're good enough, he lets you live."

"Wonderful," she said. "So basically, I have to defeat the monks--"

"Kill the monks."

"What?" Alerice gasped.

"You'll have to kill them, Alerice. There's no way they're going to let you make the climb."

Alerice moaned as she despaired the thought. "So the King of Shadows was right. The queen can be cruel."

"She's not being cruel," he said. "Not in this. Alerice, remember in Basque when you discovered that the inn master was selling children? Remember how he threatened to kill one right in front of you? You didn't hesitate to kill him, did you?"

"I had to save the child. But I didn't kill his wife. I gave her to the Reef. She was hardly innocent, but it wasn't my place to judge her."

"It's not our place to judge anyone we fight," he said. "Do you think I strolled out onto a battlefield and said, 'I think I'll kill someone bad today?' No. I fought because I trusted the judgment of those I served. I resisted the King of Shadows because he betrayed that trust. These monks are not innocent by any means, and the queen is doing a service to future men by having you destroy them."

Alerice sighed again as she mulled the moment over. "So kill the monks, and fight the Shadow Warriors, and then destroy the shrine? The Raven Queen expects me to do this?"

Kreston paused and then said, "I think she expects *us* to do this."

"Us?"

"Why else would she task you here? She knew we'd have this conversation. She knows we're having it now, and she knows I won't let you do this alone."

"But Kreston, if you fall, you'll die."

"Alerice," he said with a thin smile. "If you think that bothers me, you're wrong."

***

The night's wind slashed Kreston's face. Blowing in hard from the ocean, it whipped his salt-and-pepper hair and froze him to the bone. He longed for a hooded cloak, not that he'd need it for long. He looked up at the crags rising overhead, and heard the roar of the ocean waves below. To the side, he caught a faint trace of the cave where the monks kept the black flame. He was completely insane to be doing this again, but he was not about to allow Alerice to do this alone.

She had left him a moment ago, after Oddwyn had delivered them both via portal. The waning moon bathed the rocks in soft silver, but it would not provide enough light to find all the toeholds. Kreston would need to remember where most of them were, though years had passed since he had made the climb.

He hugged himself for warmth, trying to recall how driven he had been back then. His brigade had just been slaughtered. His lieutenant had just been murdered. He had just discovered the marshal's plot to betray his men and leave them without support as they faced an encroaching enemy on that damned hill. He had sworn revenge, which had consumed him as he sought the King of Shadows.

He had ridden to the seaside trailhead. He had found his way along the narrow path. For nearly two leagues, he had been forced to crawl, leap, and cling.

It was all appropriate, for the quest to reach the king's shrine should be difficult. Only the best men could solicit him, and the narrow path to the monks' cave was merely the first challenge. Those who were faint of heart would have turned back half-way, or better still never have attempted the path in the first place. He had, though, and fortunately this time Alerice had asked Oddwyn to deliver them to the cave mouth. If only she would return so he did not freeze to death.

Kreston felt a shiver chase up his back, one that was not born of cold. He turned about, and though the night concealed the swirling tri-colors of black, midnight blue, and deep teal, he could make out the edges of an opening portal.

Alerice stepped through, her blonde head and fair face seeming to float in the darkness that concealed her black scale mail. Kreston watched her look about to mark her bearings, and then regard the thrashing waves. She shivered as the cold struck her. Kreston advanced to hold her close, but she held up her hands to refuse.

He nodded, for words were useless. They both knew what needed to be done, and Kreston began to turn toward the cave. However, something in the sea caught his eye, which he regarded once, then twice.

The waves were breaking along a centerline, as though flowing to both sides of some great cresting object. He reached for Alerice so that he might maneuver her behind him, but she stood her ground.

Kreston moved abreast of her, and saw the Raven Queen's mark begin to glow. Panic struck him, for he could not bear the sight of the White Lady, as he had once called her. He had no idea what would happen if he beheld her or heard her voice, for unlike earlier at the Hammer Clan's village, he now heard everything.

For Alerice, the sensation was intriguing. She felt her mark pulse, but not in the typical way it did when the queen approached. She glanced at Kreston, who openly wore his worry, and placed her hand upon his forearm. He responded to her touch, and she felt it was safe enough to leave him and move toward the waves.

Kreston did not advance with her as she stepped closer to the edge of the narrow trail, watching with fascination as cream-colored shapes, illuminated by the moonlight, began to dance below the ocean's surface.

They were otherworldly figures. Alerice counted six darting gracefully. One crested the surface, which had gone surprisingly calm, although the waves further away continued to thrash. Alerice felt a breath of cool wind caress her face, replacing the cold slices that had assaulted her.

The figure was exquisitely long-limbed with hair of seafoam green that seemed tossed by ethereal currents.

Alerice could not be certain if it was male or female, for it was nondescript, quite unlike Oddwyn who clearly presented as a youth or a maiden. Another figure crested and then another, filling Alerice with delight, and though she had no idea why the Raven Queen's mark glowed so brightly that even she caught sight of it, she knew that these beings presented no danger.

"Sorgini," Kreston breathed as he approached to stand at her flank.

"Sorgini?" Alerice asked, turning her head slightly to him, for she could not take her gaze off the half-dozen wonders. Now that all had risen, they bent down to flatten the waves as chamber attendants might flatten a carpet runner.

Then, Alerice saw Kreston fall to one knee and bow his head, and she fully regarded him before she looked once more at the ocean.

A breath of warm perfumed air blew in. The scent was so intoxicating that Alerice inhaled deeply, remembering the bowl of scented flower petals she used to keep on her bureau in her room at the Cup and Quill. All traces of the salty air vanished, as did the cold, and Alerice swallowed in anticipation of something wondrous.

"Bow your head, Alerice," Kreston said, his own still low. "The mother goddess approaches."

Alerice swallowed again, her eyes going wide at the suddenly emerged sight of Imari, Mother Goddess of Water and Wind. She fell into her natural reverence, but for some reason she did not bow her head. She fully meant to, but she simply forgot.

Imari's gown was made of the same seafoam as her Sorginis' hair. The Sorgini tended its volume as she floated toward the shore. Imari's hair was light blue and silver, and was tucked into lovely folds adorned by combs of coral and pearls. Her flesh was close to Alerice's own tone, and her meridian-blue eyes sparkled.

Gentle wisps of wind played in her gown's sleeves. Small pools of glistening water formed as her feet touched the rocky path. She commanded the moonlight as though it was meant for her alone, and she bade Alerice to back away as she came forward.

The Sorgini fanned out, three to Imari's sides, and held their thin hands up toward her.

"You may stand and behold me, Captain Dühalde," Imari bade in a dulcet double-voice.

Kreston stood, and yet as he raised his head, Alerice could see tears in his hazel eyes.

"Alerice Linden," Imari beckoned as she reached out to stroke Alerice's blonde head.

Alerice could not help but feel her own tears forming, though she tried to dam their flow.

"A true Walker of the Realme," the goddess continued. "As are you, sweet Kreston."

"For Walkers are true beings, who rightly know their minds. Inspired by the gods, their worth is well defined," the Sorgini chanted.

"Indeed their worth is well defined," Imari said. "So I have observed across the ages, and have set down in my scrolls."

"A rare thing is a Walker, so, gods below: Take care! Groom them and protect them. Do not let them despair," the Sorgini chanted.

"So, gods below, take care," Imari repeated. "I am not certain this has been the case, certainly not with you, sweet Kreston."

Alerice watched Kreston close his eyes and say nothing. He stood at attention as any military man would, only his shoulders were not arched back. He merely forbade himself any response.

"I do not despair, great goddess," Alerice said to focus attention on herself and spare him.

"No, you do not," Imari agreed, her double-voice filling all available space. "And if the Raven Queen cherishes you, as I have decreed, you will become an asset far greater to her than her Eye."

Alerice suddenly suspected the reason for Imari's presence.

"Mother Water Wind, the King of Shadows was jealous of the Queen's Eye. He stole that gem from my matron. Do you believe he wishes to steal me?"

A tiny "Ah" escaped Kreston, and Alerice glanced at him, seeing his anxiety. He likely had not thought of this notion before, and now it spurred dread.

"Not even I can see the king's mind," Imari said in a coo that was as strong as it was calm. "But were he to covet you, I could understand his desire. My husband, Sukaar, desired you," she said, running her fingertip along the burn scar on Alerice's jaw. "Were you a woman of learning and spell craft, I would have welcomed you as my one devotee in generations. But you were born to the shadows, and to the shadows shall you be forever tethered."

"Regard them now, these Walkers, gods above and gods below. The Realme has kissed Mortalia, forever now, and long ago," the Sorgini chanted.

"And now I will add my kiss," Imari said. She bade Alerice come closer, and Alerice stepped forward without fear. Imari brushed the blonde hair from her brow, and kissed her forehead atop the Raven Queen's mark.

Alerice closed her eyes, for a feeling of transcendent peace filled her toe to top. She did not sense all-knowing wisdom. She did not feel a rush of power. She simply knew who she was and who she was born to be, a child of the shadows conceived in that rare set of circumstances when, as Imari's scrolls stated:

The Serpent Father Fire
Loves the Mother Water Wind,
When L'Orku's breath of thunder
'Cross the mighty sky ascends.

And yet Alerice felt as though she might be more than a Walker. She did not know how or why, or what this new feeling might entail, but she accepted it for what it was and where it might guide her.

"First a god, now a goddess. You're making powerful friends," Kreston said.

Alerice did not know what to say. Imari had receded into the ocean, her Sorgini with her, and the egress had been as lovely as the ingress. Alerice noted that they both still had tears in their eyes. She reached to Kreston, but he pulled his head away. She sniffed her own tears back.

"Why do you weep?" she asked.

He swallowed hard.

"Because when I heard her voice, I had a flash of memory. She came to me as well, here in this place, before I made the climb. I remember now. Her Sorgini were with her then too. The moon was waxing, but not far from where it shines now on the waning side. She offered her kiss to me, just as she offered it to you," he said, tracing the mark Imari had left on Alerice's brow, a blue upturned curve that wove through the short pointed oval of the Raven Queen's mark.

"She said that I was a born Walker, and that I should be cherished, but I've never been cherished. My birth was so long and painful that I crippled my mother for life. My father hated me for it. My siblings followed his lead, along with everyone I knew as a child. I had no idea I was a Walker. How could I? I ran from home. I found comrades in the army. Cherished," he commented derisively.

"But if I had taken Imari's kiss," he said. "If I hadn't been so..."

"Lost?" she offered.

"Proud," he said flatly. "I told her 'no'. I told her I didn't need anyone's kiss. I asked her where her kiss had been when my men were being butchered? Who in the world was I to say something like that to *her*, a goddess?"

Alerice noted that, for the first time since she had known Kreston, his inflection of that particular pronoun conveyed the utmost respect.

"And perhaps if you had told her yes, things would have been different between you and the King of Shadows?" Alerice asked.

Kreston nodded, sighing heavily.

Alerice nodded in response, but as they turned toward the monks' cave, she was well aware, that he was well aware, of how greatly he required the full use of his memory.

***

Alerice insisted on entering the cave before Kreston. He insisted on standing tall at her back. Neither had drawn a weapon, Alerice because she did not intend to and Kreston because he had none. He also knew that blades would be of no use against devotees who could step so quickly that he could not trace them.

The cave was empty, save for a brazier in which burned black flames. It stood on a cast-scroll metal stand that bore soaked-and-ready torches about its three legs. The cave was considerably warmer than outside, and Alerice wondered if the heavy atmosphere was meant to lull those seeking the King of Shadows into a state of unreadiness.

Kreston said nothing as he squeezed Alerice's shoulder. She stepped forward, only to be met with a series of quick rushes all about.

Kreston squeezed again for her to hold, which she did. The rushes continued about her sides in a frenzied fashion meant to confuse her, and for a moment they did. However, she focused her consciousness on the Raven Queen's mark, and she heard a chorus of howls ring out from the cave's interior.

She watched as the air about the cave seemed to swish as though several ghosted shadows had assembled, and she took one decisively defiant step toward the brazier.

"Be gone from this place, wretched girl," a voice whispered.

"Show yourself, shadow," Alerice replied. "I'll not move, and you must know that I mean to ruin this place."

"To your own ruin," came another whisper.

"Oh, stop," Kreston said. "Enough with the disembodied voices. Neither of us are impressed."

Alerice glanced up over her shoulder. "Well said."

"Thanks."

A whoosh of air assaulted them before five shadow monks appeared opposite the brazier. Their skin was yellowish-gray and their eyes were the same dark gray as the King of Shadows'. They were lean and tall and Alerice noticed that the fabric of their tunics and cuffed pants shimmered dully. Perhaps it had been imbued with dust from the crystals with which the King of Shadows adorned himself.

"Take a torch if you can, wretched girl," one monk offered.

"Ah, that's right," Kreston said. "They can't attack until you try to light one."

"Really," Alerice commented. "So we could stand here and discuss our favorite color, or make jokes, or waste time, and they'd have to stand there and listen?"

Alerice felt another volley of rushes dart past her, only these began to snipe at her face and body, nearly pushing her off balance. The rushes were definitely malevolent, and Alerice thought better of making another jest.

Kreston strode forward and grabbed hold of a torch.

"No, Kreston," Alerice said, but the rushing intensified.

Kreston grabbed a second torch and attempted to use them as Alerice might use her pixie poles, but the air ripped about him right and left, forward and behind, beating into him and forcing him down to his knees.

Alerice drew her Realme dagger and leaped beside him. She plunged it into the heart of the black flame, tolerating the heat as her blade began to glow. She sensed the rushes assaulting Kreston abate, and she held her blade aloft.

"If I take a torch and you attack," she stated, "this weapon will find you. You all know this. Stand down, warriors of the king, for I do not wish to harm you. However, I will complete the task that my mistress has given me."

"Slay us if you can, wretched girl," a monk said.

"Get them, Alerice," Kreston urged, cradling an arm about his midsection.

Alerice smiled as she closed her eyes and gave her entire being over to the

227

Raven Queen's mark. Again, she heard howls, but they faded as she heard the roar of ocean waves. She felt the power of water and wind fill her soul, and somehow she knew that she should mix this new force Imari had granted her with the love of the Realme and its blessed shadows. She conjured the image of the youthful Oddwyn waiting in the Hammer Clan's mead hall with Pa'oula and six of her Painted Women, all of whom bore short spears.

"Send them to me, Oddwyn," Alerice ordered.

In the mead hall, Oddwyn saw a portal begin to open in the Realme's signature tri-colors of black, midnight blue, and deep teal. His ice-blue eyes fixed on the aperture, and he straightened with surprised respect.

"You're getting good at this, Alerice."

Oddwyn drew his hands apart to widen the portal, and the Painted Women charged forward.

In the cave, the shadow monks all stood still as the Painted Women poured in. Their quick steps were of no use, for they could not elude spiritual eyes. The Painted Women thrust their spear tips, which the monks parried with open palms. The women parried their counter-attacks with their spears' shafts, and then riposted by slamming their spears' butts into the monks' bodies. The attack was quite effective, for the shadow monks had given up part of their mortality to attain their speed, leaving them vulnerable to spiritual assault.

Kreston thrust his two torches into the brazier so that the black flame consumed the tips. Then he withdrew and tossed one to Alerice.

"Come on!" he said as he bolted from the cave.

Alerice sheathed her dagger and called, "Pa'oula!"

The Painted Woman turned to her and grinned. Alerice held wide her arms, and Pa'oula flew toward her, leaping into her flesh in a Realme meld. Alerice steadied her balance and then opened her eyes, which had turned copper-brown.

***

Kreston stood at the base of the crags, his black flame torch burning in lurid licks. He watched Alerice sprint toward him, and was about to caution her how to place the torch in her mouth so that she could make the climb. However, he was gobsmacked to watch her do so without instruction, leap clean over him, and begin to scale the crags.

Achieving a solid hold, Alerice withdrew the torch from her mouth to shout, "Come along, Crimson Ghost."

Kreston knew that Alerice's voice was not her own. He caught the faintest trace of her eyes, and then jammed his torch between his teeth. He leaped up after her, noting that she began to ascend with surprising agility.

Alerice leaped high from her toehold near the top of the cliffs. She landed in a crouch on the upper plateau, but then her head snapped to the side to behold the basin of the King of Shadows. It rested within an open stone shrine, the eight arches of which supported a concave stone cap.

She sprinted to the basin and cast in her torch to ignite the oil-soaked peat, but then she heard a man grunt, and she hurried back for the cliff's edge. Glancing over the side as wind sliced her cheeks, she saw Kreston struggling with his hold.

"Throw it up!" she demanded of his torch.

He hurled it at her. She leaned over the cliff edge as she reached for it, but she leaned too far. Her body teetered, about to fall, when Kreston vaulted himself up and planted his palm against her breast.

He pushed her back, and Alerice regained balance. She reached down to grab hold of his arm, and with strength that seemed too great for her body to bear, she cried out as she hauled him high enough to crest the edge of the plateau.

Then she fell back to her haunches, panting.

"Get out of her!" Kreston shouted as he kicked the back of Alerice's black scales. Alerice saw him reach down and grab his torch, and then he hesitated.

He seemed prepared to kick her back again, but fortunately Pa'oula's spirit flew out of her breast, and Alerice heaved backward.

She began coughing. Kreston reached down and lifted her to her feet, but as Alerice watched him turn toward the basin, she saw the king's two Shadow Warriors standing in his path, swords drawn.

Alerice regarded them, then Kreston, and then she grabbed Kreston's torch to throw it into one of the warrior's helms. It landed within the empty space, causing the specter to shriek and recoil.

"What are you waiting for?" Alerice said as she grabbed the pixie pole cylinders from her belt and activated them so that their bladed poles popped out. She passed one to Kreston and drew her Realme dagger with her free hand.

Kreston bore his pole two-handed and charged. He laid into both warriors, but neither fought him with much vim. Just as well, for Alerice had already planned a countermeasure.

She moved behind him and tugged the back of his belt. He glanced over his shoulder, and she gestured for him to retreat. She guided him to the edge of the shrine's base, and motioned for him to step off.

"What's your plan?" he asked.

"Get clear, and I'll show you," she replied.

He did, following her lead. The Shadow Warriors reached the shrine's circumference, but did not step down.

Alerice motioned for Kreston to hold his ground, which he did as she again gave herself over to the queen's mark. She felt it pulse. She heard Imari's waves. She felt the Realme, and then she called once more, "Now, Oddwyn!"

In the mead hall, Oddwyn opened a second portal and turned to Aric and his clan. They raised their war hammers, hungry for another opportunity to do battle in Mortalia.

Oddwyn offered a "There you go" gesture, and then quickly jumped back as the broad warriors cried out and charged into the portal.

The sky swirled above the shrine's concave cap. The portal opened, and the Hammer Clan flew down from its center. They launched themselves upon the cap and began pounding the stone. The *cracking* rang out into the night, and Alerice smiled even as she winced, for the attack sent out shockwaves that reverberated inside her ribs.

Kreston led her away toward a grouping of boulders where they could watch the demolition from a safer distance. The incessant pounding fell off into the moonlit night as the Hammer Clan collapsed the cap and began assaulting the columns.

Alerice looked at Kreston, who savored the destruction of his place of enslavement.

"You could always join them," she offered.

"How?" Kreston half-chuckled.

"You're still a Realme Walker, Kreston Dühalde. You could take one of their spirits into your flesh and--"

"Alerice, stop. I've never tried a meld, and I'm not going to start now."

"Fair enough," she said.

Aric and his men began to topple the columns. The Shadow Warriors stood stoically as the first crashed down and broke apart. Aric's men downed the remaining columns, and soon the Hammer Clan began reducing all stone to rubble.

The air over the Shadow Warriors began to shift, and the king's knights dissolved into nothingness, leaving the Hammer Clan happily plying their well-renowned skills.

Kreston handed Alerice's bladed pole back to her and folded his arms across his chest. "Who'd've thought."

"I know," she said. "I actually wasn't certain they would be able to successfully destroy this place, but Oddwyn told me that they could. That's why I left you standing alone near the cave. I wanted to make sure I had reinforcements who could capture the monks and destroy the shrine. Fortunately, the Hammer Clan and the Painted Women had joined for another gathering in the mead hall, so I didn't need to chase after them."

"No. I meant who'd've thought that a woman left for dead only a short time ago could've made this all work."

Alerice smiled a bit sheepishly. "Oh. I've just always been a good organizer, I suppose."

Kreston turned to her, openly displaying his adoration, but she backed a half-step.

"Kreston, you should know that when this is finished, I'm going below."

"'Course, you are."

"It's not because of you."

"'Course, it's not."

"I don't know when we'll see each other again. And please don't say 'Course, you don't.'"

"No," he said softly.

She paused before she said, "Promise me you'll live a good life."

He nodded. She gazed up at him one final time before she turned and called to Aric. He bade her come to see what remained of the shrine, which she did.

Kreston watched her join the broad warriors. They hefted her upon their shoulders and tossed her about, which meant that more of her soul had become one with the Evherealme, a place he never wished to see again.

However, he longed to see her again. His mind began churning on some way to achieve this, but then his blood ran cold and he straightened. He was about to turn and look behind him, but *her* voice rang clearly in his mind.

"Summon your courage, Captain Dühalde," the Raven Queen said. "I wish to speak with you."

Kreston snapped to attention, 'eyes forward' as he focused on Alerice. He thought of her, and only of her. Her smile, her hair, her touch... even as the queen approached from behind and placed her willow-white hands on his shoulders.

Her touch froze him to the bone. He could only bear her presence for a few precious moments, and how he found the courage to speak to her, he had no idea. "I want to help her," he said, his voice shaking.

The Raven Queen petted the back of his salt-and-pepper head. "Because you love her."

"Yes," he gulped. "And I could be of help to her, whenever you send her back up here. If you place me in her path somehow. But... I need my mind back. She's yours, and if I'm to help her, I can't live in fear of you."

He felt the queen pet his head again, which sent shivers down his spine. No terror of a coming battle was ever as great as her dreaded caress.

"Kreston, if I unlock your mind, you will remember everything – every man you slaughtered, every task my husband forced you to undertake. I locked your thoughts away to spare you these things."

"I know." Kreston looked at Alerice, knowing something else as well. "But I need to be a whole man, White Lady. I want to be with her, even if she doesn't want to be with me."

The Raven Queen gripped Kreston's shoulders.

"So be it," she said.

Kreston felt the Raven Queen bend down and kiss the back of his head. A white light ripped across his eyes, and he saw figures come forth as though sketched in charcoal.

He saw the marshal of King Kemen of Andelous, the greedy lowlife who had betrayed the Crimson Brigade. The marshal had been Kreston's first mark, and Kreston had made his death a slow one.

Next Kreston saw the rival lords who had bribed the marshal. He saw their knights, and their squires, and so on down through the ranks. He had slaughtered them all, down to the stable hands, and from that moment he had never looked back.

After taking revenge, Kreston had done as the King of Shadows bade, moving from one battle after another, one man after another.

Kreston knew none of them. He feared none of them. His goal was to slaughter them so the King of Shadows could claim their souls, but when he had seen that desperate captain cradling the body of his lieutenant, he saw himself cradling Landrew Mülton, the younger brother he had never had when growing up on that forsaken farm where his family had blamed him for his mother's infirmities.

That captain had not deserved to die. All the fighting men Kreston had slaughtered had not deserved to die. Their quarrel lay with their foes, not with the King of Shadows, and yet the king had claimed them, for Kreston was the enforcing agent sent to butcher them.

Then in a terrible moment of recollection, Kreston saw the face of the runner boy he had stalked. Next, he saw the faces of the other boys, helpless children who could never have outfought him even if he hadn't wielded the king's broadsword.

Then he saw the nurses. He remembered how they had huddled together, bravely praying to the Raven Queen even though they knew their fate was sealed.

How could he have done all this? Had he ever attempted to deny the King of Shadows and rebel against his orders? Yes. He had, but only once, for the king had tormented him with the Crimson Brigade's loss over and over until he had capitulated.

Kreston had learned to summon ice into his veins long ago, but the ice the King of Shadows inspired had made Kreston more obdurate than the world's hardest stone.

Now he was no longer. Kreston fell to his knees on the plateau and held his hands out above his head, palms up as he begged, "White Lady! Let me atone. Show me how I may be forgiven. Show me how I may tip the balance of my defaults so that when you measure me, you may find at least one merit by which I may redeem myself. Please, White Lady. Help me!"

"There is no help for you, Dühalde," a dark voice said.

Kreston's heart seized. He felt a veil wrap tightly around him, just as it had when the King of Shadows had held him captive in the Realme's landscape of glowing blooms. The king had forced him to stand in a suspended state while Alerice conversed with him, and now that same state enveloped him and held him steady, his palms still high overhead.

"There is no atonement," the King of Shadows said. "You should resign yourself to doing what you do best, and for that you will need this."

Kreston managed to look up at the dreaded shade looming over him. The King of Shadows drew his Realme broadsword and placed the handle in Kreston's right hand.

Kreston could not stop his fingers from closing around it. He could not stop his hand from gripping it tightly. He could not move as the King of Shadows stepped in, reached to his forehead, and raked his iron fingernails across his brow.

Kreston tried to strangle a cry as the king again branded him with a mark of wide striations. He felt the Realme claim him once again. He felt his soul tethered and bound, and though he had vowed to fight the King of Shadows should he try to recapture him, Kreston was powerless to prevent his return to bondage.

Just as he had told Alerice when encouraging her to run after the Raven Queen had released her, once the Realme had him, it could always take him back.

"And welcome back," the King of Shadows said. "And welcome back to your mind. I knew if I freed you, you would find some way to pledge yourself to the girl so convincingly that my wife would free you. And you did. And it worked. But you are mine, Dühalde. You will be until the day I let you die. Now, you are ready to kill again in my name? Let's see what the girl thinks of you once she watches you do what you have always done best."

"I already know what I think of him, Your Majesty," Kreston heard Alerice say. He tried to find her, to gaze upon her, but she stood somewhere behind the King of Shadows, and he could not see her. Nor could he call out to her. He could do nothing to protect her.

To Alerice, this moment was sadly predictable. She stood, arms folded, behind the King of Shadows. She could not see Kreston, for the king had veiled him. She had been looking directly at Kreston before the king had made him disappear. Then the king had engaged in conversation, which meant that Kreston was still at hand, hidden and likely in a dire situation.

"Let him go, Your Majesty," Alerice calmly asserted.

The King of Shadows turned about to gaze down on her. He pressed his dark gray eyes into hers, but they did not affect her. He stepped forward to tower over her, but he inspired no fear. She was more than the Raven Queen's Walker now. She bore the mark of Imari and the kiss of Sukaar. She had won the alliance of the Hammer Clan, the Painted Women, and the Wyld. And she was going to help Kreston Dühalde.

"Never order me, girl," the King of Shadows said.

"Then please let me see him, Your Majesty," Alerice offered.

The king took one more step to close the distance, and Alerice arched her back and raised her head.

Locking stares with the king, she stated, "You will not dare strike at me, Your Majesty. For in so doing, you will be declaring war upon your wife. Is that what you truly wish? War within the Realme? Your wife does not wish that. Imari and Sukaar do not wish that. You have no power over me, and I implore you, with all respect. Let me see Kreston Dühalde."

The King of Shadows narrowed his dark gray gaze, but he lifted an arm so that the crystalline trim on the sleeves of his long robe caught the moonlight. Then he banished the veil, and Kreston to fell forward.

Alerice wanted to bolt for him and lift him into her arms, but she forced herself to take a measured breath and remain in locked stares with the Evherealme's master.

"Thank you, Your Majesty."

Alerice paced past the King of Shadows, shocked at her own deliberately even steps. Had this been the very shade she had met in the Hall of Eternity not so very long ago? Had he been the same immortal who had inspired her to dread herself? Perhaps, but no longer.

She crossed to Kreston, and extended her hand. He grasped her forearm, and she pulled him to his feet. She regarded him, and then regarded the broadsword set in his hand. She saw his hazel eyes begging her to leave him to his fate, but she was not about to do anything of the sort.

Alerice turned about to face the king, planting herself between Kreston and his vilified master.

"You are about to send Kreston back into battle to harvest souls for you. You will no doubt prevent the queen from locking his mind away again, and you have no care if Kreston loses it in forced servitude to you.

"But you have overlooked one last move in this game: mine. Kreston may slay men in your name. He may again become the Ghost of the Crimson Brigade, but I will be there to make certain he never goes too far. I will be his advocate against you. So as I told you earlier, two Walkers now stand before you, and neither of us will be of much use to you."

The King of Shadows looked Alerice over. "I told you that you are better than he is. Enjoy your self-assuredness, Alerice Linden of Navre. You're going to need it."

The King of Shadows waved his arm once again, and both he and Kreston vanished from the plateau.

THE RAVEN'S DAUGHTER

THE RAVEN'S DAUGHTER

Tales of the Ravensdaughter

Adventure Six

The children who knew shadows
Have risen now to fame.
They know their place and power.
They know their true acclaim.

Regard them now, these Walkers,
Gods above and gods below.
The Realme has kissed Mortalia
Forever now, and long ago.

from the Scrolls of Imari

The dawn's wind blew briskly across Alerice's cheek and tossed her blonde hair about her eyes. She shivered and drew her feathered cloak closer, for the chill chasing down her back was not borne of the wind.

The sights and sounds of two armies filled her senses. She could feel their wild energy, like two great beasts about to tear into one another. She could smell the dirt churned up by men's boots, horses' hooves, and wagon wheels. She could hear voices, some shouting, some an underlying drone.

Alerice had thought the task assigned by the Raven Queen would be simpler. She had commanded that Alerice retrieve as many souls as she could, and deliver them to the Hall of Eternity so they might be processed without guiding them in from the Convergence.

The queen had gifted her the feathered cloak for this purpose. Just as with the cloak belonging to one of the Raven Knights that Alerice had worn in the town of Uffton, she would be able to fly about the battlefield and tuck souls into the winged fabric. She would be able to dart and flit so quickly that she doubted any of the fighting men would be able to see her, let alone land a blow against her.

All the same, in addition to her black scale mail tunic, she now wore black metal leg plates along with the black gorget and pauldrons that Oddwyn had offered her when he, and she, had first outfitted her.

Alerice also bore a helm, which she tucked into the crook of her arm. Similar to a Raven Knight's, hers was fashioned in the shape of a bird's skull with a spray of metal feathers rising from the top-back of the crestline.

However, unlike a knight's helm, her visor was open. Alerice was grateful for this because she had never worn a helm before. She had never worn full armor before, and for that matter, she had never seen the dreadful sight of two massive groups of men about to destroy one another.

"Pretty sight," Kreston said from behind.

Alerice turned about to find him standing at her flank, the vanishing traces of a Realme portal dissolving in the tri-colors of black, midnight blue, and deep teal.

Kreston was dressed in gray scales, and Alerice paused, for this was the first time she had seen him in armor. His tunic looked as though it had been crafted by the King of Shadows, for it was not a solid color. Depending on how Kreston moved, the metal shifted from light to dark gray, save for one red patch on his upper left chest.

Alerice did not know the reason for this mark, and she did not wish to inquire. She surmised that, in the heat of battle, it could draw an opponent's focus to Kreston's left side, allowing him to strike from the right.

However, it could also be a reminder of his lost Crimson Brigade, and this was not a subject Alerice was about to broach.

The remainder of Kreston's body was protected by plate. As with the king's Shadow Warriors, his leg and arm plates were etched with wispy curls. So too were his pauldrons, which bore metal spikes resembling the crystals protruding from the shoulders of the King of Shadows' own long robe.

Kreston's helm, which he too held in the crook of his arm, was a single piece with angled, open eye slits and an angled nose guard. The front slit was long and pointed. Upon the brow rested an off-set square that bore the emblem of Kreston's lost Crimson Brigade, a red broadsword set point-down between two bull's horns. Indeed, any fighting man seeing him so adorned would recognize him as the ghost of that tragic regiment.

Alerice watched as Kreston looked past her to survey the battlefield. They both stood some distance away on a small rise topped by a little shade tree. His expression belied the ice that she had seen him summon into his veins. His hazel eyes were hard. His demeanor reminded her of when they had fought creatures in the Evherealme, that of a man capable of wholesale slaughter. With what Oddwyn had told her of Kreston's history – and especially now that the Raven Queen had unlocked his mind – Alerice sensed that the King of Shadows had assigned Kreston the task of killing as many men as he could.

Kreston's gaze shifted to her, and she lifted her chin. She held his stare for a moment, but then saw him draw a thin breath before his shoulders lowered.

He tossed his helm so that it turned upside down, and caught its crown in his gray-gloved palm. He placed it on his head with practiced ease, and looked again at the field.

"Stay clear of me," he warned.

"Because the king has sent you to claim souls, just as the queen has sent me?"

"Because the king has sent me to do what I do best, and I don't want you getting in the way."

Alerice looked over her shoulder at the armies. "I take it that the king enjoys this type of entertainment."

Kreston humphed. "Are you joking? This is what he *lives* for."

Alerice turned to the field as Kreston stepped up to her side.

"I'm not going to let you ruin yourself," she said.

"Too late."

"I'm serious, Kreston," she said, turning her head to him. "I meant what I told the King of Shadows. I am going to be your advocate."

"Huzzah to that."

Alerice did not wish to suffer sarcasm at a time like this, and so she tucked her intentions to the back of her mind and looked at the forming lines. Then, she focused on the standards of both armies, and concern crept into her thoughts.

One army bore the standard of her home city of Navre: four golden circles on a blue field. The other bore the standard of Navre's sister city, A'Leon: a white lion on a blue field.

"This isn't right," she said.

"If only I had a gold coin for every time I've heard you say that."

Alerice shot Kreston a scorned look, but he simply stared ahead. Seeing that he was not about to engage, she continued.

"Why would Navre and A'Leon fight one another? Their Prime Chevals are brothers, Lord Andoni and Lord Bolivar."

"Sibling rivalry?" Kreston suggested.

"Stop it, Kreston. I've lived in Navre since I was five. There is simply no way that those two would fight one another."

Horns blew and the roar of men rose up. Alerice shivered once more, but Kreston's gloved hand caught hold of her upper arm to steady her.

"Just fly fast," he said. "The way you did in Uffton."

Alerice's brow wrinkled. "How did you know I did that? You weren't with me then. You had already left Uffton and returned to the Realme. That's what you told me when we were with the Wyld."

Kreston did not reply, except to repeat, "Fly fast."

With that, Kreston charged so quickly that Alerice had difficulty tracking him. He bolted straight for the armies, drawing the King of Shadows' broadsword as he hurried toward the thick of the fight.

Then, as the first blows landed and the first men cried out in agony, Alerice felt her spine straighten of its own accord. She felt her feathered cloak spread out, and felt it bear her down into a waiting crouch.

Alerice hastily donned her helmet, for in the next moment her body sprang forward from the little rise and its lone shade tree, her cloak spreading into wings as she, too, shot for the thick of the fray.

There was no time to think, no time to reason or analyze. There were only lightning-fast flits from body to body and soul to soul.

Somehow, Alerice recalled what Oddwyn had ordered in Uffton when the faun souls were facing the dangers of the morning sunlight.

"'Gods above, Alerice. You're a Realme Walker,'" he had said. "'One of your tasks will always be shepherding souls into the Realme. Now hurry before you lose them.'"

Alerice had spread her wings back then, and darted with surprising deftness. She did so now, reaching out to catch hold of any nearby soul that rose away from its corpse, and tucking it safely within the metaphysical folds of her black feathers.

She felt as small as a sparrow, nimbly shifting course from wingbeat to wingbeat. She moved by will, her consciousness guiding her cloak to propel her forward.

She saw a Navre foot soldier gasp and collapse. His soul shot from his body as surely as if it had been cast from a sling. She caught hold of its shoulder and tucked it to her side as she might catch a coin from one of her old tavern customers and tuck it in her purse.

The wind rushed past her face, venting into her helm, and though her eyes narrowed, she retained full sight of the work at hand.

Swordsmen, axe men, and pikemen, Alerice flew above and about them as a black angel, securing souls by any means, whether they required tugging up from their mortal remains as she might tug up roots from a garden, or capturing them in erratic flight, as she might take hold of a moth desperate to escape a window pane.

Alerice did not know how many souls her cloak could bear. The Raven Queen had told her that when the cloak had reached a full tally, it would feel heavier and slow her flight.

Indeed, this did happen after what seemed a good amount of time, but from what Alerice could see of the battle below, it had not been much time at all. The men below were still hotly engaged with no signs of slowing.

"My Queen!" she called as she banked to double-back upon her last direction.

As Alerice looked ahead, she could see a Realme portal opening midair. She flew straight toward it, but as she glanced down she saw Kreston cutting, thrusting, and slicing through any nearby body, and she felt a pang of heartache for him.

Alerice flew into the Hall of Eternity. She had no idea how to land, and she crashed and tumbled forward, her plated knees striking the floor's great mosaic glyphs. Some of the amorphous spirit guides, who guided souls from the Convergence, rushed to her side. They removed her cloak and shook it out as servants might shake out the dust from a long journey.

Alerice looked up to find the Raven Queen floating toward her, and she rose to all fours and shook her head to regain her senses. She saw the Raven Queen gesture 'up' with her willow-white hand, and Alerice felt an unseen force gently help her to her feet. There, she readied her stance, for the queen was opening another portal to the battlefield.

As the spirit guides replaced the cloak about her shoulders, Alerice felt it prepare her to spring back into action, but she quickly looked about.

"Where's Oddwyn?"

"In the Convergence," the queen replied.

Alerice looked into her matron's pale face, drawing strength from her deep amethyst gaze. She nodded, ready to continue, but paused as the Raven Queen advised, "Approach with your feet before you, Alerice. Just as a bird might do."

Alerice nodded and launched herself through the waiting portal.

Alerice's second flight mirrored her first, but with many more souls to collect now that the battle was fully joined. She concentrated on those that appeared to be the most confounded, unaccepting of what had just happened to them.

Some reached out to her willingly. Some resisted her, and she had to fight to catch hold of them and tuck them into her cloak. She felt the latter kick within her feathers like a prisoner when the door slams shut, but the commotion died down quickly enough for Alerice to lift more men away from the sad world that had seen their lives' end.

Then, as she circled the heart of the conflict, she saw Kreston raise his broadsword and heard him shout, "My King!" His broadsword glowed brightly, causing men to shrink from him. She saw a Realme portal open for him, and he jumped through.

Wanting to fully understand his task, Alerice collected as many souls as were handy, and then flew back toward the short rise and its lone, little shade tree.

"My Queen!" she shouted.

As she hoped, a portal opened for her and she flew through.

This time, Alerice imagined the wild bird she used to feed when she managed the Cup and Quill. It was a pretty boy with a red breast and tan wings tipped in black. She used to place crumbs on her window sill and watch it alight to peck. She now employed that seemingly mundane observation to her advantage as she expended her legs before her so that her boot soles struck the Hall of Eternity's glyph-encrusted floor.

She landed on balance, and stood as the spirit guides came to collect her cloak. They shook it out as before, and while they shooed the exiting souls toward a waiting area near the side of the dais below the queen's throne, Alerice looked over her shoulder to find Kreston kneeling before the King of Shadows.

He extended his broadsword, which the king grasped in both hands. Then, as though drawing from a long pipe, the king inhaled the souls trapped in the steel.

His dark gray eyes widened, and his face flashed with exhilarated ferocity. He hooted and slapped his chest, and for a moment, Alerice thought he might expel a burst of power that would demolish his side of the hall.

"More!" the king shouted.

Kreston nodded and stood, taking back the broadsword and holding it ready.

Alerice saw him look at her, his hazel eyes meeting hers for the briefest moment. Then he turned and stepped through the portal that the King of Shadows had opened for him.

"Alerice," the Raven Queen said.

Alerice's face snapped to her matron's. The queen regarded the king, and Alerice saw in her expression the same suppressed anger that she had seen in many a disappointed wife come to collect their drunken husbands from the Cup and Quill.

"You may stop Kreston, if you can," the queen said softly. "But do not allow your concern for him to hinder your task. The more souls you deliver to me, the fewer for Oddwyn to sort in the Convergence... and the fewer for my husband to devour."

Alerice nodded as she prepared to take flight a third time.

Alerice again circled the center of the battlefield, for the fighting along the sidelines had become sporadic skirmishes in which few men perished. Again, she saw Kreston in the heart of the conflict, but despite possessing a Realme Walker's enhanced stamina, he was beginning to show signs of fatigue. Even so, men dared not approach him, and the only combatants he could slay were the unfortunate ones who ventured too close.

Alerice could see that a great deal of momentum had dissipated in both armies, and though she could see that more men wore white lions than gold circles, it seemed to her that the two armies had fought themselves into a stalemate.

Then a shout of "For Andoni!" rang out from a mounted A'Leon captain, which Alerice found strange. Andoni was the Prime Cheval of Navre. It made no sense that anyone from A'Leon would use his name as a battle cry.

A small cavalry unit repeated the call before they followed the captain into the final pit of activity.

They were heading directly toward Kreston.

Alerice rolled off to her left and dove down to intercept them as Kreston prepared to fend them off. As she soared low, the A'Leon foot soldiers closed in, some even drawing up the courage to approach Kreston from behind.

Alerice swooped in as a blackened *whoosh*, and the foot soldiers leaped back, even as Kreston half-turned in their direction. He held his broadsword aloft and yelled at the top of his lungs. The soldiers scurried away as Kreston quickly turned back to the incoming cavalry. However, with a reverse swoop, Alerice brushed past the lead horse. It reared and whinnied, throwing the captain to the mud.

Kreston stalked toward the downed officer, and Alerice had only an instant to stop him. She reversed direction once again to fly in low, and pushed Kreston backward before he could strike.

The remaining horses either reared or sidled into one another, fouling the charge and frustrating the cavalry. A hush fell over the field, and Alerice *whooshed* past Kreston once more, making certain that her cloak brushed the faces of as many men as possible.

"Damn it, Alerice!" she heard Kreston shout. However, his consternation made her smirk, for by denying him combat she was doing what she had promised the King of Shadows she would do: become Kreston's advocate. He would slaughter no more men this day.

Though her cloak required unburdening, Alerice banked about, extended her legs, and set her boots down into the mud. She steadied herself, and employing the old trick of bending her knees to maintain balance, she straightened her back and struck a stance, shoulders squared and head high.

"Stand down, Crimson Ghost!" she ordered.

Through his helm's angled eye slits, Alerice saw Kreston blink in astonishment. "What?" he exclaimed.

"Can you not hear me? I said stand down!" she demanded.

Alerice held her ground, but then Kreston snarled and raised his broadsword. She leaped aside, her cloak carrying her well out of his range, and drew the pixie pole cylinders from her belt. She caused the bladed poles to appear, and noted that the men about her murmured in astonishment and gave her room.

She faced Kreston, whose fatigue was becoming more apparent, and knowing that she needed to extract them both to the safety of the Realme, she *clanged* her poles together. The clear tone rang out, and several men recoiled.

Kreston cried out and turned his body away while raising a hand in surrender.

"Mercy, Ravensdaughter," he panted, his voice loud enough for all to hear. "The Ghost of the Crimson Brigade yields to you."

Alerice did not know how to respond, and so she *clanged* her poles again. She caused the mark of the Raven Queen to glow upon her brow, emitting an odd purplish light within her helm. She watched more men back away, which afforded her a few precious moments.

"*My Queen!*" she called mentally. She looked about for a portal, but did not see one forming. Hoping no one would try to claim an advantage while she closed her eyes, Alerice gave her entire being over to her mark. She felt her way through time and space as she visualized the Realme's mossy rise surrounded by columns where Oddwyn had once taken her to be healed.

"My Queen!" she called again, praying that her matron would deliver her and Kreston to safety without delay.

Distant thunder rolled across the sky. Alerice sensed it more than she heard it, but then she heard something that she did not expect – a man's deep, far-off laughter.

"L'Orku," men muttered, ruining her concentration. Alerice opened her eyes and looked about. Kreston recovered and moved close to her side as more men looked skyward and murmured, "L'Orku."

Kreston took hold of her arm and leaned in close to whisper, "They're hoping the thunder god joins them tonight."

Alerice glanced at Kreston and then regarded the men, for she recalled the army lore her father had once imparted, that if L'Orku and his brother Gäete, God of Storms, assumed human disguises and sat at a regiment's campfire, no harm would befall the men that night and no rain would fall upon the battlefield.

The laughter faded, but then lightning tore across the sky. Thunder *boomed*, startling some, and as the din rolled away, a man's voice proclaimed, "Hail to the Ravensdaughter!"

Alerice watched at least a hundred men turn to her, sending a shiver up her spine. She had never felt more exposed in her life.

"Hail to the Ravensdaughter," a few men echoed, somewhat stupefied. "Hail," more said with mounting confidence. "Hail," even more joined in until all nearby began to raise their weapons and call, "Hail to the Ravensdaughter."

The cavalry captain, half-covered in mud, came forward. He stopped before Alerice and saluted, then turned to his men and shouted, "Hail to the Ravensdaughter! She has vanquished the Ghost of the Crimson Brigade!"

Alerice cringed internally, and pressed a bit closer to Kreston. He shoved her forward and took a knee at her side, burying the point of his broadsword into the soil and gripping its handle with both hands. Then he bowed the crown of his helm onto the pommel.

Alerice wanted to kick him to make him stand up, but just then she saw something that she truly could not believe. A rider drew near, bearing the Navre standard. Next, two men rode forth.

One was the Reef of Navre, the same villain who had stabbed her on the open road and sent her body to the Realme. The second was none other than her rapist, Mayor Gotthard, who now wore the trappings of Navre's Prime Cheval.

The poisoned cup she had given Gotthard had apparently not killed him, and since Lord Andoni was nowhere to be found, it suddenly struck Alerice why men of A'Leon were calling Lord Andoni's name. If Gotthard had assumed

Andoni's place, it was a simple matter for Alerice to conclude that Gotthard had murdered Andoni in a rise to power.

"My Queen!" Alerice shouted aloud. "Great Lady Raven! I claim my prize for the Evherealme!" she said, grabbing hold of Kreston's vambrace and tugging for him to rise.

He did, and to Alerice's great relief she saw a portal open before her. Men gasped as it swirled in black, midnight blue, and deep teal, and she caught one final glimpse of the Reef's and Gotthard's astonished looks as she guided Kreston into the safety of the world below.

***

"Kreston, will you just support yourself against the column?" Alerice asked. She lifted Kreston's arm and guided his hand to the column's surface, exposing the side of his body so that she could begin unbuckling the leather straps of his scale mail tunic.

"I can get out of my own gear."

She paused and straightened to look at him. "I know you can, but you're tired, and you can't honestly look me in the eye and tell me that you don't appreciate my help."

She watched him try, but in the end he smiled and humphed a little laugh. She smiled back, and returned to her task.

They stood on the mossy rise where the 'sky' above swirled in tones of deep teal with light blue currents creating a daylight hue.

They had already been to the Hall of Eternity where the spirit guides had taken her cloak to shake the souls free. The Raven Queen had recalled Oddwyn from the Convergence, where Alerice learned that he had been more than occupied sorting the souls that Alerice had not been able to gather. There was also the natural influx of souls from other Mortalia deaths, so battles were indeed intense times for the Realme.

The queen had instructed Oddwyn to help Alerice out of her helm and plate, but given that the King of Shadows had engorged himself on the final souls Kreston had taken, there was no one to tend to his needs, and so Alerice had asked that the Raven Queen send them both to this place where she might see to Kreston herself.

The column was composed of the same silver-veined stone that formed the Convergence's arches, and Kreston had placed his hand over one of the black glyphs. A cascade of silvery glimmers flowed down about his fingertips from the column's crown, and Alerice could sense that he was already beginning to relax from his exertion. She gave thanks to any gods that might be listening that he had not suffered serious injury.

She moved to Kreston's other side and finished unbuckling his scales. Then she helped lift the tunic over his head and set it down. She noted that he watched with pleasant satisfaction as she began to unbuckle his arm plates. Then she tended to his leg plates, unbuckling them and untying them from his gambeson so that she could also set them atop his scales.

She guided Kreston to recline on the moss, and sat down next to him.

"Keeping your scales on?" he asked.

"For now," she said.

"Mmmm," he muttered, his hazel eyes fluttering even though he tried to keep them open.

"I wish I could put you to sleep," she said, stroking his salt-and-pepper hair. "If I had a potion to give you, I would. I'm just glad that those horses didn't ride over you. They, and the men coming up on your back, could have killed you."

"You should have let them."

"Don't say that, Kreston."

"Why not? It wouldn't have been the first time I died in *his* service."

Alerice noted the derisive manner in which Kreston referred to the King of Shadows. He used to use that tone when referring to the Raven Queen, but now that his mind was free, he knew where to focus his resentment.

"I don't want you to die," she said.

"It would have gotten me out of there."

"I got you out of there. And I'll keep doing so as long as the king sends you to slaughter people."

"Which," he said sleepily, "makes you dangerous."

"How so?" she asked.

He smiled as he gazed up at her. He stroked a lock of her blonde hair, and ran his fingertips along the burn scar that Sukaar, Father God of Fire, had left upon her jaw. Then he sighed and flopped his arm onto his chest.

"Later," he exhaled.

His eyes closed and he began to drift off. Alerice wanted to kiss him, but she was afraid that would imply a promise she did not wish to keep. She thought about kissing his brow where the King of Shadows had scratched his mark into Kreston's skin, but that would be making the same promise.

She decided to pet his head. Then she looked about at the mossy rise, and the columns, and their sparkles cascading down from their tops like glistening little waterfalls.

Alerice saw the maiden Oddwyn standing a small ways off. She brightened at the sight of her Realme sister and waved, taking care not to disturb Kreston. Oddwyn waved back, and beckoned for her to come over. Alerice slowly slid away from Kreston's side to join her.

Alerice and Oddwyn walked for a short while, saying nothing. As she kept her eyes down, Alerice occasionally caught sight of the hem of Oddwyn's iridescent belted demi-gown that showed off her light-blue leggings and white boots.

The path they treaded was made of midnight blue paving stones, and currents of pewter-gray ether undulated on both sides. The path seemed to go on forever while leading nowhere. It was yet another mystery of the Evherealme that Alerice was pleased to discover.

"The king is going to be furious at Kreston when I tell him that he yielded to you," Oddwyn said.

"He doesn't already know?" Alerice asked.

"I think he's had too many souls," Oddwyn said.

Alerice nodded, but then asked, "Can't you tell him that Kreston simply withdrew from the field?"

Oddwyn smiled knowingly. "The Ghost of the Crimson Brigade does not 'withdraw from the field'. He either clears the field or dies on it. If he dies, the king doesn't get his fill. Kreston's soul comes into the Convergence, and the king takes hold of it. I fetch Kreston's body, and the king melds the two together. Either way, the king always asks me how the battle went, and I always have to tell him."

Alerice patted her hand on her thigh. "I'm not certain why Kreston did yield. He could have defeated me if he had attacked me. He knows that."

Oddwyn stopped and turned to Alerice. "You're not serious. Why did he yield? Because he loves you, Alerice, and he had to find a way to avoid fighting you without losing face. Luckily, you've learned to use your cloak, and you put on quite a show, calling him the Crimson Ghost. It's natural that things of the Realme should come quickly to you now. Your soul is nearly tethered here."

"Tethered," Alerice pondered.

"Does that worry you?"

"I don't know. It doesn't feel bad, but I'm not certain if it feels right. I'm still mortal. How will I manage myself?"

"Oh, you'll manage yourself. You can manage anything. I see that now. And so does the queen."

"And the king?" Alerice asked.

After a pause, Oddwyn answered, "Yep. Kreston is right. You're dangerous."

"But I don't wish to be."

"But what choice will you have, Alerice? When things are dire and you wish to follow your own mind, especially when it comes to Kreston? Do you think the King of Shadows is going to stand by and let you rob him of his prized

Realme Walker? He keeps Kreston as a gem, just as the queen kept her Eye."

Oddwyn turned and began walking along their path again. "But that's not why I wanted to speak to you. Over the ages, I have known several Realme Walkers. Not many, because you people aren't born that often, but a few. However, I've never met a Walker like you. Perhaps it was the way you were born, or the gods who might have been involved, who knows? But you are almost able to open your own portal, and Walkers can't do that. I said you were becoming tethered. There's a way you can control how it happens. You've been kissed by the Raven Queen, but there's another kiss that will bind you to us forever."

"The king's," Alerice said, knowing this as surely as she knew herself.

"Mm hmm," Oddwyn said. "If he kisses you, the duality is complete."

"What about if you kissed me?" Alerice teased.

Oddwyn presented himself as a youth, and placed a hand on Alerice's arm. She stopped and turned to him – but then he stepped in and kissed her. He wrapped his arms about her black scales and she found herself wrapping her arms around his iridescent tunic. Their kiss was deep and lasting, and they felt their spirits mingle.

When it ended, their lips parted and they both found themselves out of breath. They swooned, and soon began to steady one another.

"That was good!" he exclaimed.

"Yes, it was," Alerice commented.

"Whoof," Oddwyn said, his head lolling as the little bursts of color in his white hair gleamed. Eventually, he recovered and looked into her eyes. "Feel like a demi-goddess?"

"Mmmm, not particularly."

"Well, it's obviously not my kiss that you require. It's the king's, and the thing is, he knows what his kiss will do to you, so you should be prepared that he might see it as his only means to control you, if he doesn't lash out at you first."

"But he doesn't need to lash out or control me, Oddwyn. Neither of them do."

Oddwyn presented herself as a maiden once again, and continued in her soft voice, "Alerice, I'm going to let you in on a truth. The only thing that the king and queen have to call their own is control. Look about you. This is the Evherealme. It's not a land of hope. It's a land of memory. All the souls here had their chance to live. Some did well. Some did horribly. But that time is past.

"Mortalia is the world of hope, and dreams, and all the happy things people conjure up. Mortals are alive to live out those things, for good or ill, and it is life's unpredictability that proffers multiple outcomes.

"Here, things are fixed. Here things are shadows of what they once were. Here, the King of Shadows and the Raven Queen have one thing: control over who gets which souls, how they dispose of those souls, and how they maintain this world of souls.

"And now the queen has an advantage," Oddwyn added. "You. Kreston is spent. There's no hiding it. He has a few years left, but he's ebbing. You, on the other hand, are ascending. You are a wonder to behold, a strange dichotomy of modesty and pride.

"But there's one more thing that makes all this truly interesting," Oddwyn said. "You have also been kissed by two gods above, Sukaar, Father Fire, and Imari, Mother Water Wind, and if the king kisses you to complete our duality, their duality might allow you to transcend what either the Raven Queen or the King of Shadows thinks you're capable of."

"That is interesting," Alerice commented. "Do you think the king or queen have considered this?"

"I have no idea what they consider. It's not my place to know their minds."

Alerice was tempted to challenge this point, given Oddwyn's constant attendance upon the Realme's mistress, but her matter-of-fact response made Alerice think twice.

"Oddwyn," she said. "If I chose to solicit the king's kiss, do you think he would grant it?"

"I don't know. As I said, he's going to be furious when he learns what Kreston did." Oddwyn presented himself once more as a youth and asked, "Does this mean you are thinking of binding yourself here?"

"I am, but there's something else," Alerice said, glancing back over her shoulder where she could see the mossy rise and its glistening columns. "If I let the King of Shadows believe he has leverage over me, then I have the 'coin' to buy Kreston's freedom."

***

"Alerice, I wish you to end the conflict in Mortalia," the Raven Queen said. "Specifically, the conflict between your city, Navre, and the city of A'Leon."

Alerice was glad to be given the task because now she no longer needed to ask her matron's permission, for along with Kreston, the problem of Gotthard in control of Navre was forefront in her thoughts.

She stood in the Hall of Eternity at the foot of the dais. Clustered at the side of the hall near the statues of women of the arts, Alerice saw souls still waiting to be measured. Spirit guides tended to them, but Alerice knew that the queen had taken time from her sorting to summon her.

Alerice could also sense the queen's disdain for the King of Shadows, who reclined sideways on his throne. The queen could not stop a momentary glance in his direction, followed by a thin sigh as she pressed her red lips into a line. Then she focused her amethyst gaze down upon her champion.

"If all elements work according to their natures, the Realme will see benefit from this task, for which I sense your eagerness."

"I am eager, My Queen," Alerice said. "From what I was able to see on the battlefield, something has gone wrong in Navre."

The queen nodded. "Then I dispatch you."

Alerice could not help but look at the King of Shadows, who readjusted his position but did not wake from his stupor. The thought of kissing him seemed as vile as the memory of how the Reef of Navre had nearly kissed her the night he stabbed her and sent her into the Evherealme.

She needed to think of something else.

"My Queen," Alerice said. "I became practiced in one skill when I managed my Cup and Quill – forcing men to cease fighting – but I must have a strong show of force to deal with two mortals waging war. May I use the Raven Knights as I did when solving the mystery of the thief of souls?"

"You may," the queen said.

Alerice saw the Raven Knights step forward, the golden glows in their helms' eye sockets brightening. How she wished she could have opened her own dual portals to send them off.

"I need one knight to fly to Bolivar of A'Leon, and one to fly to Gotthard of Navre," she said. "I ask that both knights deliver these men to my tavern, and that you send me there so I may await them."

"Agreed," the queen said as three portals began forming within the Hall of Eternity.

***

Alerice stepped into the late afternoon sun. Golden light shone on a street lined with multi-story, exposed timber homes. She knew each door as surely as she knew each family behind it. She knew each roof as surely as she knew that the sky was blue.

She was home... and yet was she?

Alerice became aware that she stood in the open and that heads were turning in her direction. Notoriety would not serve her well at this moment, and so she turned to the narrow alley that she knew was behind her, and slipped into the shadows beside the Cup and Quill.

Her blessed shadows. She had eluded so many people in this alley. It was not lengthy, only the depth of the tavern. She touched the rock of the home next door, remembering its rough surface. She smelled the air, allowing the scent of spiced cooking and roasting meats to whisk her back to a time that seemed forever ago.

But there was work to do, and as Alerice contemplated her task, she also knew that this was no longer her world.

"Chessy?" Alerice called to her cousin, who stood thumping kegs to check their levels.

She stood inside the Cup and Quill's back door, noting that the evening crowd had not begun to arrive. Cousin Chessy looked in her direction, but she remained within the shadows, her black scales helping to conceal her.

"Who's there?" Chessy asked.

"Chessy, I want you to place a hand on the bar and grip it."

Alerice saw Chessy squint, but then he reacted as though his blood ran cold, for he obviously recognized her voice.

"God's above," he gasped. "Leecie?"

"Chessy Linden, take hold of the bar," Alerice demanded in the same voice she had used when they were teens.

Chessy's hand shot out and he did as he was told. Alerice stepped into the light spilling in from the side windows.

"Leecie!" he shouted.

"Shhh," she cautioned.

"Oh, Leecie!" he said a bit softer, bolting for her and catching her in his arms. He squeezed, but then he reacted to her scale mail tunic, and released her to look her over. "What are you wearing, and what in the world has happened to you? Are..." He gulped. "Are you Leecie's ghost? Oh, please, please tell me that's not so. You feel real. You must be real."

"It is me, Chessy, and I am alive. And if I had time to tell you everything that's happened, I would sit you down and we'd drink the kegs dry. But I don't have time, and so you're going to have to do exactly as I say." She smiled then added, "But I have been on the most amazing adventure."

The front door flew open, and two black *whooshes* flew in. Chessy's eyes went wide, but Alerice stepped around to the front of the bar.

"Place them over there," she said to the Raven Knights, who appeared in the flash of an eye, one holding Bolivar of A'Leon and one holding Gotthard of Navre. "Tavern Master!" Alerice called to Chessy. "Two tankards, and they don't have to be the best. These two don't deserve it."

The Raven Knights forced Bolivar and Gotthard to the table Alerice had indicated, and then withdrew to either side of the room. Their golden eyes glowed from the shadows created by spaces between the windows.

Gotthard and Bolivar looked about to assess their surroundings, Gotthard becoming incensed.

"What is the mean--" he tried to say.

"Gotthard," Alerice interrupted. "If you say, 'of this' I swear to the Raven Queen that I will castrate you right here, right now." She drew her Realme dagger and raised it so that it glinted with sunlight. Gotthard held his tongue. "Sit down," she ordered.

The men obeyed.

Chessy came forward with the tankards. Alerice took them and gestured her head toward the front door. Chessy nodded, and hurried to lock it. Then, he turned toward the rear door while glancing at the Raven Knights. He quickened his steps and he exited, nearly slamming the door behind him.

Alerice knew that Chessy was not running away. Rather, he was heading down the alley to the front to move out the "Tavern Closed" barrel and block anyone from entering. Sure enough, Chessy moved past the front windows, lugging something heavy, and secure in her position, Alerice was ready to manage the moment.

"You're the Ravensdaughter," Lord Bolivar said. "The one my men were telling me about."

"I am," Alerice said.

Alerice nodded to the Lord of A'Leon, but then she watched Gotthard look from the rear door to her as he likely realized her identity and her relationship to Chessy.

"It *is* you," Gotthard said. "That murderous little Linden bird."

Alerice slammed the tankards down upon the tabletop, splashing their contents over Bolivar's and Gotthard's tunics. The men brushed off the brew, Gotthard glaring.

Alerice threw her Realme dagger into the table so that it sank into the wood. Gotthard reacted as though he had just been handed the advantage in a bar fight, but as he reached for the dagger, Alerice held her hand high, and it appeared in her palm.

"You think this is a common blade?" she asked as both men startled. "You think I wear mortal scales? You think *they* are not servants of the Raven Queen?" she asked, gesturing to the knights. "You are in the presence of a Walker of the Evherealme. Yes, me, the murderous Linden bird, whom the Reef murdered in return, and who has been to the world below and risen back into this world above. You are in my presence, in my power, and you both will now listen to me. I promise you that."

Gotthard scoffed, but Lord Bolivar rose and bowed.

"Ravensdaughter," he said with eager deference.

"Oh, shut up, Bolivar," Gotthard said, also rising. "She is Alerice Linden, the former maid of this place." Gotthard stared into Alerice's eyes. "A nothing. A nobody."

"Who poisoned you," Alerice said with a knowing grin.

Gotthard paused, giving Bolivar the chance to step about the table and come closer.

"But she appeared and disappeared on the field," Bolivar said. "L'Orku himself announced her. She even vanquished the--"

"Ghost of the Crimson Brigade?" Kreston said as he appeared near the bar, traces of a Realme portal vanishing behind him. He wore his gray scales, but he had left his plate and helm below.

Both Bolivar and Gotthard backed as he approached.

"Gods above," Bolivar breathed.

"You'd best say, 'Gods below'," Alerice commented. "The Crimson Ghost serves the King of Shadows as I serve the Raven Queen, and he has come to enforce my right to demand that you end hostilities immediately. The rulers of the Realme are not happy about it. This is my message to you."

"Your message," Gotthard sneered. "You will deliver no message to me. Or have you forgotten how I took you in this place?" He glanced about for the table over which he had doubled Alerice and thrown back her skirts. "Right there," he continued, pointing. "You remember the feel of me, how it must have filled you. I'm certain you recall how I had your cousin murdered right over there--"

Kreston strode forward and punched Gotthard's jaw so hard that he splayed the man to the floorboards.

Alerice saw the hate in Kreston's eyes, but she had no intention of telling him to stand down. Rather, she paced to Gotthard so that her boot rested near his head.

"Monster, I will tell you what I regret most about that moment. You took my cousin from me. You took my family from me, but more importantly, you took my good judgment from me. I regretted poisoning you, not because you didn't deserve it, but because I am a better person than that. You robbed me of my sense of self, my peace of mind, but events have a strange way of turning about, for now I have returned with such strength that I will never suffer anyone to rob me again. You are the nothing, the nobody, and if I chose to proclaim it in the streets of Navre – just as I proclaimed it on the night I gave you that cup – everyone would listen."

"It's a pity you did not kill him," Bolivar said. "Gotthard used your cup to rise against my brother. He circulated rumors that you were Andoni's spy, and extorted enough city officials that they turned a blind eye while he had Andoni murdered. This is why I've come. To rid Navre of him, which I will do now if you and the Crimson Ghost will only step aside."

"No," Alerice said flatly. "When this wretch dies, he dies publicly. If he extorted city officials and had your brother murdered, then let him stand trial for it."

"Oh, yes," Gotthard said. "I welcome a trial. Especially here in Navre."

"Where no one will convict you," Bolivar said.

Gotthard smiled. "Where no one will convict me."

"Gotthard?" Alerice interrupted in a sweetly sarcastic tone. "What makes you think the trial will be in Navre? For that matter, what makes you think it will be attended only by the living? I can guide souls up from the Realme below now. Perhaps Lord Andoni himself would like the chance to speak."

Fear shot through Gotthard's eyes. Alerice allowed it to linger before she beckoned the Raven Knights to step forward.

"I will choose the place and time to settle this matter," she said. "Until then, you two will withdraw from the field and barrack your men. If either of you advances, you will answer to me, and to my champion," she added, gesturing toward Kreston.

Kreston nodded, his expression conveying a strength that neither man dared confront.

Bolivar stood down and Gotthard looked about for a means of escape. He appeared ready to bolt for the rear door, but Kreston moved to stand in his path.

"Now," Alerice said. "Return to where you were, but always know that I have the power to summon you again."

Alerice beckoned again to the Raven Knights, who swooped in to claim their respective mortals. The tavern's front door flew open, and the knights *whooshed* out with their mortals in tow.

***

"You should have let Bolivar kill him," Kreston said. "At the very least you should have arrested him. Why'd you let him go?"

Alerice and Kreston walked along the street not far from the Cup and Quill, the evening's dusk providing enough light by which to see. It also provided enough shadows for them both to slip in and out, no doubt creating an otherworldly effect to all who watched. They sensed many eyes upon them, though no one dared approach, save for a brief moment when Chessy had found them.

He had brought Alerice's two other cousins, Clancy and Little Judd, and Cousin Jerome's widow, Millie. Alerice had spent a short moment with them, filled with hugs and a few tears. While she promised to return to the family brewery as soon as she could, she made it clear that she and Kreston needed to walk the town to challenge Gotthard's dominion.

"If I had let Bolivar kill Gotthard," Alerice said, "which believe me was very tempting, then the Reef would control Navre, and that's not an improvement. I let them both go to make their troops stand down, but I kept Gotthard in place so Navre did not devolve into chaos. When it changes hands, I will oversee it."

"But you know he's going to plot against you," Kreston said.

"I do, but he can't harm me now, and I want everyone to know it. That's why we're taking this little stroll."

"All the same, never let your enemy have breathing room."

"What can he do, Kreston? If Gotthard killed me, the queen would restore me the way the king restores you."

"That's not something you should welcome, Alerice."

"No, but it affords me the opportunity to assert my presence as I look for someone to govern the city. It can't be Gotthard or the Reef, and if Gotthard was able to extort city officials, then they're corrupt as well. Bolivar might be the right choice. I'm going to have to meet him and see what type of man he is."

"As you say," Kreston said. "Thank the gods above that I'm a soldier, not a politician, but guard your back."

"Isn't that why I have you?" she asked with a smile. Then she softened her voice so that only he could hear. "Who told you where I was?"

"Oddwyn. I asked him when I woke up, then I asked him to send me here."

"Why?"

"To spy on you."

She hid a little laugh. "Well, if you're spying on me, why are you telling me?"

"Oh, I'm a lousy spy, but the king will want to know what you're up to. If he's not watching you through me right now, he will be soon enough. I told you once that you can't trust me. Not because of me, because of him."

She nodded, then took a breath. "Listen, Krest--"

Kreston stopped and reached out to turn Alerice toward him. "No, Alerice, you listen. You still think you can persuade the king to free me, and I'm telling you that just won't happen. He took me back. He sent me to slaughter people, and he'll do it again."

"And I'll stop you again."

"For how long?" he asked. "Alerice, we both know that the only option you think you have is to bargain with the king to free me, and what would you offer? Yourself? If you did, and if the king accepted, I am telling you right here, right now, that would destroy me."

"But..."

"No buts. I couldn't live with myself if you paid that type of price. My mistakes are my own, and I don't ask other people to clean up my messes."

She gazed into his hazel eyes, knowing there would be no use discussing her thoughts on winning a kiss from the King of Shadows. Also, he was right. Perhaps she shouldn't.

"If the king is watching, should I have you here with me?"

"As long as you don't tell me your thoughts," he said. "The king has seen us together many times, and he knows that I will try to help you no matter what he orders me to do."

"Even if he orders you to kill me?"

He paused before he said, "Even if. I defied him once and he racked my brain, but I'd go through that again if I had to."

She placed her hand on his arm.

"Then, let's make sure you don't have to. There must be a solution, Kreston."

Kreston relaxed slightly. "If anyone can find it, it's you."

***

"Did you see her walking the streets?" Gotthard demanded.

"Yes, though I can't believe it," the Reef responded.

The two men stood in the Prime Cheval's suite, formerly Lord Andoni's domain. Gotthard had indeed taken hold of it by leveraging his having been poisoned. Since the attack had come on the night when he had hosted Andoni, he had claimed injury at Andoni's hand.

The fact that his wife, who had drunk more from the cup, had died only helped matters along. Once he recovered, Gotthard had ordered the Reef to arrest Andoni and sequester him in a cell that conveniently housed a murderer. With a simple slice of the throat, Andoni was no more, and with a proclamation by the city officials he held in his purse, Gotthard had declared himself Prime Cheval.

"I stabbed her with her own knife," the Reef said. "She died in my hold."

"I believe you," Gotthard said. "And now she claims to be the Raven Queen's daughter. She has a weird way about her. There's no denying it. So what is the solution?"

A disembodied voice spoke two simple words: "Kill her."

Both Gotthard and the Reef froze as they looked about. The suite was empty. However, the standing mirror caught their attention, for its pane began to frost over.

"Gods above," the Reef muttered.

"Or," Gotthard said, "gods below." He stepped closer to the mirror, seeing that the frost was not made of ice. Rather, it was made of tiny crystals that reflected the light from the suite's many candles.

Alerice and Kreston rode into the heart of Lord Bolivar's encampment. When they had arrived, two sentries had cried for them to identify themselves, but they had stopped short to find the Ravensdaughter and the Ghost of the Crimson Brigade.

Two pikemen had run up to escort them in, and Alerice had watched as one company after another stopped whatever they were doing to stand and stare.

The camp's fires had reflected on Kreston's gray scale mail, Jerome's flowing black mane, and Captain's mahogany shoulder as the pikemen had called for everyone to step aside. One of them had a deep voice that Alerice imagined could be heard for miles.

Lord Bolivar awaited them outside his tent, along with his marshal and other officers. Alerice glanced at Kreston for any recollection of how his men had been betrayed by their marshal, but he was his stoic self.

Burning logs in standing braziers lighted the area. Alerice and Kreston dismounted as the two pikemen held Jerome's and Captain's bridles. Alerice was about to approach Bolivar, but Kreston held her back. Then he turned to one of the pikemen and asked in a low voice, "How do you find your Lord?"

"Bolivar?" the man with the deep voice asked.

Kreston nodded, but gestured for the fellow not to speak too loudly.

The other pikeman stepped in to discretely offer, "He's a good'un, that one. Does right. Fine spine."

"Good man," the first added as quietly as he could.

Kreston patted the pikeman's shoulder. Then he turned Alerice to their waiting host even as he said under his breath, "Want to know a commander? Ask the ranks."

Alerice could not have been more grateful for Kreston's advice.

Bolivar's double-peaked tent was lighted by thick candles burning in tall holders. Several adorned his table, which was covered with maps. U-chairs bearing A'Leon's white lion on a blue field surrounded the table, while Bolivar's head chair bore the full A'Leon coat of arms.

To one side, Alerice noted a bureau topped with wine jugs and goblets. To the other she saw racks holding rolled scrolls. A scribe's desk stood near it, as did stands bearing swords and pole arms.

Alerice glanced at the maps, several of which outlined Navre's strategic positions. Bolivar gestured for her to take in her fill, which she did with calm confidence. Kreston kept to her flank, and Alerice could see Bolivar's officers doing their best to mask their realization that he was flesh, not spirit.

"You are welcome to everything, daughter of the Raven Queen," Bolivar said. "I have no secrets from the White Lady Below. My sister serves at Graystone Abbey, and she has written to me saying that the Raven's Daughter has risen to walk among us. I never imagined I would meet you, or host you at my table now, Alerice Linden of Navre."

Alerice acknowledged the familiarity, pleased at Bolivar's attempt to reach her on a personal level.

Gotthard and the Reef watched as the mirror's pane filled with smoke while a layer of tiny crystals grew thick enough to crack the glass.

Gotthard gestured the Reef back, and both men tensed as cracks ran along the mirror's surface. Then, the mirror shook on its stand until it burst forth in a shower of shards. The smoke exuded forth, and Gotthard and the Reef bolted for the far side of the suite.

The smoke swirled about in midair until it changed from gray to black, midnight blue, and deep teal.

Gotthard held his breath and the Reef swallowed hard as they saw a figure form within the swirl's center. It stepped forward, landing a white boot on the floorboards.

It was a youth with ice-blue eyes and white hair popped with colored bursts. He wore an iridescent tunic of turquoise and lavender, accented by indigo and pearl. His shirt was crafted from some shimmering material.

He struck a pose and stared, his eyes briefly narrowing on Gotthard before he proclaimed, "Mortals, lower your gazes in awe. Bend your knees in respect, for I present to you the King of Shadows, Master of the Evherealme."

Both Gotthard and the Reef hesitated, and the youth shouted, "Kneel! Cast your eyes down!"

They gulped and complied.

Gotthard then felt an icy blast shoot up his spine, and he could not help but look up. A tall specter wearing a crystalline crown stood where the youth had been. His long gray robe was trimmed in crystals, and more crystals protruded from the shoulders.

"Come here," the specter demanded.

Gotthard and the Reef obsequiously scurried forward.

"You want to do something about the girl?" the King of Shadows asked. "Then, do as I say. Kill her."

Gotthard shook, and yet his fear was not sufficient to prevent the slight upturn of his lips.

"The murderous Linden bird," Alerice called herself.

"As I said," Bolivar commented. "It's a pity you didn't kill him. I told you I was here to do that very thing, but unfortunately your decree has left me in a difficult position."

"How so?" Alerice asked.

"I respect the gods above and below," Bolivar said. "And you have ordered me to cease my attack. This means Gotthard will go unpunished, unless you do something about it."

"As you said you would," the marshal stated. The other officers echoed his sentiment, and he folded his arms as he awaited her intentions.

"Be silent!" Kreston shouted. Alerice saw him fix a steely gaze on them before he stared at Bolivar.

"My Lord," Alerice said in a diplomatic tone. "Prime Cheval of A'Leon. I have only one question for you."

"Ask it, I beg you," Bolivar said.

"Would you keep to my decree and leave, despite what your men, or your army, or your city would think of you? Would you do this to show fealty to the White Lady Below, no matter what the personal or political cost?"

Bolivar took a breath. "I am a pious man. And so my answer must be 'yes'. It would destroy all that I have promised my people. It would mean that a guilty man lives to commit more atrocities, but..." He paused and then added with a half-bow, "I would obey, Daughter of the Raven Queen."

Alerice smiled. "Then you are the type of man who should govern Navre and bring Gotthard to account."

Gotthard's suite was the last place in Mortalia Oddwyn wished to be, and yet here he was. The King of Shadows had commanded a heraldic entrance, and Oddwyn could not deny his duty.

Yet he longed to summon Alerice's Realme dagger and cast it into Gotthard's heart, for he knew that this was the creature who had raped her.

"How do we kill her?" Gotthard asked the King of Shadows.

"The way you kill any mortal," the king said. "She is flesh, and flesh dies."

"Until the queen restores her," Oddwyn thought.

"But I did kill her," the Reef said. "And she came back."

"Exactly," Oddwyn thought.

"Lock up her soul, and her body will die," the king said.

"Ah," Oddwyn thought, for the king had just outlined what he meant to do – have one of these worms kill Alerice, and then distract the queen so that he could steal her spirit. This meant acting against his wife's champion, which meant possible war within the Realme.

"Kill the girl," the king ordered, "and I will make certain that she does not rise."

"And Bolivar too?" Gotthard asked.

"Your mortal disputes are nothing to me," the king said. "Kill whomever you wish, only kill the girl first."

"With pleasure," Oddwyn mouthed silently as Gotthard said the words aloud. He half-rolled his eyes as he watched the greedy mortals begin to plot, suddenly understanding why weak dramas inspired nausea.

"We'll invite them to a congress of truce," Gotthard said. "In the hall below, his brother's hall. That will rankle him."

"Wait," the Reef said, noting the bruise on Gotthard's jaw left by Kreston's tavern strike. "What about that man of hers?"

Oddwyn caught sight of the King of Shadows, whose face almost seemed to flush. Oddwyn knew when to stand on guard, and he backed a step as the air rushed toward the Realme's master, causing the mirror shards to vibrate on the floor.

"He's not hers!" the king decreed in three distinct syllables. "He is mine. And he will remain mine until the day I let him die."

Oddwyn was rightly fearful of that tone. He watched the King of Shadows stand tall and order, "Herald!"

Oddwyn stood bolt upright. "My King."

"Go and fetch her. Fetch them all, but breathe one word of this to any mortal ear, and you will have failed me."

Oddwyn said nothing as he bowed low, a Realme portal forming at his back.

Setting a portal's course was an inherent talent for any Realme immortal. All Oddwyn required was knowledge of the person he wished to engage. The Realme provided the ether that transcended into Mortalia. There was no 'time'. There was no 'space'. There was only consciousness, and once Oddwyn knew where to aim his intentions, he directed his essence toward that location and the passageway formed – which was why he found himself quite shocked to feel some unknown hand grab hold of his tunic and pull him off course.

Oddwyn tumbled through his portal to land on the dirt outside a double-peaked tent. The black, midnight blue, and deep teal whisked off as if blown away by a stiff breeze. This place was not his intended point of entry, for he had meant to appear at Alerice's side.

Men-at-arms moved about and two guards stood at the tent's flap, but no one paid him heed, which was further strange, for Oddwyn was well aware of the figure he cut to mortal eyes.

He stood and looked about, and even waved at one of the guards. Then, Oddwyn felt a pleasant tingle run up his back, and he spun about to see two pikemen smiling at him.

Pikemen indeed.

Oddwyn beamed with joy and immediately presented her female self, for she stood in the presence of L'Orku, God of Thunder, and Gäete, God of Storms.

"Brothers!" she cried as she leaped into L'Orku's embrace.

L'Orku set his pike aside so that it stood upright of its own accord. He caught hold of Oddwyn and swept her up into his arms to plant his lips on hers. He doffed his mortal disguise to reveal himself as a brawny fellow whose red beard glistened in the torchlight, and whose mighty ram horns curled about either side of his head. Matted hair tumbled down his back, and as soon as he finished kissing Oddwyn, he tossed her to his brother.

Gäete had been strengthening the bands of silence and invisibility that protected them from mortal ears and eyes, but upon seeing L'Orku toss the Realme's herald in his direction, he likewise planted his pike upright and caught her so that he might kiss her as well.

Oddwyn caressed his smooth charcoal skin and drew strength from the tiny lightning arcs dancing about his bright eyes.

"I've always preferred you as a lass," L'Orku said in his deep, resounding voice.

"I as well," Gäete said as he tossed a giggling Oddwyn in his arms one more time. Then he spun her about as he lowered her to the ground.

Oddwyn looked over his toned body, noting the cache of lightning bolts that he wore at the back of his banded cuirass. The bolts were covered by the buckler he used to block his brother's head butts when they battled.

"What are you two doing here?" Oddwyn asked. She looked about at the encampment. "Slumming it again?"

"We enjoy slumming," Gäete said.

"When haven't you?" Oddwyn commented. "But what brings you here? You hate officers."

"Not all of them," L'Orku said. "That one is a decent man," he said, gesturing to the tent. "But we're here because of her."

"Her?" Oddwyn asked. Then the response struck her, and she asked, "You mean Alerice?"

"Very good," Gäete said with mocked applause.

"She's our girl," L'Orku said proudly. "And just look at her. What a woman. What a Walker. So accomplished in so short a time."

Oddwyn held up her hands. "Wait a moment. What do you mean 'your girl'?"

"Realme spirits," Gäete said aside to L'Orku. "Never that bright."

"Oh, give me my dice cup, and we'll see who's bright," Oddwyn said. "Now what do you mean 'your girl'?"

"We knew her father, Oddie-lass," L'Orku said. "Back when he served in Andoni's ranks. Tomas Linden. Simple soldier, simple man. He died saving his brothers in arms. He was worthy of a gift."

"So you blessed Alerice's birth?"

"L'Orku always blesses a Walker's birth," Gäete said, "but I added my own touch. Why do you think she can do things other Walkers cannot? That's my brightness inside her, despite her shadows."

"Unbelievable," Oddwyn said to herself. "But... what now? The King of Shadows means to kill her, and I've told her that she needs his kiss to become part of the Realme."

"She has choices to make, then," Gäete said.

"And she will," L'Orku added. "She's no fool. Go to her and warn her. She'll know what to do."

"I can't. *He* won't let me."

"That shadow thinks he can trap our girl, does he?" L'Orku asked.

"He seems determined to try," Oddwyn said.

"Don't worry," Gäete said as he assumed the guise of a messenger. "I'll warn her."

"No, I will proclaim it," L'Orku said, assuming the guise of a bulky foot soldier.

"You may be loud, but I'm fast," Gäete said to his brother. "Stay here, bellow-head."

"I'll show you how to bellow," L'Orku said as he pawed the ground, produced his horns, and lowered them in his brother's direction.

Gäete conjured his buckler and held it ready, but Oddwyn jumped between the two, for if L'Orku rammed into the shield, thunder would ring out.

"Stop it, storm brains!" she demanded.

They stood down, and Oddwyn presented himself as a youth once more. He straightened his tunic and brushed off his shoulders.

"I'll go to her first," Oddwyn said. "Then you can deliver the warning," he said to Gäete. "Tell her that Gotthard has found a way to kill a Realme Walker, and tell Bolivar that Gotthard means to kill him as well. Then he'll have a reason to offer Alerice assistance."

Gäete nodded and dispelled his buckler.

"But," Oddwyn added. "Let me distract Kreston before you say anything he might overhear."

Both gods nodded, seeming to understand this necessity.

Oddwyn looked between the brothers, then winked at L'Orku before he turned and paced toward the tent, startling the guards as he slipped out from the gods' invisibility and through the flap.

***

"You wished to see me?" Alerice asked Gotthard in a sweetly sarcastic tone.

Gotthard's reaction was an astounded loss of voice, for Alerice knew that he did not plan for the show of force she had assembled in the Prime Cheval's great hall.

Daylight flooded in through the towering windows, the arched crowns of which were framed in elegantly carved stone. Ornate hammerbeam timbers rose high overhead, each the work of a master carpenter. Man-tall candelabrum dotted the walls, and man-wide chandeliers hung from the ceiling.

The Prime Cheval's chair stood on a dais at the hall's head, but Gotthard did not occupy it. Rather, he stood at one end of a long table, the Reef of Navre at his side and a cadre of men-at-arms flanking them. Each armed man wore a blue surcoat embroidered with Navre's four gold circles. City dignitaries in formal finery stood nearby. However, every one of them was so taken aback by Alerice's company that they could do little more than stare in dumb wonder.

Kreston stood at Alerice's right, every bit the Ghost of the Crimson Brigade. Bolivar stood at her left, flanked by his marshal, officers, and a contingent of smartly dressed soldiers.

However, in preparation for what Alerice knew would be a game of 'who held the last knife', she had asked Oddwyn to help her find Lolladoe, the forest faun whom she had befriended while discovering the thief stealing souls from the Realme. Lolladoe held her crossbow ready as her hooves *clomped* on the floor stones. When she moved her head, her antler jewelry jingled.

Also present were Mutt and Wisp from the Wyld mercenary clan, their ash-and-black painted bodies striking a stark contrast to the Navre men-at-arms. Mutt growled behind the bevor plate that covered the lower half of his face, and watched the Navre men shrink from him.

Finally, Alerice had gathered two of the Painted Women, whose spirit ancestor, Pa'oula, had helped her fight the King of Shadows' monks. These copper-toned warriors bore their traditional spears while proudly displaying indigo and purple ink patterns atop shaved heads.

Alerice stood in full battle gear, save for her helm. Still, she was terrified. She had never faced a moment where she knew someone wished to kill her, and if Gotthard had found a way to murder a Realme Walker, she could not rely on the queen's ability to restore her.

She was taking a terrible chance coming here, but killing a Walker must involve the King of Shadows. Alerice's exotic allies had already fouled any plans Gotthard had of capturing her, which would force the king to take the initiative. This was her best chance to position him for a kiss.

Alerice drew strength from the men beside her. Bolivar's life was in jeopardy, and Kreston knew that if he acted against the king he would face dire consequences. Yet neither of them showed the slightest apprehension.

And neither would she. Alerice pocketed her fear, and trusted that the little amphoras she had given Lolladoe, Mutt and Wisp, and the Painted Women would tip the balance of any metaphysical conflict.

"I hear that you seek my death," Alerice said to Gotthard. She gestured to her company. "I invite you to try."

Gotthard looked about, clearly worried that his men would be no match for her odd group.

"Do something," he commanded the Reef.

"Yes, do something," a voice demanded.

Alerice looked about for a midair distortion, for she knew that voice all too well.

A Realme portal appeared at the base of the dais. Alerice waved for her company to fan out, which they did as several essences rushed into the hall. In moments, Lolladoe, the Wyld, and the Painted Women were under attack by unseen forces that struck them at vital body points, incapacitating them so that they fell to the floor.

Kreston drew his broadsword as he shouted, "Shadow monks!"

Alerice thought she had imprisoned these warriors after she had destroyed the King of Shadows' cliffside shrine, but he must have released them. She drew and threw her Realme dagger, knowing it would find its mark. It killed one monk, who slowed enough to be seen as he fell only paces from Lolladoe.

"At my side, Dühalde," the voice said from the dais.

Alerice watched Kreston disappear, only to reappear beside the Prime Cheval's chair. She held her hand high so that her dagger appeared in her palm, but then she felt hands upon her. She could not stop an invisible grip from forcing her to sheathe her dagger. Then it pinned her arms behind her back.

Alerice glanced at Bolivar, who was similarly apprehended, and then looked at her fallen friends. This game had taken an unexpected turn, and Alerice tried to think of what to do.

She focused on the still-open portal, which floated to the top of the dais, and then watched as the King of Shadows stepped from it.

The king raised a hand, and the shadow monk holding Alerice appeared, as did the one holding Bolivar and two more at either side of the table's head. The monks were not the problem. Alerice's crippled friends were, for if they could not reach their concealed amphoras, this plan would not work.

Alerice caught sight of Gotthard, who took a moment to process the situation before he beamed and ordered the Navre men-at-arms to surround

Bolivar's company. Then he strode before the dais and bowed.

"The Ravensdaughter," Gotthard offered.

The King of Shadows struck Gotthard with a shock that propelled him to the side.

"Useless mortal," the king said as he gestured for the monk to bring Alerice forward.

She did not resist, for there was no point. There was only one question she needed to ask herself, for this was the moment of no return. Was she prepared to tether to the Realme?

Alerice looked up at the king's dark gray eyes, and forced a glimmer into her own. She nodded in a deferential challenge, despite her anxiety, and asked, "Are you certain this is a good idea, Your Majesty? The queen must be watching."

"You think I don't know how to distract my wife?" the king countered. "You think that, even from this place, I can't order the herald to babble at her while I take hold of you?"

"Oh, I'm certain Oddwyn can babble most convincingly, Your Majesty, but why would you wish him, or her, to do that..." She allowed her voice to trail off as she used the queen's mark to project her spiritual voice, purring, "...When you could have more of me?"

The king looked down on her. "I already have you, girl, for I have him," he said, gesturing at Kreston. "And I will torment you with him at every turn. Your angst at his plight will be my delight. Allow me to show you." His lips twisted into a grin, and he said aloud, "Dühalde."

Kreston tensed and looked at his master.

"Kill her," the king ordered.

Kreston looked down at her, horror flashing across his face. Then he looked at the King of Shadows, hatred mounting.

"Remember, Dühalde," the king said. "You defied me once."

Alerice saw a bolt of fear shoot through Kreston, and he closed his eyes as he steadied himself. When he opened them, he recovered his ice-hard expression and locked his stare on her.

Kreston advanced, and then paced down the dais steps. He walked toward Alerice, who wanted to tell him that she still had one more play to make in this 'last knife' game. She had told him about the plan to arrest Gotthard in his congress of truce, but she had taken his advice and not told him every detail. If only her friends could break their amphoras.

Kreston came before her. Alerice held her head high, for he had been with her long enough to know that he should trust her. Alerice saw Kreston glance in her friends' direction, but when his gaze shifted back to her, she could not read his expression to know how they fared.

Kreston reached down to Alerice's side and drew her Realme dagger. She was about to call to her company, but he held the dagger to her throat. She drew in the words she was about to shout, trying to find the true Kreston Dühalde somewhere in his cold visage.

Kreston placed his other hand on her shoulder and gripped it tightly. He glanced once more at her company – and then he turned and launched her dagger at the King of Shadows.

"You want her dead, do it yourself, coward!" Kreston shouted. "Smash 'em!" he ordered before he lunged for the shadow monk holding Alerice.

Alerice saw the king catch her blade even as she felt the shadow monk release her. As the monk shot away so quickly that Alerice could not track him, she spun about to see her companions retrieve their amphoras as best they could and smash them against the floor stones. Then she saw them suffer more of the monks' attacks, but that would all end in the next moment.

Glistening clouds welled up, and in the blink of an eye, spirits of faun warriors, Wyld warriors, and Painted Women flew out to seize the monks.

Alerice saw Bolivar's men draw their blades upon the Navre men, who quickly folded, given their witness to supernatural machinations. Lord Bolivar and his marshal then advanced upon Gotthard and the Reef.

Alerice held her hand high so that her dagger disappeared from the king's grip and reappeared in her palm. Then she reached out for Kreston, elated to know that not only did he trust her, he had been clever enough to discover the details of her plan without alerting the King of Shadows.

"Get below, Dühalde!" the king roared.

Alerice grabbed at Kreston's arm. "I'm coming for you," she said as a Realme portal swallowed him whole. Then the king summoned the portal to him and stepped through.

"Oddwyn!" Alerice shouted.

A new Realme portal opened, and she charged into it.

***

The King of Shadows stood over Dühalde, inundating him with visions of every mortal he had ever killed, either in the ranks of the Crimson Brigade or on independent battlefields. His Walker fell to his knees within the Hall of Misted Mirrors, screaming as he threw his palms to his skull.

Dühalde had stood in defiance once before, when he had refused his destiny as servant. The king had brought him to heel then, and as soon as he did now, he would send the Ghost of the Crimson Brigade back to Navre with an army of souls. They would destroy the city, and slaughter the residents. They would kill the one called, Bolivar, whom the girl championed, and then kill the girl's family one by one while Dühalde forced her to watch.

The king looked at his crystal-encrusted prime pane. He wished to see his wife's pet, but for some reason he could not conjure the girl's image. She was not in that Mortalia hall where he has just been forced to appear. She was not in the Realme. He considered looking into the queen's Twilight Grotto, even though he and his wife shared an unspoken bond never to invade each other's personal sanctums.

"Are you wishing to see me?" Alerice asked at the king's flank.

The King of Shadows turned about to behold the girl, a flash of astonishment in his dark gray eyes.

"Alerice…" Dühalde groaned before he doubled over.

The king glanced at him, and then saw the girl direct the boy Oddwyn to tend him. Dühalde tried to rise up on his knees, but he slumped into the herald's arms.

The king discounted them both as he turned back to the bold child standing so proudly. "You have such spirit, but what do you think you can accomplish by coming here?"

"An end to this, Your Majesty," she said flatly. "An end to your abusing Kreston, and an end to your jealous impotence."

"Girl," the king said in a measured tone, "I could show you power the likes of which you could never fathom."

"I'm sure you could," Alerice challenged. "But you'll never have what your wife has, a Walker you respect. You use Kreston to satiate your emptiness, whereas the queen uses me to reinforce what a Walker can be."

"A Walker is an instrument."

"When correctly employed," she said. "Perhaps that's why you offered me your sword, and might offer it to me again if I agreed to take it. Of course, that would mean freeing Kreston."

"No, Alerice…" Kreston moaned.

"He says no," the king commented with a grin.

"I heard him, Your Majesty, but in truth, this is not about you or me, or Kreston or the queen. It is about the Realme. It's about my place here. When I once challenged you in the field of glowing flowers, I put us at odds.

"But we do not need to be at odds. And while I want Kreston to go above and live a normal life, I want something else as well, something only you can give me. Kiss me, and you will tether me here. Kiss me, and perhaps you will have the opportunity to take pride in me."

"Damn it, Alerice!" Kreston cursed.

The king sensed the herald forcing him to stay down. Through it all, the girl remained focused.

"Otherwise, Your Majesty," she added. "How long do you think the queen will allow you to use Kreston against me? She'll step in to cripple him again. All I need to do is distract you so she can claim him, and believe me, distracting you is *not* a difficult thing to do."

The king drew closer to Alerice, wondering what sparked her spirit. He stroked her blonde hair, for he would have her. He would also keep Dühalde, and before the girl changed her mind, the king reached to the back of her neck and drew her in. He kissed her below her ear on the opposite side of her face from where Sukaar, Father God of Fire, had kissed her, and there he held her.

Alerice felt the King of Shadows drain her breath. His kiss invaded her throat even as it invaded her soul. She hung suspended in his grasp, unable to move, unable to gasp. Yet somehow she did not feel the need to inhale or exhale. She felt the wispy smoke of his shadows fill her thoughts, and she lost track of her vision. Yet she saw things with amazing clarity.

She felt the Raven Queen's mark pulse upon her brow. She felt Sukaar's latent power rise within her breast. She felt Imari's blue crescent create inner peace – and then she felt an unstable element begin to tickle inside her ribs.

It felt like a roll of thunder. It felt like a flash of lightning, and it played within her so strongly that she began laughing.

This was joyous! Alerice felt the vastness of the Realme enfold her. She felt the coolness of her blessed shadows bathe her. She was more than the king or the queen. She was more than the gods above. She was the Realme, its Walker, not anyone else's, its champion, not anyone else's.

Alerice stopped laughing and opened her eyes. She reached to the king's face and stroked his beard along his jawline. He pulled away from his kiss and looked confusedly down at her, but she quickly reached to the back of his neck to pull him in and press her lips against his.

He resisted only briefly before he wrapped her within his crystalline robe and allowed his deeply-welled passion to flow. It was an obvious attempt to regain dominance, but fully-present in the moment, Alerice knew that this kiss was hers to control.

She was grateful for the king's gift, and she did not mind expressing it. She was grateful to have a power now that might even free Kreston. She savored the kiss until she was satisfied, and then she pushed the king away, noting that he did not have the power to resist.

The King of Shadows looked down up her in stunned shock before he attempted to recover by straightening and backing toward the center of his Hall of Misted Mirrors. His smokey eyes glared, but they could not disguise his befuddlement.

Alerice beamed a smile at him, and then she looked aside at an astounded Oddwyn and an agonized Kreston. She beamed at them as well, but then she swooned, passing into the blissfully contented sleep she could only find in this world below.

"Alerice!" Kreston called, forcing himself up. He looked at the King of Shadows, and seeing that the wretch was momentarily overwhelmed, he grabbed Oddwyn and scrambled forward.

Kreston fell to his knees at Alerice's side. He hefted her into his arms and hurriedly got back to his feet.

"Get us out of here," he demanded.

Oddwyn nodded, and quickly opened a portal.

***

Kreston laid Alerice down on the mossy rise surrounded by the silver-veined healing columns. The 'sky' above swirled in tones of deep teal with light blue currents creating a daylight hue while cascades of silvery glimmers flowed down from the columns' crowns.

He brushed Alerice's hair from her face, and though he strangled his emotions, he could not prevent his hand from trembling.

"Kreston, are you all right?" Oddwyn asked, his youthful ice-blue eyes intent upon his friend of many years.

"How would you be if you just watched the woman you love marry another man?"

"I suppose that's a good way to look at it," Oddwyn said. "She's a part of the Realme now. She'll be that way forever."

Kreston tensed to control himself, and then almost as an afterthought, he reached to his brow and felt the hated mark that the King of Shadows had scratched into his skin. He grunted in regret and then exhaled heavily.

"She didn't even win my freedom. Now that shade has us both. Why'd she do it, and why did I say 'no'? The king used it to double-back on the deal."

"The king doesn't have you both," Oddwyn said. "He has you, but not her, and now I don't think he ever will."

"What do you mean?"

"Kreston, there are other gods at work here. That's what I told Alerice earlier, and that's why she just did what she did."

"Sukaar and Imari," he said. "I know."

"But also L'Orku and Gäete. I met them in Bolivar's camp. They blessed her at birth, and now you just saw the power that gives her. The king could not resist her kiss, and she laughed at his, not derisively, but that's how he'll see it."

"And I saw what he's going to command me to do," Kreston said. "He's going to order me to kill her family. He's going to give me a soul army and order me to sack Navre and kill Bolivar."

Kreston balled his fists. "I'll stall as long as I can, but this has to end, Oddwyn. The king will deploy me against her any chance he gets, especially now if she has become as powerful as you say. If I could remove myself, I would."

Oddwyn nodded, but then both he and Kreston straightened as they felt a malevolent force invade the healing columns.

Kreston knew the sensation of the king's summons. He looked at Alerice and then at Oddwyn. "Take care of her for me."

Oddwyn grasped Kreston in a hand-to-forearm grip, both fearing this might be the last time they beheld one another.

Then Kreston vanished, leaving Oddwyn to glance down at the Realme's new Far-Walker, a mortal he knew would be able to do things according to her own volition.

"You're right, Kreston. This does have to end."

In her Twilight Grotto, where thick tree branches spreading horizontally from broad trunks outlined six window panes, the Raven Queen watched her herald move closer to her champion.

Then she glanced aside at an empty soul amphora resting on a floating stand.

***

Alerice stood on the section of Navre's city wall that crowned the portcullis. She gazed out upon the dusk landscape that streaked the clouds with orange and pink against a sea-green sky that was fading to cobalt blue.

Yesterday at this time she had walked the streets with Kreston. Now she stood awaiting his impending attack, for Oddwyn had told her everything that Kreston had said.

The King of Shadows was going to send him to Navre with a soul army. He was going to force Kreston to slay her family, which was why Alerice had gathered them in the Prime Cheval's great hall.

Her cousins, Chessy, Clancy, and Little Judd, had all wanted to fight, still beside themselves with wonder at what she had become. However, Alerice had asked them to protect Uncle Judd, Aunt Carol, Cousin Millie, and Grammy Linden. Fortunately the boys had seen the sense in her plan.

Of course, Alerice was not about to leave her family so thinly guarded, especially given that the coming fight would involve elements of the Realme, and so she had asked Lolladoe, Mutt, Wisp, and the two Painted Women to also protect her family. She had helped them all recover from the shadow monks' attacks, and they were more than ready for action.

So too were the remaining spirits who possessed the stamina to sustain themselves in Mortalia throughout the day. These included Ketabuck and a few of his faun warriors, all of whom were happy to reunite with Lolladoe and once again behold their clan's precious gem, the Heart of the Forest.

It included Pa'oula, the Painted Woman, and a few of her sister spirits. They floated stoically with spears at the ready near their mortal offspring, none of them making a fuss, for Painted Women were keen on battle.

As for the shadow monks, Alerice had sent them to the Raven Queen via the very first portal she had created herself, and what an amazing moment that had been.

Her portal had been ringed in plum and lapis, not the traditional black, midnight blue, and deep teal. She had formed it by extending her consciousness to where she had wished to travel, and then simply allowing herself to slip through. She knew that the Raven Queen's mark upon her brow guided her, but so did Imari's crescent. She knew that Sukaar's power propelled her, but so did the King of Shadows' kiss.

And then there was the unknown feeling that had tickled her ribs and made her laugh. Oddwyn had explained that the brother gods, L'Orku and Gäete, had blessed her birth, and the feeling was their gift. However, she was not certain how to process this contribution, and so she tucked it to the back of her thoughts.

Alerice gazed down at the A'Leon encampment which now surrounded Navre's gates. Lord Bolivar had arrested Gotthard and the Reef. He had taken possession of the city and organized his troops outside to await any approaching foes, but what good would they be against an army of souls?

And for that matter, what good would Bolivar be?

Alerice turned and glanced down inside Navre at the decorative cobblestone courtyard that fanned out before the Prime Cheval's hall. Lord Bolivar waited there, along with his officers and a cadre of his best soldiers. A pike regiment stood at the rear of his company. Two of the men caught Alerice's eye, even from such a distance, for they had offered her some interesting advice.

They had said that spirits who died in the world above stayed dead. They never returned to the Realme, and so Alerice should take care if she shot one with her crossbow, for shooting a wicked soul would be just. However, she must use every ounce of intuition to know if the soul was wicked, lest she shoot a soul that was being unjustly used against her.

It was a sagacious offering from two common pikemen, and Alerice wished Oddwyn had been present to confirm their counsel. However, Alerice had not seen the Realme's herald since leaving the healing columns. Perhaps because the Raven Queen wished for her to stage this fight alone. Perhaps because she had just transcended the Realme to become a Far-Walker, as Oddwyn had put it.

Whatever the reason, Alerice hugged her feathered cloak, for she had never felt more alone. She looked at the final ray of sunlight disappearing behind the distant hills, and then she looked down upon the field outside of Navre's gates. Kreston Dühalde stood there in full scales, plate, and helm, the very image of the Ghost of the Crimson Brigade.

Alarm horns blew within the encampment, and soldiers rushed toward Kreston's position. Without pause, Kreston drew the King of Shadows' broadsword and began doing what he unfortunately did all too well – killing anyone who came within range.

Alerice quickly glanced back at Bolivar and his men. She saw them reacting to the horns. She did not know if they meant to break ranks and rush out to help their soldiers, but she needed them to remain in place. Besides, she had armed them all with soul amphoras that they would deploy to tip the balance of any metaphysical conflict.

Alerice made a show of spreading her cloak so that her black silhouette stood out against the darkening sky, and as soon as it formed into wings, she launched herself and shot for Kreston.

Alerice *whooshed* past the Crimson Ghost so closely that she easily pushed him off-balance. Just as in yestermorning's battle, he recovered and looked about for her, but she had already circled and beat her cloak's wings solidly to swoop down toward him again.

She watched him focus on her and raise his sword to strike, but she darted hard to the side just before reaching him, and he sliced into thin air. Then she darted aside once more to begin circling him.

With one wingbeat after another, Alerice pushed all nearby men off their footing. Some stumbled backward. Others fell onto their rumps.

Then she alighted and appeared, standing tall as the captain from yestermorning's cavalry rode up, flanked by his mounted men.

Alerice looked up at them, and then leveled her sights on Kreston.

"Stand down, Crimson Ghost!" she demanded in as loud a voice as she could muster. "There is no slaughter for you here!"

Kreston readied his broadsword, but said nothing. Alerice could see his hazel eyes narrow behind his helm's angular slits, and watched him snarl through what she could see through the vertical slit.

She glanced about at the A'Leon soldiers, quickly assessing that they looked emboldened by her command, and the last thing she wanted was to inspire them to cut Kreston down.

Alerice looked up at the mounted captain and ordered, "Keep your men away! No one stands against the Crimson Ghost save me, the Raven Queen's daughter!"

"Aye, Black Lady!" the captain replied before he began barking orders for the soldiers to clear off.

Alerice watched them provide a great deal of room, and then looked at Kreston. She saw the mark of the King of Shadows glow upon his brow, and then heard his mental voice.

"Gods, I love you, Alerice."

She smiled, though she still stood tall.

"Take the city, if you can!" she challenged, mostly to extract him from the moment. "Bolivar and I await you."

"How I wish you didn't," he said before he turned aside and began pacing toward the Navre portcullis.

Alerice spread her cloak once more as the evening drew in, the beat of its wings creating a downdraft that inspired the soldiers to give Kreston a wide berth.

In his Hall of Misted Mirrors, the King of Shadows beheld his Walker within his crystal-encrusted pane. The girl was ready for his advance into Navre? So be it. Dühalde would have his army of souls, and the king had some specific souls in mind. He focused his remaining mirrors into different locations within the Realme to fetch them.

Kreston stood before the barred entrance to the waiting city. The great bolted timbers of the portcullis would only hinder him for a moment, for the king would surely grant him passage via portal. His army would enter any way they pleased.

And if Alerice had any sense, she would use that Realme crossbow of hers and shoot down every soul in rapid succession. The King of Shadows would no doubt send the worst of the worst to terrorize the city. They would hurl themselves into homes and make away with babes. They would wreak havoc in the night. The less of them the better, and if he could he would assist in slaying them himself.

Kreston tensed, for he sensed the advance of the king's ranks. Still looking ahead, he saw a distant Alerice alight within the city entrance and move inward toward what Kreston knew from walking with her yesterday would be the courtyard at the Prime Cheval's hall.

If that was where he must confront her, so be it. If that was where Bolivar waited, all the better.

Kreston passed his broadsword into his left gloved hand and reached to his left shoulder. His patch of red scales still felt intact, even though he had loosened them enough that all he had to do was twist a few and pull hard to snap them off their rings.

Kreston looked up as firepits along the city walls came to life. Then, he felt a presence to his right and looked aside to see a lordly soul floating next to him. Kreston's brow furrowed inside his helm, for this was not a wicked man raised from the Realme's dregs.

"Who are you?" he asked.

The spirit looked longingly at the Navre portcullis. "I am Lord Andoni of House Anzar," it replied.

"Andoni?" Kreston questioned, until he realized what was happening. "You're Bolivar's brother."

"I am," the soul said in a forlorn voice.

"Gods above," Kreston said, despite the need to maintain his battle countenance. "The king sent you to break Bolivar's will."

The soul did not respond, and in the next moment the ghost of an infantry man appeared at Andoni's flank.

"And you?" Kreston asked.

The ghost looked at Kreston, but then saw the spirit of his liege, and bowed to it. Andoni acknowledged the ghost, who turned and stood at attention.

"I asked, who are you?" Kreston repeated.

"Tomas Linden, at your service," the ghost replied.

Kreston paused, but then his blood ran cold. "You're... her father."

"Captain?" a voice questioned from Kreston's opposite side.

Kreston stood upright, for he knew that voice. He could not help but spin about, only to behold his brother-in-arms, his lieutenant, Landrew Mülton.

Landrew stood proudly and saluted. "Where do you want the men, sir?"

Kreston gulped, for he felt his army fill in behind him, and his worst fears were confirmed when he turned about to behold the entire Crimson Brigade.

That loathsome wretch! The King of Shadows had served up the spirits of men Kreston held most dear, spirits he had never sought out all these years walking the Realme for fear he would lose his mind if he ever beheld them.

And now they stood ready for him to order them into the waiting defenses of the woman he loved and the death she would no doubt give them.

Kreston had not tasted the salt of tears in ages, and yet he tasted them now.

Kreston reached to his red scales and snapped off enough to create an adequate chink. Then he tossed the King of Shadows' broadsword back into his right hand and raised it high.

Were this any other attack, he would bellow the battle cry, "For the red horns!" Now, he would rather choke on those sacred words than utter them in the king's name.

"Into the city!" he roared.

"Into the city!" his men echoed as they all bolted for the portcullis.

In his Hall of Misted Mirrors, the King of Shadows summoned his two Shadow Warriors and bade them to enter Mortalia. The warriors drew their broadswords and flew into the king's prime pane to execute their task.

On the courtyard's torchlit cobblestones, Alerice stood before Bolivar and his men. She glanced behind her at the candlelight shining from the Prime Cheval's hall's great windows, and knew that both the mortals and souls guarding her family were prepared.

Alerice looked at the men behind her, seeing that all eyes were fixed on her. She found the two pikemen who had given her advice, and nodded to them. Then she heard the otherworldly sound of howls on the evening air, and watched the spine-curdling effect it had on Bolivar's troops.

"Your amphoras," Alerice shouted as she removed the one she wore about her own neck from inside her scale mail tunic.

"Do as the Raven's Daughter says," Lord Bolivar ordered, reaching to the amphora he had tucked inside his vambrace.

Alerice watched his men follow suit, and then focused on the shadows, sensing the influx of a phantasmal army. She held her fist high, and then cast her amphora to the cobblestones.

It shattered, freeing the spirit inside. A glimmering essence rose up as Alerice heard several amphora smashes behind her, and she watched Aric, elder of the Hammer Clan, take shape before her. She saw him glance behind her, which prompted her to turn, and as more essences rose up, members of the Hammer Clan began floating above the cobblestones.

Alerice looked back at Aric, who nodded in response. Then she took hold of her Realme crossbow in one hand and the edge of her cloak in the other and shouted, "Kill only the wicked! Hold the rest for me!"

With his own otherworldly howl, that Alerice sensed bolstered Bolivar's men, Aric and the Hammer Clan launched themselves at the invading spirits, and in no time the ethereal *clang* of war hammers upon broadswords echoed through the city streets.

Alerice was prepared to act either offensively or defensively when she saw a stately soul walk forward into the torchlight. She paused, confused, for she knew its face. It was Lord Andoni, and he was walking toward his brother. Alerice wanted to shout a warning to Bolivar, for as the man locked eyes with his dead sibling, he became too overwhelmed to move.

However, just then another ghost caught the corner of Alerice's eye. She reflexively raised her crossbow as her head snapped in its direction, but she, too, stopped short.

"Da?"

A Shadow Warrior swooped into the Prime Cheval's great hall and landed before the assembly of mortals and spirits. The Linden women shrieked in spite of themselves, and the Linden men quickly stood before them.

Lolladoe fired a crossbow bolt into the warrior's breastplate, but it passed through and shot a hole in one of the great windows' panes. The faun spirits bared their antlers and the souls of the Painted Women bared their spears, and both groups launched forward to battle the shade. However, no force, physical or metaphysical, could slay a Shadow Warrior.

Drawing its broadsword, the warrior slew Pa'oula with a single stroke and then slew Ketabuck in a riposte.

Lolladoe blinked in horror, and then fired another bolt into the Shadow Warrior's empty helm. It passed through as before, but the faun then drew a breath and bugled at the top of her lungs.

Lolladoe's voice rang in Alerice's ears, drawing her attention away from her father's ghost. She turned to the commotion inside the hall, fearing for her family's safety.

She was about take flight to them when a thrown broadsword cut through her father, rendering him into a soft dust that filtered away into the evening breeze.

Alerice could not hide her alarm as she looked about for Kreston, only to watch the same broadsword cut down Andoni's soul as it reached out for Bolivar.

"Kreston!" Alerice cried.

To her side, Kreston stepped forward from the shadows. He wore no helm, and the look of utter loss commanded his expression.

Alerice watched him look about at the sight of his apparitional soldiers in the custody of the Hammer Clan.

"Kill them, Alerice," he said. "Kill them all."

Alerice saw one younger soul fly in toward Kreston, and noted that he bore an officer's uniform. On it, she saw the badge of the red, bull horns broadsword, and knew he was a member of the Crimson Brigade.

"Captain?" the soul asked.

"Hold your place, Landrew," Kreston said.

Alerice watched the young officer stand at attention, but then she saw a tear fall from Kreston's eye as he held his hand high so that the king's broadsword would appear in his palm.

"No, Kreston!" Alerice shouted as she took flight. She caught hold of Landrew's soul, and tucked it within the folds of her feathers. Then she darted about the courtyard collecting all the souls held for her by the Hammer Clan.

The clan had killed none. Therefore, none of them could be wicked – and all of them bore the patch of the Crimson Brigade. Why was Kreston leading his own men against Navre? Why had he been about to kill the lieutenant she knew he still held dear?

One of the king's Shadow Warriors alighted at the courtyard's center and *shrieked* into the night.

Bolivar and his men recoiled, but Kreston turned to face the monster. To her side, Alerice caught sight of the other Shadow Warrior threatening her family within the hall.

There was only one thing to do. "My Queen! Your knights!"

In her Twilight Grotto, the Raven Queen looked at her Raven Knights. She nodded to them, and they cawed as they spread their winged cloaks, vanishing as they took flight.

The queen then looked at the maiden Oddwyn, who gazed up at her with plaintive, ice-blue eyes.

Then, the queen looked at the empty soul amphora cupped in her palms.

Alerice watched as the sky above began to swirl with the Realme's tri-colors of black, midnight blue, and deep teal. A portal opened and the queen's two Raven Knights flew out and down, one confronting the Shadow Warrior in the courtyard and the other diving for the warrior inside the hall.

Alerice noted their immortal combat, and though she briefly considered that the contest of these servants of the Realme's master and mistress might bode true war for the Evherealme, she tucked that notion away and beat her cloak's wings to return to Kreston.

She alighted before him, knowing she should feel betrayed.

"Kreston, why did you kill my father?"

"Because the king sent him here to torment you," he said. "That's why you never seek out loved ones in the Realme. It eats at your mind and heart. The king sent your father to torment you, just as he sent Andoni to torment Bolivar, and Landrew to torment me... and me to torment you." He paused and then said, "This is over, Alerice. Now give me Landrew so I can spare him."

"No, I will spare him, and protect him, and I will have the king release you if it's the last thing I do."

"Then gods above damn you, Alerice Linden!" Kreston shouted as he raised his broadsword and cleaved for her blonde head. Alerice dodged, but Kreston spun about to cleave at her side. His stroke caught her in the scales and knocked her off-balance, and he pressed his attack by striking her across the back to splay her down to the cobblestones. He kicked her in the gut to roll her over, using his strength to deny her the opportunity to draw and activate her pixie poles.

Alerice nimbly rolled away and got to her feet, but then she saw Bolivar summon his officers and hurry forward. They would flank Kreston if she did not do something.

A tactic jumped to mind, and though she had no idea if it would work, she decided to test a Far-Walker's strength.

She closed her eyes and gave every ounce of herself over to what she knew she had become: the beloved daughter of the Raven Queen and Imari, the passionate object of Sukaar and the King of Shadows, and even the god child of L'Orku and Gäete. Then she sprang upward at Kreston to wrap her arms about his body even as she demanded that her wings beat as hard as they possibly could. She felt a powerful gust blow into them from below, lifting them both high, almost as though Gäete himself had sent a breath of stormy wind to aid her.

Alerice landed once more atop the section of city wall that crowned the portcullis. Unable to hold Kreston a moment longer, she dropped him as her boots struck the stone, but the sudden shift in weight fouled her balance and she toppled toward the wall's edge.

Someone grabbed the scruff of her scale mail tunic and drew her back from the brink. Then that same someone tore her feathered cloak off her body and cast it to the ground below. She watched it float down, but then felt Kreston grab her arm and spin her about.

He locked stares with her, and dropped his broadsword. As it clanked to rest, Kreston grabbed hold of Alerice's left arm and held her in an iron grip. Then he forced his left hand over her right, and guided it over her dagger. With a quick tug, he drew the blade and closed her fingers over the handle, his gloved hand pressing down upon hers.

"I said this is over," he stated.

"Yes," she said. "I'll yield if that's what you need."

"No," Kreston said, forcing her to lift the dagger and aim it at the chink in his red scales. "I yield." He paused and then added in the sternest voice Alerice had ever known, "Kill me."

Alerice's eyes went wide. "What?" she gasped.

"You heard me," he said, his gaze both desperate and demanding. "The king won't let me strike myself. Believe me, I've tried, but he can't stop you unless he's here, which he could be any moment, so you've got to do it now."

"Kreston," she said. "There must be another way."

"There isn't, Alerice. Please. I'm begging you. Before that wretch puts me back into action against your friends. Once my soul goes below, he'll take hold of it and have Oddwyn fetch my body. He always does, and he'll make me pay for this, but if there is any mercy, the queen will find a way to lock my brain up again so I can't murder at his command. You can persuade her to do it. I know you can." He strengthened his hold on her hand, half-crushing it. "Alerice Linden, strike me down."

He moved the dagger's tip into his armor, and Alerice felt the resistance of his body. She saw him wince, but then she saw his hazel eyes imploring her to act.

In that moment, Alerice knew it would be better for Kreston to never have known her, never to remember her once he woke within the healing columns, for the King of Shadows would only use her memory against him, and if the king would not grant him liberty, she would.

"I will see you free, Kreston Dühalde."

He smiled and said, "If anyone can it's you."

Though Alerice knew that her steel had already pierced his flesh, she kept it ready as Kreston reached to the back of her neck and drew her to him. Then he kissed her with every ounce of the pent-up passion he held for her.

He released her left arm, and she grabbed hold of his shoulder. Then, she thrust her dagger into him, feeling it drive as deeply as the Reef of Navre had driven her own dagger into her heart not so very long ago.

"Now, Oddwyn," the Raven Queen ordered in her Grotto.

The maiden Oddwyn conjured a portal and disappeared.

"I should have known!" the King of Shadows shouted at the foolish scene playing out in his prime pane. Both it and the other eleven mirrors shook in their smokey tendrils. Yes, he would make Dühalde pay for this idiocy. By the Realme, he would.

The king focused his prime pane on the Convergence, for Dühalde's soul would appear there any moment. He drew a breath to summon the Realme's herald to fetch his body, but just then the maiden Oddwyn appeared to his left.

"Go and bring him," the king ordered. "That girl child thinks she can help the queen lock his mind away again, but I'm not about to let that happen a second time."

"Yes, but My King?" Oddwyn said, perhaps a little too sweetly.

"What?" the king asked.

"You see, the queen... She has asked me to... You see..."

In her Twilight Grotto, the Raven Queen conjured the sight of the Convergence in one of her windows. Kreston's spirit appeared there, looking about. Then his spirit closed his eyes, held wide his arms, and hung his head back awaiting his fate.

The queen curled her willow-white fingers into the palm of one hand while holding the soul amphora in the other. Kreston's spirit flew through the window to her. She caught hold of it, and gently directed it into the amphora, managing every moment of its glistening descent.

"The queen what?" the King of Shadows demanded.

The maiden Oddwyn curtseyed deeply so that her knees touched the floor, but looking up into the king's dark gray eyes, she rose to her feet and stood with her shoulders back.

"The queen commanded me to do something."

"Well, what is it?"

Oddwyn paused one final moment and then said, "Distract you, My King."

The King of Shadows thought the command curious, until he spun about and looked into his prime pane at the sight of an empty Convergence. Then he altered the image to that of the city wall where the girl child knelt beside his fallen Walker.

Alerice withdrew her dagger from Kreston's side and looked about. All she could see were storm clouds rolling in against the moonlight. Fires burning along the wall highlighted Kreston's body, and she could see the blood trailing from below his gray scales and pooling onto the stone. But she saw nothing else.

"Where are you, Oddwyn?" she called into the night. "Oddwyn!"

She felt Kreston's face. It was cold, and his complexion was growing pale. The clouds above moved with surprising speed, and she looked about once again.

"Oddwyn!" she called again.

Lightning split the night, and Alerice recoiled. When she looked up, she saw the King of Shadows standing over her.

"She's not coming," the king said. "He's not coming. Neither of them are coming. My wife has Dühalde's soul. He's dead."

Alerice looked at Kreston in disbelief. Then the truth struck her, and she felt a flash of anger as she scrambled to her feet. She raised her bloody dagger against the king, but then she caught sight of Kreston's broadsword.

As another bolt of lightning flashed and a clap of thunder rolled out, Alerice tossed her dagger aside, swept the sword into her grasp, and aimed it at its master.

"So now you claim my blade," the king said, the crystals on his crown and standing out from his shoulders seeming to reflect the after-traces of the lightning above.

"Yes, I do," Alerice said, her expression hardening. "But not in your service. The gods above and you below have blessed me, and I am no longer yours. I am the Realme's."

"I am the Realme," the king said.

"No, you and your wife are the personifications of the Realme, but you are not the world below. It is boundless, and you are fixed, and I will walk past you both. I will carry this sword with me – though I will never draw it again. I will never allow you to enslave anyone else with it again. This is the last time you will ever see its service. I promise you that."

"And how do you think you can accomplish all this?" the king asked.

"With a little bit of help," two voices said – L'Orku in his deep, rolling tone and Gäete in his higher tenor.

The three immortals locked stares before L'Orku lowered his torso and presented his great ram horns. Then he charged at the King of Shadows, colliding with him so soundly that thunder rang out atop the wall as he sent the king toppling off into the night.

Gäete reached out to steady Alerice from the percussive shock. As she grabbed hold of his arm, he reached out with a charcoal hand to touch the broadsword. His lightning-ringed eyes danced as he ran his fingers up the blade from hilt to tip, causing it to crackle with dancing dynamic.

Gäete then smiled at Alerice, who looked at the sword's many arcs before she looked up at the brother gods. Then she stood upright before them and raised the blade in salute, her back straight as she lowered her weight onto her rear leg in her classic reverence.

"Do use it," Gäete said. "Use it well."

Alerice nodded, but then she looked down at Kreston's body. There was only one proper way to send him off, and so she raised the lightning blade high so that it sparked in the night sky. Then she brought it to her, turned its point down, and slammed it through the heart of Kreston's gray scales.

A blast flashed brightly, and yet this time Alerice did not feel any repercussion. She saw a brilliant wave spread out from Kreston's body, and though she needed to glance away for a short moment, when she looked down, Kreston's body was gone – as were both L'Orku and Gäete.

***

Alerice stood atop the small rise that was capped by the little shade tree. Stretching out before her was the flat expanse where two mornings ago, two armies had joined battle. Kreston had stood beside her then, and she had promised him she would be his advocate.

Now, the battle was done. Lord Bolivar was the official Cheval of both Navre and A'Leon. He had ordered his men to clear the field and bury the dead. What remained were mounds where groups of the fallen lay.

Alerice stood quietly in her black scales. She bore no gorget or plate. Her Realme dagger rested at her hip, opposite her crossbow. Her pixie pole cylinders hung from her belt, but she also bore another belt – a man's belt, Kreston's belt.

Strapped to it was the sheathed broadsword he had been forced to bear. The weapon was hers now, infused with Gäete's lightning, and she intended to keep her vow that the King of Shadows would never again use it to enslave someone.

The king would likely find another champion in due course. There were always men willing to seek him out, but Alerice doubted he would ever find another natural Walker. As so many others had told her, her kind was not born all that often. The king might seek one out, but Kreston Dühalde had been a unique fellow, a combination of talent in both the worlds above and below, and yet a man driven to try and right the wrongs he had suffered.

A small red bird alighted on one of the shade tree's branches. It sung for a moment, and then cocked its head to spy down on Alerice. She smiled as she gazed upon it, and watched as it looked into the distance and darted away.

Then Alerice saw a Realme portal begin to open beside her, and she looked once more upon the field.

A youthful Oddwyn appeared and lifted his hand in salutation. Alerice saw him from the corner of her eye, but did not acknowledge him. She waited for him to approach, which he did. He held something in his hand, but she did not look closer to see what it was.

"I..." Alerice paused before she said, "I should have let myself love him more, Oddwyn. He deserved it. He was a good man who endured bad things. He should have had a better life."

"It's always sad when mortals don't get the life they long for, but that's the way things often happen. You gave him what love you could. He wanted more for a while, but he resigned himself in the end. And you did give him love, Alerice. And he was grateful for what you had to offer."

Alerice thought of Kreston's hazel eyes and the way he laughed when he was truly himself. Her tears began to well up, and she closed her eyes to think of something else.

She sniffed to collect herself, but when she opened her eyes, she saw Oddwyn looking out upon the field, tears in his.

"Oh, Oddwyn," Alerice said, holding her arms open to offer an embrace. Oddwyn glanced at her, then turned toward her and stepped in. She held him close and cradled him softly as he pressed into her shoulder and allowed himself a rare moment of raw feeling.

"I'll miss him, Alerice," Oddwyn said. "Yes, he was a good fellow."

"You knew him better than I did," Alerice said.

Oddwyn gave Alerice a long squeeze, and then withdrew to wipe his face. "I did," he said with a sigh. "You're right. He didn't deserve to be treated the way his was. For what it's worth, the gods above did their best to keep Kreston from dying his whole career. It was their way of hiding him from the King of Shadows. It was also his lucky charm in battle. Just when he thought the game was up, he'd sidestep a fatal blow. He was known as the pride of the Crimson Brigade long before he was known as its ghost."

"But then his brigade was destroyed," Alerice said.

"It was," Oddwyn agreed with a far-away look. "And nothing could stop him after that. He climbed the cliffs to the king's shrine, and the rest you know."

Alerice paused, trying to imagine the dashing Captain Dühalde before disaster had struck. "I wonder what he was like when he was younger."

"Charming beyond belief," Oddwyn chuckled.

"Maybe I would have fallen in love with him back then."

Oddwyn looked Alerice over, seeing that the moment was perfect for a frank assessment.

"I don't think so," he said. "I don't think you'll ever let yourself fall in love with anybody, Alerice Linden. There's a part of you that's locked away, perhaps for a good reason. I don't know why, but let's be honest. Wearing that scale armor came naturally to you."

Alerice sighed thinly and said, "Perhaps you're right. Did you take my cloak back to the Realme so what's left of the Crimson Brigade could be safely placed?"

"I did," Oddwyn said.

"And Lolladoe, and Mutt and Wisp, and the Painted Women?" she asked.

"All back where they belong. We can always go seek them out, if you like, both here and below."

"Perhaps we will," she said.

"Perhaps you will," he offered. "When I said we, I meant as walk-about friends. You don't need me any longer."

"No," she said before she drew and released a deep breath. "Before she sent me to Navre, the Raven Queen said that if all elements worked according to their natures, then the Realme would see the benefit. But what benefit, Oddwyn? Losing Kreston is a benefit to the queen, I suppose, because the king can't use him against me any longer, but the queen has lost me too, in a way."

"Hmmm," Oddwyn mused, looking Alerice over. "And yet you still wear her scales."

"Because I choose to," Alerice said most heartfully.

"Then perhaps that's another benefit," Oddwyn said. "The queen has a colleague in you now, and so does the Realme. Perhaps in time you and the queen may find a different type of relationship. She's not exactly the 'motherly' type, but she may see you as her daughter. She set you on your path. She gave you wings. Either way, the Realme benefits, and I'm happy for that."

"Mmmm," Alerice said. "It's always been about the Realme for me, hasn't it."

"I'd say so," Oddwyn said, a twinkle in his ice-blue eyes.

"Do you think, then, that the queen knew all this would happen?" Alerice asked.

"I don't know. I told you, it's not my place to know her mind."

Alerice nodded.

"So, what's it like?" Oddwyn asked sweetly, presenting her maiden form. "I've never met a Far-Walker."

"It's... strange," Alerice said, reaching out to take her Realme sister's hand. "Sometimes, I feel the full might of each immortal working in tandem within me. Then at other times, if I concentrate, I can call upon each immortal separately, though I doubt I'll ever call upon the king or the shadows he commands."

Oddwyn patted Alerice's hand, and then presented himself as a youth once more to tuck the item he was holding into her palm.

Alerice looked down to find Kreston's soul amphora, and she gulped back a sob. Then, she curled her fingers about its smooth surface and held it tightly.

"You can always wear it," Oddwyn offered.

"No," she said. "That will only tempt me to open it and see him once again. He's gone, Oddwyn. He wanted an end to this, and now he has it. Let's let him be." She turned to Oddwyn and asked, "Yes?"

"Yes," Oddwyn said.

Alerice smiled and closed her eyes. While holding the amphora in one hand, she reached down to release her crossbow with the other. Then she concentrated on Imari's blue crescent that wove into the Raven Queen's mark upon her brow.

A pleasant breeze blew in, warming the morning air with a gentle perfume. Then a low fog swelled about the field, covering the mounds.

Alerice opened her eyes and watched the two layers play against one another, the wind churning up the top of the mist so that it looked like some apothecary's preparation.

Alerice allowed a few moments to pass, and then raised her crossbow and took aim at the distance. The bow string pulled back of its own accord, and a gleaming black bolt appeared in the flight groove.

"Throw it," Alerice said as she passed the amphora to Oddwyn.

Oddwyn took it, and then hurled it as far as he could. Alerice took aim and fired.

The bolt struck home, shattering the amphora in midair. Alerice felt Oddwyn come next to her and snuggle a bit as she watched the amphora's contents cast the field with a glistening cascade.

The wind scattered the evanescent particles about so that they dusted the top of the mist, and then the wind blew in just a bit more to waft the mist away.

As Alerice looked out, she saw that new grass had begun to sprout on the field. Also, tiny little ground scrubs had begun to grow, each of which bore clusters of miniature red flowers.

Alerice could not stop the tears from rolling down one cheek and then the other. Oddwyn balled his iridescent sleeve into his hand, turned her toward him, and wiped them from her face. Then he tickled his fingertips along the jawline scar left by Sukaar, Father God of Fire.

Alerice sniffed, and then ran her own black sleeve across her face. She reattached the crossbow to her belt, and found her hand naturally curling about the handle of Kreston's broadsword.

Oddwyn smiled, and opened a small portal beside them. As when riding along the ridgeline after giving Alerice her black hat, he reached into the vertical slit, diving deeply so that his arm disappeared up to his shoulder.

"Ah... ha!" he exclaimed as he withdrew two foaming tankards and handed one to Alerice. "To you, Dühalde," he said, raising his.

"To you, good friend," Alerice said, raising hers.

Together, she and Oddwyn lowered their tankards, poured a bit of brew out onto the ground, and then touched rims before they drank.

Alerice savored the flavor, for it was rich and pure as she knew any Realme nourishment would be from this moment forward. She was a Far-Walker now, but a Realme Walker first, and she was forever tethered to the world below. When she finished drinking, she saw Oddwyn looking at her lovingly.

"You wanna go below?" he asked. "The Hammer Clan is having another feast. Lots more brew."

Alerice smiled, then gave her full concentration over to visiting the mead hall, where she knew Aric and his kindred spirits would be happy to see her. Her own portal opened in a swirl of plum and lapis, and she found no difficulty maintaining it in the mortal world.

"After you, Oddwyn," she said.

"Hmmm, race you for it." Oddwyn presented herself as a maiden one final time to say, "Last one there pays!"

Oddwyn charged into the portal. Alerice looked after her confusedly.

"Oddwyn, the brew is free," she said before she smiled to herself. She paused and raised her tankard once more before saying, "Gods above bless and keep you, Captain Dühalde."

Then a smile flashed in her gray-green eyes as she strode into her portal, calling, "We'll see who pays!"

Tales of the Ravensdaughter
will continue with
Collection Two

Author's Suggestion

In honor of our beloved Captain Kreston Dühalde and to play out *Tales of the Ravensdaughter Collection One*, please search for the song "Summon Your Courage" by the Steel City Rovers.

PLEASE REVIEW THIS BOOK:

If you enjoyed *Tales of the Ravensdaughter*, please leave a review.

AMAZON

GOODREADS

AUTHOR'S WEBSITE

Thank you and blessings,
Erin Hunt Rado
ErinRadoAuthor.com

ABOUT THE AUTHOR

Erin Hunt Rado

 Erin Hunt Rado is an action writer who crafts unique fantasy adventures. You can expect fight sequences mixed with humor, moral dilemmas, and psychological struggles. Erin crafts character-driven stories that take readers to fresh new worlds. Buckle up and enjoy the ride!

Erin is also a mindfulness artist. Having always been interested in medieval and renaissance culture, Erin began drawing original Celtic art in 2008. She began showing her Celtic collection at renaissance fairs and art festivals, and observed that users kept entering a mindful state each time they worked with her products. Adults struggling with tension or anxiety would sometimes experience breakthroughs, and children diagnosed with behavioral disorders would often remain calm and engaged.

Erin added Finger Labyrinths to her collection in 2016. They were Erin's first digital collection, and represent a stylistic difference from other labyrinthian art. Erin now produces both Celtic and Labyrinth mindfulness art in workbooks, travel cards, and specialty gifts and apparel.

Finally, Erin loves graphic design. Her newer digital collections include original Irish-Scottish-Welsh designs, Judaic designs, and a full line of Pirate Arrrrt! You can discover all of Erin's creativity on her webstore,

BOOKS BY THIS AUTHOR

Tales Of The Ravensdaughter

When Alerice Linden dies at the beginning of a story... you're in for something good.

But for Alerice, death is just the beginning. After being stabbed, she wakes in the Evherealme, only to learn that she is a Realme Walker, a mortal who can traverse the world below and the world above.

After pledging herself to the Raven Queen, Alerice embarks on a series of adventures. Assisting her is Oddwyn, the Realme's wonderfully witty gender-fluid herald, and Kreston Dühalde, a former brigade captain with a tragic past.

In her journey of discovery Alerice exposes a two-faced Beast in the town of Basque, stops a Thief from stealing Souls, forces a Wizard and Wyld Mercenaries to come to terms, prevents Rips in the Ether from destabilizing the Realme, challenges the King of Shadows to play the Game her way, and finally realizes her true potential as the Raven Queen's official Daughter.

Gray Warrior

Two fate-locked men - Traevis Airlight, Swordson of the Rhuelands and Rowland Mont-Lestarre, the self-destructive heir - must take on the mantle of the land's magic, though both are tormented by loss, the appetites of a demonic blade, and an ancestral foe who refuses to remain dead.

SCAN ME

ErinRadoAuthor.com

Please Visit My Website For News, Giveaways, Goodies, And More!

Made in the USA
Columbia, SC
18 January 2025

ff635868-c8d8-4648-bdce-f4e355f1f84cR01